Barefoot in December
A Novel

Cindy Sigler Dagnan

ISBN-13: 978-1717047069
ISBN-10: 1717047068

<u>Dedication</u>

For my Beloved. Each year we have loved each other better, even through the days that we drive each other crazy. I can't wait for the next 25 years. That you would read this "chick book" and make sure I had those cop details correct, means the world.

For Eden, my oldest Blessing, the one which began my adventure with motherhood. What a joy it is seeing you be a wife & mommy now too. And for Nick, my favorite son-in-law who made her both of those things. Tylan, Grey & Daxon – Nana sure loves you!

For Emmy, my fellow lover of history, books, cozy nights and the most likely Blessing to text me random things that will crack me up.

For Ellie, my third Blessing, with Boppa's eyes and my child most likely to be sporting something from my closet. I wouldn't have it any other way.

For Elexa, my final Blessing. There couldn't be a better caboose. I am taking heart pictures of all of our drives together to school.

For my two Blessings that are in Heaven. I'll hold you someday; that is the Father's promise.

For Mother & Daddy: my biggest fans, best examples and shapers of what I became. There aren't words. Daddy, if you can't be here, I'm glad you are Home.

Father God – Author of marriage, Maker of the stars & Holder of my heart. Thank you for everything. Literally.

Prologue

*P*ersonally, I have never made a post-coitus sandwich while standing naked in the kitchen, no matter what the Danielle Steel novels say. However, my husband Max and I are in the kitchen after some pretty good lovin', if I do say so myself. But we're not naked. Entirely. Too many little people in our house throw a damper on that sort of thing.

Max pops the top on a can of Diet Coke for me and I fix him a turkey and Swiss on rye. I throw some chips in a bowl and we head upstairs.

Snuggled next to each other in bed, we eat our snacks. Max reads snippets from *Police* magazine to me while I try to be engrossed in a quiz from some women's magazine that promises to gauge my happiness level.

Question 1. I consider my work to be:
   a. A fulfilling task which lets me enjoy what I love every day.
   b. A reasonable and equitable division of tasks which I enjoy most days.
   c. A duty to be performed for a paycheck to provide basic needs.

Unsure what to circle, I snort under my breath? What paycheck? I quit working to work harder than I ever have, staying at home with our babies.

Question 2: My most recent pleasant exchange of non-work ideas took place:
   a. Yesterday or today.
   b. Three days or longer.
   c. A week or more.

Well, let's see. Every day is my life's work lately, but I guess a graham cracker smile, a drooly kiss or a craft project covered with lots of glue and prominently displayed on my end table qualify as very pleasant exchanges.

Question 3: When I wake up in the mornings, I feel:
   a. Well-rested and raring to go. *[Well – laugh out loud!]*
   b. Focused and ready to dispatch my To-Do list.
   c. I want to sleep; my days are draining.
Of course I want to sleep, precious quiz crafters!

   "Max. Listen to this one. 'Question 4. If your relationship were described as an inanimate object, it would be a:
   a. Surprise box from a mail order company – you never know what you'll be getting.
   b. A favorite quilt—snuggly, comfortable & broken in.
   c. A buzzer joke toy—you're not really getting each other these days."
I turn expectantly to face him, tilting my body back so I can gauge his expression. "Well? Come on."

   "Huh uh. No way."

   "Please, Max? Come on. Play."

   "Nope."

   "Why not?"

   "Two reasons. Past experience, and I'm not stupid."

   "Very funny. Play. I won't get mad. Promise."

I straddle him and threaten to tickle him; he hates that.

   "Okay, okay. Umm…the quilt, I guess."

"Great. We're boring." I am in full pout mode and roll off of him.

"No, Deena, wrong thinking. I love our life. It's comfortable."

"Boring. Max, you just said our life is boring!" I hit him with the pillow, letting it lie on his face.

Max lifts it off, pretends to spit out feathers and pulls me toward him.

"See?" He kisses the tip of my nose. "That's why I don't play. Can't win."

~~~~~~

And so it started, the crazy, ordinary, yet not ordinary at all, year that changed my life forever...

Chapter 1

It was the birth of my third child that did me in. I'd barely recovered from the flab of reality that was my stretched-out stomach, only to be greeted by my cheerful five-year-old daughter, Caroline, blue eyes widened and black curls bobbing as she observed, "Mommy I thought you were going to the hospital to get a baby *out* of there, so how come it looks like he's still inside?"

From the corner of my eye, I saw my husband Max furiously making slicing motions across his own throat in Caroline's clueless direction. Fat chance. Poor Max. He's trying, but he just doesn't get it.

After attempting to make a fashion statement with the accordion pleats on my stomach, I rediscovered that quintessential difference between Regular People Tired and Mommy Tired. There's really no comparison. This was an ankle-weighted, biblical millstone tied-around-your-neck-thrown-in-a-lake-and-left-for-dead sleep deprivation that felt worse than when I'd worked three jobs and carried twenty-one hours of courses in college.

Somebody is always awake. *I need to nurse. I want you to do the rock-bounce-pat-the-diaper waltz while touring the house at 3 a.m. Come wipe me. I had an accident. I had a bad dream. I can't sleep.*

By the time my precious son was five weeks old, I'd snap at anyone within ear shot every time his plaintive newborn wails dragged me out of the solid four hours of broken sleep I was getting each night. And each night I resorted to playing a sick game with my husband. Though neither of us ever named it aloud, it was called: Who Can Pretend Best They're the Best Sleeper. I am usually the big loser.

Sometimes a well-placed elbow somewhere in the vicinity of Max's ribs could do the trick. But most nights he either played the game better than I or was truly able to sleep through the wails and all five lights from the nursery monitor blinking directly in our eyes.

Tonight, I trudge wearily to the nursery to change soggy diapers, flop down in the rocking chair and grope for the nursing flap buried in the voluminous folds of my dumb maternity gown with ugly pink and blue rocking horses on it. Baby Eli has a similarly ugly drawstring gown; both gowns were gifts, courtesy of my mother-in-law, Dora.

Aren't we an adorable pair, Eli and I? Perhaps Dora wanted to make sure I'd not be having any more babies any time soon, because I am fairly certain this ensemble could turn off a prisoner who hadn't been with a female in twenty years.

In these dark watches of the night I want to know: where are the mothers that are in the ads of parenting magazines? These mothers always have long, glossy hair (think Jane Seymour as *Dr. Quinn, Medicine Woman*; doesn't *their* hair fall out in clumps during the great post-partum hormone reduction?!). They are model Madonnas, attired in white peignoir sets, resting cheeks blissfully against an infant's downy head. Cheeks rosy, lips parted and slightly glossy. Those model mommies don't look sleep-deprived. They look fulfilled. Serene even. Sane.

A quick glance in the mirror shows I'm not measuring up. There's a Lilly Munster-like pallor about my skin. My lips are dry and chapped. One side of my hair is smashed flat against my head; the other side looks like a nest for small burrowing animals.

The soft nighttime lamp with glowing stars and a moon casts a spotlight on the edge of one of these stupid magazines, open to a ridiculously impossible ad for infant detergent. I glare at the faux mommy.

And she's wearing *white*?! This proves, beyond a shadow of doubt, that she cannot possibly be an actual mother to a newborn. I mean come on, wasn't she sent home with the same arsenal of Tucks, hemorrhoid cream and diapers for grown-ups as the rest of us? Isn't she worried about ruining her gown? How does she nurse in that thing?

I think these cranky, bitter thoughts and my heart races, the way it used to race whenever I'd meet Max for lunch somewhere, or his car would turn in the driveway, or his hand would brush mine and the look between us triggered every smoke alarm in the place.

These days, my biggest heart palpitations come from trying to unscrew the too-tight lid from a jar of gourmet mustard. That's not to say that I don't find my husband incredibly attractive, because I do. And he swears that I look just as good to him as the day we met. [Which is kind of him to say, since the mirror I'm looking in shows all body parts sticking out a collective tongue at me in vicious mockery -- Na,na,na, na,na,nah, it taunts. It fairly shouts, WHAT THE HECK HAPPENED TO YOU on a daily basis.]

So, attraction's not really the problem. Sleep is. Or rather the lack thereof. By the end of the day, given a choice between sleep and fifteen or twenty minutes of sex, give or take, I've been choosing sleep, hands down. Not the greatest way to maintain a passionate relationship, I admit.

Kissing the precious tip of Eli's tiny nose, I lay him down in the cradle and pad back to our bed, falling asleep with one leg hanging off the bed. He'll be up at least two more times before morning. It's the same routine every night.

And last night (or was it morning -- who keeps that straight anymore) Max suggested that I go back to an old B.C. [Before Children] ritual I used to enjoy -- writing out my feelings in a journal. An update with a twist; I should post a blog for all the other mommies out there in Neverland. I protested that I do not have time. He reminded me that I always said that writing clears my head of confusion and gives me a safe place to pour out all of my feelings and frustration. I think he's just seeking whine relief.

But still. As if I have time to write or even think coherent thoughts these days. Max walks in on me, discussing life with myself, and smirks that smirk which I used to find sexy. Now I merely find it irritating. I feel all the embarrassment of the lady on the television commercial who gets caught belting out, "YOU MAKE ME FEEL LIKE A NATURAL WOMAN!" into her hairbrush. Okay, so a blog journal it is.

All of this brings me to this morning where I am now rummaging around in the kitchen Everything Drawer (I can't bear to call it a junk drawer) and find half a pencil with an eraser top that looks as though it's been gnawed by termites. I hop up on the breakfast bar stool and ease sleeping baby Eli (of course, he's sleeping -- it's time for me to get up) onto my left shoulder. I open a blank spiral notebook, fold it back until the flimsy covers touch, the way I did when taking notes in high school. I have to suppress an urge to doodle hearts and flowers around the lined paper edges. Here goes nothing. I will gather my paper thoughts for later posting.

Blog Spot Post by Pajama Mama
January 12, 2010

*Good morning, Blog land and fellow sleep deprived mommies.
Will try to ignore the fact that when I slouch on this stool to
write, a small ridge hangs over the edge of my underwear.
Huge white grandma panties. Wooly plaid robe that has
definitely seen better days. Speaking of, are days of pleasing
pastel lacy matching bra and underwear sets finally gone
forever? Help!*

*Here are the facts as I see them:
It's been 5 weeks since I quit my job at the University to be a
full-time mom to my three kids. I've never worked this hard
in my entire life! Basically, I'm either housebound or hauling
around various small people and unwitting objects [tubes of
washed Chapstick; an arsenal of stale Cheerios and petrified
French fries; lost Barbie accessories], and sometimes our
orange and white cat, Butternut Squash, an unwitting,
underpaid chauffeur.*

*I'm toying with the idea of calling this blog, Diary of a Plaid
Housewife -- ha. What do you think of that? And do I really
expect an answer?*

*Anyway, back to life. Good luck with yours,
Pajama Mama*

Comments:

*I feel your pain. Thought I was the only one.
~Formerly Hot*

Nope. Right there with you. Three-packs of Grandma panties on sale this week at JC Penney.
~Chocolate Guru

This will be fun! Just what I need to read.
~First Time Mommy

Last night I went to get baby Eli for the third mid-night feeding. I was much too sleepy to nurse in an upright position, and laid down with him in our bed. We faced each other tummy to tummy, his tiny toes stretched, kneading my leg. I must've fallen asleep because next thing I heard was the alarm clock going off to the local radio station blaring. I'm switching it to the nature sounds option tonight.

"Gooood morning! It's time to stretch and get ready for work. But first -- it's time to play another round of Name That Sound!"

The D.J. sounds annoyingly peppy. I reach out to slap snooze button. I am stopped in mid-air by the prizes -- $50.00 cold hard cash and a gift certificate to *Olive Garden*. Two things I have sorely missed since stoppage of pay check -- money of my own and dinners out to grown-up (read expensive) places. Places where French fries are absolutely not served.

"Listen. I'll play the sound twice, and then caller number five, caller number five -- if you have the correct answer -- you're our winner!"

"Okay," I say aloud, "I'll play." I strain, listening to the tinny ancient clock radio. Riiippah. Riiiappah. I know the answer! I *know* this! I hear it a hundred times every day! In my elated, sleepy stupor, I reach too quickly over baby Eli and he stirs and grimaces, irritated with the interruption. Using skills all mothers possess, I pat and shush, leaning with my other elbow between his scrawny frog-bowed legs. This, of course, he sleeps through.

I dial frantically, my finger repeatedly smashing redial after each busy signal. Unbelievably, I get through.

"Good mooorrning, KWAS! Yooooou are caller number five! Who am I speaking with?" Irrationally, I think of correcting his grammar. *With whom am I speaking.*

"With Deena," my voice sounds morning-husky, like Karen Carpenter with a bad cold.

"Alright, Deenie," chirps D.J. as though auditioning for part as newest member of the *Wiggles*. "I'm going to play the sound one more time. Tell me what you think it is!"

Riiippah.

Piece of cake. "It's a diaper tape being unfastened."

"Are you sure about that Deenie? Is that your final answer?" He chuckles with the ease of Road Runner after pushing Wiley Coyote off the cliff [my favorite childhood cartoon], only constipated. Beep. Beep!

"Yes I am."

"What makes you think the diaper tape isn't being *fastened*?" There's a loud snort of laughter from the D.J. I wonder how much he gets paid for this.

"Look, I'm postpartum and I'm sleep deprived. Don't toy with me. Just give me the money." I'm unsure if I said this aloud.

"Congratulations, DEEENIE! Tell us what station just made you a winner!"

"KWAS." A yawn splits my answer. I stay on the line to give the D.J. address, last name and other pertinent information. Kiss the tip of Eli's nose in silent apology.

I turn around to see Max, lying on his side, propped up on one elbow watching me as if I have truly lost it. I picture for a moment what he must be seeing. Me sitting on the floor beside our bed, clutching the cordless phone and Eli, surrounded by the mountain of decorative throw pillows flung from our unmade bed. Shortly afterward, he reminded me to keep up with my blog. This, he said, will give me a concrete record of my days at home.

I write a rough draft for another post, half-heartedly and haphazardly, trying to recall the bittersweet humor surrounding Eli's birth. How about that? One crazy day, and I'm instantly whisked away from the order and stateliness of old University buildings, of grade books and flow charts and faculty meetings into the chaos of sticky oatmeal and sticky floors, endless sleepless nights, car pools, wading pools and a flannel jammies wardrobe. Seriously, you'd think a woman on her way to a doctorate could somehow manage to be showered before noon. I curl my hands around my University logo mug and hang on for dear life, rolling my eyes.

~~~~~~~~~~~~~~~~~

My pencil lead breaks in the middle of my reminiscing and I knock over the juice glass next to my mug with my elbow. Ugghh!! Leaning across the breakfast bar, Max winks at me and leers. "Six-week check-up today, huh, sweetheart?" For a detective, he's oddly oblivious to the spreading puddle of orange. Glad I hadn't yet powered up my little notebook computer to make a post.

I nod, listlessly wiping up the spill with a perky Easter dishtowel. I cannot believe I'm looking at bunnies marching through piles of pastel eggs in January. He kisses my cheek, gives my bottom an exuberant pat and fairly waltzes out the door. "Can't wait!"

You have got to be kidding me, I think for the third time in my life. What doctor in his right mind would ever give clearance for a woman to be looked at, much less touched, a mere six weeks after giving birth? This never ceases to amaze me, nor does Max's remembrance of this crucial date after the births of each of our children. Anniversaries and birthdays might slide right by Max. But Safe to Have Sex Again Day is indelibly burned in his memory files. Figures.

Just feel lucky he still wants you, I chide myself.

After a too-quick shower, I walk down the hallway to the girls' room and gently shake Caroline and Zoe awake, folding my tummy over the wooden railings of the bunk beds. I must ready them for a play date with my mom, the Perfect Woman. No school for them today (Teacher work days, incidentally, are no good for parents), so they'll get to play with grandma while I have the unmitigated joy of slipping my winter-roughened heels into the doctor's stirrups. Ugh. Ride 'em cowgirl. No one should have to see my mother and be a cowgirl in the same day.

****

Sunday, our first outing to church with Eli, turns out to be a disaster. My eyes are bleary and I am bone tired. Zoe throws a fit about having to wear tights, even after I point out their merits when it's only 22 degrees. Caroline calls her a baby and Zoe, in an uncharacteristic fit, kicks Caro's shins, lies down on the floor and sobs.

It's all I can do not to join her. All mothering sense has deserted me. I sit on the floor next to Zoe and point to my own grey cable knit tights that I'm wearing with my shapeless denim jumper. "Look sweetheart!" I make my voice unbearably perky. "Mommy's wearing tights. See? It's cold outside. That's just what we girls do in the winter."

"Daddy doesn't have to. Not ever." Zoe is down to just sniffling, so I feel somewhat gratified.

"Daddy's a *boy*, silly." Caroline retorts smugly.

"Caroline Elaine!" Max's voice requires instant obedience and a humble apology.

"Sorry, Zo." She gives her the smallest hug. "But he *is* a boy." Caroline is the champ at making sure you can always hear a seed of rebellion and she always has the last word.

"You could wear pants," I suggest.

"I like dresses." Zoe's lower lip forms a ledge. Fine.

It takes an unbelievable amount of time to get Caroline's Bible and track down her quarters for offering (actually, I couldn't find hers, so I dug around under the couch cushions and presented her the change I found there along with a smashed piece of stale popcorn. Blew off the lint first though). Then fetch Zoe's Toddler Bible replete with attached pink handle from their bookshelf, replenish Eli's diaper bag with wipes, Pampers, two changes of clothing, pads and a lipstick for me.

Oh yeah, and a water bottle. I dash back inside to fetch one from the fridge door, remembering Dr. Ellison's admonition to drink more fluids while nursing. Privately, I think if I don't cut back on the fluids, my breasts are going to explode while standing on the third verse of *How Great Thou Art*. Hence the shapeless denim jumper. I miss my real clothes. I miss my old life. Shoot. I miss real life. I'm also desperately afraid this might be real life.

I lean my head against the headrest and doze on the short drive to church, only vaguely aware of Max and the girls chattering. Max drives around under the covered canopy to drop us off.

We are swarmed the moment the door opens. "Oh, Deena, you come right over here and let me see that little fellow." I surrender my blue-blanketed bundle. "You done good girl!" Big Mr. McKenzie holds Eli's tiny overall clad self. Eli mirrors his standard Sunday attire in miniature.

"Thank you, Mr. Mac. If he grows up to be half the gentleman you are, I'll be pleased." I pat his arm and he flashes his toothy grin. If I didn't know him better, I'd think "Shucks!" would be next out of his mouth; under those overalls is a heart of refinement. He pats my shoulder and presses two pieces of his stash of Bazooka bubblegum in my hand.

Next in the informal admiration line, Sharon and Karen Rossman, the sweetest seventy-year-old spinster twins, take turns cooing over Eli. Leaving him in their capable hands, I excuse myself to drop Caroline and Zoe off in Junior Worship.

Back in the main wing, Max has rescued Eli from his admirers, and stands there holding our son, beaming. "Hey, Deena Bean. Let's go get a seat."

"Deena Bean," overhearing, Miss Violet pats me in approval. "You have a good man there. Yes, you do."

"I know it." I press my cheek next to her soft, papery one and make "let's go" faces at Max.

"Near the back, please." I snuggle under his arm, toting Eli's tan and blue striped diaper bag, which now doubles as my purse. Max's arm squeezes my softness under my jumper, not seeming to notice my squishiness or my lack of fashion.

Vicki and Zeke have apparently been watching for us and wave us into a pew just two rows from the back on the right-hand side.

"How goes it?" she bends in and whispers, eyes laughing.

"You know perfectly well how it goes," I sniff in pretended offense. "I can't believe I haven't gotten to church before Eli is five weeks old; I am struggling with everything, more than I ever remember with my other two. It's just been easier to let Max take the girls while I stay home and sleep whenever Eli will let me."

"Gotcha." Vicki is all sympathy. I love that girl.

Max and Zeke roll their eyes at us and Max hands Eli off, football style, to Zeke. "Don't get used to that, Buster," Vicki pokes Zeke. "He's mine in about two seconds."

She pauses and with comic timing, demands, "Hand him over."

Max puts his arm around my shoulder and scoots me close. I lean contentedly against him. My softness against his muscled hardness is a contrast that always delights me.

The last notes of the prelude fade and Pastor Sherman takes the stage. We sing. Take up an offering; partake of communion. I note with amusement that Mr. Mac has slipped another piece of gum for me into Eli's diaper bag. There's a sermon and I'm sure it's good, because it always is. I'm just so incredibly sleepy.

In moments, it seems, Max is poking me awake. I gather our things. The last thing I shove into the diaper bag is the list I scribbled on the back of the bulletin, my gum stuck into a folded down corner.

Grocery List

Tucks
Always with wings
Try Astroglide?
Newborn Pampers
Sticky Notes
Frozen Pizza
Baby Lotion
Baby Bath
Baby Shampoo
Diaper rash ointment
24 pack of Crayolas
Diet Coke
Gallon of vanilla ice cream
Junior Mints
Cheerios
Barbie Pop-tarts
Deodorant for Max

Chapter 2

My eyes barely open, this time to the accompaniment of the buzzing alarm (nature sounds my foot) instead of Eli's hungry cry. Time to get Caroline to school. Slap the snooze button as I cannot bear the thought of getting up in this cold darkness. Max got called out twice during the night and after all this time, I still don't sleep well when he's gone. Like I sleep well at all these days.

Without the focus of classroom preparation and department meetings, all my days run together like Bert's sidewalk chalk drawings in *Mary Poppins*, Caroline's current favorite movie. She goes nowhere without her parasol.

MondayWednesdaygroceryshoppingpreschoolchurchPTOlau ndrydustvacuumchangediapersThursdayFridayweekendwher edidtheweekendgoIwishIcouldsleepuntilIdidn'tfeelsleepyany morewowIreallymissadultconversationandfeelinglikethere'sso methingproductiveinwhatIdo.

I wake up sometime later with that awful feeling you get when there's way too much light filtering through the window for the time you were *supposed* to be awake.

I stumble to the bathroom and open the medicine cabinet reaching for the tapered bottle of Visine. Definitely need to get the red out. I tilt my head back, already anticipating the relief that the cool liquid will bring. But on second glance while putting the bottle back in the cabinet, I groan and slide down the wall in disbelief. I have just squirted baby Eli's Stuffy Noses baby nose drops [he has a little cold] directly into my eyes. That's right. Snot. Direct sourced to my eyeballs. Pink eye, here I come.

The phone rings and I snatch it up. "Yeah."

Vicki snorts on the other end. I must be rubbing off on her. "I just saw your lights come on upstairs. You're running late, girlfriend. Better get a move on!"

"You are so the anti-Christ." I hang up to the sound of her giggles.

I glance quickly into Eli's cradle and note that wonder of wonders, he's still sleeping. I fling myself into the shower, flooding my hair and body with some sort of peppermint all-purpose soap I got from my Christmas secret pal at the University. The scent woke me up and caused me to tingle all over! Ouch. Ouch. Ouch. Too strong a scent for soap. I dance around in the shower, quickly rinsing off.

Perhaps the fragrance layering that the magazines always talk about will put me in a prettier mood. I go for the matching peppermint lotion, twist my short ponytail into a passable updo and throw on my worn jeans and favorite pink sweater.

Downstairs the coffee maker is sizzling, giggling and whispering like it has its own pleasant secrets. It is also evidence that Max is up and out the door and I didn't hear a thing.

I wrestle a tired, tearful Caroline into a warm swing top and leggings set featuring bright bluebirds and their green and brown nests. I smooth her long straight hair into two pig tails, tying a green and brown ribbon around each. I'll allow her to eat a chocolate Pop-Tart in the car on the way and scoop Zoe and Eli into their car seats in their footed sleepers. What a rotten mommy. What happened to rising early and greeting their little faces with my freshly scrubbed and made up one? Pancakes and bacon or biscuits and gravy for breakfast? My mother always did it.

The drive is always pleasant though. There's a small college town feel, with lots of older homes, set back from the road on over-sized lots. Mature trees grace the edges of most lawns, waving oak, maple and walnut trees provide cover for wooden play structures, lawn sets and barbeque grills.

Main Street boasts a *Ben & Jerry's*, an old-fashioned café, *Delia's Downtown Diner*, that's been around since 1933, a tiny one-screen movie theatre, city hall with its adjoining police and fire departments, the quarry stone courthouse with its impressive clock tower and a few trendy boutiques and a one clothing shop, trying to hang on with the competition of a temperature controlled mall.

A few miles out from Main Street is our school complex, with an elementary, junior high and high school sharing a square mile of tree-lined streets and charming stone walls. The web of towns tucked next to our central town of Southern Hills, Missouri have their own smaller districts.

Across town, is a mall and a Target, my personal haven. Adjacent to campus is an eclectic coffee, pastry and gift shop called *The Rooster*. I usually stuck with the *Starbucks*, one street over, drinking my coffee and my ever-present can of Diet Coke there nearly every morning of my academic life, watching my students stroll by in a colorful blur of backpacks, bicycles and iPods. Of course, at this time of year, the entire landscape is unrelieved gray, dirty snow and chilly rains.

Pulling into the school lot, I notice that Eli has something dried and disgusting looking all down his flannel clad leg. I don't remember the girls' diapers leaking this way. Ugh. I won't be walking Caroline in today. Again. She turns around at the door and waves to me. All is forgiven over chocolate breakfasts and a car ride. I'm blessed she's like that.

We start to head home, but at the last minute, I remember some things I've forgotten at the grocery store, a habit that's becoming more and more frequent, despite my ongoing lists. I lug Eli's infant seat inside, the huge purse that Max calls my luggage smacking my rear, dangling from its long straps. Zoe is holding my other hand, skipping along, oblivious to the dingy, sullen piles of snow and the bitter cold. She looks the most like me with her shorter brown curls, upturned nose and sprinkling of brown sugar freckles.

"Can we get some donuts, Mommy? I loooove donuts, right? I do. 'Specially the pink kinds with the sprinkles. I'd like some donuts. I didn't get some Top parts like Caroline had." Her face grins up at me expectantly, and I reply with my own answering grin at her reverse name for Caroline's beloved Pop-Tarts.

"Alright then. Donuts it is, Zoe girl!" I know what this is and I don't like it in myself. It's a guilt offering. After all, the donuts are not for a special occasion or a treat, they're a constant bribe for good grocery behavior or a gift to somehow make up for the fact that even though I'm at home, I don't feel like I'm really there at all. I don't know where I am either.

Hefting Eli and seat into the cart and letting Zoe hang onto the front and ride, I quickly dispatch most of my list. And I throw some things in the cart just because. New Nora Roberts paperback. Ruffles potato chips with French onion dip. Nutty Bars. Junior Mints. More vanilla ice cream. Breyers vanilla bean, to be specific. I throw in another package of Pampers and a triple value pack of baby wipes.

The nice clerk smiles at me in the check-out lane. "Your children are darling! It's tough having two little ones at once. I remember when mine were small..." Her voice trails off in sympathetic reminiscence.

I schlep the kids back to the car and buckle them in, receiving sugary kisses from my sweet Zoe. I peek inside Eli's flap to coo at him briefly and he sneezes right in my face. Lovely. My cell phone, permanently set to the loudest setting, the better to be heard from the depths of diaper bags, coat pockets and the luggage that is my purse, blares *Stayin' Alive* by the BeeGees. And isn't that too apropos?

"Hello?"

"Hello. How's my best girl?"

"Max." I sag against the car, sudden tears stinging my eyes.

"Honey? Everything okay?"

"Um yeah. Mostly. Rough morning, I guess." My English Lit degree has deserted me and I can't think of words to articulate my lostness.

Wedging the phone under my neck, I bend over and kiss the tip of Eli's nose and give Zoe's knees a quick squeeze as I hand her a notebook and the ever-present baggie of Crayons from the little pocket in the back of her seat.

"I know exactly what you mean, Deena Bean. We've been making arrests and taking reports like crazy, and I've only been here since seven." Radio traffic sizzles in the background. Max responds and I'm uncertain whether or not he's talking to me. I hear pops and distracted, protracted patches of silence.

"Max? Max?" Why? I wonder. Max isn't even in patrol now. He's back in detectives.

"Well, Babe, I was just picking up some coffee at *The Rooster*. Gotta go." He hangs up in the middle of my unformed sentence. And the other thing I want to know is, whatever is he doing on *my* side of town? I wonder some more. I feel a sudden tug of longing for the order and schedule of the University campus. Some coffee at *The Rooster* wouldn't be bad either.

I hang up the phone. *I love you to the max*, is lodged in my throat, stuck there, choking me. I feel ridiculously rejected, forgotten. I am the gummed up back burner of the stove, desperately needing maintenance, but whom nobody sees.

I wheel into *The Rooster* just to have an excuse to go by campus. And remember.

Back home, the day stretches into the infinite sameness of all my days since being home. I should be more grateful, and I know it. But I don't feel grateful, only bored. Full of haywire hormones.

I load the washing machine with baby blankets, sheets, burp rags and impossibly tiny clothes. Adding two of my bras and a pair of hose, safely zipped inside the mesh delicates bag, I pull the knob and pour in the cup of Dreft.

I build, knock over, and pick up seven different block towers with Zoe and cut a peanut butter and jelly sandwich into four neat triangles for her lunch.

"Mommy, I need some magic powder on my applesauce, please." Zoe grins at me with a peanut butter rimmed upper lip and I dutifully sprinkle cinnamon on top of her current favorite. For good measure, I add a kiss to her sweet-smelling head, pour her another glass of milk and absently eat a few handfuls of Cheetos from the bag. Surely a Nutty Bar is close to a granola.

When lunch is all cleaned up, I put the dishwasher on delay, read *Bunny My Honey* for the hundredth time and lay Zoe down for her nap.

Eli gurgles at me from his perch on the coach, safely ensconced in the handy u-shaped Boppy pillow. Max was so happy to buy me a manly looking navy-blue version with race cars. "Your turn, little man." I scoop Eli up and settle in the recliner for nursing and snuggles. I inhale that indefinable baby scent, powder, Johnson's baby lotion and something that is ephemeral and sweet.

Rocking and patting, I glance around the room. The worn overstuffed couch and chair are covered in denim. A cheery red pot filled with orange Gerbera Daisies holds court on the square, pine trunk serving as coffee table, still the same one that Max and I got at an estate sale the day we came back from our honeymoon. I haven't found anything I like better.

The afternoon light floats in lazily through the enormous picture window that faces the front porch, spotlighting the dust motes in their slow waltz across the denim slip-covered couch. I really need to mop. And dust, for that matter.

Eli sucks too quickly, flooding his little mouth with milk and breaks off, choking and then sneezing. His expression is comical in its rage. I pat his back, making silly faces and murmuring words of comfort. "Son, don't be so greedy." I nuzzle under his neck and his tiny hand fists itself in my hair. He is Max in miniature. I rock us both to sleep, thankful for a quiet hour before time to pick up Caroline from school, supervise her sight word flash cards and start some kind of dinner.

Max is late coming home again and even though I know this is just how it is with police work, my frostiness surprises me. I hear the garage door go up and the noises of Max taking off his shoulder holster, storing his duty weapon, popping the top on a cola. I roll over in bed with a huge sigh.

It's just that I look forward to his homecomings now more than ever. He is the cavalry, the reinforcement, the bedrock, the playmate and the rescuer all wrapped up into one fantastic package.

But even so, he'll never understand how long it can be from 3:30 to 5:30 every afternoon. If he's late, it's worse.

He came up to kiss me goodnight before retreating back downstairs to unwind in front of old cop show episodes, but I pretended to be sleeping. How else could I keep back the hateful, resentful words that sprang to mind: *No problem Max. Way to be everybody's hero but mine.*

The next morning, I reluctantly call my mother for babysitting duty again. I have no choice since my right eye is crusty, itchy and swollen shut. I'll have to go to the doctor's office. Mother agrees to put off her facial peel until another day in order to babysit. I get my own mini-facelift by rolling my eyes at her meticulous beauty regimen.

Mother doesn't breeze in anywhere, despite her diminutive size. She dominates every situation. I know that's a terrible thing to think about your own mother, but just seeing her wears me out.

If she hadn't seen me first [actually, she saw Zoe, playing with her baby dolls on the entry way bench right next to the front door] through the narrow glass window on the side of the door, I wouldn't have answered the door bell. I would've had Eli already in the car ready to make our getaway and allowed Zoe to let her in. Okay. Maybe not.

She's impeccably dressed as usual, wearing soft gray flannel pin-striped slacks and a baby blue cashmere twinset. Her only ornaments are a pair of pearl studs and her giant diamond wedding set. She swoops up Zoe in a single motion and covers her sticky face with kisses. Mother loves her grandkids, I'll give her that.

"Deena, darling." She kisses my cheek, concern in her eyes. "I don't think you've been getting enough rest." You think? I don't say this aloud.

"You go on and don't worry about a thing here. I'll change the sheets on the beds and see about dusting. I'll have the best little helpers here and I'll check the fridge for lunch — you do have groceries, don't you?" Whew.

"Nana," Zoe interrupts, pulling on her slacks. "When I'm a redult, I can have a house and you can babysit my kids too, huh?"

Mother and I exchange brief knowing smiles over her head. "You can do anything you want, sugar," Mother assures Zoe. "Now Deena, about getting enough rest and things. You really do need to take care of yourself. Max and the child--"

"You know how it is, Mother." I interrupt what I see as a lecture. "Anyway, thanks for coming over to watch the kids this morning. It's just so much easier to sit in the waiting room without them. I'll take Eli though. He'll just sleep in his seat. I have to run. Late." I lean in to kiss her cheek. For a second, I think she looks disappointed.

But I'm outta here anyway. I'm going to get take out from *Delia's Diner*, my favorite cafe. A grilled steak sandwich with green peppers and onions. Smothered with provolone. A side of garlic fries. And the largest peach iced tea they can muster. If I have flavored tea instead of my usual Diet Coke, I can practically count that as a serving of fruit.

And if I leave my sunglasses on, nobody will know I have the reddest, goopiest eyes in the Midwest. I read once that starfish can vomit up their stomachs and grow a new one. Wonder if it's possible to do the same with a pouch that stores part of your life you don't want any longer, or simply can't hang on to anymore.

I scarf down the café lunch at stop lights and just before I go into the Southern Hills Care clinic building, I flip down the visor mirror to wipe garlic salt and parsley from my lips and reapply some gloss. "Come on, son." I heft Eli's seat and let it bang against my knees, deftly slamming the door with my pinkie and a well-placed hip thrust.

Inside, I check in at the window and take some papers to update my information. I write down my insurance number and check that my contact information is still the same. There's also a box for checking whether or not you're sexually active. I laugh, glancing at Eli and wonder if they'd notice if I check-marked 'no.'

Waiting for it to be my turn, I leaf through a new magazine and oh joy, a few pages in, I see that Nike scientists have studied how breasts move during exercise (a figure-eight type motion; go figure) in order to design the Cadillac of all sports bras. I'll rush right out and get one.

"Deena Wilson?" A perky nurse pokes her head out the door wielding an enormous pink Lucite clipboard. When she spots me rising and gathering Eli in his seat, she motions. "Come on back!" I feel like a frumpy game-show contestant.

The nurse takes my temp and blood pressure, coos over Eli, and tells me someone will be right in. Right. At least this is the kind of doctor visit in which my clothing can remain on my body. In a surprisingly short amount of time, an extremely tall woman with her hair cut in a stylish page boy enters the room, brisk and capable and white-coated.

I chat with her, telling her the story of Eli and the Stuffy Nose drops and she chuckles. I feel an overwhelming urge to grab her arm and beg her for a prescription for the uncharacteristic heaviness in my soul.

"Yep. That's pink eye all right," the nurse practitioner confirms. She scratches out a prescription for an antibiotic eye cream and some drops, shaking her head in amusement. Ha. Ha. Hahahaha.

Eli and I run through the prescription drive-through lane at Walgreen's on Broadway, right before Main Street. I'm slurping the last of my peach tea and thinking about going home. What is the matter with me that I'd just rather sit here in the minivan?

I feel lonely, but I don't want company. And the work at home overwhelms me. I don't remember feeling that way when I worked. I could point to concrete evidence of all that I accomplished. This adjustment to being home full-time seems strange.

I feel like I live with my own little band of pirates who don't do anything. See Mommy dust. Dust Mommy dust. See Mommy cook. Cook Mommy cook. See Mommy vacuum. Vacuum Mommy vacuum. See Mommy try and try but get more behind every day. See Mommy disappear. See Mommy forget who she was. See Mommy sweep everything under the table and run. Run Mommy run.

Placing my insurance co-pay and enough more to pay for a treat, into the little plastic cylinder, I wait for the return medicine and the box of Junior Mints and bottle of Diet Coke I've talked the pharmacist into shoving in there too.

And we're off. I talk aloud to a sleeping Eli just to hear myself talk. In my head, I think of witty responses and what someone would say if they were with me all day to banter. To care about the myriad small tasks which make up my current job. Professional Mommy.

About two miles from Main Street is the turn off for our subdivision. I signal a left-hand turn and slushy snow spurts underneath our tires. Usually I like our neighborhood of hodge-podge houses. Everyone keeps their yards nice and in the spring, flowers abound. Today, though, everything is flat and gray.

My flats echo on the stone breezeway and Mother meets me with a finger to her lips. Zoe must be sleeping. I hug Mother awkwardly, and she slips out the front, shutting the door with a crisp, quiet click.

True to her word, Mother has everything under control on the Homefront. The army of dust bunnies have been captured and quarantined in the kitchen trash. The coffee table and the mantle gleam with a fresh coat of Murphy's Oil Soap. Five of Max's shirts are ironed and hang down from the sides of the ironing board like a miniature army. Zoe is down for her nap. Mother has left a tray of freshly washed and chopped fruits and vegetables – evidence that she is worried about me. She has even cleaned out Butternut Squash's litter box, a task I know she loathes.

You'd think I'd be grateful for the help, but it seems just another thing to brand me inadequate. Look at all you can't get done even though you've freed up seven extra hours every day by not being at work.

Irony of ironies, Mother leaves *me* with a To Do list. "Little things I've been noticing that would likely make things a lot more pleasant for you, Deena dear." Dear Lord, please, please don't let her have made it to my closet. The little list is clipped to a bag of goodies she's left for me. Dumping it on the counter, I inspect the contents.

An anti-aging serum from a high dollar make-up counter. Exfoliating sugar scrub with grapefruit seed. Concentrated eye cream. A compact of shimmery bronzer. A scented body lotion. A carob-coated organic energy bar. Blech.

If she knew me at all, she'd have left a freezer bag with some vanilla bean ice cream, some Junior Mints and a thirty-six pack of Diet Coke. Gift certificates to the movies? A massage? Twelve hours of uninterrupted sleep?

And the list in Mother's impeccable flowing handwriting:

- Get a different color bin for each bed's sheets. When you fold them, place the set inside the pillow case. {*Bed, Bath & Beyond* have some stylish ones on sale this week}
- Put a dimmer switch in your bedroom; ambience for your private quarters & not as much shock when you have to get up with Eli in the night.
- Make sure you're drinking your water; our skin doesn't glow without proper rest and hydration.
- Have you been exercising? Perhaps you can try a new kick-boxing class with me.
- Use the exfoliating scrub before applying your self-tanner; sun is terrible for your skin! *Gosh and here all this time I was thinking that tan fat looks better than pale fat.*
- Thought you might like these new energy bars; I know busy young mothers need snacks.

On anyone else's list, a smiley face might have gone there.

I'll tackle another project after we get Caroline from school. Something mindless. Something that no one suggested. Probably something upstairs.

Later that afternoon, Eli back in his crib for a late afternoon nap, I sit on the floor in the girls' room, surrounded by piles of their stuffed animals, alphabet blocks and books: *Dr. Seuss, Junie B. Jones, Owl Babies, Good Night Moon, Guess How Much I Love You, Five Little Monkeys, Little Critter's Just a Thunderstorm, The Berenstain Bears Get the Gimmies. Winnie the Pooh. The Country Bunny and the Gold Shoes, Little Bunny's Loose Tooth. If You Take a Mouse to the Movies. Olivia and the Missing Toy.*

I ponder alternate Mommy lit titles: *The OB/GYN Doctor of Doom; Guess How Much I Love to Sleep; Children Behaving Like Five Little Monkeys; All the Children Who Climb in My Bed During a Thunderstorm; Winnie and Poop; If You Take a Mom to the Coffee Shop; Mommy and the Missing Mind.* Not productive at all.

On a lower shelf, tucked in a corner, are some books that belonged to me, things I wanted them to have when they grow older. *Little Women.* My yellowing copies of the *Nancy Drew* mysteries. An ancient boxed set of *Little House on the Prairie. Rebecca of Sunnybrook Farm. Anne of Green Gables.*

I am determined to bring order to their haphazard system of three and five-year-old room cleaning. If there isn't a semblance of order somewhere, I too will be one or more whatevers over the cuckoo's nest. There's more of my mother in me than I'd like to admit.

In January of 1815, the U.S. Library of Congress acquired Thomas Jefferson's personal library, consisting of 6,457 volumes. I'd love to have read each one. This current little library, housed on the five pine planks of the girls' bright white bookshelf, with decoupage daisies and baby farm animals, is a far cry from that one. Or the one at the University, for that matter.

What I'd give for a moment or ten to devour a biography. To reread one of my favorite classics. To attack a new Pulitzer Prize-winning novel. A novelty paperback by Nicholas Sparks. Even to start writing on my own. At least the eye drops are already making my eyes feel less weepy and irritated.

Sigh. These days, I'm limited to extra-curricular readings of Shel Silverstein poetry or leafing through a few pages of *Parents* magazine while I nurse Eli. Everyone wants a piece of me, some more literally than others.

I try grouping the books by binding, by author, by series. Wonder if they'd be more apt to put them back by color, height or board book versus staple stitch? I wonder why I care so much.

Caroline and Zoe scamper in and I hear the *Veggie Tales* closing theme song drift up through the vents. Zoe scrambles up on my lap and sits down hard. Caroline bends in to lean an elbow on my shoulder.

"Hey, Mommy. Whatcha doin'?" Caroline inquires pleasantly.

"Yeah, whatcha doin'?" Zoe parrots.

I lay on my back taking both of them down with me and wrestle them to their backs. "This is the Tickle Monster!" My voice is deep and pseudo-scary. "I am cleaning up your bookshelf because you little girls live in a pig pen!"

They writhe and giggle, so I continue. "In fact, this room is abominable!"

Growling, I nibble at their sweet necks, making pig-like snorting noises and pretending to play concertos on their rib cages. "Pigs with culture," I tell them. Their delighted howls fill the air.

"What's 'bominable?" Zoe laughs, hiccupping.

"It's this." I gesture around their room, an exaggerated frown on my face. I'm breathing hard so I just lay back with them. Caroline nestles close to my heart.

"I like you Mommy," she says.

"I loooove you," Zoe tops her.

"Ah, my girls…"

Blog Spot Post by Pajama Mama
January 27, 2010

Good Tuesday afternoon, fellow sleepy moms.

According to the Farmer's Almanac, 88% of adults make New Year's resolutions, but only 20% keep them. The most popular resolution of course, is to eat healthier. And here I am, sitting at my laptop, spoon deep into a pint of vanilla bean ice cream, a bowl of PMS Cheetos on the side.

For all you other guilties out there, my devotions landed me in Leviticus this morning. The graveyard of Bible study. I feel properly chastised that my housecleaning efforts aren't nearly up to par. Mildew. Check. Pile of ironing with blended fabrics. Check. Unidentifiable gunk under my washing machine. Check. If it's not supposed to be in my house, I probably have it. They say that dust is mostly skin cells. If that's true, I have company sleeping over under my couch. Anyone else?

People do say that motherhood will change your life. Obliterated is changed, right? Still, my two girls have a clean, organized bookshelf. Ta da.

Well, gotta run pick up some more stuff at the store.

Back to life. Good luck with yours,
Pajama Mama.

Comments:

My under-the-couch company could come and have a play date with yours!
~Dust Diva

Ha! Beat everyone. A giant AND a band of dwarfs are living under my furniture.
~First Time Mommy

Another winter evening, another night at home. When I was teaching at the University, I loved nothing better than to come home. I like our well-worn nicked pine floors and the collection of antiques Max and I picked up on our weekend jaunts to little towns.

When the girls came along, I treasured the long afternoons with them and the evenings spent rocking them or curled up with them in my arms, watching a movie at home with Max. Ah, popcorn, Junior Mints and relaxing. But now it seems like this is just a cozy prison. I am not free to leave except to run errands that all have something to do with here and will all eventually lead me back here. I am boredom personified; unless that's an oxymoron.

But there's one thing I still love to do here; I love to stare at the fire. I'm lying on my stomach in front of the fireplace, no lights on but for the floor lamp by Max's leather recliner. For once, I'm not even reading. All the children are mercifully in bed and blessedly asleep.

Here's an ugly truth: sometimes taying at home is not what I pictured it to be. Some days I feel stuck in the grown-up equivalent of a job where all you do all day long is say, "Do you want fries with that?" Of course, I'd have to ask, "Do you want a pacifier with that?"

The fire snaps and sizzles. Warmth creeps from the hearth bricks and settles over me. I should be content. I can will myself to be content. I will.

The stairs creak as Max comes down to join me. He's been up there talking after yet another call regarding a search warrant of some sort.

He says nothing, just sits down by me and begins to rub my shoulders and my back. I could be cynical and assume that he's just after the usual thing, but I can sense tenderness of another sort. Max seems changeless. Still lean, toned from his running, a 6'2" man's man. His sandy hair and lake blue eyes are just like Eli's. And he can still make my pulse race.

It seems odd to me that so much of mothering, which after all, is born of romance, or at least passion, strips one of the same. Conversations that seemed unlimited in possibility are reduced to the color and frequency of bodily functions and the daily report of chores accomplished and left undone. Of the exchange of schedules and activities which seem to be more important than any that is done on Wall Street. Crazy, really.

Rolling over to more easily face him, I study his face, looking for the Max who fell in love with a girl who's buried so far in diapers and nursing bras, board books, sippee cups and snack baggies of dry Cheerios, she might not exist anymore.

His eyes turn instantly darker as though my attention alone has rekindled a fire in him that's never quite gone out. Max reaches up and does one of my favorite cinema moves, unclasping the tortoise barrette holding my hair in an unruly knot and it falls. His arms move around me and his lips take mine on a moan. My hands travel up to his hair and I whisper against him, "Love you to the max."

Max skillfully finesses away buttons and ties and wraps and hooks. There is an urgency to this prelude of our intimacy that I want to capture, but don't quite understand.

I turn to face him and marvel at how perfectly we fit; how Max's desire for me can cause me to want him back. We fit together and I decide this is a good time to surrender.

<u>Grocery List</u>

~~Tampons~~
Pads aka Diapers for Grown-Ups ☹
Toilet paper
Highlight shampoo
Milk
Bread
Size 1 Pampers
Diet Coke (2 cases)
Baby Bath
Diaper cream
Gallon of vanilla ice cream
Ink cartridge
Valentine candy
Valentines for the girls' class exchanges
Frosted animal crackers
Hot chocolate mix
Little Debbie Nutty Bars
Cheetos
Junior Mints

Chapter 3

Blog Spot Post by Pajama Mama
February 2, 2010

I love my life! Children are adorable today! Love taking Caroline to school, twirling her parasol the whole way, chatting with other mothers, doing the domestic thing while Eli naps in his swing and Zoe "helps" me with her toy broom. I adore picking Caroline back up and smelling her Kindergarten smell of paste, applesauce and playground sweat. Is there anything more wonderful? Am delighted that it's Groundhog Day. With children, it's possible to celebrate absolutely anything!

We pinch the edges of store bought sugar cookie rolls to resemble ground hog legs. I let Caroline and Zoe throw on some leftover Christmas red hots on for eyes. And oh my goodness, all of Zoe's critters look like an advertisement for Chicken Pox Groundhog.

Sweet, candy life. Good luck with yours,

Pajama Mama

Blog Spot Post by Pajama Mama
February 3, 2010

I hate my life.

Comments:

Don't say 'hate', darling. Loathe is better.
~ Mother

Is she for real?
~Dust Diva

You have no idea.
~Pajama Mama

I can read this.
~Mother

February seems to be the love month for everybody except mothers of newborns. Even Vicki and Zeke have plans. I have assured her that it's no problem for her kids to join us since we have no plans that I know of and once you have three kids, what's a few more?

True, it's a full ten days before the date on which Hallmark and restaurant chains everywhere have decreed we shall celebrate love in a romantic Hollywood fashion, but Max hasn't so much as acknowledged that we're in a new month.

Of course Eli will also be two months old on the fourteenth. Not exactly conducive to a romantic getaway, but dinner and a night time movie? There's just something romantic about dressing up and going out at night. Daddy would caution me about the colossal waste of money; a matinee and the special off a lunch menu would be much more economical.

This paradox from the same man who believes that money spent when he *wants* to spend it, is the fix for every situation and the only gift to give. Sigh. He loves me though. Can't say I feel the same vibe from my mother. Sometimes I think she wants me to be a top floor showcase piece but I'm more a bargain basement disappointment.

If I don't watch it, I will hostess my own pity party and it will be a doozy. Only nobody will come because even *I* am tired of myself. One day I adore being here at home, baking bread from scratch on occasion, and feeling that I've mastered Eli's schedule and the minutiae that comprises the rhythm that is home.

I know how many places I can take the children in any combination before a full-fledged meltdown will commence. I make a menu of sorts and have even begun putting a red star by Max's favorites. I'm certainly cooking [and ordering pizza from *Pizza Palace* – with coupons, though] more than I did when I was at the University.

I've let Caroline and Zoe help tear up lettuce for salad, use strips of yellow, green and red peppers, along with radishes and cucumbers to make leafy faces. They've delighted in spreading tomato sauce and grated cheese all over pizza crust – with their fingers, I might add. Good Mommy. Responsibility lessons combined with tactile experiences. All this I've learned at library parent days and from reading all the articles I wanted to read in the magazines but never had time to before.

Other days I feel like a glob of failure, no shape, even around the edges. I'm not even talking about the shapelessness still present in my physical body. If I were a horse, there'd be a burr under my saddle. As it is, I feel like there's a pebble in my shoe or worse, a wedgie of wearing-too-small-underwear–the-same-day-you-break-in-a–new-pair-of-blue-jeans proportion. It's likely just the baby blues. Or so everyone tells me. Whoever "everyone" is.

Maybe chocolate would help; can't hurt. I rifle through my secret cabinet for some Junior Mints. The world's largest box of chocolates was 3,226 pounds, created by Marshall Field's in Chicago. It contained 90,090 chocolates. I wonder what Max is thinking of getting me for Valentine's Day. Pouring myself a handful of the small chocolates, I chew slowly, waiting for the desire to scream and cry to abate.

Nope, here it comes. A three-Kleenex box, *Casablanca/Gone with the Wind/Sleepless in Seattle*, popcorn, vanilla bean ice cream, Junior Mints, haul out the old yearbooks and photo albums, cry myself into a stupor party. I am permanently out of sorts. Even *I* am disgusted with what brought this on: a combination of the Valentine's Day blues and the thought of wearing warm weather apparel, already arriving via the catalogues in my mailbox.

I sit at my dining room table, laptop in front of me, supposedly taking in a few mommy moments and writing on my serious work. I check Facebook for important updates, but all the new pictures confirm what I suspected: everyone's life is more exciting than mine. Instead I troll the Internet for facts about stuff. It prompts me to make an unexpected post.

Blog Spot Post by Pajama Mama
February 7, 2010

Okay, girlfriends! It's the month of love. Just in case your sweetheart has forgotten big time plans to romance you and sweep you off your feet [or at least sweep your kitchen] here's a list of some romantic sounding places:
> *Lovelady, Texas*
> *Loveland, Colorado*
> *Love County, Oklahoma*
> *Lovelock, Nevada*
> *Love Valley, North Carolina*
> *Loves Park, Illinois*
> *Loving, New Mexico*
> *Romeo, Michigan*
> *Valentine, Nebraska*

So, there you have it! Just for fun, why not research whether or not there are any Bed & Breakfast Inns in those places and invite your mother-in-law along to babysit! Seriously, cyber moms, have to go clean those toilets!

Back to life. Good luck with yours,
Pajama Mama.

Comments:

Last time we had a romantic getaway, I had my third daughter. Think I'll stick with cooking.
~Chocolate Guru

Children are a blessing!
~Mother

Mother – quit commenting! Please.
~Pajama Mama

This is as good as the blog!
~Dust Diva

No comment.
~Formerly Hot

That's a comment.
~Dust Diva
Desperate for adult conversation.
~Dust Diva

This is pretty far from "adult."
~Anonymous

And no such luck with the distraction. The same things pop right back into my head. It's February, the longest short month in the year. Spring clothing catalogs are already in my mailbox, but just like winter feels never ending, I feel decidedly settled in frumpdom. Seriously, I irritate myself.

My body just feels foreign to me. I mean really. Pregnancy and nursing have made my breasts what a bodice-ripper-writing novelist with zero real-world perspective would call, "full and lush." Oh puhleese! Why can't people just call 'em like they are? Can't anyone spell "swollen and cantaloupe-y?" Well, maybe that just doesn't sell.

Stuffing mine into a sports bra for aerobics workouts just gives me a serious uni-boob effect which makes me cringe every time I attempt to get in any exercise at all. Which isn't much of the time. Too much effort to bundle up Eli and Zoe and drive to the mall to get in a walk. Somehow, driving to exercise seems stupid. Frankly, I'm just suffering from a deplorable lack of interest.

As usual, whenever the land line rings, I'm startled back to reality. "Hello?"

"Hey, Babe." Uh oh. When Max greets me with nothing else forthcoming, he's usually going to tell me something I don't want to hear. Silence. But I can outwait him.

"Deena Bean?" Max plows ahead. "I volunteered to go ahead and work a bit later on the fourteenth. Is that okay?"

"The fourteenth that is Valentine's Day? *That* fourteenth? Well, sure, Max!" my fake voice sails across the wires. "Isn't that what you're supposed to say when someone tells you something that isn't okay *at all*, but you're trying to be polite?"

"Yeees, but you don't generally tell the person that's all you're doing. The polite thing, I mean. Your technique needs work."

"Um hmmm. I'll get right on it. You did mean the fourteenth that is Valentine's Day? And our son's two-month birthday?" I throw in that last part just to be mean. Of course Eli won't have the slightest idea that's his two-month birthday. It's not like an official celebration or anything.

"See, Deena, that's exactly why I thought it'd be okay. We could use the extra money. You aren't going to want to go away or do anything big anyway. Because you wouldn't leave Eli. Right?"

For the briefest second, Max's silence makes me feel small. He is right. Sort of. But still. I'd just like to be given the option. As in, *Hey, Deena Bean! I've arranged for my parents to come down and stay with the kids. Thought we'd drive the hour to Branson and stay at Big Cedar Lodge. Hang the cost. We'll take in a show, sit in the whirlpool tub and drink champagne. I've already decided we can talk to your heart's content after we make love. Oh – you can have all the Junior Mints you want too.*

Okay. We can't afford Big Cedar Lodge. We don't drink. And with my luck and my crazy hit and miss periods these days, the whirlpool *and* sex would both be out of the question. But still

I sigh heavily. "Probably. But Max, I just would have liked to have been asked. Or surprised with something. Something." My voice trails off and we hang up awkwardly, as though there's no history between us at all.

****

I hear the key turn in the lock at eleven o'clock Valentine night. Butternut Squash opens one eye and goes back to sleep. Why isn't Max coming in through the garage and the stone breezeway? I'm on the couch, attempting to read the new bestseller Vicki brought me as a thank you (bribe?) for keeping Christopher and Canaan while she and Zeke dined (with reservations Zeke had made a month in advance) at the new Greek restaurant.

She floated in about an hour ago, flushed and glowing, and scooped up Christopher and Canaan already set for bed in their Spiderman footie pajamas. "Here you go, Deen. Thanks, thanks. It was, um, great to be out." She *doesn't* tell me how lucky I am to have my mother so close for things like babysitting; she knows me and my mother.

That's when she handed me the book, all tied up with a red heart ribbon and a tiny box of Valentine candy taped to the top. Knowing Vicki, she'd probably had it all bought and ready for weeks.

Her red sheath dress topped by a classy black sequined shrug made quite the contrast to my pink fuzzy jammie bottoms plastered with red, purple and white hearts, topped with one of Max's old undershirts, yellowed under the pits. *Thou shalt not envy nor begrudge thy best friend a night on the town with her hubby while you sit alone tackily attired.*

"I'm glad you and Zeke had fun, Vick." And I am.

Lovely. I look lovely and now I kind of wish I'd put on something with at least a piece of lace on it somewhere.

I see the briefest edge of Max's coat as he steps in the door and looks around, probably not expecting me to be up. He gives the family room the most cursory of glances; I always keep the antique milk jug lantern lit, so that wouldn't tip him off. He tiptoes, (*tiptoes?*) to the kitchen and I hear the unmistakable sound of a match striking and some smaller rummaging and clanking sounds.

I can't help myself. I can no longer sit on the couch, sulking, waiting for Max to go upstairs and discover I'm not there. I walk into the kitchen and stop.

Max turns around, a boyish grin lighting his face when he sees me. From his expression, you'd think I was dolled up like Reese Witherspoon in any of her romantic comedies. He is obviously pleased with himself.

He opens his arms. "Happy Valentine's Day, Deena Bean! You're the best wife in the world. Really. You are."

I walk right into them, so ashamed of my attitude. I nuzzle my face in his neck and he kisses me deeply. When I open my eyes and push away from his kisses, I have to smile.

Max has lit a fat orange pillar candle and placed it on the kitchen table. "It's the only one I could find," he grins sheepishly. A box containing a heart-shaped pizza, a six-pack of Diet Coke and a box of Junior Mints are arranged in what I assume is supposed to be an artistic fashion. And in a vase is the most lopsided arrangement of hastily purchased end-of-the-Valentine's-rush roses that I have ever seen.

"Oh, Max." Really, what else can I say?

"Do you forgive me, Deena Bean? I just didn't get it. This probably sounds lame, but I don't need a special day to remind me of how much, or why I love you. I love you every day. Sorry I'm not always good about showing it."

And this is why I have to love Max.

We sit down and munch on pizza, and talk about everything and nothing. Our ice cracks and pops as the warm Coke fizzes over it. The candle sputters and our makeshift dinner is illuminated with additional help of the sputtering long florescent bulb above the kitchen sink; clearly, it is about to burn out.

"Want a fire?" Max wiggles his eyebrows.

"Why not?" I *do* want a fire. Both kinds. All kinds. I desperately don't want to burn out, but oh, I long to burn with some kind of passion.

****

Well, shorts weather followed by the ever-dreaded swimsuit season is upon us. The children are beyond restless, shrieking like the March winds on the blustery days that keep them inside and shrieking even more loudly if possible, than on the rare days that Vicki and I have been able to haul them to the park.

It is unseasonably warm today and Vick and I are on a blanket surrounded by the remains of an early picnic lunch. The kids are playing in the enclosed climbing area, except for baby Eli, who naps under the shade of his stroller.

We're attempting to paint our nails, an unparalleled luxury. This is no easy feat, as one or the other of us has to keep swiveling around on the blanket, to make sure the children are still in the central play area of Fielding Park, a large conglomeration that includes slides, rock walls, covered platforms to use as forts, pretend steering wheels and monkey bars. I'm trying to keep all that scooting from adding mulch and gravel to our sitting quarters. We have promised to push the kids on the swings as soon as our nails are dry.

A few other mothers have also determined to bust out of their winter hibernation, and we trade distant, if conspiratorial smiles acknowledging our desperation for spring. We're all pushing it, wearing capris and various brightly colored long-sleeved tees. A wee bit ahead of that season. Perhaps if we will it by our collective fashion efforts and trips to the park, springtime will arrive in earnest instead of the days teasing us, like the promise of a colorful kite that is trapped high in the branches of a bare tree.

Zoe hurtles down one of the concrete pathways, some treasure in hand to show me: a bird's nest, a pretty rock, an interesting twig. Canaan is just a beat behind her, sand streaming from his pockets, toy cars clutched in both hands.

It is one of those calendar moments when your heart snaps pictures like crazy. Zoe's face is turned up, the sun and branches dappling her face, framing it in pure joy. This morning she begged to wear one of the new outfits I picked up for spring [Target. $14.99], a pair of navy blue capri pants with white eyelet and a matching navy cardigan with red cherries on it, a rim of white eyelet tank top peeking underneath. Her dark hair keeps falling down into her mischievous blue eyes, so like Max's eyes.

Canaan is all boy—Vicki's promise son. His golden curls are straight out of a 1940s picture book. His chubby little legs, pumping hard under their long denim boy shorts, do their best to hide the muscle underneath. His tee shirt is that quintessential striped boy staple. How can a face that dirty be so adorable? Add that to the mysteries of children.

"Hey Mom! Lookit what my trucks can do!" Canaan puts one into Vicki's outstretched hand and crashes his other truck into it. A smear of berry colored polish dots the truck. "Mooom! You ruined my truck!"

I laugh. His little face is so affronted and never mind that Vicki's thumb and forefinger now have bare spots surrounded by ridges of still tacky polish.

"So sorry, son," Vicki drawls.

"S'okay, Mom. I forgive you." A quick hug and he wriggles away. "C'mon Zoe, let's play."

"I brought you a present, Mommy!" Zoe's eyes glow. "You should guess."

"A picture? An offer to babysit Eli so Mommy can take a nap? Junior Mints?" Her head shakes after each guess.

"Do you give up?"

"I do."

She solemnly presents me with five broken twigs, varying in height and thickness. I can't imagine what they are supposed to be, but I know from experience that an explanation is coming.

"I choosed them for you, Mommy, just so you could remember how much you love me when I am three!" She is jubilant.

"Zoe Irene, thank you! Thank you, my sweet Zoe girl. Mommy doesn't know what to say. Tell you what," I finish, tugging her down on my lap, "as soon as we get home you can help me choose some ribbon and I'll tie them up and put them on my dresser in a very special place."

"Yay, Mommy!" She wiggles out of my grasp. I want her back.

Canaan stomps gravel all over the blanket and tugs on her hand. "Zoe! Let's. Go. Play."

"Whoa there, son. You'll be waiting on women your whole life. Be patient."

Vicki and I watch them go and replace the caps on the polish. Manicures are not gonna happen. I have gravel-as-decals imbedded in my nails. Slowly we walk toward the swings where Zoe and Canaan have called us over, pushing Eli who is oblivious in his stroller. The wheels crunch, turning gravel and mulch in an odd rhythm.

"So, Vick. You're kind of quiet today. What's up?"

For a moment, I don't think she's heard me. But when she turns, a clear sheen stains her eyes. "I'm just trying to soak this up. To feel blessed. Caleb is already in school, Canaan is four, Zoe is three and Eli looks bigger every day." She stops and draws in a deep, deep breath.

"Baby Eli just makes me want to have another one. I'm running out of time and I try not to dwell on it and anyway, I did ask God for Canaan and promised I'd be content after that, but it just consumes me some days. You know?"

"Oh Vick." I put my arms around her shoulders and squeeze her. This isn't the moment to flippantly offer to let her borrow Eli rent-free at three o'clock in the morning. "I can't imagine. Knowing how much you want more children and all those miscarriages..."

"It'll be okay. I'm thirty-five and well, they say all kinds of problems can happen after that anyway."

I clear my throat. "Ahem. Kindly remember that I just had Eli at thirty-six! You're a young pup compared to me." I lean in and hug her, wordlessly hurting with her, my dear friend who would raise a dozen children in her immaculate house if she could.

If I were Vicki, I'd suggest praying. Deep down I have a hard time believing God is really interested in anything I want Him to do these days. He just has a plan and wants me to get in it. Right now I imagine He's fairly disappointed in me. Guess God and Daddy will just both have to be disappointed for now.

Vicki swipes the back of her hand across her nose and straightens up. "What about you, Deenie? What do you want these days?"

I laugh. "Easy. To see the bottom of my laundry basket? Do you know that laundry procreates without benefit of marriage?" I adopt a shocked tone.

"Yeah, but seriously." She looks at me expectantly.

"Okay. To sleep the whole night." I glance at her and her arms are folded.

"Spill it."

"I don't know—to feel like anything I do is worth something, I guess." It's as close as I've managed to telling someone how false my life is becoming.

"Deen, you *are* doing something worthwhile. Seriously, you won't get it back. This season of your life will only come once."

"Thank goodness!"

She drills me with a look.

"Kidding. I'm kidding." I throw my hands up. "I know."

We push Zoe and Canaan languidly until they notice we're not really into it, visiting or staring off into space. They cajole us into being better mommies and they reach and push, tips of little toes trying to touch the edge of the sky.

I look at my watch and as though he can read it, Eli promptly wakes up, letting me know it is lunch time this instant.

We load up the minivans and head our separate ways. Vicki has to run to the grocery store and I need to get home and transform myself into the Dairy Queen. If I wait and feed Eli here, I might be late to pick up Caroline.

Forty-five minutes later, Caroline sulks the minute she opens the minivan door. "Mommy," she accuses, "I see McDonald's cups. Did you go without me?"

Before I can explain, Zoe pipes up. "Uh huh. I got a Happy Meal and we went to the park too! With Vicki and Canaan!" Zoe rats me out.

And the sulk is on. Driving home, I notice that some wit has put a notice up on their nursery sign: **Spring, where R U?** Yes, where are you? Stop teasing and sulking and come to stay. I need a million more days like this one.

I reach in my purse and crumple this week's list in my hand and throw it on the floor. There.

<u>Grocery List</u>

Flowers
Get a life
Get a new attitude
Write something serious
Spiral notebook
Paper clips
Zit medicine
Anti-wrinkle cream

Chapter 4

Only two weeks ago, I was pushing Zoe on the swings at the park. Now Morning Glory Circle, along with the rest of Southern Hills, is tucked in under another blanket of snow. The sky is still gray though it's nearly noon. It's a friendly gray, though, no menacing threats of still more inches of snow.

From my view on the porch steps I see a few stray flakes lazily float here and there in no particular hurry. Down the street near the cul-de-sac end, I can hear the shouts of children pulling sleds and organizing snowball fights. Small pieces of yellow and vibrant green daffodils valiantly poke through the snow around my sidewalk. Max didn't have time to shovel this morning, and only the deep impressions of his boots have left a mark in the sidewalk.

I feel like a child myself, carefully fitting my feet inside those hollows. A wave of loneliness, of missing Max, flows over me. Stop it. You can't miss Max, you *live* with him. The air is still and crisp. My breath curls up like miniature chimney smoke and when I reach the street, the cold makes me jog.

I dash back across the street from Vicki's sprawling ranch where I have been gone for approximately 3.5 minutes. Eli's safely in his crib and I just needed two eggs so we could bake something and make memories on this snow day. I open my door to chaos.

"Mommy! Mommy! Come upstairs, 'cause I got something really pretty to show you!" Zoe thunders down the stairs on her sweet chunky three-year-old legs.

Caroline stands at the top of the stairs, hands on hips, looking old and sage for a Kindergartner. She shakes her head. "You won't like it. I can tell you that right now."

Chubby hand tucked in mine, Zoe pulls me up the stairs toward the bathroom. Uh oh. She points proudly to the toilet where Felix the fish swims happily in the bowl, above an assortment of bright orange and turquoise gravel. She beams at me. "Should we save it for daddy?"

A quick mental picture of what happens the moment someone tinkles on Felix and then flushes, makes me choke on a giggle. "Zoe girl, can you tell mommy why you did this? Putting Felix in the bowl?"

"He looked squishy so I wanted him to have more room. This is more room, right?"

"It's definitely more room Zo." I sigh. "Felix has five more minutes and then he has to go back to his bowl okay?"

Zoe's lower lip trembles and I explain the dangerous situation that Felix is actually in. "I told you so," Caroline gloats.

I shoot Caroline a sharp glance and turn back to Zoe. "Actually, Zo, you'll be a rescuer, saving Prince Felix the Fish from the sewer monsters, okay? Okay!" I swing her up, tickling her, pretending to be a sewer monster. Sunshine breaks over her face. Whew. Crisis averted.

The phone rings at the same time that Eli awakens from his nap. I can hear his snuffling and grunting; a few minutes of that always precedes a full-blown come and get me cry.

Leaving the bathroom, I scoop Eli from his crib in the nursery and sprint for the phone just as the machine is picking up. *Hi! You have reached 260-3392. We're having way too much fun to answer the phone, so leave a message and we'll get back to you as soon as we're not!* It seems like a message from another lifetime.

"Hello?" I gasp into the phone, breathing heavily from trying to reach it before the machine picked up.

"Wow," Max grins through the phone. "I just thought I was calling home. No idea I'd accidentally dialed a 900 number!"

"Very funny, Max. What's up?"

"Just wanted to give you a heads up. I'll be late tonight. Not sure when I'll be in. We're waiting for confirmation on a search warrant. Briefing's in about an hour."

"Thanks for the warning." I try to be upbeat and supportive. "Um…maybe we'll just order in pizza since you won't be home for supper." I can hear the teary edge to my voice.

"Sounds great, Babe! I'll see you when I see you. Kiss my boy and my princesses for me." He signs off with his usual cheerfulness. Max loves his job and that's probably why he's so good at it. But some days it seems like I'll never get used to the unevenness of his hours, never develop an immunity to his absolute passion for it. A passion that I'm sometimes jealous of.

I remember our courtship days, both of us in school, broker than broke. We played *Clue* and *Sorry* and *Scrabble* and ate popcorn by the truckload. We married on semester break because Max couldn't wait for the honeymoon to begin.

I relished our early days, decorated with the furniture that Mother's tastes outgrew and I made it ours by supplementing with flea market finds and a whole lot of stenciling. Our carefree, laid back existence was quite the contrast from the ultra-regimented tone of my growing-up home and I enjoyed that so much that I refused to take any of the money daddy was always offering us. "Just til you get your feet under you, Deena girl." That didn't stop him from hiding the occasional fifty or twenty in my car's ashtray or under a vase in our kitchen.

Trying to stuff some of that back in my mind, I became an odd hodge–podge of manners and decorum, combined with a wide sarcastic streak and the persistent notion that I was trying hard to live as a Type B person, in a Type A mind, clearly of my parents' making.

I succeeded in living in a maze of orderly piles until I heard my Mother was coming for a visit. Then, how I flew around our studio apartment. *"Deena, I do believe that comforter is just a tad crooked dear." "You're not leaving those dishes in the sink are you? It only takes a few moments more to do that job properly." "What are you doing with your hair these days?"*

I managed to take a few breaks from mother's orders at the *Dairy Shack* with Daddy, who I think, had a secret fondness for my independent streak.

Because when Mother and I sat, we just sat. We didn't really get along unless we were doing something: shopping, trying out a new tea room, having a spa treatment or something. Then of course, she wondered about when grandchildren might come along. I remember wondering why she wanted some so badly when she barely seemed to tolerate the child she had.

At any rate, I soaked up Max's attention and sense of fun, feeling that my days of awkward, over-achieving, warped identity seeking during adolescence and early college were finally over. Max made me feel I had finally come home.

When Max finished his four-year degree in law enforcement, concurrently with graduation from police academy, he brimmed over with enthusiasm for his job. I devoured books alongside him, trying to finish my own degree, but eager to soak up the details of his day.

"Let me guess," I'd tease when he came home from working on a difficult case. Adopting an exaggerated Southern accent, I'd throw back my head. "It was Miss Scahlet in the conservatory (dramatic pause and big breath) with-gasp—the candlestick!"

Max became the inspector in a melodrama, dipping me backward toward the threadbare rug, castoff from my parents' basement. "Miss Deena, I do believe my suspects are disappearin' at an alarmin' rate!"

We laughed and our youthful repartee always ended in passion. The difference almost embarrasses me now. Last week Max worked eons of hours with only a few at home for sleep. I actually called him on his cell phone and begged for him to come home and I wasn't thinking about intimacy at all.

"Max!" I had wailed, a sharp bundle of edgy hormones. "Those bodies are going to stay dead! Please just come home and help me!" But as usual, a family feud over a will gone bad and the resulting double homicide, took precedence over something as normal as post-partum blues, and Max labeled evidence, helped photograph the crime scene and interviewed half the town.

******

I change and feed Eli, more quickly than I'd like. Felix the fish needs to be rescued; dinner needs to be started. That is, I need to chop some quick veggies for a salad to go with the pizza that is becoming our standard meal.

The swollen board from last year's leak under the sink has made that part of the kitchen floor uneven. It creaks underfoot as I open the cabinet for soap to start the dishwasher.

About 45 minutes later, the pizza delivery boy greets me like I'm his favorite aunt. "Here you are, Mrs. Wilson! See ya soon!" I press a few folded up dollar bills into his hand and wave him off.

"I think *Pizza Palace* loves us, don't you, Mommy!"

"Don't talk with your mouth full, Caro."

I don't want to think about it. Where are the healthful from-scratch meals and the consistent family dinners I'd planned on creating with all my extra time?

I leave the pizza boxes on the table and when I come back downstairs they yawn at me, mocking me for the mess. Turning my back on them, I head for the family room, a book and a fire.

If Max isn't going to be home, then I don't feel like doing anything.

****

The weeks alternately scamper and drag by, like walking a new puppy on a leash. Some are hesitant and sleepy; some rich and full of new discoveries and eagerness. Too bad I never know which kind they're going to be.

School time. Errand time. Chore time. Lunch time. Nursing time. Clean up. Nursing time again.

Nap time. Somehow, I have fallen asleep facedown with a terrible case of morning breath in the afternoon. I am aware that I'm not alone and I reach down to feel what size feet have joined me. Zoe feet. That's right. Caroline is at school. Caroline is at school!

I bolt upright and look at the clock. Unbelievable! School dismisses in one minute. Shove on my coat and pink fuzzy slippers. Wrestle a startled Eli and grumpy Zoe into the minivan and their car seats. I don't even remember any of the scenery on the way there.

"Oh, Caro," I smother her face with kisses. "I'm sorry, so sorry Mommy's late. I just got caught up in, I forgot...." I trail off lamely.

"That's okay, Mommy. I'm used to you. You know? My teacher says that when you're around somebody lots you're used to them," Caroline chirps. Children are nothing if not humbling.

She prattles on about a mommy who's a banker, one who works at the mall and one who sells cell phones. I recall that it's "jobs day" at the school. I used to have one of those too. Well then.

I look around the school cafeteria where the students who are parent pick-ups are supposed to wait. Only two other children are still there. I feel sorry for them; I feel sorry for their mothers.

Mrs. Henderson, the matronly principal, comes over and shakes Caroline's hand. "Well, how nice, Miss Caroline, that you have such a nice Mommy and little brother and sister who will come and pick you up!"

I could just hug her for being so nice. "Mrs. Wilson?" She shakes my hand too. "I believe we met at Open House back in September. And didn't you work the Book Fair?" I nod, so grateful that she doesn't point out the discrepancy between Deena Then and Deena Now.

"Caroline loves it here, Mrs. Henderson. This is a great school."

She inclines her head and then winks at me, leaning in with a conspiratorial whisper. "Once, when my third child was born, I forgot I had three children and left the new one in the nursery at church. My husband and I had driven separately that morning since I was running late. I didn't even notice until I'd almost pulled into the restaurant. Still go to the same church; still haven't lived it down. Sleep deprivation will do things like that to you." Her smile is gracious and I don't feel quite as stupid when we all pile back in the minivan for home.

I look back over some of my posts and realize that I've been a slacker here too. Alright, I'm on it.

Blog Spot Post by Pajama Mama
March 14, 2010

"If it weren't for the grace of God, I'd be in heaven right now," is the pithy quote on my devotional flip calendar this morning. Again, I'm fairly certain it says something ugly about me that this sits on my bathroom counter. And after this afternoon, I'm certainly in need of grace.

Anybody ever driven to pick up their kids from school and have no idea how you got there?

Here's my list of things I miss:
- Sleeping in
- Pedicures
- Not feeling guilty about having time to myself
- Not feeling guilty period.
- Having a bigger thrill than finding a place that takes double coupons on Pampers
- Wearing my regular jeans minus the permanent zipper tattoo after I take them off
- Having sex without listening for the baby or watching the doorknob to see if a toddler is trying to gain entry
- Free time
- Pre-child brain, pre-child body
- A paycheck
- Feeling like anything I do is making a difference

So, what's on your list? How do you deal with Mommy Guilt? Should we just put life for ourselves on hold for the next eighteen or so years?

Duty calls, fellow sleepy moms, so back to life. Good luck with yours,

Pajama Mama

Comments:

Lists? Who has time for lists?
~Dust Diva

Lists are the best tool for staying organized.
~Mother

Mother. Seriously. P.S. Lists are the bane of my existence.
~Deena

For what it's worth, I kinda agree with "Mother."
~Formerly Hot

You would.
~Dust Diva

Now girls...
~Mother

Oh, brother! Signing off comments with a huge eye roll. Mother,
don't you dare say a word about wrinkles.
~Pajama Mama

Later, I sit leafing through the book of trivia that Max got me one year for my birthday. He said I always amaze him with my penchant for facts. What I actually am is a veritable storehouse of completely worthless information. Oddities and bits come at me at the weirdest moments.

The most common day of the week to have a heart attack is on a
Monday between 4 a.m. and 10 a.m.

In 1973, only 27% of hospitals allowed dads in the delivery room.

Clark Gable & Vivien Leigh had to use a moving wooden platform
during their dancing scene in Gone with the Wind.

No babies have ever been born within the borders of Vatican City.

E-mail was introduced to the White House in 1992.

Maybe I like knowing facts because my daddy always told me that knowledge is power. He was so proud of me when I graduated at the top of my class and then went on to get my Master's degree. When I got the position as English department head at Southern Hills University [on the provisional condition I would start my doctorate program within the year], I don't think I'd ever seen him so proud of me.

There's a picture that mother had printed for me and I framed it and put it on my desk at the University. I'm in my cap and gown, my hair and nails done for the occasion, an early graduation gift from Mother. Max is on one side of me, arm wrapped around my waist; Daddy is on the other side, his arm grasping my elbow and a genuine smile on his face.

Just before she snapped the picture, Daddy leaned in and told me, "Deena girl, if I haven't told you, I'm very proud of you. You have what it takes to keep going, no matter what." That's a speech for Daddy; Mother is the speech maker in our family. I love that picture. I love the evidence that Daddy was proud of what I had done and the career path I was on. The next spring, I found out I was expecting Eli.

****

It's green day at school. St. Patrick's Day and all that. I've agreed to bring shamrock cookies for Caroline's class snack time. "You wear green too, Mommy! Don't forget!" she calls over her parasol-toting shoulder as I walk her into school this morning.

The Irish ironically used to think that wearing too much green was a bad thing, as it increased your chances of being kidnapped by a leprechaun. Figures.

I dress Zoe in her denim jumper with the school house appliquéd on the front and a green turtleneck underneath for good measure. Eli gets a miniature green sweatshirt with his tiny jeans.

Pulling into the school lot, I beat out another mom for a pretty close parking space considering it's a party day. I shrug into my coat, hold the diaper bag handle in my teeth, release Eli's seat from the base and tell Zoe that I need her to hold my hand. The cookies. Rats.

I lean in to tug the white bakery box of shamrock sugar cookies dressed in green-sprinkled edible glitter. I see them slide as if in a slow-motion movie sequence. The box isn't heavy, just awkwardly balanced and it does a double gainer off the seat onto the parking lot.

Asphalt chunks mingle with green sparkly cookie pieces from the cookies that managed to slide out the side when the box hit. The ones still in the box are mainly broken, cracked as if along floral fault lines. There's not enough icing on the premises to make these guys whole again.

Another mother rushes past me, breezing past with her own basket full of jauntily made treat bags, green pencils peeking out the tops like mile markers for an Irish country road. I don't recognize her from PTO. Taking a second glance, she turns around. I see the brown suit, the two-toned peep toe pumps and the nametag—Amanda Billingsley—from Southern Hills Bank. She has one of those hip mom brown and blond stacked-in-back bobs too.

Looking at the mess of sticky sprinkles and icing, some of which is sticking to my dull black loafers, I want to call after her. I too have some cute suits. They're just hanging up in the "I have a dream" section of my closet. Not that I have any use for them at home. See I was somebody important; I was a department head at the University. But how pathetic would that sound?

I stick my tongue out. Unbelievable.

I'm crouched on the ground, debating whether to turn around and pretend I've forgotten about the party, when I see a pair of cool mom sneakers, putting the finishing touch on a really cute turquoise sweat suit. Looking up from my squatting position amidst the green glitter cookies, I meet a pair of friendly gray eyes that are trying hard not to laugh. My benefactor leans down and inspects the mess.

"I've seen worse. Let's see, I've got a few extra treat bags here…what if you put the pieces in them and told them about leprechaun treasures and pots of gold? Or something like that."

"Sold!" I put out my hand. "I'm Caroline Wilson's mom, I mean, uh, I'm Deena Wilson. Thanks for helping me."

"No problem. I'm Wyatt Jansen's mom. Joan. I just happen to work at the mall right now. *All Athletes.* Obviously." Joan smiles. "Don't feel bad. Seriously, one time I was bringing in a cookie cake for Wyatt's birthday and all my girlfriends had been complaining about the ants in their kitchens and I was so proud that I didn't have any in mine.

"Well, that's because they were all *inside* the box eating the cookie cake and I didn't *discover* that little problem until I got to the school. The box had been sitting on my kitchen counter all night and," she shrugged, "that's my story. Complete and utter humiliation."

We walked into the school laughing, which makes me feel better about being snubbed by Perfect Barbie Mom. I survived the party and even managed to tell some of the other moms about it without crying. Kids being kids, they thought their last minute "pots" of leprechaun magic were great fun. "Scope for the imagination," as Anne with an 'e' Shirley would say.

Max thinks it's very funny when I tell him about it over dinner that night. "Nice save!" He pulls me down on his lap. Within seconds Caroline and Zoe are crowding me out.

"That's okay." I hop up off of his lap. "Snuggle with your little women, I've got stuff to clean up in here anyway."

"Deal. You go feed my son and clean up; I'll get the girls their baths and then," he grins in his Max way, "then, I'll help you get yours!"

I swat him with a dish towel and clean up the kitchen, cleaner than it's been since Christmas.

****

I am lying securely in Max's strong arms, my head snuggled on his shoulder. A few cold stars have braved the chilly velvet March sky and are winking at us through the blinds. My gaze travels around the room and comes to rest on the stack of clean laundry towering on the rocking chair. South of that, I can see the world's largest colony of dust bunnies. I don't notice the cozy braided rugs or the warmth of the punched tin lantern; I'm too distracted by the clutter I've failed to conquer.

We've just made love and Max's tenderness awes me. I'm not sure why, but I'm crying.

Max feels my tears leaking all over his bare chest and he rolls on his side, head propped up on his hand, elbow crooked. "Hey, now," his hand smoothes my hair and he draws his index finger across my brow, soothing me. "That's not particularly the response I was going for."

My silence hangs between us; my throat is full of inexpressible longings and aches. I shrug against the pillow. "I'm sad." I say it like it's an announcement.

"Why, Babe?" Max puzzles.

"I don't know." My eyes sting, my nose runs and I know that full-out sobbing isn't far behind.

"That's weird." He sees my face. "Orrr, maybe not."

He pulls me to him again, muffling my sobs against his chest as he rocks me back and forth. I think of my favorite Robert Browning quote: "Ah, love-you are my unutterable blessing...I am in full sunshine now." This was printed on our wedding napkins.

The fact that the shelter of Max's arms does not bring me any sunshine this time pulls a dark, heavy blanket over a huge section of my heart.

My sobs subside into hiccups and soft whimpers and he whispers into my hair. "All better, Deenie love?"

I have no reply.

Blog Spot Post by Pajama Mama
March 31, 2010

Almost time for spring jammies, cyber girlfriends! I'm thinking of offering a contest for anyone who can guess how many times I've locked myself out of the house this month alone. Yes, my neighbor has a key; I just can't manage to do stupid things at the same time she's home. Flowerpot key is not a good idea given what my husband does for a living. Tried a fake rock one time, but could never find it after the neighbor's dog moved it.

I'm too humiliated for the police department to come rescue me anymore.

They say that each pregnancy steals away some of your brain cells. If any of you see any of mine for sale on eBay, please, please do NOT buy them. I need them all back.

Speaking of back, it's time to get back to life. Easter outfits to hunt, eggs to dye, hair to pull out. Good luck with yours!

Pajama Mama

Comments:
Let's just dye our hair instead.
~Formerly Hot

Aren't those chemicals damaging?
~First Time Mommy

How old are you?
~Formerly Hot

LOL.
~Dust Diva

<u>Grocery List</u>
Extra house key
Toilet paper
Paper Towels
Tea Bags
Pampers Size 2
Flour
Sugar
Butter
3 dozen eggs
Easter egg dye kit
Easter basket for Eli
Turquoise grass for baskets
Chocolate bunnies
Slice & Bake Cookies
Fish sticks
Chicken nuggets
Microwave French fries
Applesauce
Can of Mandarin oranges
Whipped cream
Grown-up Movie with No Animated Characters

Chapter 5

I've been up since sunrise. The color from the eastern sky is reflected in the west, as though the two sides have played a friendly game of paintball. The east had more brilliance, but a faint pink smudge ran down into the western clouds.

It's my favorite time of day to nurse Eli. Nursing is our private conversation. I love Eli's little smacks and hungry noises. The way his eyes crinkle in pleasure and the way he smiles around my breast and lets a bit of milk dribble from the corner of his tiny mouth.

It's a very powerful feeling knowing that Eli's sustenance, though it's about to be supplemented by rice baby cereal, comes solely from me. My body was his hotel room for nine months; now my body sustains his life.

I stare down at him. His eyes are mostly shut, but they occasionally flutter open to stare at me with a sleepy expression of adoration. I am his life. This is when I feel most fulfilled. It's the rest of the day I struggle with.

Vicki has invited Zoe over to play this morning. She says it's because she has a new craft to celebrate spring being just around the corner, but I know better. She can sense that I'm just a few gallons of vanilla ice cream away from a total meltdown if I don't have some grown-up time to feel productive, or at least semi-alone. I'm afraid I may have forgotten how.

Eli and I walk her over and I drag my feet the short distance back across the street. I miss me. Perhaps it's just an adjustment period like Vick says. After all, dryer sheets are not exactly an aphrodisiac and it's true that children and laundry have overtaken my life.

Throwing a load of laundry in and putting this morning's breakfast dishes in the dishwasher, I sit down with Eli and read him a board book about Clifford. I rock him until he falls asleep and lay him down in his crib. What to do? What to do? Be productive.

I halfheartedly throw in the new workout DVD I found on sale at Target. Shopping the sales at Target, which Vicki calls Pottery Barn for Poor People, has become my favorite pastime. I'm racking up charges on a Target card that Max doesn't even know I have. I have sets of fluffy turquoise and lime green towels; pieces of beach in soggy, land-locked Missouri. I have a cute new coral tank top, some denim capris and a bracelet with tiny gold and coral beads dripping from it.

Over the past two months I have bought adorable polka dotted swim suits for Caroline and Zoe; a miniscule pair of baby swim trunks for Eli. Some nautical placemats, matching napkin rings and a set of new glasses to make my table look just like the one in the bazillion by sixty glossy poster suspended over house wares.

I purchased two new novels and a few DVDs that I thought the kids would enjoy. I bought snacks, magazines, darling travel size Kleenex, greeting cards and make-up. Somewhere in there were a few birthday gifts and a basket with baby robins on the fabric liner. Therapy shopping at its finest.

Right now, I walk and kick and do side-steps to Leslie Sansone's pray walk DVD. (An in-home walking program and how cool is that?) Zoe is usually attempting to do it beside me. Every now and then, she'll look up at me and grin. "We're doin' extracise, huh, Mommy." Normally, I could squeeze on that girl all day. Normally I love any workout of Leslie's. But today, everyone looks too perky and toned in their colorful spandex and I just look frumpy.

At the end of the last mile, I see the monitor lights from their perch on top of the television set, before I hear little Eli's snuffling against the crib. Weak protests grow stronger, and I give up, pressing eject.

I trot upstairs, picking up Eli for kisses and a diaper change. I decide to put Eli in his Exersaucer, the life saving device that lets him sit up in a chair of sorts, and bang away on toys attached to the tray, and lug them both through the front door. Butternut Squash runs out between my legs, a furry flash of orange and white, and stretches out in a sunny patch on the sidewalk. He squints one eye in skeptical feline supervision.

I'm going to vacuum out the minivan so I can have order in some small segment of my life. There are French fries under the car seats that would qualify as dating from the Paleolithic age if I believed in such nonsense.

Eli babbles and gurgles, staring at the toys neatly arranged on his tray and looking quite comical with the arrangement of Boppy pillow and blankets it takes to keep his wobbly self in place. Satisfied that Eli is safe and content, I put Max's Shop Vac to excellent use. I fill up half a kitchen size trash bag with abandoned fast food toys and wrappers, broken crayons and markers whose lids have long since taken up residence elsewhere. Receipts. School papers imprinted with small dirt-gray shoe tattoos. Wadded up napkins smeared with disgusting unidentifiable stuff.

Inventory: six pennies; 1 dime; the back to one of the remotes; four Barbie shoes; one and a half pencils; a hot pink plastic snack cup with some remaining Cheerios and a sippee cup whose nearly solid and fermented contents would qualify the girls for underage drinking.

I toss and move car seats and vacuum vigorously, taking a few quick breaks to steal some sugar from underneath Eli's sweet neck. He laughs. I've just finished the floor mats and squirted some sort of pineapple car scent (Target) underneath the seats when I feel Zoe's breath against my ear. Even though I can't think of anyone else it would be, it still makes me jump.

Just back from Vicki's house, Zoe puts her little hands on her hips and announces: "It must be really fun to have *her* for a Mommy!"

"Well, Zo! Glad you think so. Good to see you too." I straighten up, wiping my hands on my jeans. Glancing across the street, I see Vicki waggle her fingers and shrug from the edge of her yard. She hurries back in, probably to keep Canaan from shaving the dog.

In consternation, I pick Zoe up and kiss the sweet spot under her neck. In return, she proffers the craft that she and Canaan made under Vicki's watchful and creative eye. A washed-out soup can has been transformed into a vessel for holding writing utensils, using magazine strips rolled up to add color and texture, and evidently, a plethora of Elmer's glue.

"This is for you, Mommy. You can use it for your writin' stuff. Cause Vicki says you're gonna write a book one of these days." She turns Max's blue eyes on me and that glue-y creation is guaranteed a prominent spot on my little kitchen desk.

"Thank you, Zo. You can help Mommy fill it up with pencils and pens as soon as we get inside. Can you help me pick up Eli's toys?"

She eagerly gathers them in chubby hands, stopping to smack a loud kiss on Eli's cheek and run her fingers through Butternut's fur. I motion for her to stand way over on the sidewalk and I pull my newly made over minivan into the garage.

Back inside, I settle Eli on the floor for some tummy time, which he hates. I won't have long. I scoop up Zoe, plunk her on my lap, flip open my laptop and log onto Facebook to scrawl Vick a note.

Well, friend – Zoe just came in from your stinking house and announced with a blissful sigh: "It must be really fun to have her for a Mommy! Christopher and Canaan are lucky." I am choosing to regard this as a commentary on my excellent taste in friends rather than as a pronouncement on my poor (in comparison) mothering skills. Thanks for that. A lot. LOL.

That will make Vicki's afternoon, I am sure.

Blog Spot Post by Pajama Mama
April 3, 2010

I've been pondering the larger questions of motherhood:

1. Why do children never truly want your attention unless you're in the bathroom or on the phone?
2. Why are the only people with perfect bodies in your home the ones who began the ruination of yours?
3. If you're one of the lucky ones who gave up your career for the full-time Mommy adventure, why do they trip over you like you're furniture and yell, "Daddy's home! Daddy's home!" at the end of every day?
4. And, finally, from Caroline's ridiculous book of "Would You Rather…" – how about one for us: Would you rather have stretch marks or varicose veins?

That's enough philosophizing from me for one day.

Back to life. Good luck with yours,
Pajama Mama

Comments:
Stretch marks. No bikini is ever touching this body again.
~Formerly Hot

Can I pick neither?
~First Time Mommy

Two words: plastic surgery
~Lexus Mommy

Mother?
~Deena

A jealous Butternut Squash huffs off after finding Zoe on my lap. I laugh as Butternut pretends to stalk an errant dust bunny, dismisses it as too tame and lies across my feet.

Blog Spot Post by Pajama Mama
April 3 – Take Two

Forgot to lament about the whole basket of Easter issues. All this and the time change too. Spring forward. Oh, joy. If it's one thing we mothers get too much of, it's too much sleep! Why can't we just fall back until we get ten hours of shut-eye? Anyone with me?

Hurry, scurry, back to life. Good luck with yours. Again. Sleepier than usual,

Pajama Mama

Comments:

Define sleep.
~Lexus Mommy

Ummm…slip. Slop. Slope. Slep. Oh, you said sleep?
~Dust Diva

Emma is sleeping 6 hours at a stretch.
~First Time Mommy

Girls, I think we can take her.
~Dust Diva

An Easter outfit shopping trip. I'm glad Easter is a bit later this year. Maybe it'll be warmer. I'm browsing all the displays of stuff and new arrivals in between consulting my list. Sidewalk chalk shaped like bunnies. A jump rope with pink and blue wooden bunny handles. According to the National Confectioners Association, 76% of Americans feel you should eat a chocolate bunny's ears first. I throw some of those in my cart too. All those will be good additions to the girls' baskets, along with the Resurrection story book and Bible CD I picked up for them at *Life Source* bookstore at the mall.

I find Eli a little Sailor suit that will be perfect with white long dress socks and his little shoes. Caroline and Zoe get baby blue and baby pink sheath dresses, respectively, overlaid with white eyelet, little white shrugs, lacey socks and white patent leather shoes.

I don't indulge myself with an Easter outfit; Max still hasn't seen my Target statement from last month, though I've thought about coming clean on the credit card. If I don't stop this, I'll be forced to admit I need help. Nah. Still cheaper than paying some counselor to talk to me. Probably.

Naturally, Easter morning dawns chilly, temperatures down near freezing and we all traipse off to church with our winter coats on, an incongruity with our pastel outfits. Caroline and Zoe are quite grumpy about it and Max and I have to sternly remind them about the point of Easter.

"That would be Jesus rising from the dead, Zoe. It would not be 'show off Zoe's new dress' day." Maybe I've had a slight role in creating these monsters.

On the other hand, my mother made a big deal over our Easter outfits every year. All three of us got something new to wear and most of the time I got taken to the Sears Portrait Studio for coupon pictures. Once Mother and I got our pictures taken together; I was six. I don't remember seeing a picture of just the two of us after that.

I'm not too disappointed about the winter coats; I'm sad that I didn't get to see the glorious burst of sunrise over the baby animals and spring green grass that trumpets this time of year. Instead, the sky is chalky gray and I think it should be ashamed of itself for greeting Resurrection Day with such a somber reception.

At any rate, I'm thankful that my parents go to a different church across town; we won't be joining them until the traditional ham, asparagus and scalloped potatoes dinner at their house. Then we'll inspect Easter baskets and have a little egg hunt for the kids in their front yard and take our sugar-laden, over-indulged children back to our house for naps.

The sanctuary is beautiful though. The lights have cast the stage in a golden glow. Pots of Easter lilies flank its edges like a regal floral guard. Soft flood lamps illuminate the stained-glass windows on either side of the auditorium and the praise band leads off with a trumpet rendition of "Christ Arose." The congregation rises spontaneously and Pastor Sherman greets us. "The Lord is risen!"

"He is risen indeed!" we respond with one voice.

Pastor Sherman's sermon is captivating, pointing out that because we have a Savior who has conquered death, our ultimate enemy, we can rest assured of victory over any other problem we will ever face. And there in that sanctuary, surrounded by other believers, it is easy to believe that I too am a conqueror.

Super Mom, able to change diapers with just one hand; can lift and juggle car seats, human toddlers, diaper bags, purses, bag packs, lunch boxes and water bottles and possibly a sack or two of groceries as though they were mere packages of Pampers; can dazzle in-laws and parents alike with organic, made-from-scratch meals and flawless table settings; manage the PTO budget, repaint her house and make a grown-man cry in the bedroom – her husband, of course. Ah, but then there's kryptonite: a steady dripping reality of bills, drips, creaks and overload.

After the service, Mr. McKenzie, sporting a new gingham shirt under his overalls, seeks us out in the fellowship hall over biscuits and gravy. I love this little brunch thing the church has going between services on Easter morning. I'm trying to get the girls to eat some fruit and at least a few bites of sausage biscuit instead of the cream cheese Danishes that are always present at this feast.

"No takers, huh?" Mr. Mac chuckles and pulls up a chair at our table, right between Caroline and Zoe. They're hoping for gum. Our kids and our stuff take up an entire table for ourselves.

"Nope," I confirm shaking my head. "They take after their daddy." Okay now I'm lying through my teeth. Max could pass on sweets any day. Of course, that's why he's all muscle-y and I'm just now reaching my abs of Styrofoam level, four and a half months after delivery.

Mr. Mac put a large square of the Bazooka Bubble Gum he always carries in his front overall pocket in front of each of the girls' plates; he adds one for me. I open mine instantly, loving this sticky sweet pinkness of childhood. I tuck the comic away for later.

"Tell you a secret, Miss Caroline and Miss Zoe – I got me a sweet tooth too, and I'm tellin' you, folks that like sweets just have a better disposition. That's the truth!

"My Sadie, she made pie for after nearly every one of our dinners and we were married for a good sixty-four years. She knew I liked two kinds of pie: hot pie and cold pie! I think that was our secret, right there." He chuckles, winks at the girls and looks at Eli with longing.

"You go ahead and take him around for a bit, Mr. Mac. He's fussy since we rousted them all out of bed to go the early service; we're meeting at my folks' for dinner."

"Will do, Miss Deenie." He cradles Eli carefully, gets the girls to magically fall in by his side, and they're off, touring tables, visiting with folks and showing off their Easter finery.

Looking around for Max, I see him talking to another one of his cop buddies from a smaller, nearby department. Max is scowling and concentrating; obviously it's work stuff and not church business.

Vicki, Zeke and the boys are a few tables over from us, sitting with Miss Opal, our Bible study teacher. I'd really like to get to know her better, but I've put it on my shelf with the other Things I'd Like to do Someday When the Children are Older.

From the corner of my eye, I see Caroline and Zoe scamper off from Mr. Mac, holding hands, having spotted some friends from Sunday School at a table across the room. I find myself with a rarity – time alone with good coffee.

"Hey, sexy. I see your good for nothing husband deserted you. How 'bout coming home with me?" Max has snuck up on me, bending over my shoulder to whisper in my ear.

"No way, buster! I'm a married woman. My kids are all with somebody else, so I'm going to drink this cup of coffee alone." I smirk and turn my back on Max.

Max pouts. "Well, I was considering hiring house help, aka seeking Vicki and Zeke's assistance with the kids, and taking this beautiful woman out to a movie, complete with movie theatre popcorn and Junior Mints and the largest cup of Diet Coke they sell."

"Oh really?" My voice arches. "And what is this woman's name?"

Max whispers in my ear and I blush furiously. "Max!" I smack his arm hard. "We're in church!"

"I know that, Deena Bean. But you know, it is God's invention, after all. I hardly think He's shocked that I'd proposition my wife."

"So sweet, Max, but it's Easter Sunday. Therefore, we can't impose on Vick and Zeke."

"We can't?"

"Nope. It's in the friend rules."

"Plan B. We'll leave them with your folks for a little while after dinner."

Sold then. I can leave behind trouble for a few hours. Heaven knows I'll need it after Mother is done inspecting and commenting on my dress, my hair, my skin, my lack of rest, general discipline and what not.

Dinner at Mother and Daddy's house is laborious. If it weren't for the children who serve as unknowing buffers, I think I would have thrown every piece of china out of her cabinet. The food is delicious as always; the table set impeccably.

Mother makes polite conversation, though most of her comments seem like criticism to me. "Deena dear, do you think you ought to be letting Eli have cereal already? You don't want to upset his little tummy."

"Deena, I've heard they're building a *Curves* center out by Main Street. That might be something fun we could do together—workouts." Over my dead body.

And here comes the unwitting tag team. "Deena. How are you enjoying your sabbatical? When do you think you might go back to work?" my father wants to know.

"Daddy, I'm not planning to go back, at least not until Eli's in Kindergarten. Anyway, it's not like you just call up the University and announce you'd like to return."

"*Would* you like to return?" Mother and Daddy chorus in unison.

"Deena is doing a superb job managing our household and being there for the children. I'm very proud of her. She certainly makes life easier for me." Max comes to my rescue.

My turn to tag team by changing the subject. "Well, Daddy, if you and Max want to hide the eggs, I'll help Mother with the dishes and then Max and I can catch the matinee. By the way, thanks for agreeing to take the kids."

"Why, Deena!" My Mother looks surprised. "You know that we'd gladly watch any of the children any time. They're so well-behaved."

But are they *fun*, Mother? I want so badly to ask. That's the thing I don't remember about my childhood. I don't remember being adored by her. The closest I can come to that feeling wass going with Daddy down to his accounting office and being given quarters for the vending machine. And the outing for donuts during my birthday week. Daddy always acted proud of me and Mother always had me outfitted like a living doll. I just don't remember *playing* with her or snuggling on her impeccable lap.

Suddenly, I can't wait to escape. I whiz through the dishes, washing the delicate china much faster than I know Mother would like. On to watch Caroline and Zoe hunt eggs while Mother watches from the screen door with Eli bundled in her arms; it's much too chilly for Eli to be outside.

Caroline and Zoe don't even notice the chill, dashing here and there, baskets in hand (already emptied of their loot from the ubiquitous Easter Bunny) looking for the most eggs. Daddy has hidden a few plastic eggs in addition to the ones the girls dyed; these he has filled with $5.00 bills.

Max senses my desperation and he coughs loudly or points conspicuously with his foot when the girls are about to overlook an egg. We finish in record time; I will reward him later.

I kiss all the children good-bye, hug my parents and collapse in the seat next to Max in relief.

Two hours of snuggling during a big screen romantic comedy and snacks, followed by one incredibly adolescent make-out session in the parking lot and I am a lot more ready for life. Just not ready to face my parents. Easter Sunday is over. Max goes in after the children and I ponder how I'm going to get through the long months ahead.

I dread Mondays. Not for the usual reasons that working people hate Mondays. No. I hate Mondays because loneliness sets in. I drop Caroline off at school, listlessly run a few errands, go to story time at the library with Eli and Zoe, and usually end up with a shopping trip to Target.

It seems like I live life on hold, trying to get from special occasion to special occasion the way some people need to get from paycheck to paycheck or drink to drink. I simply have not established a joyful rhythm to my days; in fact I don't have any rhythm at all. I am finding that trying to substitute order for joy isn't any way to live.

To Do List:

Go through Caroline's spring clothes & box as hand-me-downs for Zoe
Make list of spring clothing needs for both girls
Clean out pantry
Soak refrigerator shelves
Laundry
Make Good Will sweep through all the rooms
Take donation box to donation center
Get a life

Grocery List

Toilet paper
Baby Wipes
Pampers Size 2
Milk
Soy Milk
Orange juice
Ground beef
Rice
Black beans
Tomatoes
Salsa
Sour Cream
Taco shells
Shredded cheese
Junior Mints
Bleach (check out "green" cleaners)
Clothespins
Nora Roberts paperback

Chapter 6

I sit listlessly on the porch swing, watching Caro and Zoe frolic in the front yard. Tall sticks of frothy milkweed and yellow dandelions dot the yard like noxious lollipops. I've dutifully collected all of them the girls have brought me, lining them up in tiny bottles on the porch railing.

The girls occasionally smile and wave, their laughter punctuated by shrill calls to "Watch us, Mommy! Watch!" As if I could do anything else. I feel as bitter as an unripe crabapple with crankiness to match. So far, the month of May has worn me out.

Their choruses of "watch mes" are matched only by my stunning capacity to referee.

"Caroline! Be nice to your sister. I mean it."

"Zoe. Share. Nobody likes a pouter."

And with each infraction, my voice grows slightly shriller. I hate yelling, but I do it.

Caroline comes up on the porch insisting that I see their sidewalk chalk creations, an artistic phenomenon overtaking our driveway. Checking Eli, snug in his seat, I take her small hand in mine and leave the sanctuary of the porch for the softness of spring sunshine. Warm rays pour down my shirt like melted butter. It feels glorious. So what is my problem?

"This one is my sunshine and I..."

"I have a sunshine too, Mommy! Come see." Zoe interrupts.

"You are an interrupter, Zoe Irene." Caroline stamps her foot.

"Girls." It comes out in an unpleasant tone, close cousins to a hiss, although I am not raising my voice.

"Stop yelling at us, Mommy!" Caroline is adamant in her instruction, hands on hips.

I look at her in surprise. "Honey, I'm not yelling at you."

"Well, your eyebrows are."

"Oh, sweet girls. Come here." I squat down and gather them to me and little faces press warmly into my neck. They smell like outdoors and fresh grass, dirt and chalk. All is forgiven. Childhood has that kind of magic to it. I remember, hugging my girls, why I have chosen to stay home. Truly, I haven't given up much in comparison. My attitude needs work.

I just need to be more conscientious about making memories. At this rate my obituary will read: *Deena Renee Wilson. Wife. Mother. She willed her collection of dust bunnies to the local museum for their room on domesticity through the ages. Oh, and she was really good at pathetic pity parties.*

I run inside for a glass of tea, jot a few lines down in my writing folder and create a new post on the laptop, my current substitute for conversation with grown-ups.

Blog Spot Post by Pajama Mama
April 29, 2010

My libido has gone AWOL. If found, please return to owner; husband would greatly appreciate it.

Back to my hidden spark life; good luck with yours,
Pajama Mama

Comments:

Ugh. What a topic. Maybe all of ours have gone to hang out together.
~Dust Diva

A vacation trip away usually helps.
~Lexus Mommy

With what money?
~First Time Mommy

You go, girl!
~Formerly Hot

Wait. We agree on something?!
~Dust Diva

I surrender myself to the remaining hours of the afternoon. I stop trying to compare myself to mother, or Vicki or any other mom I've ever known. I decide to leave the dishes, the dust bunnies and the detergent alone.

We play Mother May I and blow bubbles. I go inside for an old quilt and we spread it across the front lawn and lay on our backs, sunglasses on [Dora the Explorer, Blue's Clues and polka-dotted, respectively] and find shapes in the clouds. Pirate ships. A fire-breathing dragon. Clifford the Big Red Dog. A plate of chocolate chip cookies. We take Eli for a walk in the stroller and blow still more bubbles.

Max got home, took one look at me and agreed to take over dinner; it may have had something to do with my charming disposition.

Max loaded the dishwasher after dinner without being asked. All this after coming home and barbequing spare ribs with his special dry spice rub. I can't tell if he's romancing me, trying to bring me out of this uncharacteristic depression or something else.

I wonder briefly if Max has an interest in someone more interesting than me, but quickly dismiss it. Max is more loyal to us and more committed to his family than any officer I've ever met; any other *man* I've met. The fact we've been married only to each other is a novelty in this department. Actually, in most departments.

The screen door slaps gently, a sound I've always loved. Max scoots me over with his hip. His arm rests behind me and for a minute I relax against it, imagining that all is right with our world. Deep down, I believe Max still thinks that it is.

I look around me, trying to decide what's gone wrong. I have a husband, a home and three healthy children. We are drifting, Max and I. And I'm having to work so very hard at being consistent in enjoying or appreciating anything.

But if you could paint the world in spring, today would capture its essence. The temperature is balmy, enough coolness for comfort with just a hint of the coming summer's breeze. The air has that marvelous smell of freshness. My border of yellow tulips and daffodils are bowing and nodding to each other as if requesting a dance in a long ago ballroom.

As the sun fades, Morning Glory Circle is bathed in equal parts shade and rich lemon light. Many families are outside after dinner and the sounds of neighbors visiting and children squealing and playing waft along the air, borne by the sheer energy of their busyness.

The trees display their brand-new baby leaves, some already fleshed out into early adolescence. The grass is a carpet of emerald and even the dandelions that Max despises look festive.

Caroline, Zoe and I have planted the tiniest garden in the side yard: a few heirloom tomatoes, cucumbers, squash, radishes and watermelon. Tiny shoots of green mist the dark, moist earth, a canvas of life. We won't be harvesting anything monumental, but I hope that digging in the dirt, soaking up the sunshine, tossing a few weeds and watching things grow that will later be on our table will be both a fun and educational experience for them. Besides, it gives me something to do.

Our cat, Butternut Squash, walks restlessly back and forth underneath our feet, carefully avoiding Eli's loud squeals from his Exersaucer. Eli sees him and throws a plastic block.

"Look out Squash! My boy's got a good arm," Max warns. Max calls him Squash, mostly he says, from his personal dream of the cat's demise than from any true affection. Butternut Squash raises his tail and marches away in disdain. Max throws back his head and laughs his bold laugh.

From across the street, Vicki cups her hands around her mouth, calling over from her porch with a request for a quick shopping trip to the mall; she has gift certificates she's been hoarding and wants me to go with her. "Come on, Deena! Zeke says he's got a project to do with the boys and to go with his blessing. Let's make a break for it!"

"Go!" Max stands and shoos me away from the house. "Please go." He leans over the railing. "Take her away Vick. And don't bring her back until you find my wife again!" Max is joking, of course, I think, but still the comment stings. I suppose I've been indulging myself in the vain hope that no one but me has noticed my struggling and the daily fluctuations of my moods.

"Okay," I warn darkly, "but don't be surprised if we never come back."

Max swats my backside. "Not worried."

I scurry inside giving my hair a cursory glance in the mirror and grabbing my purse off the sea of detritus that always sets up an eco-system on my kitchen table despite my best efforts.

Vicki and I talk a hundred miles a minute in her Explorer on the way there. "I just don't like her," I say, about Kay in our Tuesday morning Bible study. Well, it's not really "our" Tuesday morning study anymore. I haven't been in ages.

That doesn't stop me from griping about perky Kay Tupper. "When she hosted at her house, she had a scale in the Master bath that talks in three languages! Who wants one of *those*? I don't want one that tells me my numbers in *any* language! That's just wrong, Vick. Wrong."

Vicki laughs. "But seriously, you need to give it another chance. I think you'd really like who's teaching now; it's Miss Opal. And it would be really good for you to get out. You haven't been since December, you heathen, and there's only a few weeks left until we break for the summer."

I roll my eyes and promise to take her suggestion under advisement. We're at the mall and finding a decent parking place is always a challenge.

In the dressing rooms at *JC Penney*, we try on swim suits, our claustrophobic cubicles next door to each other. "Ugh," I groan. "What is *with* department store mirrors? These would make Calista Flockhart's butt cheeks look like two pigs fighting under a blanket! You'd think they would *want* you to want to buy their stuff."

Vicki snorts from the room next door. "I heard that, Vicki! Let's drown our figure woes with a box of warm *Krispy Kremes* on the way home if the hot light's on."

"What you need, girlfriend is to get out more. Come with me to Bible study Tuesday mornings again! You'll love it."

I hedge. "I don't know, Vick. Aren't there people there? Blech."

"Very funny. I thought you were starved for company. This is the best Miss Smarty Pants Department Head can come up with?"

"*Former* department head. Former. And it's a valid excuse! Bleeeech."

"It can be tough when you first start staying home, Deena. Give yourself a break. Get. Out. Of. The. House. It's not bad, it's just, it's just different."

"I'll say. I think I've figured it out though—the only downside to being a professional stay-at-home mom is that usually the kids are there too!"

We laugh boisterously, managing to shop at *Old Navy*, *American Eagle*, *Gymboree* and the *Gap*. We don't buy much, but the time away from everything is a blast. And by the time we leave the mall for home, via *Krispy Kreme* (the hot light was agreeably on), I've agreed to give Bible study another shot.

The next morning I'm slightly happier getting into blue jeans with a regular sweater instead of one of Max's oversized dress shirts or a comfy pair of sweats. I choose my three-quarter sleeved soft peach cashmere set (the color looks good on me even if mother did pick it out) and even add the tiny diamond necklace that Max bought for me on our tenth anniversary.

Vicki's vehicle purrs in the driveway and before I get to the door, she's standing there grinning, offering to take Eli off my hands. "So where are you for three a.m. feedings?" I demand.

"You don't know how blessed you are, Deenie. But my equipment doesn't work anymore." She waves a hand around the general area of her chest. Underneath her joking, I know is pain.

Zoe sits by Canaan, both of them twisting around in their five-point harness car seats. They chatter senselessly, Canaan telling her all about the kids at Bible study in a superior way. Zoe is excited to make the craft. She takes over the conversation and chatters at either Eli or Canaan the whole way to church. Compared to Zoe, both boys are quiet.

"Mommy, I don't think Canaan and Eli are very good listeners!"

"They're men, honey!" Vicki and I laugh. I twist around in the seat and see that Eli has drifted off to sleep. Canaan is studiously ignoring Zoe, playing with his beloved toy dump truck.

We arrive just five minutes late, which for me these days, isn't too bad. Vicki directs me to the childcare counter, where I sign my girl in on a clipboard and Zoe skips off happily with Canaan, without a backward glance. Go figure.

I tote Eli along in his seat; he's still little enough to sleep and not disturb our study.

Miss Opal, a lovely older woman with the lightest English accent and beautiful dark hair, swept up in some sort of elaborate roll, reminiscent of the 1940s, has clearly just finished prayer time. She greets us with a welcome glance, but doesn't embarrass me by calling me out.

I have seen her before around church, of course, but just haven't really gotten to know her. She took over when Misty Callahan's husband got transferred to Detroit. I remember that her last name is something like Drew, though everyone I know has always just called her Miss Opal.

"In the Bible," she relates, "are 1,260 promises from God. Promises. What does that precious knowledge speak to you today?"

Several hands go up, some timid, some bold.

"That God can supply my every need in Christ Jesus," the perky Kay-with-talking-scales relates, quoting chapter and verse. And where is a barf bag when you need it?

"I like the one about God being our husband and maker," relates one woman I've never seen before. Vick whispers that her name is Reagan McCabe. "My husband left us three weeks ago. He says he's not happy being a husband and dad right now. I'm, I'm pretty sure he might be seeing someone else." She dabs her eyes with a wrinkled tissue.

One woman puts her arm around her and another offers a small packet of purse-size tissues.

Tandy Walker shares that she loves that God is our Great Physician and Healer, then quietly mentions that she's having a needle biopsy done to check for breast cancer. I didn't know that. Her husband Macon is stationed in Afghanistan right now. She's my age. I resolve to pray for her and instantly decide that I'm not going to share anything with this group. My problems are paltry in comparison. Miss Opal jots down the requests in a notebook and opens our study with prayer.

While Vicki never shies away from sharing, she seems content to soak up the responses of others and glean whatever insights she can from Miss Opal. We're talking this morning about the Patriarchs and the problems Jacob had with his tricky father-in-law, Laban, and his two wives, Rachel and Leah.

"You would think, wouldn't you, that marrying Jacob, who had such a legacy of experience with God, would have blessed these women. But they had their own problems. Let's read this morning from Genesis 29:31 through Genesis 30:24."

We each read a few verses, marveling at this Old Testament soap opera of dishonesty, barrenness, rejection and bargaining for the right to sleep with your own husband. I wonder about the mandrakes. If the herbal shop in town stocks them, I might see the return of my libido.

"What was it that Leah lacked?" Miss Opal queries. Her eyes land on me. "Deena." It's her firm invitation to answer.

"She doesn't have Jacob's love."

"That's absolutely right. Can you imagine having to compete with your beautiful younger sister for your husband's love, knowing that he hadn't wanted to marry you in the first place?"

We murmur and nod and whisper all around the table, trying to picture ourselves in Leah's position.

"Alright, then, what about Rachel? Surely she had everything going for her." Miss Opal's gentle leading reins us in.

Vicki's answer breaks my heart. "No. She wanted children and she couldn't have them. In *that* culture, it branded you a failure in every way."

"And she blamed her husband for that and it just made Jacob angry with her," Tandy adds.

Miss Opal folds her hands and then opens them, spreading them on the table as though beseeching us. "Ladies. What is it this morning that makes you feel inept, inadequate, unloved, incomplete? I don't want you to answer out loud, I just want you to think about it and then spend this week petitioning God for it, rather than blaming someone else or feeling put upon by your circumstances."

Well, ouch. But Miss Opal's spirit isn't condemning, so we can take it. We linger a bit longer over flavored coffees (I look around in vain for a cooler of cans that contain cold, brown, carbonated liquid) and then break up, mindful of how long this study hour must seem to the nursery workers. I am in dire need of a Diet Coke.

When I stop back by to pick up Zoe, she is in the front play area, sliding down a bright orange and blue Little Tykes slide and munching on the Fruit Loops strung around her neck on a piece of yarn. Canaan is on the floor, crashing two trucks together and making motor noises. Two other little girls are tugging on the same plastic alphabet block, howling and wailing.

Next to the check-in desk is a newly laminated sheet of pink paper with typing on it:

Toddler Property Laws

1. If it's mine, it's mine.
2. If it looks like mine, it's mine.
3. If I can take it from you, it's mine.
4. If I had it first, it's mine.
5. If I'm building something, all the parts are mine.
6. If I had it a while ago, it's mine.

7. If you put it down and I can pick it up faster than you, it's mine.
8. If I want it, it's mine.
9. It's all mine.

-Unknown

Vicki appears next to me. "Isn't that *great!*"

"It is. You know a mother with MPS must have written that!"

"MPS?"

"Yeah, um, it's my newly invented acronym: Multiple Preschooler Syndrome!"

"I love it!" Vick squeezes my shoulders in a sideways hug, hoisting Canaan on her hip.

Zoe is still admiring and munching on her necklace while Vicki and I sign out our children on the clipboard sheet.

We agree on the McDonald's drive-thru on the way home. Zipping us through the drive-thru, I notice a help-wanted sign on a neighboring fast food establishment sign: "Looking for Dependable Days." I snort to myself. Well, me too! Oh well, something about a Happy Meal makes everyone happier. At least temporarily.

Grocery List

Index Cards
Kleenex
Toilet paper
Ground Beef
Sloppy Joe mix
Sesame seed buns
Chips
Pretzels
Grapes
Oranges
Blueberries
Cheerios
Baby food – assortment
Celery
Carrots
Ranch dressing
Milk
Bread
Pampers
Baby Wipes
Baby Shampoo
Volumizing Shampoo – me
Deodorant - Max

Chapter 7

Big grey clouds threaten the sun like a bully with all talk and no action. The wind postures and blusters, but not a drop of rain falls. Summer's tentative beginning sits on us, sulking. The weather is in a holding pattern and so is my life. I wish it would rain. That something would change.

Restless, I pace through the house, always coming back to stare out the enormous window facing the sunrise. I am weary.

Dolphins can't allow themselves to sleep too deeply or they'll drown. They've learned to compensate by training only one half of their brain to sleep at a time. Isn't that what we mothers do? Seems like we're always half awake. Listening for the baby to cry. Making endless lists of things we need to do/can't forget/must return/answer/purchase. Endless multi-tasking. Making lunch while I talk on the phone. Doing leg lifts in the shower.

I feel like I'm living half asleep. And so this morning, like most mornings, I am having trouble getting myself going. The kids are up and at it; I'm merely up.

Sitting in the floor by Eli and Zoe, I wind and rewind the Jack-in-the-Box for what feels like the thousandth time. It never fails to draw one of Eli's precious baby giggles after he first startles and turns his large blue eyes on me. Zoe really still likes it too.

It's the final teacher work day of the school year, so Caroline is upstairs, grooming and dressing all of her Barbies, enchanted by the new sets of evening wear that my mother brought by earlier this week.

The phone rings and I grunt my way into a standing position, grabbing for the phone, leaving my youngest two angels on the cherry red and yellow braided rug. It's new from Target this week. "Zo, can you please wind that up for your baby brother? Mommy needs to talk on the phone." I step over the cadre of dust bunnies that march from beneath my couch as I hurry past it.

I see the University number on the Caller ID screen before I answer. "Hello," I greet in my most professional voice.

"Hello back," a deep, amused voice registers with me and I grin before I can stop it. It's Dr. Thomas Hunt, the Dean of History at Southern Hills University. "This is Thomas Hunt, Southern Hills University. I wasn't sure if you'd remember me." He sounds teasing.

"Dr. Hunt. Of course." I keep my tone even, like I'm not starved for conversation with a colleague, a grown-up, anyone who understands and loves written words. Surely it's not normal for our UPS guy to drop our packages on the front porch and run back to the truck like crazy. Of course lately I've nearly tried to chase him down, begging for news of the real outside world.

"Call me Thomas, please."

"Sure, uh, Thomas. What's going on?"

"I have a proposition for you. We're putting together a new curriculum proposal; possibly start it next fall. I'm sure you know, the modern-classic mind meld hasn't been as successful as administration thought it would be. Students do not understand the connections between past events and current outcomes." He breathes deeply and continues.

"Sooo, they're suggesting a multi-disciplinary approach between the history and English departments and they'd like some input this summer especially, and then continuing a bit through the school year. Ideally, we'll get ideas from people with backgrounds in both departments. Didn't I read that your minor is in history?"

I'm unreasonably flattered that he would remember. "Actually, Thomas, I'm not on the faculty anymore. I've been home for several months on a, well, on a sabbatical of sorts." I take a deep breath and blurt out the less fancy version. "I've decided to stay home with my children."

"I'd heard something like that, but I'm authorized to hire you temporarily, as kind of a consultant. You know the University; it won't pay the big bucks, but hey — I thought maybe you'd like to do just enough to keep your hand in.

The English faculty and some of the history gang will meet with us sometimes, but the bulk of the work will just be in committee or smaller groups. I'm heading up the project, and the prof who replaced you will be in England, working on a paper about Jane Austen this summer. So as you can see, we need you."

We need you. Simple words. I drink them like a dehydrated spring in the desert during a rare rain. It's not like I'm *not* needed at home, it's just more a neediness that can sometimes drain the life out of you.

"That sounds intriguing," I say in my most adult voice, trying not to reveal that I'm doing the happy dance with my feet while peering around the corner spying on my youngest two, willing them to stay quiet and contented for just a few moments more. "I'll need to discuss it with my husband, of course and make some arrangements for childcare…"

"I'm sure we can work meetings around whatever you need."

"Well, sometimes, Max can take them – depending on what's going on at the station. I mean, he's not on that type of shift anymore and…" I need to stop rambling.

"Factory?" Thomas' voice holds the slightest bit of condescension.

"No, nothing like that." I bristle, and oh, man if that isn't a bit of my Mother's judgmental bent creeping into my psyche. "Actually he's a police detective with the Southern Hills force." I can't help it; pride creeps into my voice. I can complain about Max if I want to, but I don't want anyone else casting him in a bad light.

"I see. That's great. So, are we on?"

"Very likely. When and where is the first meeting?"

"Tomorrow at noon. Top conference room in the library. I hope I'll see you."

I hang up, brimming with soul bubbles. I don't stop to consider why I'm the last-minute add-on.

I walk to the mailbox on my way over to share the good news with Vicki, and wave to Gloria the mail lady as she drives away. Rock Hudson was a mail carrier in Winnetka, Illinois, home to that older TV show I loved, *Sisters*. Walt Disney was once a substitute mail carrier too. I can't remember where.

I pound on the door, bringing Vicki in a hurry. She seems excited for me and agrees to watch the kids for me tomorrow for the first meeting at the University. Now, the wait for Max to get home. The hours will drag along like a flat tire limping to the side of the road.

I decide to make baked spaghetti, tossed salad and garlic bread for supper. It won't hurt to make one of Max's favorite meals. Sooner than I think, between naps and picking up toys and paraphernalia from every floor in the house, I hear the garage door go up and Max's footsteps in the stone breezeway.

"How are my favorite girls?" Max picks up Zoe and Caroline, swinging them in concert and kissing my lips with tenderness. He looks at me holding Eli and leans in to him as well. "And my boy!" Eli purses tiny lips and blows bubbles. "A sign of intelligence."

"Definitely," I agree. "Come sit down and eat. I have lots to tell you today!"

"Of Pride and Prejudice or Poop and Pampers?"

"No," I bristle, and then remember my resolve to be pleasant, entertaining and interesting. "Actually, I got a call from the University this morning. From Dr. Hunt, to be specific. I've been recommended to serve kind of like a consultant for a new curriculum committee this summer and possibly a few weeks through the school year too."

"I see."

"What's that supposed to mean?" I am hypersensitive to any sign of disapproval. I said I would ask Max, but honestly, I've made up my mind that I want to do this desperately.

"Nothing. Nothing at all. Do you know who's watching the kids?"

"Don't know anything yet, except that Vicki said she'd watch them tomorrow at noon for the first one. I thought maybe most of the meetings might be when you're home?" I make it a hopeful question.

'Humpff," Max mumbles with his mouth around a piece of garlic bread.

"Max! You don't even seem excited for me at all!"

He swallows. "Deenie, I am if you are; I guess I just thought that you wanted to be home."

"Well, I am, and I do."

He arches a brow.

"Want both, I mean. I'm just, I don't know--restless, I guess."

"I guess." He agrees with me in a flat tone.

"Don't be placating, Max. It's insulting." Wiping my mouth off with my napkin, I get up and start clearing plates. Loudly. Thunk, slap, dishes in the sink. If I could make the water ring louder, I would. Bang! Go the cabinet doors with the dishwasher soap inside. Snap! Goes the lid of the dishwasher closing. Smack! Goes the pantry door as I replace spices and boxes.

And Max, being Max, calmly takes the kids into the family room to play, leaving me to work off my sulk. I clean up as quickly as I possibly can, retreating to the front porch, my refuge.

Crickets sing an evening symphony and stars come out shyly. A sliver of moon sails along, cruising past filaments of cloud. Morning glories are drooping their heads, leaning on their chests for a good night's rest.

The wind picks up a bit, causing the few leaves and grass piles swept into the street to chase their tails like puppies.

I linger a moment longer, leaning on the porch railing. Contingents of early fireflies wink on and off like a crazy display of Christmas lights. They fill me with an odd excitement. Could things be looking up? Or does just the thought of donning big people clothes and going back out into the real world provide me with an instant mood makeover?

Either way, I'm reluctant to leave. To go back inside and face the soaking pots and pans and laundry and mundane responsibilities. Instead, I duck inside and locate Eli on his blanket where Max is watching *Max and Ruby's* springtime video with the girls. I smile my apologies, gently tuck Eli in my arms and go back out to the porch swing. He makes sleepy baby sounds of protest at being disturbed from his cozy nap.

I hold him close to me and drink him in with my eyes. A tiny fist shoots out from his soft blue blanket and bumps against my cheek. I slide my finger into it and he grips it with fierce tightness. "The sweetest flowers in all the world — a baby's hands," wrote Algernon Swinburne. And ah, yes, he's right.

When I hear the credit music roll through the screen door, I step inside and work side by side with Max, preparing the children for bed, tucking them in, reading them stories and hearing their prayers.

Back in our room, I sway against him and try to kiss him. He's really not receptive and we drift off to sleep in a semi-truce, after I trudge off to the bathroom, removing all my make-up and brushing my teeth since Mother insists that every night you neglect your nighttime routine adds a year to your face.

The next day at high noon, with my children safely ensconced in Vicki's capable care [I did not care to explain this to my mother, or to get my father's hopes up about me returning to work], I drive to the University. A familiar drive, but this time, it seems infused with freshness.

We're having a luncheon round table discussion about which works of literature that combine a dose of historical legacy or contemporary culture ought to be incorporated into the plans for cross-curricular development. Black plastic oval trays hold sliced sub sandwiches, chicken salad, fruit salad and the requisite dry cookies. I take half of a chicken salad sandwich and a Diet Coke.

Sonya Weatherby, poster child for American feminism, suggests a contemporary title which I tried to read last year, but whose language so offended me I was unable to finish. It is a rare thing for me to stop before a book's end. She crosses patent red and black leather sling back pumps and displays a set of mean calf muscles.

"You can't mean that," I blurt out, not a diplomatic word in my mouth. Perhaps I've been away from adult company too long. Perhaps I shouldn't be here at all.

The table looks at me; Thomas Hunt with particular interest. I forge ahead. "My experience with that book shows a deplorable lack of creativity by the overuse of one particularly vile swear word. It is such an overused mechanism that it's even a sloppily profane way to express mild irritation. It's not even bold; only foul."

Unlike many colleagues in my field, I'm not a literary snob. My summer reading list has, on occasion, included the likes of LaVyrle Spencer and Nora Roberts. Both of them have a superb command of dialogue. I devour them, not just like chocolate, but as a course of study I can't get enough of. Like many in my field, I dabble at writing, and harbor a dream of writing that illusive novel someday.

But until my once upon a someday arrives, I do keep meaning to write Nora a letter taking her to task over some language issues. Max laughs at me: "Sweet Deena, you'd be appalled at how many people use language like that daily."

"In *your* line of work," I retort haughtily, "I'm certain that's true. In *my* line of work, I expect better."

So, I remain happily glued between the pages of wonderfully crafted conversations with other people whose problems are nothing and yet everything like my own. Looking around the table, I'm certain now isn't the time to mention those particular authors.

Sonya gazes at me over red polka-dotted reading glasses. "Let me guess. You don't like *The Catcher in the Rye* either. You know, Salinger did an excellent job of exploring adolescent themes and—"

"Oh puhleese. Salinger exploited teenage angst and threw in a few symbols as a simplistic backdrop for some of the crassest language known to man. In my humble opinion, people who feel the need to express themselves in that manner may as well carry a sign admitting their poor command of the English language and plot structure, or at the very least, their impoverished vocabulary!" This is one of my pet peeves and I've forgotten professionalism.

Sonya unsheathes her claws. "Perhaps it's just as well that you've decided to take this little, er," she coughs behind her hand, "sabbatical to stay at home with your little ones. Perhaps you could use the time to cut *your* teeth on some new literature."

No one else around the table is even pretending to jot down notes or rifle through file folders. Sandwiches languish on the edges of paper plates with pale tomatoes and wilted lettuce leaves. The group is watching us with absorbed interest. I have not made a good showing, but clearly I *have* put on a good show.

Thomas steps in, intervening with the copies of the next meeting's agenda and tasks, and smoothly guides the conversation back to topic, even managing to suavely put in a word about the superior reading backgrounds of children who have mothers devoted full-time to their care.

I resist the impulse to stick out my tongue and quote author Tony Campolo's wife whenever she was asked what it was she did all day as a stay-at-home mom: "I am socializing two homo sapiens (in my case, make that three) into the dominant values of the Judeo-Christian culture so that they might become the kind of citizens fit for dwelling in the eschatological utopia which God has ordained from the beginning of creation." So there.

I unball the napkin from my hand and shred it into tiny pieces, letting them drift from my hand, covering my chicken salad like paper snow. Max would know I am about to blow my top.

The conversation enters safer ground, including a compilation of short stories. We debate the merits of symbolism in Raymond Carver's short story, "A Small, Good Thing." "Eating is a small, good thing," the baker says to the couple engulfed in the tragic loss of their son. Someone mentions the line aloud.

"Eating is always a good thing," Jeremy Templeton, who was new to the University during my last semester there, pats his not inconsiderable girth and simultaneously reaches for another cookie. I never got to know him very well, but now I instantly like him. Evidently *he* doesn't mind a little levity even in the midst of an academic gathering.

"What about plays?" offers John Claxton, another veteran of the history department. "Say, *Death of a Salesman*. Arthur Miller."

"Too pedestrian. Should have been done in high school." Sonya Weatherby.

"You must remember though," Thomas redirects, "what are college freshmen except fifth year high schoolers?" We all laugh.

"Isn't that the one about the traveling salesman who cheats on his wife? I avoided that one like the plague in high school." This from Clare Samuels, resplendent in one of her *Garanimals* for grown-ups outfits, this one a yellow gingham ensemble embroidered with dragonflies.

"Infidelity is both a timeless and a timely theme, I suppose," Sonya concedes.

"I think it's about much more than that. More." I stop, struggling not to convey my odd identification. "It's about his restlessness, his dissatisfaction. Not just with himself or his circumstances, but his soul!" Oops. I've given something of myself away.

I am quieter for the rest of our meeting, jotting down notes about what I need to have prepared for next time. I decide that quiet observation is better until I figure out this meshing of personalities and agendas. Then, perhaps, I can better do what is expected of me as a "consultant." I am to be an outsider with background knowledge. I've been demoted from faculty to community member.

All too soon it is over, as I was borne away discussing books and words, two of my very favorite things, right up there with bright copper kettles and warm woolen mittens.

I can tell I have been granted preliminary acceptance as a vital part of the committee by everyone except Sonya Weatherby, and frankly, she didn't like me when I was department head and, I think holds it against me that she wasn't recommended as my replacement.

Thomas Hunt walks me to the minivan, appearing to enjoy every bit of my conversation. Whenever the subject of books comes up, I have a tendency to gush. I tell him this as though it's a secret confession.

"Gush away, then, Deena. Your spirited opinions really brought something to the table this afternoon. I'm going to enjoy working with you." He opens the door for me and the heat from his hand as he helps me in, sears the small of my back. I am at once thrilled and scalded. For some reason, I feel the tiniest bit of guilt.

I roll down my window. "Thank you again for allowing me to help. I'll be seeing you, Dr. Hunt."

"Thomas," he reminds. "And count on it."

I drive straight to Vicki's house and pick up the children, giving her the most complete lowdown that I can with Eli pulling my hair and earrings and the girls clamoring for my attention. "Thanks, Vick. Really."

"Anytime, Deen." She waves me away and I back out across the street to our own drive.

Blog Spot Post by Pajama Mama
May 10, 2020

Guess what, cyber girl friends? I'm going to break out of jail for a few times every month! Get to do some consulting related to my former job. I got to wear big people clothes and engage in adult conversation. It has already improved my mood ten-fold, even though there are idiots on the committee. Have you noticed that a grown-up idiot is still an idiot?
Oh, well, my standards are getting preeeetty low. Adult company is adult company.

Back to life and good moods in yours,
Pajama Mama

Comments:

You have standards? I'm pretty much best friends only with the UPS guy. He's the only grown-up I see until after six o'clock when the hubs gets home.
~Chocolate Guru

Will he update you on real world news if you bake something?
~Dust Diva

You bet.
~Chocolate Guru

I meant the UPS guy.
~Dust Diva

Beware of lowering your standards, "Pajama Mama."
~Mother

I can hardly wait for Max to get home that evening, even though I've barely beaten him home by an hour. I've already called the number for *Pizza Palace*, and hope that my enthusiasm will gloss over the meal.

Max raises his eyebrows at the sight of cardboard pizza boxes yet again, but he does lean forward and pay attention as I babble on and on about the meeting, the hoity-toity Sonya Weatherby and Dr. Hunt. Thomas.

"Well, then, Deena Bean, sounds like I'll be hearing a lot about Sonya and Thomas this summer." Max leans back in his chair, his elbows bent, fingers laced behind his head. "I hope this helps you."

"It will, Max, it will. I just can't tell you how wonderful it was to discuss – even argue—about books."

"Mommy loooves books, daddy," Caroline says with authority. Max and I grin at each other.

"You don't say," Max says drolly. "But not as much as she loves me." He winks.

"Did you read them *Goodnight Moon*, Mommy?" Zoe queries, her earnest freckled face tilted upward.

"No, silly, that's a baby book!" Caroline is disdainful.

"Nooooo, it's NOT a baby book, cause Eli can't read it and he is a baby!"

"Girls," Max intervenes, "let's go upstairs and you can both read it to me."

Eli and I are left with the dishes and I don't mind. Words and conversation and Sonya Weatherby jam my brain as I clear the table. And perhaps just a bit of Dr. Thomas Hunt creeps into my thoughts as well.

The days seem to fly by and I find myself browsing the stacks and old micro fiche and Googling possibilities for the next meeting on each trip to the library for story hour with Eli and Zoe. It seems like my clothes fit better and my mind is alive. I'm being allowed back out beyond the symbolism of *Good Night Moon* and it feels good.

Vicki seems to understand how much this committee work means to me. She loves to read and lets me bounce book ideas and course lists off her whenever a new thought occurs to me. I find myself livelier around home too. This is good for Max, because it's good for me. Between the committee work and the weekly Bible study, I'm getting my groove on.

After Bible study Tuesday morning Vicki and I stand outside the childcare room discussing the lesson. Miraculously rescued from cruelty and enslavement by the Egyptians, God's chosen people still spent forty years in the wilderness, aiming for the Promised Land, complaining about the food, the provisions and pretty much everything. Petulant and disobedient. That's exactly how Miss Opal described them. "Those Israelites! They're such whiners." I laugh.

"Pot, kettle, black!" Vicki retorts.

I smack her with my Bible. "I do not whine. I protest."

"Whatever."

"What's that supposed to mean?"

"It means that up until the last few weeks, you've been hosting big, fat pity parties almost weekly! 'Poor, pitiful, misunderstood, underappreciated, misses her books and her academician University friends Deena.'" She mock sniffles, acting pathetic and holding her nose in the air, opening her purse and pretending to catch crocodile tears in the bag.

"Very, very, funny, Vick."

Miss Opal walks up wearing one of her gracious, aristocratic smiles. She is elegance personified in her soft orange sweater, brown slacks and gold jewelry. "I couldn't help but overhear you two. You're very blessed to have such a candid relationship. 'Faithful are the wounds of a friend,' King Solomon wrote. It's good that you have each other as such friends. I'll see you next week."

She walks to her car. "I want to be just like her when I grow up," I tell Vicki, only half-jokingly.

"I know what you mean." And then she breaks our serious thoughts. "Fat chance, though!" She snorts and we race to the nursery to pick up Canaan, Zoe and Eli.

I wonder, and I wonder if I'd listen if Vicki ever truly needed to wound me.

<u>Grocery List</u>
Roast
Carrots
Potatoes
Dry onion soup mix
Vidalia onion
Quick bread mix
Creamed corn
Frozen peas with pearl onions
Toilet paper
Tide
Stain stick (make that 2!)
Birthday gift for present box

Chapter 8

Vicki and I sit on her back patio performing our first day of June ritual. We're painting our toenails some shade of shocking red. It's a bit of a stretch for a favorite-color-pink-plain-vanilla kind of girl like me. Still we do it and it brings a light-hearted, youthful quality to the day, as though we can shed the responsibilities of being wives and mothers even as we shed our wool socks and boots for sandals and flip flops.

We actually ventured out to the beauty supply shop this morning, browsing through the aisles of bottled color. I chose *I'm Not Really a Waitress*, and Vicki has *O'Hare & Nails Look Great*, labels which crack us both up. (Vicki was a hairdresser, and a darn good one, until she quit to stay home with the boys.) Honestly, who thinks up this stuff? Our all-time favorite was a scarlet color called, *Frankly My Dear. Gone with the Wind* with its Rhett, Scarlett and Mammy drama, was one of our favorite movies as Jr. High girls. Although we didn't grow up together, we've discussed it many times. How we loved the romance, the dresses and the grand elegance of life in the 1860s. Naturally we never thought about the slavery issue then, or the uglier side of war: the dysentery, the death, the deprivation.

Trouble is, my mother was busy trying to raise a Melanie while my inner thought life was totally Scarlett. Vicki's mom, on the other hand, just told her to love Jesus and be whatever she wanted to be.

Mother's generation spent a lifetime licking the formaldehyde polish on their nails, trying to get them to dry faster. Perhaps that's part of her problem.

Daddy loved me more as I was than mother did, I think. But he had my doctorate and a University teaching position all lined out for me from the moment he heard me express an interest in education. Enough of that.

"Summer afternoon," penned Henry James, "The two most beautiful words in the English language." This afternoon, I concur. I stretch and wiggle my red toes.

"Did you know that ninety-three different insects use dandelion pollen as food?" I ask Vick out of the blue.

"Deenie, you need to get a life!"

"I'm trying! I am trying!"

I fill Vicki in about my first day of official consulting meetings back at Southern Hills. In the elegant oak-trimmed library conference room, I am handed a pristine yellow legal pad in case I want to jot down any notes. I frantically dig around the bottom of my purse to see if I have anything other than a chewed on American Girl doll pencil or Caroline's favorite purple pen topped with a plastic replica of Cinderella's slipper and a feather to write with. I don't. I go with the purple feather pencil just to spite Sonya Weatherby.

Vicki laughs. "How typical. My how things have changed. Welcome to *my* world!"

"So what's on your table tonight?" I ask, hoping for some culinary inspiration, seeing as how making dinner ranks just below scrubbing the bathtub grout with a toothbrush on my list of favorite things to do.

"Um, laptop, permission slips, *Good Housekeeping*, all the receipts from the bottom of my purse, a package of lime green pencil toppers and a can of pepper spray. We're dining out."

"Huge help. Thanks, Vick."

"What are friends for?"

I lie back against the surprisingly comfortable, but durable bright print of Vickie's polished cotton lawn furniture cushions and sigh.

Blog Spot Post by Pajama Mama
June 1, 2010

Well, girls, wondering what's on your table tonight? Anyone else out there having a hard time mustering up the desire to cook dinner? What's your favorite take-out place? Anchovies on pizza, yes or no?

Here's to great pedicures and a summer full of bright things!

Back to the mundane side of life, good luck with yours.

Pajama Mama

Comments:
Chinese takeout! And definitely – anchovies!
~Lexus Mommy

Cereal.
~First Time Mommy

Aha. It's catching up with you! No anchovies. And we're having pizza tonight.
~Dust Diva

Pie. That's all. Also without anchovies.
~Chocolate Guru

I don't like pizza.
~Anonymous

No wonder you're anonymous.
~Dust Diva

Watch your figures, girls.
~Mother

Later that evening, after the girls are tucked in, Eli has nursed and I've had the luxury of a steaming bubble bath, adding the secret snack of a bowl of vanilla bean ice cream, Max and I connect. It's wobbly and tenuous, and yes, naturally it leads to sex. But I am heartened. Maybe I am not crazed after all; maybe this wild up and downness, this irritating contentment followed by raging, itchy boredom and anything *but* contentment is normal.

****

Tuesday morning is our last Bible study before summer break. Miss Opal asks for praises to close our study and I decide that this I can share.

"I'm so very thankful that God provided me with this consulting opportunity for the University. We'll be meeting a few times a month all the way through December at least, and those outings are a lifeline for me. I really appreciate the chance to talk shop with colleagues and fellow word lovers."

Miss Opal inclines her head and smiles. "That's wonderful Deena. I'm certain that the University is taking advantage of a wonderful asset in your energy and love for language and literature. I can tell you miss it."

"Sometimes, I do, yes."

"That's just fine, honey. But remember that what you're doing these days at home cannot be duplicated. That's fine work too. Worthy."

"I've never, never felt that way about staying home. That I miss working, I mean. Of course, I *do* work, I just don't earn any money," jokes barf bag talking scales Kay. "Motherhood is just an awesome privilege. I feel blessed to have the time to make cookies and volunteer at school and have more time with them and energy for my husband."

"Whose world does she live in anyway?" I lean over and whisper to Vicki.

"Not the sticky floor world we live in. Her tile wouldn't dare!" Vicki answers.

I roll my eyes and then carefully look down at my Bible to stifle my growing need for an outburst.

"That's a wonderful attitude, Kay," interjects Miss Opal Drew, queen of diplomacy. I like her more every week. "It's important to remember though, that all sorts of factors, from the age of your children, to your previous involvement in a career, to the amount of spousal support you have can affect your outlook at home.

One thing I'm sure we can all agree on, is that it's a blessing to have the opportunity and the option to stay home with our children if we so desire."

"That's for sure," says the newly single mom, whose name, I remember, is Reagan Anne McCabe. And yes, she prefers to go by both first names. She mentioned a few weeks earlier that her husband is still undecided about what he wants to do and she still doesn't get anything in the way of child support. My empathy meter is twanging.

"It has its moments," Vicki and I agree.

Betty Mitchell, county knitting champion, and some of the other older women look at us with indulgent glances, mixed with a bit of wistful remembrance. I have a flash of insight: though it seems endless, this will be fleeting. I am, however, grateful to have a break from Kay. She gets on my last nerve. God save me from perfectly coiffed, too perky, over-organized, under-analyzed, mother-of-the-year types. Even Vick has the occasional off day.

We join hands, circling around the scuffed, white and gray-flecked Formica table for prayer. I haven't done a prayer circle since summer camp when I was a kid. I'm ready for a break, but will miss having Bible study too. It started me on my upward road out of Swamp Stuck.

Kay comes out, not looking at anyone, swinging her perfectly coifed and stacked bob, pulling her toddler and preschooler by their little hands, clicking the remote unlock button on her ivory Jeep with a manicured finger. Yes, a break. That's what I need.

But backing out of the church parking lot with the children, I already feel lonely. Cold dread slides down my throat. What will I do with all of these endless summer days?

Blog Spot Post by Pajama Mama
June 7, 2010

Okay, spill it. What do you girls do with someone who gets on your last nerve? That's legal, I mean.

I'm trying to allow someone to go on with their life [meaning I won't back over them in the church parking lot] and go back to mine. Can't wait to hear!
   Pajama Mama

Comments:

Feed her pizza with anchovies.
~Chocolate Guru

Days back into more days and slide over one another with maddening sameness. Hot. Humid. Sidewalk chalk, bubbles, play dates at Vicki's, pizza take-out, nap times and still more chapters of Junie B. Jones.

"What do you guys do all day now that you get to be home and play?" Max asks me, all innocence.

"You wouldn't understand," I answer coldly. I didn't realize how much of me I had tied to being someone professional. Someone who knew her stuff. And for the first time in our marriage, I lock the bathroom door when I bathe and dress in my pajamas.

Blog Spot Post by Pajama Mama
June 18, 2010

Have escaped to porch. Sheer noise level present inside my house was overwhelming. Sat down on the porch swing anticipating a fifteen-minute wait until Max's arrival home from work. I contemplate my nails, woefully inadequate by anyone's standards. Shove down memory of twice monthly manicures -- a past treat to self when actually earning money from University.

Tucking the offending appendages under my thighs, I leisurely push myself with my toes. Imagine myself to be a glamorous wealthy lady of privilege, indulging myself in idle pastimes, awaiting my husband's return and then dinner at a swanky cafe, smoky with candlelight and awash with ambiance.

My fifteen-minute wait drags on into 45 minutes, punctuated by glances at the portable baby monitor and the slap of the screen door approximately every 2.3 minutes by one or another of the children. "Mommy? Whatcha doin' out here?" "Mommy, Caroline took my Barbie!" "Moooom! Make Zoe leave me alone!" "What time is dinner?" "Is Daddy home yet?"

I marvel that mercifully the baby sleeps through all of this. A new, restless, dissatisfied Eeyore side of me pipes up. *Probably means you'll be up all night though. Play now, pay the piper later.* Shut up Eeyore. And great. Nursery rhymes are invading my thoughts right along with Eeyore.

The minutes slow to a traffic jam creep of the mind, the kind of slow-motion visual where morbid curiosity seekers and ambulance chasers crane their necks out windows to see every grisly detail. I begin to imagine every kind of horrible scenario.

Shake my head hard to knock out morbid nonsense. Wouldn't Freud have a field day? My paranoid reverie is interrupted by Max's car pulling in the driveway. I won't have to be a gracious widow after all. He's holding something behind his back. I see wilted green tendrils peeking around his arms like the tentacles of those green space aliens in 1950s horror flicks. He proffers a sad bouquet of formerly fresh tulips and daisies, bound with yellow ribbon. The color of sunshine. The color of the bridesmaid dresses at our wedding. The color of hope. And, I'm beginning to think, the color of nothing we are anymore.

Max has arrived, so back to life. Good luck with yours,
Pajama Mama

"Sorry I'm late babe. You wouldn't believe the trouble at. . . ." I am already tuning him out. Sorry for it, and sorry that I can't feel sorrier, and feeling it impossible to stir the interest I should have and wanted to feel, as Max's wife. Sorry that my interest in such things seems to have dried up, withered and fallen off like the stump of Eli's umbilical cord.

I'll have to come back and change some identifying details on the blog later, before I post it.

Blog Spot Post by Pajama Mama
June 24, 2010

Okay. Just for fun, I made a list of stuff I did today. To my knowledge, I didn't leave anything out. How'd your day stack up?

Nursed Eli. Changed Eli. Nursed Eli on the other side. Attempted to shower in private; forced to watch musical number by Zoe and Caroline through the curtain instead. Got dressed. Mostly. Did laundry. Folded towels. Realized I forgot to put bra on and went back upstairs to change. Helped the cat with a fur ball. Helped Caroline make a collage of things beginning with letter Q, using old magazines from the recycle bin. Made slice and bake cookies. Ate four of them raw. Explained to the girls why eating raw cookie dough would *not* be good for *them*. Asked forgiveness for my hypocrisy. Asked my neighbor about the correct substitution for buttermilk in tonight's recipe. Gave up and took the kids to the store anyway, via the library and Target.

Pulled two dandelions. Fixed peanut butter and jelly sandwiches cut into triangles with a side of grapes and Goldfish crackers for lunch. Held my nose and drank milk for calcium needs. Spoiled? Forgot to check expiration date. Tricked Eli into eating strained peas by pretending that rubber coated spoon was a spy plane. This entertained my girls far more than Eli.

Noticed that Eli has a sweet, tiny tooth breaking through his bottom gum. Nursed Eli again and considered quitting nursing because of said tooth. Took Eli and the girls for a walk around the block. Explained to two telemarketers why I do not need a set of knives or a "free" magazine subscription. Two more loads of laundry.

Built six block towers with Zoe. Gave myself a face lift with raised eyebrows trying to nicely explain to Caroline why I did NOT think it would be fun to play house. Four readings of *Pat the Bunny*; one of *Bedtime for Frances* and three Chapters of *Junie B. Jones is Not a Crook*. Took break for two more loads of laundry and five diaper changes in between. Sorted through my underwear drawer and threw away an amazing amount of holey, discolored, and elastic-less undies.

Practiced spelling word flashcards with Caroline. "Ate" some of Zoe's Play dough ice cream. Folded and put away clothes. Bent down and picked up toys from interesting places in six different rooms. Wondered why given such activities, I don't have firmer thighs.

Found a Slinky, a rock and seven Fruit Loops in a closed Tupperware container under Zoe's bed. Did I mention they were under water? Changed another diaper, approaching blow-out status.

Wiped Zoe when her big girl potty duties were too much for her. Saw my son do a wobbly, rocking, army crawl just a short distance for the first time. Sat down and cried.
Pajama Mama

Comments:
A dried lizard in my little boy's jean pocket.
~Dust Diva

Gravel. Lots of gravel.
~Lexus Mommy

Good for you!
~Chocolate Guru

Was that supposed to be snide?
~Lexus Mommy

Not only supposed to be, it was!
~Chocolate Guru

Aw, this was a sentimental post. Emma is growing too fast already.
~First Time Mommy

Better get used to that.
~Formerly Hot

<u>Grocery List</u>
Vanilla ice cream
Toilet paper
Paper towels
Scrapbook
Print pictures from memory-card
Glue sticks
Junior mints (do they come in a case?)
Moth balls
Baby hangers
Pampers
Little Debbie Nutty Bars

Chapter 9

This morning, the committee gathers at *The Rooster* for coffee and raspberry muffins. Naturally, I am having a Diet Coke with mine. The front counter is covered with old barn wood and chicken wire. Stained pine shelves line the rooms with various carved, painted and porcelain roosters, hens, chicks and eggs. An enormous stone rooster carries the framed chalkboard advertising today's pastry specials and coffee flavors right by the entrance. Gift items from notepads to kitchen timers, all with a rooster or farm theme are scattered attractively throughout the shop on shelves, tables and wooden crates.

I am seated at a round table across from Thomas and I find myself ridiculously attuned to him. Each time my eyes roam around the table, his eyes meet mine.

Breaking my muffin into pieces and spreading them liberally with butter from those tiny white rectangles covered in gold foil, I watch him when he goes to the self-serve station for a coffee refill. It's too warm for the black wool overcoat I always saw him in. Without it, I can check him out in greater detail. He's tall and dark and thinner than Max. His eyes are a rich brown, but they are aloof. Observant, but unemotional. His hands are slender and they look tender to me; I don't see any of Max's physical strength.

His hair has a bit of sophisticated gray at its edges and his jaw always has a rogue-looking shadow of hair. He does have a bit of the scoundrel about him. Max is the clean-cut, clean-shaven All-American hero. There is no pretense. He's rugged and manly and forthcoming, unless he needs to hide something for a case.

Thomas has the reserved air of an enigmatic Bronte sisters' hero. He seems European in manner, though I know he is not.

All comparisons aside, though, there's something magnetic about Thomas. He is confident, smooth and well-read. I remember seeing him, on his contemplative walks around the lake on mid-week afternoons, rehearsing his research notes, crafting his lecture into dynamic, living pieces of history. Students always sign-up for his classes.

It's a much quicker meeting this morning, since we're basically all assigned to come up with collegiate level lesson plans using a novel that pairs with an era in history or was written in a specific period and shines as an example of literature and topic during that period.

A few of the group are assigned to come up with composition assignments and blue book essay tests that will comprise a combined history-English grade. Some get American history assignments; others, World history. I hear rumors that we'll be compiling ideas for an on-line version too.

The committee will have a larger final meeting to choose the final selections and present them to the board right around the holidays. If we have spring semester meetings, those will be reserved for fine-tuning and ordering texts.

When Sonya Weatherby has to leave early for another meeting, Thomas casually moves into the seat next to me. I am surprised, but no one seems to think anything of it. His knee occasionally bumps into mine and after a bit, he leaves it there.

I'm startled into doing nothing, since he seems so unaware. I would hate to make a big deal out of it, so I leave my legs right where they are. After a while, they tingle and I seem aware of Thomas in an oddly physical sense.

Thomas wraps up the meeting smoothly by assigning each of us a partner to narrow down topics and hone the major concepts into student-friendly bites. I am concentrating on the faint yellow blobs of hardened muffin, scattered on the table like anemic tumbleweeds.

"I'll go ahead and work with Deena Wilson since she's the temporary consultant here and we won't have as much time to get her valuable opinions," Thomas decides.

He turns to me and smiles a Pierce Brosnan smile. "Is that all right with you, Mrs. Wilson?"

My index finger rests on a brittle crumb and it snaps under the pressure. I choke up for a moment, startled into feeling like the wallflower that is chosen to dance with the most handsome, popular boy in school. "Certainly," says my voice, in a tenor I've never heard before. "That will be fine."

No one ever discusses the possibility that you might someday be attracted to someone who is not your spouse. I'm in unfamiliar territory and very unsure what, if anything, to say to anybody. I decide that I'm being silly and acting normal would be the wisest course. *Acting* normal?

My cell rings on the way home from the committee meeting and Vicki instructs me to go straight home and get my suit. Since she has the kids anyway, why don't I just come over and swim? "I can't wait to hear all about it." Her voice lilts with the enthusiasm I need these days. "By the way, the kids were little angels."

"I'll do it," I tell her. She's the only friend I'd knowingly allow to see me in my swimming suit. "Just give me a second to pee and change," I thank her. "I've been meaning to get over there and lay out in all of my child-free time –" I interrupt myself with snorts. "Because we all know that…"

"Tan fat looks better than pale fat!" We finish together. "Jinx. Owe me a Coke." We'll put on sunscreen, though, and mourn the days of laying out on tin foil, our bodies slathered in baby oil.

Throwing on my suit and cover-up and tossing some ice pops and Diet Cokes in a Target sack, I head on over. I love times like this and I instantly relax.

Vicki's backyard is amazing. The boys' swing set is encased by railroad ties, the underneath of which is piled with mounds of cushiony mulch. The lawn is so neatly trimmed I wouldn't have been surprised if my mother had been there with the manicure scissors.

The concrete area around the pool has gently beveled edges and is flanked by huge copper pots of bright red and yellow poppies and green leafy ferns. *Pottery Barn* striped umbrella tables in rich shades of chocolate invite gatherings. Even Zeke's grill is properly shined chrome. Yet somehow the sense of order soothes, rather than accuses. I feel at home here. I guess the atmosphere is all about the people who live there.

The radio, piped through a speaker on the side of Zeke's tool shed, plays quiet pop tunes. Occasionally a song from our high school era causes us to sing along and we laugh, each quietly remembering other times. Simpler in some ways, harder in others. I love that Vick and I can either chatter like magpies or just *be*.

I've sailed baby Eli through the shallows in a plastic blow-up baby float, shaped like a bunny. Held Zoe underneath her back, trying to get her to keep her ears in the water so she can back float. Canaan is interested only in splashing and riding around on the swim noodles. Christopher is over at a friend's house from church. Caroline gingerly dips her feet in, preferring to sit on the side and look at books or walk around the shallows to cool off. She is so like me.

We've only been in the water for about thirty minutes, when the sky grows dark in an instant. The wind whips the water into choppy waves and makes the umbrella tables tremble.

I quickly help Zoe out and wrap her in a thick kid-sized Blue's Clues beach towel, her snuggie of choice. Canaan scrambles up the ladder calling out, "I don't need help, Mom!"

"Me neither, Mom," Caroline tosses over her shoulder and for that second, I notice and mourn that she has imitated Canaan and called me 'Mom' rather than 'Mommy.'

Vicki hands me Eli, wrapped in a blue striped towel. He howls, angry at being too quickly snatched from the fun of splashing in the water and feeling independent, floating around in the bunny. He pushes against me, little legs flailing.

"Hush, Son. Mommy's got you." I pat him and he reluctantly lays his head on my shoulder.

A huge crack of thunder fills the air at the same time that a sheet of lightening splits the heavens.

"My goodness, here it comes!" Vicki gives up looking for her other flip flop and grabs Canaan's pudgy, sweet little boy hand.

As we run for the safety of Vicki's sunroom, I see the storm pushing together a rainbow in the pool, comprised of colored foam swimming noodles. A remnant of one of God's promises that we talked about in Bible study a lifetime ago.

I dry everyone off and slip our cover-ups on. "Let's go, kids! Head 'em up and move 'em out!"

"Yeah, head 'em up and head 'em up," Zoe echoes, a misquote which always cracks me up.

"Thanks, Vicki," I call over my shoulder. "You're a gem."

"Well, don't run off."

"Nah, don't want to wear out our welcome, and besides, I want to grab a few things in town before Max gets back."

She nods in understanding and I see her relief that some relative peace will reign in her house for a few hours at least. Inviting kids over indoors is a whole other world from inviting kids over outdoors, even if they are with your best friend.

Arriving soggily in our driveway, instead of dragging them all back in the house for baths and clothes changes, I go ahead and buckle them into the minivan.

Max has been away at a training conference in Jefferson City for a few days, so I surprise the kids by wheeling into the video store and telling them they can choose a movie. Eli gurgles over my shoulder, secure in his Snugli, and Zoe and Caroline whoop it up in the aisle displaying *Blue's Clues*, *Strawberry Shortcake* and a variety of Disney pictures.

Keeping them in my sight, I browse the new releases, and then the older classic cowboy films, thinking I might treat Max to a testosterone- laden action film and some welcome home sex. Last week I distinctly heard him use the words "sex life" and "terrible" in the same sentence. I tuck two possibilities under my arm and after glancing at my wristwatch, call the girls to come on.

Getting no response, I walk over to their aisle and try to be patient with their dickering, bickering and pseudo-compromises. "Girls, come on. I want to swing by and pick up pizza. Daddy should be home any time now. Move it."

They act as though I'm not there. "Caroline! Zoe! I said choose your movie and let's go." Eli drags his sleepy face back and forth across my shoulder; I feel the beginnings of a fuss coming on.

"Just a sec, Mommy!" Caroline chirps.

"Yeah! I need a sec too, Mommy," Zoe chimes in.

"No. No MORE SECS! I'm running out of patience so I AM ABSOLUTELY DONE WITH SECS!" I haven't realized that my voice has gotten louder and shriller until I sense the absolute silence in the store.

Other customers begin snickering at me and I realize what else 'secs' sounds like. My face flushes and my ears flame.

I snatch a *Blue's Clues* that we don't already have at home, hoist Eli's buns a little bit higher in the Snugli, and drag both girls by the hands to the counter. For good measure, I throw a family movie value basket on the counter. It has a super-sized buttered microwave popcorn bag, two boxes of movie candy and a 2-liter of Diet Coke. I hand over my credit card and try to hold my head high.

At the exit, someone is already holding the door open for me and even as I start to brush past, I sense him looking at me. I look up into Thomas's amused brown eyes. "Absolutely no more, huh? I wouldn't have taken you for that kind of woman!"

I drop Caroline's hand, adjust Eli and try to check on my hair. I sure haven't taken time with myself since we were just out for two quick errands and I'd planned to grab a few minutes for reconstruction before Max's arrival. I am suddenly conscious of my sheer white gauze cover-up and how short it is. I position Zoe in front of my hips. Three year olds are great camouflage.

"Uh, I'm not, generally. Sometimes these little guys," I ruffle Caroline's hair, wave Zoe's hand and kiss the top of Eli's head, "make me a little crazy. Sorry to run into you like this." I gesture to my cover-up and flip flops.

"I'm not minding anything I'm seeing. I'm just grateful to get to see you again this soon. Our private meeting already seems a long time ago." His eyes drill deeply into mine, trying to find answering desire.

He has not touched me. At all. But my knees are water and my breath comes short.

"That's sweet, Thomas." I fumble and drop my eyes. "I, uh, I really enjoyed talking with you. But I better get my crew home now. Soon," I say in closing and surprise myself by how much longing there is in that statement.

"Soon, then," Thomas echoes and he salutes me as I scurry out to the minivan, trying not to get the movies or Eli wet under plump drops of rain.

"Who was that Mommy?" Zoe asks before the doors even close.

"That was Dr. Hunt, from the University."

"Are you sick?"

"No, silly girl. Not that kind of doctor; it just means he's been to school a long time."

"Does he like you?" Caroline asks suspiciously.

"I would hope so, pumpkin. We have to work together on a project."

"I don't like him."

"Caro! That's not nice. What would make you say that?"

"Cause I think he looks gushy at you like daddy looks at you." There is a possessive note to her voice. And I wonder at the perceptions of a five-and-a-half-year-old girl.

"Alright, Caro," I sigh. "I don't think so at all; let's not talk about it anymore." I don't want to listen to what I know. Caroline is right. Something is different, but I'm better off not naming it. If it has a name, I might have to stop and this giddy feeling is the most alive I've felt in months.

We make the rounds, pick up the pizza and when we pull into the driveway, Max's car is already there. My pulse feels thready and weak. I can't determine if it's excitement that he's home or a guilty-giddiness over my odd conversation with Thomas.

"I thought you guys had deserted me," Max greets with his usual energy, hugging all of us tightly. He kisses my mouth soundly. "Have you been swimming in *this*?" He glances over his shoulder and gestures out the window to the rain-drizzled panes.

Butternut has entered the fray from wherever it is that he hides himself, and winds around Max's legs. He steadily ignores me; traitor cat. *Pot, kettle, black,* I hear the echo of Vicki's words.

"No, daddy!" Zoe and Caroline giggle and fill him in on the sudden storm and the video store.

"And we brought pizza!!"

"What a surprise," Max says dryly.

I find myself holding my breath, hoping neither of the girls will mention the encounter with Thomas. I can tell him about it later, if I need to. And besides, I didn't exactly tell Vicki the truth about last night's late meeting.

They don't say anything about it though, reveling in having their daddy home. I share small daily anecdotes from the home front and Max tells a few amusing stories about his training on investigating juvenile crimes.

"After the kids go to bed, I have a surprise for you," I tell Max.

His broad grin makes my stomach do flip flops and I marvel at myself. "I will like that surprise *very* much."

"Actually, I have something else, but sure, um, we can do that too."

"You bet we can," Max growls and pulls me to him. "In fact, let me put the kids down and you can go get out of your suit and into something—else." He leers.

Later, I sit on the couch, shoulder to shoulder with Max. I'm enjoying the comfortable familiarity of having him home. I've brought home *Open Range*, a cowboy movie with Kevin Costner. At a critical point, Charlie's boss says, "It's a pretty day for makin' things right."

I latch onto that statement and consider telling Max that I think I might be attracted to Thomas. But then, I'm not really in the mood to fight, and I don't have an indiscretion to report exactly.

I blush thinking of last night's impromptu meeting beneath the jauntily striped umbrella tables of the outdoor student union. In a flash, my traitorous mind movies take me there. Thomas inquires as to my preferences and returns with a warm apple hand-pie, one of the cooks' specialties, Diet Coke and hot chocolate. feel spoiled. It is not often in my new job as waitress/referee/psychologist/nursemaid/full-time mom that anyone waits on me.

In an effort to deflect the charged atmosphere, I clutch the hot cocoa mug with both hands and gulp too quickly, scorching the roof of my mouth. My tongue feels as if tiny sharp potato chip shards wearing little socks are marching over it.

Thomas is solicitous, proffering my icy Diet Coke, standing so near that the warmth of him spreads to my shoulder.

We've been speaking of the basic University philosophy. It seems that where both relationships and curriculum are concerned anything goes. Whatever. I look at him and am conscious of an odd danger; I could adopt that philosophy all too easily.

Not a single piece of dialogue stands out in my mind. I am seventeen again, crushing hard.

Maybe the connection of all that we have in common – our love of literature, history, academia, the lure of foreign travel—would be as delightful as I imagine it might have been were I not a married woman. *Married*, Deena, I remind myself forcefully.

I think of *Ethan Frome*, a classic literature favorite among my students. "*Serves him right, the idiot,*" I remember one particular female student blurting out, incensed. "*There's no excuse for cheating, not ever!*"

"*You're too much of a prude,*" retorted a male student. "*You might cheat too if there wasn't anything left of your relationship.*"

"*Yeah, I mean what a self-absorbed hack!*" This was backed up by a male chorus of "*Go for it! Go for it!*"

I think of the story's ending. Maybe not. The movement of Max's solid arm around my shoulder bolts me out of remembering and back to reality. Max smiles down at me.

"Okay, babe?" I nod and he turns back to the movie.

And what if Max makes me quit the committee and consulting? I love those excuses for putting on big people clothes and using my brain for more than determining the symbols in our check book, inventing bedtime stories and trying to keep Butternut Squash off the counters.

With horses whinnying and clomping around on the screen in front of me, I decide that I don't truly have anything that needs to be made right; no wrong has been committed. *Yet*, a nasty voice hurls in my head.

And when Max pulls me to him to make love, I find myself having to willfully refuse to think of someone else.

*****

Over the next few weeks I have a wave of body consciousness and am trying like crazy to walk consistently, to do something that will firm up the casualties of childbirth and too little sleep. I have already fallen into the take-it-for-granted rhythm of Max being home and being with all three of the children for endless hours is wearing on me.

Blog Spot Post by Pajama Mama
July 2, 2010

Gleefully leave children with my man as soon as he walks through the door. Feel guilty and relieved at getting out of the house. Almost just as guilty seeing my own husband and not wanting to sit down with him and ask about his day.

I take a brisk walk through our neighborhood, struggling to clear cobwebs from the jumbled attic that my thoughts have become.

I see an enormous woman chasing a toddler, attempting to keep him from running into the street. She's huffing and puffing. I run interference, scooping up the tot with a practiced maneuver and handing him back to his mother. She smiles wearily, pushing her hand through over-processed hair. "If I could just bottle 1/10 of his energy. . . ." Her voice trails off and I nod with understanding. I pick up my pace and think uncharitably, *if you'd lose about 50 pounds, maybe you'd have some.* The scripture from Matthew about logs and specks and your own eyes comes up from the depths of my soul to haunt and convict. I have a strange sense of foreboding. I am a fraud. In fact, were I a security exchange, I'd be shut down for fraudulent activity.

What about that kind of life, girls? Any fakeness going on out there in mommy land?

Back to my so-called life, good luck with yours.
Pajama Mama

Comments:

Hey, fake can be great, so don't knock it!
~Lexus Mommy

No way can I be critical of extra pounds. Man!
~First Time Mommy

I hear that.
~Dust Diva

We eschew doing anything for Independence Day this year, save for sparklers in the yard. Max has volunteered to take someone's shift, an officer whose wife just had their first baby.

Mother and Daddy are disappointed because we aren't going to the lake with them; Max's parents are disappointed because we aren't driving there to see them. So, I can just disappoint everyone with one fell swoop.

The day drags on. I miss the big bar-b-que scene with homemade ice cream, burgers with little toothpick flags sticking out of the buns, potato salad, coleslaw and an assortment of chips, brownies and sun tea. I imagine everyone else having fun with family and friends and feel sorry for myself. Vicki, Zeke and the boys drove to Gatlinburg to stay with her parents.

This is a strange, endless summer with flat patches of extreme boredom, punctuated by the sharp thrills of my encounters with Thomas.

It seems far too long between meetings at the University. Thomas surprises me one morning, meeting me at the minivan on the back lot of the library, holding a huge chocolate bar and a six-pack of Diet Coke, and wearing a broad smile. His face is summer tanned and looks, well, yummy. If you act like an adolescent, I suppose your vocabulary follows suit.

"A little bird told me your birthday is almost here, and since I won't have the privilege of being with you on your special day, I just wanted to acknowledge it."

"Thomas!" Impulsively, I throw my arms around his neck and about two seconds later, realize the absolute impropriety of such an act. I push away from him, flushing. "Sorry. I mean, thank you, I just didn't expect, you shouldn't—no, I shouldn't have…Thank you. Really. It's very sweet of you."

His arms encircle my waist and he just stands there so I can't really move outside the circle and the only thought I think is how we really shouldn't be seen like this. Only that. Not that I shouldn't even be standing there.

"I'll collect later," his voice is husky, promising things I don't fully understand.

Honeybees communicate about where nectar is by doing the nectar dance, spinning in circles, wagging their little abdomens and vibrating their wings. Sadly, the thought of seeing Thomas makes me feel like doing a honeybee dance of my own. Happiness wriggles out of me, drawn to the nectar of Thomas' attention and frank admiration.

He steps back from me and I get my things from the van, trying to force the heat from my cheeks, trying to understand myself.

We walk separately into the meeting, evidently by unspoken agreement. I am greeted by Sonya Weatherby's arched eyebrows and I don't remember a thing that was discussed.

Back home, Vicki has left a simple Mason jar filled with some of her black-eyed Susans on my porch. Tied to the ribbon around the vase is a coupon for five hours of girlfriend time, one per month for the rest of the year. One hour for every year we have been friends. A note in her precise, sloping hand read, "I happen to know you'll be busy tomorrow [she's drawn a winking face there] so this is a day early." I am touched by her elegant simplicity. I also wonder what it is she knows about my plans for tomorrow.

And, I do lunch with my mother. She takes me to a ritzy Greek place, the same one where Vicki and Zeke celebrated Valentine's Day, and then presents me with a certificate for a massage and a spa facial. Most moms I know would love such a gift; to me, it just seems an unspoken criticism. We engage in stilted, shallow conversation. I'm certain I've felt more warmth from a stranger. The upside is that Daddy will come get me for donuts sometime this week, I know. He has done so every birthday week of my life.

I have not ever been one to dread birthdays, and I don't exactly dread this one because of the numbers. I dread it because there seems to be no luster. Not the grand anticipation of presents that you have in childhood, nor the sweet remembrances that marked the first half of my married life. Rather, it seems bland. A day like any other day and frankly, I have far too many of those.

The morning of my actual birthday dawns in muggy splendor. I tiptoe out in my robe and slippers, enjoying a brief stretch and some muted birdsong on my way to throw a few bills in the mailbox. A shimmery haze already hangs over Morning Glory Circle. The heat is thickly visible and sits on the black asphalt like a bad-tempered fairy.

The flowers that border the sidewalk look exhausted, and the colors less brilliant, like a favorite yellow shirt that's been through the washer too many times. I know the feeling. As usual, I park myself on the white pine porch swing, scooting over to the side with the fattest cushion and less peeling paint.

Giving myself a little push with my toes, I sway gently and listen to the sounds of the day waking up. A few rebellious crickets (toddlers, likely) refuse to go to sleep making a bit of sleepy morning music.

The screen doors of those odd morning folks slap gently, as they bend to retrieve their newspapers. Pet collars tinkle as they're let out to do their morning business. Birds are the quintessential early risers, pecking the lawns for worms, scolding their young (an unavoidable part of breakfast with offspring of *any* kind, apparently) and trilling a cheerful ode to the day. The low rumble of the far away garbage truck reminds me that I probably need to get a move on.

Back inside, I relish the fact that everyone appears to still be sleeping. I shower quickly and stand staring into my closet for a ridiculous amount of time. What a strange year this is turning out to be. Ordinarily, I would have dressed up a little on my birthday. Today I just opt for jeans and my most comforting tank top with my pink sweatshirt over it. Max will want me to keep the air conditioning cranked today for sure.

Blog Spot Post by Pajama Mama
July 15, 2010

My 37th birthday is marked on today's calendar. Next to it, I have noted that the trash gets picked up today. Typical. So, what do you fellow mommies do to celebrate your birthdays, as it's a given that on those days celebrating the little people to whom you have given birth, you're busting your tail to rent a clown/pony/magician and trying to make sure Junior has a great time while attempting to show up all the other competitive mommies in your circle? Happy birthday life to any of you cyber girlfriends out there who might share mine.

Back at it, and good luck with yours,

Pajama Mama

Comments:

Happy birthday!
~First Time Mommy

Yes, happy birthday. Jungle Jym birthday party. 22 four-year-olds. Don't do it.
~Dust Diva

That calls for chocolate!
~Chocolate Guru

Doesn't everything?
~Formerly Hot

I log off my little notebook computer, lean my elbows on the breakfast bar and try to will breakfast into materializing.

Max tiptoes behind me, sweeps my hair across my shoulder and plants a kiss on my neck. "Glad you have a hoodie on," he says, grinning at my pink sweatshirt from Old Navy. "Because I'm gonna sneak around and put things in it. See?" He grins and plops a banana and a hair scrunchie from the fruit bowl in the hood of my sweatshirt. "You're planning your day and I'm planning mine."

I roll my eyes. "Honestly Max. Don't you have anything better to do? Besides how do you know I'm planning my day?"

"Because I know you and nope, today, I don't. I took the day off!"

I gape. Max never takes a day off.

"You never take the day off!"

"But I did." He looks extraordinarily pleased with himself.

"Why?"

Now he looks hurt. "Because unlike those ridiculous television shows, it actually takes fifty-four hours to process a sample of DNA, so I'm really not going to get anything done anyway, and it's your birthday. This day is my gift to you. Now, get in the car."

"Max. We have children."

"Not today, we don't. They will be in good hands, including the bottles you pumped that I took from the freezer and have already included in Eli's bag." I am astounded to discover that the silence I mistook for sleeping was Max surreptitiously getting everyone ready for my surprise.

He dares me to voice an objection, and of course, I can't. We drive the few minutes to my parents' luxurious home on a wooded acre and surrender the children to their squealing delight.

At the last minute, Caroline turns around and runs back to the car. I open the door to her and she clutches my neck with every ounce of strength in her little body. "I love you extra much today, Mommy. Have fun with all the surprises Daddy did!" Her blue eyes twinkle and mine answer hers, but with a sheen of tears.

She races back down the sidewalk and I roll down the window to blow kisses. "Good-bye! Be good for Nana and Poppy. Eli – don't grow any more while I'm gone." These days it seems he is changing before my eyes and I can remember why I ditched the University. I would have missed all this.

I turn my attention back to Max, determined to try. To be grateful. To behave. To *not* think about Thomas.

We start the day with strawberry-covered Belgian waffles at a little diner I've never seen, tucked in next to an antique store. When we're stuffed, we visit that next. We browse like we used to, holding up the ugly items and grinning, seriously considering a few things we might actually like. Although Max tells me I can pick something, I just can't make any decisions.

On to a matinee of a chick flick that Max would never voluntarily see. Popcorn with Junior Mints and Diet Coke. I feel awkward with Max, my hand strangely disembodied from any feeling when he holds it. We finish up what should have been the most magical day with Max letting me choose a new sundress from my favorite shop.

"Want to go to Target, too?" He fixes me with a look that clearly says I'm busted. Max is not one for idle words.

My look is instantly guilty. "No, thank you."

"I know about the Target card, and I cancelled it." He grins wryly. "I love you, Deena Bean. I think maybe I've been forgetting to show you that."

I am undone, yet strangely ambivalent. I don't let myself think about what this might mean. Max leans down and kisses me hard, full on the lips. There is a question behind it, a claiming that is nearly tangible in the force of this kiss. Max doesn't do PDAs either. I tiptoe up to him and try to surrender.

We pick the children up from my parents' and spend the evening playing *Chutes and Ladders*, *Candy Land* and *Old Maid*. The kids make a big production of giving me their homemade cards, flower seeds, a set of copper pots and a big bag of potting soil. It's actually a pretty sweet way to end the thirty-seventh anniversary of my birth.

Then it's the weekend, and thus a moratorium on meetings for the University. I am astounded at how bereft that certainty makes me feel. Where is the unbounded gladness for Max at home and family activities? Is it just that all of my days have a sameness to them?

Saturday passes in a lazy mix of chores. Lawn mowing. Sheet changing. Grocery shopping. Walking around the neighborhood with Max, the children in strollers or on bikes with training wheels, sporting huge baskets with flowers on them.

Sunday's sermon is on marriage. "Marriage is not about being happy. Not necessarily," Pastor Sherman explains. "It's not even about *finding* the right person, so much as it is about *being* the right person. Other excuses for failure are exactly that – excuses. I'm not talking about abuse or unfaithfulness, that's a different topic entirely.

I'm speaking of the penchant we have as a society for looking for fulfillment in anything other than God. It is not possible for anyone, no matter how perfect, to fill up a God-shaped vacuum. We do our spouses great harm and our great God a great disservice when we attempt to hold them responsible for our happiness."

Sweat beads and rolls down between my breasts. My white sundress with the multi-colored straps and colorful sandals feels constrictive. There is absolutely no way that Pastor Sherman could know of the outstanding compliment that Thomas paid me this past week as we met at *The Rooster* to compare notes over coffee.

Thomas' eyes lit up with pleasure as he stood to pull back my chair. "Deena, you could light the University commons without assistance in that dress. I don't believe I'd let you out of the house if you were my wife." Odd that this reference to the housewife I've actually become doesn't rankle. In my vain imaginings, life as simply someone's wife doesn't sound like drudgery if I were to accompany them on research trips, traveling to fascinating places and assisting with ground-breaking revisionist history.

No reason for our preacher to know I've transferred allegiance from my usual Starbucks to *The Rooster*, the more trendy college hang out on the opposite end of town. It might seem particularly damning that I didn't frequent that place even when I was full-time faculty at the University.

Max leans over. "Deena Bean? You alright? Too hot?" With a thud, I crash land out of my thought life with Thomas, and back in the red-cushioned pew.

I shake my head in protest, ignoring eye contact with him in a righteous fit of uber listening. I lean forward, Bible open on my lap, elbows on the pew in front of me, intent on the sermon.

I am in panic mode when services are over and I think of the long, lazy afternoon in front of me with Max. I can only favor even Mr. Mac with a quick sideways hug and thanks for the five pieces of Bazooka. There are only so many naps to take; so many excuses I can make to go to the University. I ask Max if he'd mind rounding up the children from Junior Church and getting Eli from the nursery and I'll just meet him in the minivan.

"Spend the afternoon," Annie Dillard wrote. "You can't take it with you." I text Vicki and implore her to meet me at the mall. I want to get out of the house and oddly enough, I crave the chaotic anonymity of the food court.

"See you in sixty,"she texts back. What a friend. I'm at the mall in record time, having left a bewildered Max at home making grilled cheese with applesauce for the kids. I wait impatiently, drumming my ragged nails on the scratched table top and wishing *Chick-fil-A* was open on Sundays.

I finally see her and wave her over, gesturing to the two gooey slices of cheese pizza with olives, green salads and ginormous Diet Cokes on the table in front of me. *Sbarro's*. I know what my dearest friend will want to eat and I am on it.

She slides into the booth bench across from me, and I attempt to fill her in on things. She laughs about the "no more secs" story. I don't mention the little birthday trinkets from Thomas.

"Be careful, though, Deen. I see an awful lot of enthusiasm whenever you're talking about Thomas. Which you do. A lot. 'Thomas this and Thomas that.'"

"Vick – get over it. You know I love Max. I'm just, restless – dissatisfied somehow – and I want something. I want – oh, I don't know! Something *else*."

"Something like what?" Her eyes narrow.

"I feel like getting a tattoo or devouring a sack of warm *Krispy Kremes* all by myself. Doing something so out of my little good girl character – surely some heathen on our block has Tivoed *Desperate Housewives* and I could watch them all, or something!"

"Wow. That would be something."

"Vick. I'm serious. It's just the chance to consult. Wear cute clothes. Have coffee at *The Rooster*. Be happy for me." I am pleading.

"I'll be happy; *you* be careful."

I roll my eyes. "Come on, as long as we're here, let's go spend my *Bath & Body Works* coupons."

Two hours fly by while we try on different scents, scope out the clearance sales and rate the window displays from grand to tacky. I'm in a considerably calmer mood when I get back home. Max and I read to the children and then curl up in bed, reading by each other. He pulls me next to him and I'm surprised when he falls asleep, his book open across his broad chest. I lie awake for a long time.

Weeks go by with meetings and e-mails and glorious stolen time with Thomas. I don't feel guilty, exactly, because we haven't done anything inappropriate, but underneath it all, I sense something is changing. Max might be oblivious, but Vicki is not. She watches me like a hawk.

Her warnings clang like empty bells in my mind. I don't want to listen to her because I don't want her to be right and I don't want to stop having meetings with Thomas. That's all they are. Meetings. About books.

As the days go by, it seems that Vicki is determined to save me from myself. A large part of her Deena rescue program seems to be getting me out of the house [for something other than University meetings, no doubt]. She coerced me to Bible study in the spring, and now that we're on summer hiatus, she's pulled together a girls' movie night after the children are in bed. Ironically, some deal about a "perfect" wife.

Blog Spot Post by Pajama Mama
July 19, 2010

Go see the remake of *The Stepford Wives* at the little old-
fashioned theatre on Main Street, with two of my
girlfriends, one of whom I don't actually care for very much.
She and her husband are the kind of people who store 2-
liters of Coca Cola in an over-sized cherry wine rack and
then pass it off in a "This ole thing?" tone of voice. "Came
with the house, you know?" Puhleese.

Sit at a table in Books-a Million Joe Mugg's Café afterwards
and share pieces of gorgeous iced triple-layer cakes. The
kind I once envisioned I could and would bake once I was
home full time. Discuss the merits and dubious
philosophical underpinnings of the film. Decide that we'd
prefer loving a real-life mate, flaws and all, over a perfect
malleable one. We *think*. That's the consensus anyway. I
am too quiet. I say all the right things; I don't say anything
that really matters.

Want to weigh in on Stepford Wives? Want one yourself to
take over your duties? What do you know that really
matters, cyber girlfriends? I'm confused about my life, but
back to it.

Good luck with yours,

Pajama Mama

Comments:
Great movie!
~Lexus Mommy

Oh brother.
~Dust Diva

Sorry, Lexus. I'm with her.
~Chocolate Guru

Wait – that was about me!
~Formerly Hot

On the way home from the movie outing, the sky is a stainless-steel bowl inverted, emptying its soggy contents on an unprepared populace. I drive home, thinking crazy thoughts to the rhythm of the windshield wipers slapping against the rain. The automatic carwash went crazy today, so the manager gave us all the extras for free. And now ironically, the rain will ruin it. Too bad that's one of my biggest thrills these days. Wonder what life is like in Boring, Oregon. Or Trickem, Alabama. Lonelyville, New York or Possum Trot, Kentucky.

Butter. Mutter. Putter. Flutter. Cutter. I'm feeling fidgety as all get out, as Mr. Mac would say. And resurrecting my bad rhyming habit to boot.

I wonder about all the little erosions in marriage; the slow drip of things that can carve canyons in the landscape of a marriage. The differences in how you squeeze the toothpaste; what you expect from foreplay; how you define romance; whose parents you want to spend the holidays with; who should take out the trash and fix the dinners. The mundane details that make up more of life than you could ever imagine when life is spread out for you like a brilliant feast, all the offerings there for your choosing.

I wonder why love alone is not always enough to make it, not if you're depending on your own strength.

Grocery List

Hair ties

Play Dough (check on metallic kind?)

Self-tanning lotion

Milk

Pampers

Toilet paper

Cereal

Baby food/Baby Oatmeal

Chips

Shaved ham

Gourmet mustard

French bread

sliced provolone

Diet Coke

Junior Mints

Chapter 10

It's Midwest summer hot. The temperature continually hovers around 99 degrees and I feel like I've been misted with a spray bottle every time I step outdoors. The record for highest temperature in the Midwest is a tie: both in the summer of 1936, both 121 degrees. Steele, North Dakota and Alton, Kansas. I'm glad it's not 1936 for a variety of reasons.

I'm inside feeling pent up and restless, trying to use up all the fruit that Max's folks brought us on a whirlwind visit and my counter is a wreck.

Flour dust litters a neighborhood of torn wax paper held captive by mixing bowls, while cookie cutters and pie pans occupy it like the remains of a ghost town.

The phone trills and I grab it on the first ring. "What are you doing?" Vicki inquires.

"Baking pies and thinking about taking up swearing. You?"

"Nothing that interesting. I wish it would just rain already. This is driving me nuts! Wanna break outta here?"

"Sure. What'd you have in mind?"

"*Bounce with Mouse.*" She mentions a local bounce house filled with various blow-up slides, ball pits and pumped-full-of-air castles. "The kids can get rid of all this pent-up energy and we can sit and watch them and have Mommy drinks in the air conditioning!"

"Whoo hoo! See you in ten." I hang up. Beats making pies.

The phone rings again and I can't help it. When I see the caller ID readout for Southern Hills University, my heart wings. It could be any of the committee members, but I hope not. Deep inside, I know not.

"Hello!"

Thomas' rich voice fills all the available space on the lines. "Hello, my brilliant consultant! How about having a meeting at *Pacino's*? Linguine. Garlic bread that'll melt in your mouth and a Caesar salad with homemade croutons and for you, the biggest Diet Coke in the Midwest."

I call Vicki back, before logic sets in, and beg for a rain check, already plotting how to keep the kids decently occupied at a table. But Vicki agrees to watch the children along with Christopher and Canaan. Fortunately, Eli will stay asleep in his carrier.

I'm answering the irresistible siren call of someone who has already noticed my penchant for vanilla things and Diet Coke. I am in love with being desired.

I drive the kids to *Bounce with Mouse*, run in to pay and sign the permission slips, double checking that they have on socks, leaving the diaper bag and my sanity with Vicki.

"If it's just a lunch meeting, I can't imagine it will take long; I'll just come back here and pick the kids up at the end of the bounce session."

"No problem," she waves me off. "Just know that I'm collecting on the later rain check for adult conversation. By the way, that's quite a dress for a meeting. Tell me you weren't making pies in *that*!"

Shrugging I toss out a glib line. "Gotta be professional. Thanks again, Vick." I smile, suddenly giddy and unaware of the sultry weather.

"Um hum," she says. "And sit on the other side of the table from Dr. Hunt."

I can't drive to *Pacino's* fast enough.

We see each other instantly. Thomas waves me over to the table. It's like we have this weird radar for spotting each other. Or at least I do.

"New dress?" Thomas eyes me appreciatively and the admiration washes over me like a welcome breeze.

"Nope. Very old dress. Let's just say, I like how it looks on me some years better than others."

"Good year." Eyebrows arched, Thomas tips his coffee mug to me in a salute.

A flush heats my cheeks and for a moment, I feel awkward. "Um, where is everyone else?"

"They couldn't make it."

"Couldn't make it?" My confusion is everywhere, a tangible thing. "Um, why not?"

"Mainly because I didn't tell them about it!" His boyish grin erases the awful vibes I should have been feeling.

"I, uh, I see. Is there something that our partnership is working on that I've forgotten?" I need to convince myself of the legitimacy of this meeting, because otherwise there is the issue of my erratic heartbeat.

Thomas settles back in his chair and assesses me. "I *am* working on it."

I blush furiously and know that I should reprimand him and leave. Just walk out. No one would blame me; I could tell Max and he'd take care of it in a heartbeat. But I don't.

Instead, I sit there for an hour, leisurely enjoying fabulous Italian food and charming company. Thomas tells me stories of trips to gather history research and amusing anecdotes of students.

I tell him some of mine and we compare favorite authors, genres, periods in history and poets. Thomas loves poetry; I wish Max adored poetry. I conveniently forget that Max adores me instead.

Our time is saturated with the warm smells of garlic and fresh bread. The terra cotta walls in a distressed finish are alternated with wrought iron gates and enormous black and white photos of old world Italy. The Trevi fountain in Rome. The markets. The Colosseum. The vineyards. The candlelight that *Pacino's* uses regardless of whether it's lunch or dinner, complete the illusion of a romantic, leisurely lunch in Europe.

When I finally look at my watch, I feel a bit like Cinderella. "Oh, my goodness. I have to go pick up the children, they're at," I realize I have to finish and how ridiculous it will sound. "They're at *Bounce with Mouse*."

Thomas laughs and pays the check and walks me out of the restaurant, his hand on the small of my back. I'm slightly uncomfortable, wondering what anyone would think if they saw me, if they saw us. I keep my eyes averted, unwilling to see who else might be seeing us. Then again, Thomas would probably come off as the perfect gentleman.

Then again, perfect gentlemen don't put the moves on other men's wives. Is that what he's doing? Am I going to let him?

Back home from *Bounce with Mouse*, I change into some shorts and plop down on the floor between Caroline and Zoe. I promised to cuddle with them and watch a *Max and Ruby* video. I wonder idly where Max and Ruby's parents are.

I'm clearly not paying close enough attention as Zoe and Caroline keep poking me. "Isn't that funny Mommy?" I don't know what to say.

I look down at the line of my stomach folded over the top of my jean shorts and laugh until the tears leak in lines down my baby blue t-shirt.

I really, really need to get serious about these last baby pounds; I want to look attractive for Thomas. I mean, Max. I mean myself. I'll do it for myself.

****

Blog Spot Post by Pajama Mama
July 21, 2010

MUST lose rest of baby weight. Start Special K jump start diet. Am through with it by four p.m. when I inhale 19 cheese Doritos and half a Nutty Bar, followed by Diet Coke chaser.

Besides, I looked inside the box which advertised a coupon for a free pair of blue jeans in some boxes; mine reads, "Sorry, this box is not a winner." Naturally not. Story of my life.

Back to my baby pounds life. Good luck with yours,

Pajama Mama

Comments:

You can get jeans from a cereal box? Get out!
~Formerly Hot

How can they fit them in there?
~First Time Mommy

Um…finish reading. It's a coupon.
~Dust Diva

That wasn't nice.
~Mother

 Dressed in my most raggedy pair of shorts, I pop in a Denise Austin aerobics DVD this morning. Zoe is standing next to me, determined to do some "extracise" with me. Caroline is on the couch looking at books.

"Come on," Denise exhorts, "you'll get nice, firm, sexy arms!"

"Sexy arms!" Zoe parrots. Great. I mute Denise.

Truly, it's hard to get in any kind of a decent workout trying to keep Zoe from hitting Eli in the head with her little soup can weights. I give up.

"Let's get out the stroller and go for a walk!"

"Yay! Yay!"

Eli blows raspberries and I promise Caroline ice cream later if she'll put up her book and walk with us. "Can I bring my parasol?" she wants to know.

"Yes, Mary Poppins, you may. What would a walk be without one?"

She sighs and carefully places one of those paper bookmarks featuring the Dewey Decimal system, and a grinning rodent inside her newest *Junie B. Jones*. It's the kind of marker that elementary librarians are so fond of passing out on library day after explaining about book manners.

A refreshing breeze tickles our faces and teases our hair. Eli looks surprised by it, waving little starfish hands and kicking. Zoe reaches out as though to touch the wind. "God's breathing on us!" she exults. "Feel it? Do you feel it?"

"I do, sweet Zoe girl!"

The cotton clouds hurry the sun along, pushing it into the folds of blue blankets as though preparing to tuck it in bed. A plane drones, the jet stream line like an Etch-A-Sketch mark across the sky.

We walk all around the neighborhood and when I get back, my cell phone is making the obnoxious tone for a text message.

I click the view button and scroll down to read it. "Enjoyed our meeting; it was the highlight of my week. Already looking forward to the next one." T.H.

I should delete it. Text him back and tell that this has to stop right now. But I don't. I save it, in case I should want to savor it later.

Turns out, I won't have to savor just one and we spend the sultry month of July texting each other like teenagers with a giant crush.

For example:

Thomas: What's up?

Me: Up 2 my elbows in arranging fresh roses & choosing the crudités for 2nite's dinner, obviously.

Thomas: 2 funny. Ask me.

Me: Ask u what?

Thomas: What I'm doing.

Me: Shoot.

Thomas: Nope. Thinking of all the soliloquies that should have been wrytn 4 u.

Me: No one txts that wd.

Thomas: U wound me.

Me: I'll redeem myself.

Thomas: I'll remember.

Sigh.

Blog Spot by Pajama Mama
July 22, 2010

Grapefruit! That's the ticket. Rummage through silverware drawer for the only spoon not gnawed on by the garbage disposal, aka our spoon sharpener. Dig in!

I don't have a life, so I'll let you get on with yours,

Pajama Mama

Blog Spot Post by Pajama Mama
July 23, 2010

Had no idea it was even possible to be so thoroughly sick of any one fruit.
Ah, well. It's good for sharpening the disposal blades.

Back to the diet life; good luck with yours,

Pajama Mama

Blog Spot Post by Pajama Mama
July 30, 2010

Have lost 2 pounds. Whoopee. Somebody want to explain to me why moronic diet gurus tell you that not getting enough sleep can impair weight loss or even cause weight gain? What are the suggestions if you have kids?!?!?!
Frantic to wear whatever I want from my closet.

On with my cranky life; good luck with yours,

Pajama Mama

Comments:

Fruit is a diet food. Skittles. Fruit-flavored.
~Dust Diva

I've given up. My saddle bags are named Hoss & Silver.
~Formerly Hot

Shudder. I swear by Zumba.
~Lexus Mommy

Sounds like exercise to me. Yuck.
~Chocolate Guru

Beauty means pain.
~Mother

"Hey, Deenie?" Max summons me from the kitchen table where he is paying the bills as he always does.

"Yes?" I wander into the kitchen walking slowly, while reading from a new book which Thomas has recommended to me. It's a fascinating novelized biography of Franklin Delano Roosevelt and his forbidden attraction, and later affair with Lucy Mercer.

Max's hair is standing on end, his lake blue eyes puzzled. The wood creaks under my feet. All across one end of the kitchen table is spread the checkbook, various envelopes and statements, stamps, pens and a calculator. I can see a bit of Caroline's printing etched into the wooden table top, driven there when she presses too hard with her pencil in supreme concentration.

I stare at it, wishing it could take me someplace else. I wonder if I pointed it out to Max if he'd be too distracted to continue. Between his thumb and forefinger is the envelope from our cell phone company. Is it too late for honesty? Too soon?

"Who is this? I didn't even think you texted that much." And then he jokes, "You and Vick get tired of your Facebook accounts and pitiful girly e-mail forwards?"

He holds up the last two pages of our cell phone bill and my heart drops. His finger traces line after line of the same number. My silence is so large it fills the house. I think I can see C-A-T scratched on the table just above the roll of stamps. Maybe Caroline wrote it in honor of Butternut Squash.

"I'm waiting, Deena." This is delivered in Max's stern work-mode voice, oiled steel.

I pretend I'm trying to recall, which is clearly stupid. "Uh, I believe that is Dr. Hunt's number."

"I see. And he needs to text you this frequently and you need to respond every time?" He's still using his work voice.

If someone didn't know Max they might think him dull, as though he's clueless about the possibilities. At best they might admire his supreme self-control. I know better, but I can't seem to stop myself from playing the game.

"He is in charge of the committee, Max and we've also been working on a few specific assignments together." I go for lofty and imperious, failing miserably.

"I see. And if I were to pull these records from the company or even just look at the history on your cell phone, exactly what would I see?"

"Feel free to look, Max. You'd likely be bored out of your skull." I am bluffing and my mouth is so dry I cannot swallow.

On Max's face is a look I have never seen before. It's undecipherable. Mistrust and the shock of feeling that he's needed to feel that. A shadow of doubt. An undercurrent of anger.

"Mmm hmm. I see."

His face closes and I can see that he does not believe me, nor is he finished. He's just done for now.

I stand there for a few more awkward moments and turn to walk upstairs. "Max," I turn back. "You don't believe me?"

His eyes burn me. "Deena. My experienced, skeptical police mind tells me no, I do *not* believe you. But for our kids, for us, yes, I'm going to believe you. I will not accept the alternative."

This cannot go on. I trudge to our room, huddle with a notebook and pencil on the floor of our walk-in closet and do the most normal thing I can think of – write out this week's grocery list.

Grocery List

Pampers [check on kind with elastic legs for crawlers?]

Baby oatmeal

Peaches

Watermelon

Milk

Bread

Toilet Paper

Cheerios

Junior Mints

Ground beef

French Bread

Iceberg lettuce

Onions

Check for tomatoes at Farmer's Market

Vanilla for cheesecake

Muffin tin liners

Diet Coke

Coffee

Chapter 11

A plump random raindrop finally falls on the sculpted head of the robin foraging for breakfast on our lawn. He looks up, surprised. Then a sudden pelting of furious drops jump around the concrete drive and freshly shorn grass like a bunch of crazed Mexican jumping beans.

The robin tilts his beak upwards and scolds. It reminds me of something.

Oh yeah. Me. Lifting up my pathetic little head and scolding God. *Scolding* God. Can you imagine? I hang my head as my arrogance strikes me just like those raindrops. I'm asking Him to deliver me from myself when I won't demand my own cooperation. I turn away from the window in disgust, and head back toward the kitchen.

I am living in limbo. Vicki hasn't called me for a few days and oddly, I haven't felt the urge to call her either. I want to hold that golden luncheon with Thomas close to my heart. To mull it over, occasionally take it out to turn it in the palms of my soul, admiring my ill-gotten treasure: feeling needed, feeling beautiful. Desired. Sought after.

On the Homefront, my silent feud with Max smacks of those stomach twisting moments when you're a little kid in trouble and your mother says, "Just wait til your father gets home!" Or the teacher sends home a note of displeasure about the fact that you spent the last hour of class standing in the corner and you know she'll be calling your folks later that night to make sure you gave it to them.

I've put off a conflict for now, but Max is brooding, simmering underneath the surface and I know that something is coming. Something has to give.

I think while I go through the motions of getting together breakfast. Setting out the white dishes splashed with the yellow border and the bright clusters of cherries. The ones that I so gleefully registered for at *JCPenney*, a lifetime ago when Max and I were just beginning. Sigh.

I dump haphazard cups of pancake mix into a Pyrex measuring bowl and angrily stir the sides. The griddle hisses when I toss a few water droplets on it, letting me know that it, at least, is ready to do breakfast.

"Only dull people," Oscar Wilde maintained, "are brilliant at breakfast." I'm so unbrilliant that I must be utterly fascinating the rest of the day.

Eli bangs a Zwieback toast piece on his high chair tray spreading a mushy trail from ear to ear. My elbow rests on the counter as I wait for breakfast to bubble enough to turn over. Pulling my elbow off the counter, I feel it clothed in something sticky. I don't want to know.

Daddy is out of town. Watch mommy make pancakes. From a mix. Requiring only water. Adding pre-cooked bacon to paper plates. Okay, make banana slice faces with raisin noses and chocolate chip mouths to assuage guilt. Bad mommy. Bad, bad mommy.

Mornings are never my best time, and Caroline is going through an almost unbearable knock-knock joke stage.

"Mommy!" her voice is lilting and her little feet bang against the edges of the breakfast bar. "Got a new one for you."

"Can't wait."

"Knock, knock."

"Who's there?"

"Dinosaur."

"Dinosaur who?" Cares, I add silently.

"Dino SORE because she fell down!"

"Ah, that was a good one, Caro." I absently ruffle her hair, but she's pouting.

"You didn't laugh, Mommy. That's okay," she brightens. "I'll try another one!"

Note to self. Laugh at the next one. Laugh hysterically. Manically even.

"Knock, knock."

"Who's there?"

"Amoeba."

"Amoeba who?"

"Amoeba wrong, amoeba right!"

I laugh in earnest, mainly because I don't even think she knows what an amoeba is.

"Mommy? Do you know what an amoeba is?"

"Hmmm....why don't you tell me?"

"Okay! It's a one-celled orkanism."

"Wow, Caro, that's right!" I'm pretty sure I was still on colors and numbers in Kindergarten.

The kitchen radio which seems possessed with a mind of its own these days (or maybe just possessed) crackles on. A country station. How long since the days I listened to either Bruce Springsteen or country tunes with Max, closing out many a night slow dancing with him beside the car. On the porch. In the family room. Or the kitchen. Or the bedroom.

A catchy tune plays and I stand for a minute contemplating whether or not "save a horse ride a cowboy" is bad or not. I reach over and turn it off. Can't make up my mind. I do remember reading that most American car horns beep in the key of F. Wonder if that song is in F.

I pace back and forth from the land line phone to my cell phone. It does not ring. I'm not even sure who I want to call or who I expect to call. Max. Thomas. Or even my friend Vicki, who seems preoccupied these days.

When the phone rings, I rush to pick it up. "Your village called; their idiot is missing." Her voice is grim.

"Vicki?"

"Who else?"

"What's that supposed to mean?"

"We need to talk."

"About?"

"See? The very fact that you've never, not once, in almost six years asked me that, tells me you know exactly what about."

Fuss, cuss, truss. I'm back at it, rhyming under stress. Bam. Cram. I'd better stop there.

"Vick. Maybe you'd better just tell me what's up."

"What's up my dear *friend,* is that you went to lunch at *Pacino's* – *Pacino's*! with a man who is not your husband and there was no meeting at all. *At all,* Deen. What is the matter with you?"

"What's the matter with *you,* Vick? I told you there was a meeting and you agreed I could leave the kids with you at *Bounce with Mouse.*"

"Yes, well, what you didn't tell me is that no one else would be there."

"I didn't know that until I got there, Vick. Truly. Want to tell me how you know this and why you're making such a big deal out of it?"

"Two things, Deen: one, was this a date, because—"

"It wasn't a *date*," I interrupt, my tone dripping with defensiveness. "Dr. Hunt happens to be the—"

"Maybe he is *on* the hunt." She sighs. "Deen, I'm sorry. Let me back up. This is not the conversation I wanted to have. It's just that I'm you're my friend and I'm--"

"Stop it. I am not Christopher or Canaan, Vicki. Don't you dare call me up and chew me out without any reason!"

"I'm sorry, Deena. Really, I am, but to me there *could be* reason. This could get so out of hand. The whole idea of him being interested in you...Deenie, be careful."

"He is not interested in me, Vick. I already told you that the committee is paired off for extra work sometimes. Who told you all this anyway?"

"I don't want to tell you that."

"You always tell me stuff eventually."

"Maybe. Not today though." There is a pointed, hurt silence.

"I'm sorry, Vick. I should have called you from my cell and let you know that plans had changed." Really, I should have left. She's right and I feel it on a level I'm not comfortable exploring. Still though, there's a stubbornness that I just can't shake. I'm defensive and cold.

"Deena..."

"Thanks for the warning, Vick. But there's nothing to worry about."

"Promise?"

I hang up gently, admiring my self-control.

Crow with a side of evidence is a hard meal to eat and I'm not feeling terribly hungry yet.

*****

"Don't give up," trumpets my flip calendar, staring at me from the bathroom counter where I have gone with the cordless phone. "Moses was once a basket case!" So am I.

I listlessly flip open my little laptop notebook and power it on. I type my login for Facebook and look through my posted pictures. There's an album of pictures I've scanned of Max and me starting out. Before children. Our courtship. Our awkward but beaming wedding photos. A snapshot of us on our honeymoon in Branson. Our cabin in the Ozark Mountains. Our too-poor-to-do-anything big trip. I look at those pictures and remember.

When Max and I met, he coached basketball for underprivileged children. I checked out an old playbook from the library and threw out phrases from the side-lines to seem like I knew anything at all about the sport. I craved his attention.

I learned about rebounds and three-pointers. We watched *Hoosiers* and played H-O-R-S-E. The feel of his arms around me teaching me how to shoot and listening for the thwump of the ball smacking the backboard followed by a satisfying swoosh was a prelude for the overwhelming love I had for Max.

He seemed larger than life and I tagged after him, relishing everything from trips to the shooting range where he laughed himself senseless at my pathetic aim, to quiet walks through the park.

I couldn't imagine not loving him and truthfully, I can't imagine not loving him still. But then, why don't I just come clean with Vicki? Why don't I tell her about the empty hollowness of my soul? The disconnect with Max? The fact that as soon as Thomas called me I suspected we would be the only two at the meeting and I didn't stop him?

For that matter, I really should be telling Max. What in the world is a thirty-six-year old (Shoot. Birthday, hello? Thirty-seven!) woman with three children and a husband doing texting some college professor and sneaking around for fancy lunches like we're both seventeen only with more money?

Perhaps because just now, I lack the imagination to see anything better. A friend request pops up in my invitations. Dr. Thomas Hunt. Gently, I refuse the request. Though I am "Facebook friends" with a few others at the University, I can't do that. Not yet.

Blog Spot Post by Pajama Mama
August 16, 2010

Day dream number 171. About the professor. Again. I am giddy with junior high emotions. I think about us at the University café. The outdoor table. The steaming hand pies, dripping with apples and old-fashioned charm. The way he indulged me with both a mug of hot chocolate (hey, it was a chilly night for summer!) and an icy bottle of Diet Coke. It's nice to feel spoiled. Nice to flirt. Nice to...

Imagine for a moment that he drops some files by the house. I answer the door, wearing only a towel. Make it one of those new lime green ones I bought at Target for the upstairs bathroom. I look good in lime green. He brushes a water bead from my tan shoulder. And then. . . imagine for a moment he might see me naked.
Nope. That would be adultery. Plus also, (to quote *Junie B. Jones*, from my daughter's favorite books in the whole world) Thomas doesn't know about the stretch marks. Claim scripture about taking every thought captive. I am tired of my mental double life. Anyway, these days, don't even want my husband seeing me unclothed. Wait a minute -- shouldn't I worry more about what my husband thinks than someone whom I have yet to exchange kisses with? Dangling words be hanged.

I power down my little notebook with disgust. I can't post this as a blog. I cannot. I don't even know why I wrote this. I don't want to admit to myself how my thoughts are taking on a life of their own. I'm investing more time in my imaginary big screen life than I am in my own. How long? How long do I have before this crashes around me?

I plunk Zoe and Caroline down in front of the television for a DVD of *Berenstain Bears*. They'll watch happily with a few handfuls of Goldfish crackers while Eli goes down for a nap and I head for the shower. Perhaps some serious soap and scrubbing will do something for my frame of mind.

The shampoo bottle instructs me to lather up two times if needed. I hunt in the under-sink basket for lotion and notice that my Kotex strips are also printed with life tips: *Staying active during your period can relieve cramps.* Super. Everyone needs life advice from their feminine products.

When I go downstairs to start dinner, on the lid of the sour cream is written: "*Simple pleasures are easily found.*" *Fresh thinking from Daisy Sour Cream.* Oh brother. I put it back in the fridge, noting that no, I have not defrosted the stupid chicken breasts in the fridge overnight and I hate that rubbery texture they get when you try defrosting in the microwave.

At any rate, 2,000 people every year are injured while trying to pry apart frozen foods. Obviously, I can't make dinner; it's a safety issue. We can order pizza. But first I have got to get out of this house. Out.

And we're off to the library for the last summer reading program. Crafts. Storytime. Supervision for my children for ten minutes while I browse the stacks or scribble writing ideas on my legal pad. During summer, I don't discipline myself with my usual academic reading load for class, not that I have any need to this year. I read pop fiction and I read just for the thrill of it.

There's a special display near the front circulation desk under the pithy banner, "The Joys of Summer." I scan the titles. *The Joy of Sex*, *The Joy of Knitting*, *The Joy of Cooking*...my eyes blur and I begin to think there's no joy in anything for me. Guilt is a joy stealer. I know this, even as I convince myself I have nothing to feel guilty about.

It's all I can do not to fall apart right there at the counter while the children gleefully check out Disney DVDs, Learn-to-Read books and Eli gnaws a library board book. I can't think about this. I will not. I will just focus on improving myself and praying harder for contentment. I can't bother God too much about a mess I've gotten myself into.

Blog Spot Post by Pajama Mama
August 17, 2010

Could there be a shallower blog on the face of the planet? No carbs are making me cranky. This cannot have been how God intended people to eat. I NEED white flour. I ADORE white sugar. I look once more in the mirror and notice that my thighs look like a mixture of the two and that they have hail damage. Can't decide which is worse to view-- that or my sour face.
Go downstairs, make and eat entire batch of No-Bake Cookies. Yum. Feel much better. Follow with chaser of Diet Coke. Bottoms up, girls.

Back to life. Good luck with yours,
Pajama Mama

Comments:

No-Bake Cookies? I haven't had those in forever. Will go remedy that right now.
~Chocolate Guru
Sorry you're having a rough time, Pajama Mama.

~First Time Mommy

Thank you. I'll get over it.
~Pajama Mama

Blog Spot Post by Pajama Mama
August 20, 2010

Get new issue of *Ladies Home Journal* in the mail. Flip pages and browse through an article about Faith Hill. Note that she is the same age I am. If I were more shallow, and less mature, I'd give her a Sharpie mustache. Is she for real?

Comfort myself with mean-spirited thoughts of plastic surgery, make-up artists, stylists and personal trainers. Add household help and air-brushing and at least *some* sleep to the list of what Faith surely has and I do not. So there.

In the same magazine, there is an ad for some sort of diet snack, "Staying between you and your fat pants," the slogan announces. Now doesn't that just slay you?

Seems to me whenever I start comparing my life to somebody else's there's always that small print thing that jumps out to bite me. The really, really small print which reads: Results Not Typical.

And doesn't that just seem typical of life? Well, back to it.

Praying no fine print in yours,

 Pajama Mama

Comments:

Typical is boring.
~Lexus Mommy

Oh no! We agree on something! JK
~Dust Diva

I got a free workout band in my box of Oat Puffies! Whoo.
~Formerly Hot

Gonna use it?
~Dust Diva

You are evil.
~Formerly Hot

The last day of August Max comes home early and I'm pleased to note that I actually feel human. I've showered and put on the new birthday sundress that he bought me. Seems like that day was in the dark ages. I give myself a mental shake hard enough to cause a concussion. *Stay focused.*

The children and I are assembled in the stone entryway and Max's eyebrows raise in happy surprise, but he lifts one shoulder in an apologetic shrug. He's on his cell phone and clearly, it's not something he can defer until later.

I hear him responding in one word answers and then asking for an address. "Umm hmmm, yes, really?" His eyes crinkle and I can practically see him trying to solve whatever is being told to him on the other end of that phone.

He reaches me and wraps one strong arm around me and I surrender my head to his shoulder. Sensing that they should be quiet, Zoe and Caroline hug him around the knees and I hand him a delighted Eli, who goos and leaves snail patches of drool on his shoulder.

In my pocket, my cell phone vibrates. That I have begun carrying it with me, speaks the volumes that silent mode cannot. I wriggle out of Max's arms.

"Goodness! This project is getting involved. It's the University again. Excuse me. I need to take this." Too late, I realize that I have not yet taken the phone out of my pocket.

Grocery List
Pampers – size 2
Special K
Grapefruit
Baby carrots
Low fat ranch dressing
Celery
Yogurt
Dried banana chips

Chapter 12

Seven o'clock on a September evening is a bad time to be driving straight west, but that's the direction of the University, so here I go. The sun is a brilliant autumny yellow, alternately fascinating me and causing me to squint and grimace, blinded by its harshness.

Alibi means elsewhere in Latin. Even though I'm going to be exactly where I said I would be, I'm not going for the same reasons anymore. I mash the gas pedal, anxious to be on the University commons, anxious to stamp out the guilt I am feeling. Thomas and I haven't done anything inappropriate, nothing *physical* anyway, I argue with myself. A few fleeting accidental touches. The way my heart pounds when he looks at me. Max could use the time with just the kids anyway. Stupid conscience.

I remember what Max always says about bad guys tripping themselves up: *If you tell the truth, you don't have to work at remembering anything.* But here I am, constantly wondering whether or not I've said something stupid, or allowed the impatient anticipation I have whenever it's time to go the University [whether I just make an excuse or invent an opportunity] to be glaringly obvious. What am I, in covert operations? It's just a stupid meeting. It is. That's all it is.

During the stupid meeting about updating Shakespeare (as if), I catch sight of a poetry volume containing works by the Brownings. Mentally I compose my own: *How did I lose my libido? Let me count the ways:*

- Listening to spousal bodily noises in bed
- Wearing socks during sex
- Missing sleep – what's that anyway?
- The annoying way you crunch your stupid pistachios, straight from the bag

- Comparing the life I've chosen with the mental adventures of what might have been

I catch Thomas looking at me quizzically and my face burns hot. When I see him, I think I could overcome my lack of interest in sex and then I am horrified by having such thoughts in his presence. Up until now, I've managed to confine such fleeting thoughts to daydreams and an occasional anonymous blog post. I didn't even post the last one.

After the meeting, Thomas and I take our notes and laptops to a table outside the student union. We don't mention it; it's as if there's no question that I'm not going home. Not yet. He ducks inside and returns with a Diet Coke and a piece of warm apple pie topped with ice cream and caramel sauce. He sets it down in front of me, his lean hands wrapped around a mug of straight black coffee.

We don't say anything, but it's not a strained silence. He scoots his chair in and our knees brush. He sighs "So..."

"So. Why don't you tell me more about how you met your wife, about what brought you here? About...you." An abrupt transition, but I figure that's always a safe topic. Mother always said that people love to talk about themselves and I know it to be true.

His face schools itself back to a classroom demeanor. "What do you want to know? There's not really a lot to it. I'm a fairly straight forward person, Deena."

"But you have a story. *Everybody* has a story."

"And you, Deena, love the story. I'll wager it's a large part of why you've racked up all those degrees in literature." He leans his chair back, hands clasped behind his head. "In fact, I'll bet there's a writer in you somewhere."

I blush in silent acknowledgement. "But I asked about you!" Occasionally a student tosses off a brief comment to Thomas as they walk through the commons and he answers them genially, the interruptions flowing as smoothly as his words. He tells me about his travels to Greece and Italy. The fascinating work on his volume of Depression Era interviews at Ohio State. His courtship days and his love of teaching.

"Yes, but what on earth brought you down here? I mean, you don't really seem like part of the Ozarks." I take in his tailored jacket, impeccable leather shoes; his English country gentleman demeanor.

The commons' crowd thins out and his eyes close momentarily. "I was still back in Ohio, when my wife, Caryn, was killed on an icy road on her way to the grocery store. She was expecting our first child. I nearly drank myself out of a job that second semester; when contract time came around, nobody was particularly interested in renewing me and I was equally uninterested in remaining. I didn't want to stay in that house, in that town."

I watch him in that private glaze of pain and then his eyes open, his professional mask back in place.

"So. There you have it."

When his gaze turns back to me, he focuses absolutely. I feel undone. Shy somehow. Until now, we've been carrying on a mild flirtation with lots of desire and on-the-border text messages, but no physical contact. I wonder when was the last time that Max and I have focused on each other with such intensity. "Thomas. How awful! I don't, I don't know what to say."

"Sometimes, there's nothing to say. Your turn."

I shrug. "I don't have anything that can touch that. I'm an only child. My parents have high hopes for me and I'm afraid I'm a chronic disappoint to one or another of them. I got to be department head here at Southern Hills two years ago with the stipulation that I'd complete my doctorate the next year. I was nearly finished with it, and then I got pregnant again. Don't get me wrong – I love Eli. I adore all my children.

I guess I just miss the purpose of my life here. The interaction. The concrete record of my days, always knowing what I got done and what I still need to accomplish. At home all of that sort of blurs together and well, there you go."

He grins, a slow grin, not accompanied by Max's bold laugh. I find it intriguing, these differences. I remember all that we studied in Sunday school last spring. *If you find yourself unduly interested in meetings with a member of the opposite sex, if you spend extra time on your appearance, or find yourself going to places where you might run into that person, beware.*

I stuff all of those thoughts back into a far compartment of my mind. After all, Thomas and I are here on business, right in the garden commons where anyone, anyone at all could see us. And then I notice his hands. His fingers are long and tapered and I wonder what they would be like touching me. He looks so handsome in his suit.

The distance he normally wears like armor makes me wonder what you'd have to do to get closer. The armor is softer though. I sense it. I have no business thinking such things.

"It's a beautiful evening. Let's walk for a bit." He stands up and pulls my chair back for me, carrying my briefcase. We amble toward the faculty lot and he puts the case inside my passenger seat. I stash my purse in a hidden compartment and pocket my keys. My actions speak my decision, but I stammer out a feeble excuse as to why I shouldn't be doing this.

"I should be going, seeing how the meeting is over and everything." I sound weak and I know it. He stands watching me. "It is a beautiful place to walk though. I guess I could count it toward my work out and I could..." I'm rambling and finally just shut up.

His eyes pin me, not unkindly, but with an intensity reserved for romance novels with improbable heroes named Rafe and villains named Rawlings.

We walk professionally side by side until we get to the paths in the back part of campus, winding gravel trails with periodic stone benches, rose arbors and hidden copses of trees. It looks fresh, green and new. The colors are rich and vibrant, leaves beginning to turn; the trees lush, not yet skeleton-armed. The grass has settled into the deep emerald tone that bridges Indian Summer, just before the splash of autumn and the barren season of winter snows to come.

It looks like I feel just now. On the verge of discovery. Fresh. Plumbing new depths of my soul. Treasure-hunting for pieces of me that I've lost. I like this feeling very much.

He asks me only one question breaking the companionable silence. "What are you thinking about?"

My gaze roams around the oaks and maples, backlit by the spotlight of the dropping sun. "Don't laugh," I warn. "I'm thinking of the view – 'Autumn, the year's last, loveliest smile.'"

"William Cullen Bryant!" We speak the writer's name in tandem and laugh.

"It's a breathtaking smile, to be sure." Thomas is looking directly at me. I duck my head, suddenly shy.

We're back far enough where we can't be seen, heading toward some of the science department fields and gardens, when Thomas takes my hand.

It feels like the most natural thing and other than my heart thudding so hard I think it must be visible, I don't think at all.

"Tell me then, Mr. Buttoned-Up Professor, Mr. I Am Absolutely Always In Control," I say in a voice so playful and light I don't even recognize it as mine, "since you don't ever show emotion, how did you ever let Caryn know you were in love with her?" Good gracious, am I flirting?

He stops abruptly, his oxford shoes crushing the gravel. An odd mixture of frustration and longing flashes in his eyes. I think about the commercials I've seen for the slot machines at the casinos that sprout up like mushrooms in our area. All of the winning images pop up with startling clarity: a row of cherries; a run of carousel horses. A nervous giggle starts in my throat.

I turn so I am facing him directly and he sighs heavily. I sense an almost tangible boundary, a wall of reserve and careful self-control. This will be the moment that I can pull away and things will go on as they have been, or I can stay where I am and resolve will shatter like bone china on tile. I choose by my indecision.

"You think I don't show emotion. Don't show *emotion*?" His voice is a low growl, words charged, voice thick with unexpressed desire. "I'll show you emotion." His eyes sweep my mouth and my heart pounds.

Although I am already facing him, he grabs my elbows and hauls me against him. Our chests are melded together and his mouth crushes mine. He doesn't kiss like a professor. He tastes like fruit and coffee. Lyrical, sweet and tart, the way Skittles taste when you move them under your tongue.

I kiss him back with every muscle straining toward him. I fear my libido has returned and I'm shocked by the breadth of my own desire. I stop, literally having to put my hands between our mouths, my palms pressing against his lips.

"Don't," I whisper in a strangled voice. "Please don't."

"Deena," his voice is a husky movie whisper. "That didn't feel very much like a 'don't.' I won't do anything you don't want me to do."

"Oh, I want, Thomas. I want, alright. But we can't do this. Not   now.   Not   later."

"No?"

"No. I love my husband."

"One more thing then, Deena. If you're so in love with him, what are you doing here kissing me?"

I pull away and literally run back up the beautiful paths through the arbor to the faculty lot, pelting and nearly tripping in the dusky light of the fading sun. I frantically push open the door to the minivan and scramble inside, buckling up with a fury. I see Sonya Weatherby heading toward me and I start the car and put it into reverse, all but squealing out of my parking place.

My heart knocks underneath my ribs all the way home. Euphoria and consternation alternate residence in my brain.

My cell phone rings but I can't see the number since the deepening of the sky has blurred my vision. Clearing my throat, I answer. "Hello?"

"Hello there, favorite committee member, and not incidentally, kisser extraordinaire. I can still taste you."

"Oh, hi." I squeak. "Thomas. Don't talk about this. I don't want to…Um, you probably shouldn't call me on this right now. I mean, don't call me. This is futile. It is folly."

"Convince me."

"You can't. I mean, I can't. What we did—it wasn't right. We both know that."

"We did it, nonetheless. You're not happy. I could tell."

"That's not really any of your business, Thomas."

"You made it my business when you kissed me back."

There's nothing to say.

"Think about it, Deena. I know I will be. Good night." Dead air.

Afterwards, I hear my own whisper. Good night.

My turn signal flickers in the lane by Wal-Mart. I have to go there. I'm sure we need a few things and besides, I need to do something normal. Ordinary. I need to remind myself that I have responsibilities. Big ones. Important ones.

The bottom line is that I cannot go straight home from having just kissed another man.

I wheel the cart around aimlessly, tossing random items in. Light bulbs. A value pack of double AA batteries. Toothpaste. An extra stick of Max's favorite deodorant. Scrapbook stickers. I don't scrapbook. Gum. Junior Mints. Milk. Pampers. Always Pampers. Bread. Toilet paper. There. That should do it.

Standing in the check-out line, I read the bad news: according to the tabloids, one of my parents might have been an alien. (Quiz inside) Eek. Eek. On the other hand, I'd love any excuse for my behavior; I know there is none.

I arrive home and skulk in the garage door, crossing the stone entryway, trying to keep the rustle of bags to a minimum. In the next room, I hear the weather channel droning on the television.

I wonder what it would sound like if it were to forecast moods. "Mommy storm squall on the horizon. Possibly able to break with bribes of Krispy Kremes and vanilla ice cream. All fronts restless with a rise in spirits predicted pending offer of Happy Meals and Daddy's return."

But the home weather has shifted; it's more serious than that. "Tsunami about to break loose on peaceful marriage. Disturbing waves seen off shore. Vessel has been drifting off course for too long. Damage unpredictable. All parties should evacuate."

I breathe deeply, steeling myself for seeing Max in his favorite chair in the family room. I walk in. Nothing. Back to the kitchen. No Max.

I head upstairs with reluctance. Max is standing in front of our open bedroom windows. His shoulders are curved inward. This is not the Max I know.

"Good evening, Deena. Welcome home." He doesn't turn for a moment. When he does, his eyes are dark. "I was beginning to wonder if I needed to come after you."

"Oh, Max," I force a laugh, but even to my own ears, it comes out stilted and harsh; false and bright. "You of all people know how meetings can go. They're never what you expect."

"I disagree. Meetings are boring and predictable. I always know what to expect. Anyway, I called the night switchboard and the meeting was over two hours ago." He takes several steps toward me. "Two *hours* ago."

"Well, I took a walk and then I went by Wal-Mart. I'm thinking they'll name an aisle there after me, I'm there so often."

"And you couldn't call?"

"Of course, Max. I'm sorry. I just didn't think of it."

He raises his eyebrows as he's done frequently, of late. He closes the gap between us and gathers me so close to him I feel crushed.

His cheek leans against my hair. We still fit perfectly together, at least in height. I wonder if unfaithful thoughts have a smell. I am tempted to blurt out that I have kissed someone else.

I am not quick enough. Max dips his head toward and kisses me. A claiming kiss. One that marks and remarks me as taken. My hands reach up toward his hair, my fingers fisting, clenching. Max breaks the kiss, my breath hitches and my tears freeze.

"Don't think I won't deal with this." Max is deadly quiet, the way he always is when he is consumed by a case. "I know there's something, Deena. Something is wrong with us. I'm going to work on it, find out. And when I do, things will be different." He turns and strides out of the room, my purposeful, make a plan and make it work husband.

I walk into the master bath and turn on the shower, shedding my clothes and trying to shed my guilt. A scant five minutes later, I'm out, drying off with one of our new lime green towels and reaching out for a nightgown that I know will not send Max any signals. I just can't make love with my husband tonight.

A restless seven hours later, I make one of my promises to myself that today will be better. I assure myself that I can certainly continue my consulting work; I just can't sit by Thomas. Can't look at him. Think about him. I will be in control of my thoughts. I think about all this while I stand in front of the mirror, brushing my teeth and watching my eyes, checking, I think, for signs of insanity. Isn't that what living a double life will do to you?

I glance down, and read, "People are comfortable with Jesus being their Savior as long as He doesn't try to run their lives." That's what it says on my flip calendar this morning. I fold it over the little spirals that keep it standing upright. And then I rip it off, leaving spiral paper crumbs all over the counter.

Good intentions just aren't cutting it. My thoughts are consumed with Thomas. I wonder what he's doing and whether or not he truly believed me when I told him not to call me anymore. I assure myself that I was plenty firm last night and this will all stop.

Glancing at the clock, I can see that I'm way too late to get Zoe to preschool today; I went back to sleep, since Max offered to take Caroline to school this morning. He was polite, distant. He obviously slept downstairs on the couch and I was glad for it.

I scooted downstairs to kiss Caroline good-bye over toast crumbs and went back upstairs just to rest for just a few minutes more, and it's been way more than that. With a start, I remember that I did not kiss Max good-bye. We have never before left without a kiss.

I tiptoe into the girls' room just as Zoe is scooting herself up from a tangled heap of covers in her miniature toddler bed. Her hair is wild, sticking up everywhere, but it seems to me that her face is already losing that precious pudge of toddlerhood and her legs are getting too long for that bed.

Unbelievably, we're already in the second week of another school year. First grade for Caroline, preschool three mornings a week for Zoe. Eli is working hard on cutting more teeth and doing a hilarious army crawl to get where he'd like to go. Where did the time go?

"Good morning, Zoe girl! Guess what? You're not going to go to pre-school this morning, we're just going to have a mommy-daughter day!"

"Why?" Zoe is clearly not impressed. I'm going to have to sell her on this because she adores her pre-school class at The Flannel Goose. Miss Carrie and her awesome sand and water table and endless stores of patient creativity have stolen Zoe's heart. Butternut Squash pads in the room and curls up tightly on Zoe's slippers, looking much like a discarded sweater ready for the laundry hamper.

"Oh, I just thought it would be fun," I fib. "Daddy took Caro to school this morning already."

"Can we go without Eli?" Zoe is plaintive.

"Weellll, no, not exactly. Eli can't stay by himself. But Eli's too little to count. He'll just sleep in his stroller and you and Mommy will go get you a new school dress and have lunch at the food court and maybe we'll even get you a book!" My voice trills with all the enthusiasm I can muster.

"I guess," Zoe warms up to it. "It'll be funner if we can get a chocolate dip cone from at Dairy Queen."

"Deal." We shake on it and I head down the hall for Eli. He's been sleeping in lately, naturally just when I am sleeping restlessly or not at all. We need to move it. It's almost ten o'clock.

A few hours later I am thrilled to be leaving the mall. This has been a disaster. Zoe and I are both splattered in chocolate, Eli has been fussy and has lost a shoe. Zoe has asked for something at every store we've been in and I am cranky and unfocused.

Plopping Zoe into her car seat and buckling her up, she has a full-blown meltdown. She kicks and cries and yells, arching her back in protest. My sweet Zoe girl! I am shocked, then angry.

"Zoe Irene!" My hand spats the side of her chunky thigh and my finger wags in her little face. "I will not tolerate this behavior; do you understand me? When we get home, you are going to the time out chair for the long haul!"

"Noooooo, Mommy," Zoe wails and I feel like every other mother on the parking lot is staring at me. The incompetent, shrill, distracted mommy. "Not the long haul! Let's do the short haul! What even is the haul?"

This makes me laugh so hard that my eyes smart and I have to turn away from the minivan, my bottom smacking against the door and my laughter turning into hard coughs. My eyes are watering when I turn back to Zoe.

Her little eyes widen in surprise. "Oh, Mommy, since we're both crying we prob'ly shouldn't do the time out haul."

I kiss her on the end of her nose. "After we get home we'll talk about it, Zo." And I wish I could get my life in gear with the ease that I back out of the mall parking lot.

Back home, I set a penitent Zoe, who only spent the short haul in time out, along with Eli in his Exersaucer, in front of a *Wiggles* video so I can finish up the dishes in the sink.

Almost the moment the dishwasher is loaded, I get a phone call from Max. He really is good about trying to check in with us every day and apparently, he's determined that this one will be no different. But beyond all this, I feel like we're playing house. Playing at being married. We are characters in a poorly written novel. We are trying too hard. Nothing about us feels natural anymore.

"Hey good lookin'. What are you up to?" He sounds almost normal, but I can hear the caution in his voice.

"I'm dancing the Ubey Doo with Dorothy."

Knowing my loathing for that particular song from *The Wiggles*, Max bestows one of his hearty laughs.

"You're just jealous, Max. Bet you can't do it there at the department!" I am trying so hard.

"It would make for an interesting roll call, that's for sure. What's for dinner tonight?"

"Um. I thought I'd pick up pizza with the coupons some kind soul hung on our front door knob this afternoon."

I hear radio static in the background and a distracted Max ends our conversation in typical cop fashion. "Sounds good. Gotta go."

"Good bye, Max," I say into the dead phone.

It's a long night, full of Caroline's first grade homework help, walking the floor with a teething Eli and reading *Hooway for Wodney Wat* to Zoe.

Max calls right in the middle of rocking Eli to sleep and of all nights to pick, Eli objects loudly and is instantly wide awake again. "Just calling to tell you I'm not sure when I'll be home. Sounds like you're busy. Got to go."

"Wait!" I want to yell like a child running after their parent who is leaving, backing down the driveway, leaving them behind. "Should I wait up for you?" But I can't. I put the phone down quietly and resume rocking Eli whose weighty eyelids keep fluttering open just to make sure I'm still there. His little fist clutches my shirt tightly and stays there long after he is asleep, bound.

Hours later when I climb into our bed, Max is not there.

*****

The sun strings out its rays as though it is clapping encouragement: "Wake up! Wake up, everyone!" I'd like to slap it silly.

Though it is only 10:30 in the morning, we are sweltering in the park for Caroline's sixth birthday. Her third one in the park. She loves it. Max is lining up small party guests for turns whacking the ruffly black and yellow bumble bee piñata and I sit with Eli in my arms, taking an occasional one-armed picture, smiling and helping Eli clap his little hands.

I see new lines around Max's eyes and I am impressed that he is this energetic. Knowing Max, he didn't bother going to sleep, just got home in time to shower and get dressed.

Vicki's Christopher is up next in the piñata line, and the bottom finally begins to tear away from the bumble bee, courtesy of his practice time in Little League, no doubt. "Oh, Max. No! Wait!" I rush over from the picnic table bench and whisper in Max's ear. Too late. It's open now and nothing is coming out.

"Miss Deenie?" Christopher looks at me, perplexed. "How's come there's no candy fallin' outta here?" He cranes his neck, trying to peer up the bee's insides.

Caroline comes alongside and tears begin quickly. "There's nooooooo candyyyyyyyyyyy!!!" She dissolves into dramatic sobs and buries her face in Max's waist. Max's, not mine. This is her commentary on my brand of preoccupied motherhood. What kind of mother forgets to put candy in the piñata? My kind, evidently.

The kind of mother who lives life divided between the home front and the University life where the chance to flaunt my knowledge of literature and academics pales in comparison to the chance to engage in witty banter and hushed exchanges and one kiss I can't get out of my mind with a certain history professor.

Vicki, ever prepared, moves into the small circle of children, surreptitiously opening up bags of Tootsie Pops, miniature candy bars and bubble gum from her stocked tote bag and dropping them on the ground. "Would you look at that? Come and get it kids!"

There's an instant scrambling and stuffing of loot into pockets and cheeks stuffed wide like chipmunks. Crisis averted.

"Where did you? How did you?"

Vicki laughs. "I had the Vacation Bible School candy leftovers in my tote bag."

Right now, I like my friend Vicki better than I like myself. And for that, I hate her.

Max and Zeke call the children over to them and begin scooping out ice cream cones with supplies from the cooler. Zeke hands me a vanilla cone as I stalk by the picnic table. No self-respecting birthday party would be complete without ice cream, especially since Missouri is one of the top ten ice cream-producing states.

They say it takes about fifty licks to finish off a single scoop cone. Not if you're angry; I think mine is gone in about twenty licks plus about six bites. I let the end of it drop to the ground. A happy beagle, cheerfully running away from its aggravated owner, stops by me to wag its tail, scarf down the cone, and takes off again.

I sit down alone on a swing when the corner of a dark grey BMW glides by. My head snaps up and my heart pounds. It is Thomas. It has to be. I look beyond the line of trees that border the little park's south side and see it in between the wide trunks.

Instantly, the cell phone in my pocket sounds its text tone. I take it out of my pocket, still swinging.

Thought I could make it without u. I can't. UR terms.

My toes drag the ground, stopping the swing and I try for composure. I rejoin the short party goers and ooh and aah over Caroline's gifts. Max stands on the other side of the picnic table from me. It might as well be a continent away.

Our eyes meet and I know he has seen the car too. But he cannot know it is Thomas' car, can he?

I wait until later that evening before stealing into my closet and texting back.

OK. Meet u on University walking trail tomorrow, but it has to be just business.

Who am I kidding? I guiltily, quickly leave the kids with Vicki, telling her that I just need to pick up some resources at the library, and it'd be faster without them. Thomas and I meet and walk and talk in a torrent of words. He seems to know he shouldn't kiss me just now, though I see that his eyes are filled with longing. I would bolt like a deer. This tentative step is bold for me.

Stolen moments with Thomas fill me with an ebullient lightness, a vicarious sense of importance. But I love Max. Truly I do. I am simply not happy. Not with my home. Not with my marriage. Not with myself. I can be friends with Thomas. In fact, I tell myself, this connection with my former, professional self will make me more appealing to Max.

Shakespeare said, "All the world's a stage," but it is an odd thing to both star in and direct the play of your life. Yet, I feel pulled in so many directions that I am in danger of snapping off like the inflexible limbs of Caro's Barbies.

I can't get away as often as I need a Thomas fix, so we text like giddy teenagers. I text from my closet, my back porch, the minivan. I have convinced myself that as long as I stay at the level of flirtation, I'm not doing anything wrong.

And then the doorbell rings one morning and on my porch is a ridiculously huge vase of vanilla and pink roses. I read the card: *Sorry, I don't think I can ever go back to just business.* Just one of many reasons that I can't seem to stay away.

What is he thinking? All the same, I bury my nose in them, pluck one perfect petal to press in my beloved copy of *Pride and Prejudice*, and bury the rest in the bottom of the trash, using an empty box of Little Debbie Nutty Bars and one of Eli's dirty Pampers as headstones.

******

Running Saturday errands is not usually my favorite thing to do, but Max is working on those burglaries, and we have a list today. It curls up on my stationery with the border of perky red cherries running around the edges, sitting on the seat next to me, part of a stain from a coffee cup on the bottom edge:

Drop off Max's shirts at dry cleaner's
Return library books
Laminate flash cards for Zoe's pre-school sight words
Hobby Lobby
Target

Zoe and Caroline are in the back seat, little legs stretched out in front of them. Each of them have one of my cookie sheets across their laps and they are attempting to spell things with their basket of colorful alphabet magnets.

We are jamming to a Veggie Tales CD, my personal favorite of all the girls 'collection, *On the Road with Bob and Larry*. There's just something about hearing animated vegetables sing Willie Nelson. I tap my hands on the steering wheel in time to the music and glance at the girls in the Mommy's Helper rearview mirror. Even Eli is gurgling and kicking his little feet.

To a casual observer, it would seem that we are the perfect family. Mommy gives up her shining career to live an equally fulfilled role as fulltime CEO on the Homefront. I do feel like I'm regaining a bit of myself, partly thanks to losing five more pounds and partly thanks to the meetings and yes, the thrill of my secret moments with Thomas.

I am strangely giddy these days in my University life; that has become my real one, and at home, my pseudo-life. Anton Chekhov, a favorite playwright, wrote that "people don't notice whether it's winter or summer when they're happy." And right now I feel seasonless.

My Mommy euphoria lasts until our final stop at Target. I choose one of the oversized carts so I can strap Eli into the little part with the leg holes and the girls can each choose one of the plastic bucket seats facing me. To say that our little band is unwieldy is like saying hemorrhoids should be kept private.

I tug and pull, stopping at the Starbucks counter to snag a Vanilla Cinnamon Dolce Latte, flavor of the month. "Uh, make that non-fat," I add at the last minute. "And, Grande."

Caroline is sitting like a perfect little lady and Zoe is sweetly perched next to her with two middle fingers in her mouth.

"You're being such good little girls, would you like a kid's hot chocolate?" Hey, for only a dollar and some change each, I'm thinking this would be an excellent bribe for good behavior. I bend down to hug them, nuzzling Eli's toes while I'm at it. What fun it is to be a mommy. Why would I want to be at work missing all this?

That was before. In my zeal to reward my beautiful and beautifully behaved family, I let Zo and Caro get out of their seats in the toy section. Big mistake. Huge.

It's as though they are released from a catapult. Amid the gleeful squeals and attempts to drag out the things of which they are most fond, a brown stream squirts from Eli's diaper. A full scale blow out.

Of course I did not bring the diaper bag in with me because I thought this would be a relatively quick stop and it was the last stop of the day. You'd think a veteran mom would know better.

"Girls," I try getting their attention pleasantly. My voice is sing-song-y and fake. "Girls, we need to quickly take Eli over to the baby aisles." No dice.

I wade into their sea of tea party paraphernalia and tiaras and stuffed animals and grab their arms. "Come on!" They are so engrossed and enthralled that they just don't respond. It takes some ugly-voiced commands on my part, issued just low enough to qualify as proper store etiquette.

I seriously think of throwing myself to the floor or just leaving. I think about my favorite cartoonist, Cathy Guisewite's description. "The story of a mother's life: Trapped between a scream and a hug." Yep, that's my life and currently the screaming is winning out.

Tearful and sniffling, they follow me. I lay a baby blanket from the layette section on the floor and place Eli on it. Unfastening his little pants, I rip open a package of Pampers and another of baby wipes, all the while looking up into the security camera saying, "Don't worry! I'm going to pay for this!"

Ten minutes later and fifty dollars lighter, we are back in the minivan on the way home. I don't bother with the radio and the girls' quietness floods me with fresh guilt.

Max hasn't called to check on us at all today; Thomas hasn't texted me either. I feel permanently out of sorts.

When Max finally does come home, he is preoccupied and goes back to the department almost immediately, something about a string of burglaries he needs to get to the bottom of. When he arrives home again, it is late. And in the morning, he is already gone.

After we drop Caroline at school, I am busily lining the kids up to go for a walk around the lake – maybe we'll run into Thomas--I hear a muffled song from the bottom of my purse.

The cell phone. Vicki's ring tone. Flipping it open, I skip any opening salutation. "Trying to leave." I don't bother disguising my annoyance.

"And how does one try to leave? Either you are leaving or you're not."

"What do you want?"

"Craaaaaanky!"

"Yes, I am."

"Oh, put your happy pants on and play nice," Vicki is genuinely puzzled, but trying to be her usual gracious self. "I just wanted to see if you wanted to do something with the kids together today."

"I'm sorry, Vick," I sigh contritely. "It's just that we have to be going. I just, we have some place we have to be." I don't offer my usual explanations.

"I see." She sounds hurt.

"We'll do something later this week. Promise." Gently, I lock my phone.

I hit every red light on the fifteen-minute drive to campus, frustrated, agitated, because I know that there if I don't get there at a certain time, Thomas won't be taking his customary walk around the lake, settling his research into his brain before working out his lecture notes.

The tires squeal a bit as I turn too sharply into a parking place and unload the double stroller, buckle Zoe and Eli into it, and hand Zoe the plastic bag of bread crumbs for feeing the ducks.

I zoom them around the lake, speed walking and forgetting to stop at the outcropping, a miniature dock with a beautiful bench. "Mommy! Mommy! You forgot to let me throw these at the ducks!"

"We'll do it on our next lap, Zoe girl, okay? Mommy was hoping to see someone from my committee."

I finally spot Thomas on one of the benches across the little lake, talking on his cell phone. He doesn't see me immediately and I feel ridiculously jealous, wondering who is on the phone.

We slowly stroll there and I decide that if he's still on the phone when we reach that bench I will not stop. My steps crawl.

"Faster, Mommy! Ducks!" Zoe enthuses.

"Ucks." Eli parrots.

I have to laugh. "We'll get there."

Thomas sees me and his face lights up and when he takes in the stroller and everything else with me, an odd expression coats his face, almost as though he'd rather not be reminded of this part of my life.

I wonder, just for that instant if Thomas would want me as much if he thought of us as a package deal.

"Well, then, it's been a pleasure talking to you. I'll get with you again later." He clicks his phone off and rises from the bench, kisses my cheek.

I press my hand to it, startled, and suddenly awkward. Zoe is scowling and is so like Caroline, I laugh.

"Only daddies can kiss mommies." Zoe lectures Thomas.

"Zoe, that wasn't nice. You remember Dr. Hunt from that day in the video store. He was just being polite."

Thomas bends down to shake Zoe's hand, but he is stilted and obviously ill at ease with children.

I want to talk to him, but I can see this won't be at all like I'd hoped. "Well, we're off to feed the ducks. I'm sure you're terribly busy, and--"

His eyes soften a bit, and he recovers his usual polish. "Never for you, Deena. I have a lecture in about thirty minutes. I'll see you Friday at *The Rooster*."

"Friday." And with that one word, I recover from my disappointment.

Zoe, Eli and I finish the lap and sit down on a bench to feed the ducks, laughing at their antics, their greedy snapping, their honking and their elaborate dives, fluffy, feathered bottoms sticking up out of the water.

Sonya Weatherby is leaving from the other side of the lake, near the bench where I have just talked with Thomas. I make it a deliberate point to catch her eye and wave. See? I am not doing anything wrong.

I wash the kids' hands off with baby wipes and drive them through McDonald's and stop at Target. I want a new shirt to wear to Bible study tomorrow. It begins again after the summer hiatus, and just the thought of having to deal with perky Kay awakens my shopping gene.

I am happy with my soft peach tank. I found it on the clearance rack. It's perfect transition wear, as summer settles into fall like a weary child nestling into a feather-topped mattress. I'll just add my brown cardigan in case the church's air conditioning is too chilly.

We've wandered around the aisles of Target so long that we have to go straight to pick up Caroline from school.

When Max arrives home a few hours later, Zoe flies off the porch where we've been lazily playing and leaps into his arms.

"Daddy! Guess what? Mommy took us to feed the ducks at her old school and someone kissed Mommy's cheek. But it's okay, 'cause he was just being polite."

That little tattle tale. Max looks straight at me. "Just Dr. Hunt, no big deal Max. We ran into him at the lake and he reminded me about the meeting on Friday at *The Rooster*."

Max shoots me the look that clearly says this is not the time or place to get into it. Caroline makes an awful face. "I don't like him," she says vehemently.

Neither Max nor I correct her. I don't want to bring up the subject; I have no idea what Max thinks. Dinner is a quiet affair. Max disappears into the study, and by the time I hear him creep up the stairs, I am in bed, pretending to be asleep.

******

All night, Max has ADD toes. His legs are restless, bumping into mine, his head clearly full of unpleasant or at least very active dreams. I give up, easing out of bed and into my fuzzy pink robe.

Making the rounds of the children's rooms, I look in on Eli first, smiling at his gentle breathing and rump-in-the-air sleep. Down the hall into Zoe and Caroline's room I survey the neat bins and baskets of blocks, dolls, stuffed animals and dress-up costumes. The ordinary supplies of childhood which I so often take for granted.

I lean over each of them in their matching canopy beds (Zoe's is currently sans canopy as she thinks that scary things hide on top of it during the night and she's only recently graduated from her toddler bed), smoothing their hair and kissing their cheeks. Zoe turns over and snuggles under her covers; Caroline's eyes flicker open for a brief second and she smiles at me.

"It's okay Caro punkin; Mommy's just checking on everybody." I pull the covers more tightly around her.

I creep downstairs and stick a spoon into my half-gallon carton of Breyers vanilla bean ice cream. I eat my spoonful, dropping the spoon in the sink to keep company with a few dried-on Cheerio's and a fork with yesterday's lasagna, still soaking in the pan. Still I cannot sleep. The first pink fingers of dawn filter through the family room window before I head upstairs to sleep for the scant thirty minutes I have left.

Vicki and I meet in my driveway after dropping the kids off to school. It's Zoe's and Canaan's pre-school day, so it will just be Vicki, Eli and me.

Climbing in the passenger seat after buckling in Eli, I blow my bangs out of my eyes. "Someone should just tell children that if we're still in the car we are NOT there yet!" I lament to Vicki. Her laughter warms me. "Seriously, we take the same route to school every single day and you'd think they were commuting from here to South Dakota!"

"I know exactly what you mean."

"What is this semester's study on?" I ask. "Eli was screaming during announcements on Sunday, so I didn't catch the topic. Not that it matters, with Miss Opal teaching, I might even be up for a study on Leviticus!"

"She's a gem, isn't she? But are you sure you don't just miss Kay's housekeeping tips?" Vicki swipes a sideways glance at me.

"Topic please. That's the only thing I've asked you for. I don't want to think about Kay for," I glance at my watch, "the six more minutes I have left."

"Party pooper. We're going to be tackling spiritual disciplines, I think."

"Ugh. I'm not having luck with any discipline of any sort. I gained back two pounds. And I think I have that furniture disease."

"Furniture disease?" Vicki knows something's coming.

"You know, Vick, it's when your chest falls into your drawers." Vicki snorts and I continue. "Nursing for the third time sure is hard on the girls." I glance woefully down at my chest.

"I hear you. I like that tank top, though. Peach is a good color for you. Is it new?"

"Yep. Target."

"Of course."

Vicki pulls into the church parking lot and offers to unbuckle Eli. He's old enough to disturb our study this semester, so I guess I'll take him to the nursery, although I hate to be without him.

"Yoo hoo, girls!" Kay is already on the parking lot and waves us over. "I'm glad you came today. Reagan Anne brought her famous apple caramel coffee cake. I've already been in and dropped my kids off. I just came back out for my notebook."

We walk in and Kay goes with us most of the way, chattering non-stop. I kiss Eli and reluctantly surrender him to the nursery workers who can't wait to get their hands on him. Obviously, he won't be hurting for attention.

Seated around the scuffed tables, Miss Opal guides us through prayer requests. Tandy Walker seems quieter and thinner than ever today. I just don't keep up with people during the summer. Seeing them from a distance and waving on Sunday mornings isn't the same as Bible study.

Tandy has just finished the first round of her radiation treatments, designed to shrink the tumor before surgery. "I'm scared, but I know God has a plan. My, uh, my double mastectomy is scheduled for October 19th. That's a Tuesday, so I won't get to come that morning. They're going to try and fly Macon home as soon as they can, but, well he hates flying." She's trying to be humorous, making light of the military's red tape and her own fear. Her voice is shaky but resolute.

Miss Opal tells Tandy that we'll just move Bible Study to the hospital lobby and be praying for her.

Kay pipes up. "Richard has been working just awful hours, you know? You guys can just pray for me because I'm really ready for him to come home and help with the kids by dinner time. I haven't been able to try anything from my new *Southern Living* cookbook all summer! I don't know about you guys, but I like the routine of school. Miss the kids of course!"

Yeah, yeah, yeah. Around the room a few other requests are shared. Someone's grandfather having a knee replacement. Someone is looking for part-time work now that all of her children are in school.

Miss Opal's kind eyes land on me. "How about you, Miss Deena? Still enjoying your consulting?"

I shift in my chair, knowing that it is asked with genuine interest. But Miss Opal's innocence accuses me. It's not just about the consulting anymore, and I know that.

"It's --- fine. Fine. I should finish up most of it by December."

"Wonderful." After looking around the room, making sure she has not missed anyone, Miss Opal bows her head and prays.

"This morning we're going to be talking about God's discipline. Girls, please turn in your Bibles to Hebrews 12:11."

Perky Kay volunteers to read. "'No discipline seems pleasant at the time, but painful. Later on, however, it produces a harvest of righteousness and peace for those who have been trained by it.' That's the truth! I've had the hardest time getting on my treadmill these days!"

Polite laughter echoes in the room. Tandy gets up for a second piece of Reagan McCabe's coffee cake. Her hip bones are jutting through her khaki pants and my heart goes out to her.

"That's certainly one aspect of discipline," Miss Opal is gracious. "But I want to focus on the disciplines we need in our spiritual lives. Anyone?"

"Prayer is one thing, for sure." Vicki is unequivocal. "I know I should pray, but lately, I haven't felt like what I've prayed for has made any kind of difference, so it's hard for me to stay with it."

"You're saying that if God doesn't respond how you'd like for Him to, then it's hard?" Reagan's voice is kind. "I remind myself daily that God is my Husband and Maker, but honestly, it's hard when child support is late and I'm lonely with just the kids and me. So, I bake. Lots. As you can see." We give her sympathetic chuckles.

Vicki flushes. "Well, not exactly. I guess I'd just like some confirmation that He's there, that He's on it, even when I can't see it."

"Oh, Vicki," Tandy speaks up. "I so understand that. But I promise you He is there. He is faithful. Always. Even when we can't see it. Even when He answers, but not in the way we'd like." Tears stand in her eyes, a full crescent, ready to flood the banks, and yet her confidence is impressive.

I wonder at Tandy's new-found resoluteness. And feel shame that I have been so caught up in my double life and Vicki's growing disapproval that I don't even know for sure what things she is talking about. Not in the way I once would have.

"That's an excellent truth, Tandy. Or worse, not on the time table we'd like. But rushing ahead of Him, assuming that we know what's best for us can cause us to act very foolishly." Miss Opal emits a rueful laugh, and I know there's a story there.

"I wasn't entirely honest before. It's the waiting," Vicki says quietly. "That's the hardest thing. That's what gets to me and it had to have gotten to David." She looks down at the table for a moment and draws a shaky breath. "If only we could know how long it will be before God acts."

For long moments we are all quiet, each of us contemplating what it is we are waiting for, and the manner in which we are longing for God to act.

Miss Opal directs a discussion about things that can happen to derail us and cause us to doubt, especially when God's discipline is in a painful area of our lives. I think I spaced out a bit, because before I know it, we are closing in prayer.

I squeeze Vicki's hand and I know that she has forgiven me for my distance, my secretiveness, and my silences of this summer. Still, it feels more like a truce, not a true mending. And that's because her transparency has shaken me. It's the first time that she has been translucent; I am merely opaque. I am missing out on vital parts of her life, and even though I know it's my fault, I feel hurt that she has not confided in me.

It's odd living in these awkward truces with my best friend and my husband. I'm just not sure what to do about it. Or, maybe it's that I know exactly what to do about it, I just don't want to.

Blog Spot Post by Pajama Mama
September 21, 2010

Daydream number 223 -- Pierce Brosnan approaches me at the community pool with his devastating, debonair Bond, James Bond smile. I am comfortably, (sexily?) reclined on chaise lounge. "How's it going?"

I beam my brightest smile back at him. "Absolutely gorgeous day, Dahling. Sunshine. Blue sky. No bloat even!" *No bloat? No BLOAT? My conversational skills have dwindled to the lowest possible common denominator--bodily functions?!* **Groan.**

"No bloat, eh?" That killer accent. He looks pitifully toward me and raises his head, searching around the pool for greener pastures. Flatter bellies. Thinner thighs. Oh, yeah, and non-psychotic, unmarried women are probably more his type. What is the matter with me? What is this insistent longing? And why isn't it aimed in the direction of the man who fathered my children, who sleeps on my pillow, who looks hopefully in my direction every time I undress for bed? Who looks like he lost his best friend when I pull on the blue and pink rocking horse mother-in-law number again (okay, it *is* comfortable) and tell him how exhausted, how *unbelievably* exhausted I am. Again.

Henry Ward Beecher said, "A person without a sense of humor is like a wagon without springs — jolted by every pebble in the road." I'm thankful that this former English professor can laugh at her ridiculous daydreams. Pierce Brosnan. As if.

Well, cyber girlfriends, have to quit daydreaming and start on nighttime dreams, as it's getting late.

As always, real life calls. Back to it! Sweet dreams in yours,
Pajama Mama

Comments:

I'm a Brad Pitt woman, myself.
~Dust Diva

Johnny Depp.
~Lexus Mommy

Team Edward. Team Jacob. Potato, potahto. I'd be okay with either."
~Formerly Hot

I make the rounds, tucking the girls in and praying with them. It's hands down my favorite time of day with them. Eli hangs out on Max's shoulder or in his lap, watching sports on the television downstairs.

In their room, I pray with Caroline and read her a chapter of *Junie B. Jones is a Beauty Shop Guy*. Then, snuggled on Zoe's bed, we read from her pre-school devotional book. The lesson is about Solomon obeying God. I finish reading and we sing to the tune of "The Old Gray Mare":

> *Dear God, teach me to use my hands to help today,*
> *Share my toys when I play and be ready to obey.*
>
> *Dear God teach me to fold my hands, to bow and pray,*
> *Just 'cause I love you so.*
>
> *Dear God, teach me to come when Mommy says to come, help my feet to jump and run,*
> *Help me say, "Yes! Here I come."*
>
> *Dear God, teach me to go to bed when day is done, knowing You love me so."*

My cheeks are wet. Zoe reaches up her hands and pats my face. "Don't be sad Mama, 'cause you love God too! Just like me. Don't you, Mommy?" And this is why God likes children better than us.

"Yes, Zo. I do." My voice breaks and cuts out entirely. "I do." And how, I wonder, can you love God and love your husband and be so utterly wrong in what you do about it.

******

Max spends slow weeks working long hours, filling me in with snatches about the odd burglaries he's working, how frustrating the leads are. I only know that he is getting called out routinely and that on one level, I'm glad. He can't be focusing on me and how *unfocused* I am.

This morning he is distracted and in work mode even as he kisses the girls and me good-bye. "Max?" I follow after him. I am hesitant to bother him, as though we are roommates, rather than lovers, soul mates, husband and wife.

He turns to me at the door. For a fraction of a moment, his eyes soften. "Yes, Deenie?"

"Well, I just wanted to, I mean, I'd like to hear about—never mind. Max? I know you need to go. Have a good day. I love you. Be safe."

"Always." He brushes my forehead with his lips and squeezes Eli's knees. When the door closes behind him, I want to cry.

We drive to school, rather pleasantly, taking Caroline in her bright plaid shorts and yellow blouse to Roosevelt Elementary first, and then dropping Zoe off for her morning pre-school at The Flannel Goose. Zoe is entirely herself, thrilled that I broke down and let her wear her ballet leotard with her ruffed pink skirt and orange sequined flip flops. Some things are just not worth a battle.

Eli is a happy baby too this morning, allowing his sisters to haul him around proudly, looking every inch a little man in his denim overalls and little red t-shirt. Every teacher oohs and aahs over those tiny toes and his ebullient squeals.

When I pull back in our driveway, I can't bear to go inside yet. It is the loveliest of days, this last Friday in September. The air no longer holds summer heat, but it is not yet chilly. I unbuckle Eli, loving his enormous drooly grin and those five and a half Chiclet baby teeth. He kicks his little legs and squeals with delight when he sees the stroller. My boy loves to go on walks.

I wave at Vicki as she backs out of her driveway, but she is clearly on a mission and doesn't even see me. Eli and I turn right at the end of our drive and begin a leisurely stroll through the neighborhood.

Sun-dappled front yards sport hay bales and vibrant potted mums. A few pumpkins grace porch steps all along Primrose Lane. At the end of Morning Glory Circle, a jaunty scarecrow in torn overalls is propped up by corn stalks on Mrs. Matthews' porch; she's got the jump on the autumn season. The grass is green and lush, there's a pleasant coolness to the air and the sun kisses my face.

Eli waves his hands and kicks his little bare feet in ecstasy. By our second lap around the neighborhood, his grip has loosened on his teething biscuit and his sweet drool-drenched, crumb-dotted chin is lowered onto his red t-shirt, eyes closed in slumber.

I push the stroller up Goldenrod, the hilly street just before Morning Glory Circle and the cul-de-sac. On the corner is a small section of split-rail fence festooned with our street's namesake flower and vines and pert rows of bright orange marigolds lending a fall feel to the landscape.

There's a wheelbarrow and rake lying in the middle of the yard, and I can see Mr. Chitwood stacking wood in the side yard. Although Mr. Chitwood stubbornly clings to the Baptist church across town after his best friend "deserted" him to attend Southern Hills Christian Church, he is still good friends with Mr. McKenzie.

I throw up a hand in greeting, but seeing me, he peels off his work gloves and heads over, beckoning to someone. Mr. Mac and his overalls, obviously there to deliver a truckload of wood. Mr. Mac grins at me and immediately reaches in his bib to pull out a handful of Bazooka, which he deposits in the basket of Eli's stroller.

"Mr. Mac!" I hug him with great affection. "Thanks for the gum. I'll need it."

Not to be outdone, Mr. Chitwood pouts, walks quickly over to the wheel barrow. He returns to hand me a net bag of daffodil bulbs and reaches out one flannel-clad arm for a hug too. "How's the prettiest little gal in our neighborhood, 'sides my Margaret?"

Mr. Mac snorts and cuffs him on the neck. "You're still an old flirt. Not much better than in our service days and here you are an old married thing!"

"Don't pay him any mind, Miss Deenie, you know how Mac is. And yes, I am – going to be sixty-two years of wedded bliss next month." Mr. Chitwood beams.

"Congratulations! And you two, you'd never know you were best friends the way you carry on!"

"Pshaw, Deenie, that's how you know we're friends! Somebody's got to keep this ol' boy in his place."

"And I suppose you think you're the one to do it, Chitterbox? I'll have you know that if my Sadie were still alive, we'd have you beat with sixty-*three* years!" Mr. Mac rolls his eyes at his buddy, winks at me and peeks in the stroller at Eli. Looks about ready to join the Marines! How old is the little man now?"

"He'll be ten months soon!"

"He's a fine one," Mr. Chitwood chimes in. "He'll be just like his daddy."

"How are you and that Max, anyway?" Mr. Mac queries.

"Max and I?" my voice squeaks. "Um, we're good, of course, Mr. Mac. Why do you ask?"

"Well, now I'd have bought that answer if it weren't for your face. What's wrong Deena girl? Max working too many hours?" Mr. Mac's weathered face reflects genuine interest and concern.

"You tell us if we need to get after him!" Mr. Chitwood admonishes, slapping his gloves against his palm.

Mr. Mac unwraps another piece of Bazooka. "Open up, Deenie. You got to get some sugar in that mouth to sweeten that sour expression."

My eyes spill over and on the corner of Goldenrod and Morning Glory Circle, I plunk down on the curb, set the brake on Eli's stroller and cry my eyes out. Before I know it, Mr. Mac and Mr. Chitwood have hiked up their flannel sleeves and overalls and sit on either side of me. Seems they've both lived long enough and had enough experience with female tears not to be undone by mine.

Soft murmurs of "There, there," and "It'll be alright", are every bit as comforting as the familiar taste of Bazooka bubble gum.

When my head comes up, Mr. Mac unfolds the miniature comic and reads it to me. "That Bazooka Joe, he has himself some adventures," Mr. Mac's thick forefinger taps the slick plastic strip for emphasis.

I turn to look at him, vaguely recalling that the Topps Company began including the little comic strips with their gum in 1953. I don't see what the adventurous life of Bazooka Joe has to do with me.

"Life's an adventure too, Deenie, especially married life. Sometimes you're right on the mountaintop, convinced you got yourself the best deal ever; others, well you're in a valley so low you can't figure why you'd ever done this thing to begin with." Mr. Mac pats my knee.

"All true, though it pains me to agree so readily with Mac here," Mr. Chitwood chimes in. "But I promise you this, whatever it is, you stick with it, Deenie. There's always sweetness comin' in after those hard times."

"Truth to tell, sometimes keeping your marriage vows can hurt, but nothin' like *not* keepin' them."

Mr. Chitwood nods slowly and amidst much knee popping, they rise to their feet and help me to mine. I stare at their stained, scarred work boots and see the same kinds of wear on their older, wiser faces. My twelve years of marriage are just a wisp compared to their more-than-a-century combined marriages.

Mr. Mac taps a rough but gentle finger on Eli's fist which startles and opens in his sleep. Eli's baby hand grips it so tightly. Soft tenderness lights Mr. Mac's face.

I smile at these two angels in overalls. "Thank you," I say. "For the gum and the counseling session." Mr. Chitwood hands me a dusty navy-blue bandanna and I wipe my face.

"You're welcome in our house or on our curb anytime, Deena. You know that."

I watch Mr. Chitwood and Mr. Mac amble back up to the side yard and the wood pile, giving each other a hard time the whole way. "Margaret have any pie?" I hear Mr. Mac ask. "I do love pie…" His voice fades as they walk.

I love those two guys, but especially Mr. Mac with his brave heart, every inch the gentleman in overalls, pluckily carrying on without his precious Sadie.

I park Eli's stroller and gently lift him out, willing him not to wake up before getting his nap out. His face nuzzles against my neck and I cradle him to me, gently patting his Pampered bottom, kissing the top of his fuzzy head. He smells like baby lotion and little boy.

Opting to go in through the stone breezeway, rather than jostling Eli by digging for my house key, I tiptoe, skirting two big copper pots of burnt orange mums, kicking a Holiday Barbie and miniature set of shoes out of the way, and carefully opening the side door, bumping it open with my hip. I make it all the way up the stairs, my chilly bare toes sinking in the plush ivy carpet.

In the nursery, I lay Eli down in his crib and he scoots his little overall clad self into the corner, sighing with sleepy contentment. I give him his blanket lovey with the silky corners and cover him lightly with the blue Benjamin Bunny quilt that Grandma Dora made. That woman can sew anything.

I am walking downstairs with unnecessary care. I don't want to do the chores that await me. Don't want to think about dinner. Don't want to think about Max and Thomas. Don't want to think about *not* thinking about Thomas. I want to treasure the nuggets of wisdom that Mr. Mac and Mr. Chitwood left me, like extra pieces of sweetness mixed in with the stroller basket of Bazooka gum.

I walk down each stair with exaggerated stealth, sliding my hand over the oak banister, peering around the edge at the fireplace and family room to my left and the uneven grey stone of the breezeway, past the kitchen to my right.

Bright autumn sunlight dapples each floor, making parallelograms, polka dots and squares depending on the surface through which it refracts and the arrangement of the tree branches which usher it into our house like the thick bumpers on the lanes at the bowling alley.

Dust motes float lazily, defiantly in front of the glass panes. Seeing Eli's tiny fingerprints and even a nose print on the one low windowpane in the family room by the window seat, makes me smile.

Butternut Squash squints at me, stretches lazily from his contented place on a rug directly in a patch of sunlight and gets up to wind his tail around my legs, purring loudly. I bend down and give him an absent-minded scratch between his ears.

This is the house for which Max and I saved. It was the first thing we have truly owned together. We are still making it ours, slowly furnishing and perfecting it, allowing the collection of memories and toys and furniture and things we have found together to burnish not just the walls, but our souls, with a rich patina of shared history.

Of course, Max would not define it in such a romantic way; Thomas would. But would life even be like I imagine it if there were no Max? I am not ready for such a step, am I? A stiff breeze pushes all the clouds in a bank like all the bed covers and sheets on sheet changing day suddenly piling against the sun and every sunny shape disappears just for an instant.

I hop lightly from the last step just as the phone rings. It seems too jangly, too disruptive and I don't want it to waken Eli. It's probably Max checking in and I run for the kitchen line, snatching it up, old married woman disapproval in my voice. "Hello?"

"Deena? Sergeant Rivers here." In an instant, my blood chills. Before I can get out a word, he continues. "I'm not in the habit of calling officers' wives, because they always assume something is wrong, so I want to say up front that everything's okay. I just want to tell you what happened."

"Okay?" My voice trails off, part question, part bewilderment. What could this be? Max is obviously not physically injured. Sergeant Rivers has never called our home phone before. I've met him no more than half a dozen times.

"I want you to know that your husband got complained on. We did an internal investigation and I took care of it. He's not going to be in any trouble, but apparently, he threatened a local college professor by the name of Dr. Thomas Hunt. Ring any bells?

Because now there's a note in his personnel file, Deena. Max is a valuable employee at the department, a top notch detective. It's none of my business what's going on, but when personal life starts affecting my business, then it becomes my business and I need you to make it stop."

I slide down the wall, landing on the floor with a thud, clutching the phone in both hands. My hands are clammy, shaky. A cold ball of dread sits in the pit of my stomach, the same way that pasta salad sat there and gave me heartburn at the faculty picnic when I was expecting Eli. Only this is much worse. I cry, my breath coming in fast hitches.

"Obviously there's something going on, Deena. If there's anything I can do to help, let me know; otherwise I'm going to stay out. But Deena, this can't happen again.

"Yes, Sir. I, I, I understand." I wipe my nose with the back of my hand, staring at the receiver and imagining the pulse of its disconnecting tone as the warning tone for my life.

I'm not sure how long I sit there unable to move. My tears dry, making uncomfortably tight tracks on my cheeks.

I turn the phone over and push the numbers for the University switchboard. I'm not going to hunt up my cell phone and I need to ask Thomas what really happened. It's been a few days since our last meeting and I haven't talked to him. Of course, this might explain all that, if I could figure out what happened.

"Southern Hills University for a bright future! How may I direct your call?"

"Extension 287, please." My voice has its professional quality back, although clogged and distant sounding, leftover from my crying jag. And mercy, those are becoming more and more frequent.

"Certainly. One moment." I hold for the clicks and dials. Instantly, I know that Thomas is deep in thought as soon as he answers. I picture him in those ridiculously tiny offices at the history building, surrounded by reference books, historical atlases, a miniature coffee maker, his brown laptop and stacks of student papers, as well as his own research and lecture notes.

"Dr. Hunt here." He is brisk, businesslike and obviously wants this to be a short phone call.

"Thomas? It's me."

A few seconds of awkward silence pass and for a little bit, I get the sense that he's not sure of who this is.

"Aha, Deena." His voice is much cooler than I've been accustomed to when we talk.

"Well, yes, I -uh- I got a call from a sergeant at the department today, something about a professor that complained on Max. Max, my husband." My explanation of who Max is seems forced and stupid.

"Ah, yes, the ubiquitous Max Wilson. He did indeed pay me a visit."

"There? At the University?!" I am incredulous.

"Yes, Deena, here. At my place of employment. Apparently, he was on campus to ask some questions regarding a burglary and he stopped in on his way out. Took off his gun and badge and made some comment about being off the clock now that his shift was over. He threatened me, Deena. He *threatened* me if I did not leave you alone." Thomas is all offended bravado, but I detect something else in his tone. Fear.

Some of the debonair shine is lost, hearing that fear. And I marvel. Max has fought for me. My arms chill. I don't know what to make of it.

Thomas grows impatient with my silent self-examination and processing of events. "Deena? Are you there? I cannot have this sort of thing occurring."

"What sort of thing is that, Thomas?" Something pivotal hinges on his answer.

"This sort of complication that hampers my career. My image." There is no mention of me. What Max must think. That it is my marriage on the line, not his. There is no mention of how this could hurt me at all. Him. Him. Him. It strikes my consciousness that Max has been all about me, me, me. My chest tightens with a hurt so heavy it feels as if *I* am the one wearing Max's bullet proof vest.

"I see." Slowly, my finger pushes the button to end the call. Eli's voice babbles at me through the monitor on the crumby gray-flecked kitchen counter.

Where does this leave me? Why have I not noticed this side of Thomas? Why don't I have a lightning bolt realization that I have been a very stupid woman?

One of my favorite writers, Anne Lamott, says one of her best prayers is "Help, help, help." So here I am with my one word (or is it three?) word prayer. It's all I can manage, but I hope, oh, Lord, I hope You can hear it. Help. Help. Help.

******

It's already 11:32 a.m. by the time I pull myself together and I am about to be late for Zoe's pick-up time at The Flannel Goose. Luckily Miss Carrie is so patient and won't inquire about my sunglasses except to tell me how cute she thinks this shade of pink is.

Apparently, crying jags aren't good for your sense of time or your sense of style. My eyes are so dry and hollow that they sting. What a mess this is.

Zoe hurtles toward my knees with an exuberant hug as soon as she sees me. I can't help but grin as she tugs me toward the minivan, barely giving Eli the tiniest greeting as she shows me all of the work she's completed this morning and tells me all about the pre-school's pumpkin painting party next month.

"See Mommy?" She says, thrusting a garish orange reminder in my hand. "I will be soooo excited about that!" Zoe starts skipping toward the double doors, painted lavender and orange respectively.

I catch Miss Carrie's eye. She is surrounded by a gaggle of parents as always, but quickly breaks for just a few seconds. "You seem like you could use a pick-me-up today, Deena. I saved something for you; Zoe says you like country music."

"Guilty," I laugh.

She hands me a women's home and family magazine with Tim McGraw on the cover. "By the way, cute pink sunglasses!" She waves me on.

"Thanks!" I glance down. And I don't care if you are Tim McGraw. Pin tucked shirts on a guy are just wrong. So wrong.

I feel wrung out, as though all of the crying and pretending have wrung me out like an old sponge that is now dried and curled up on the edges, leaving tiny frayed bits of itself all around the rim of the sink.

The ball of dread in my stomach is sitting there like dough that is too heavy. I need to rise, to lighten up, to process. We'll just kill some time at the park until time to pick Caroline up from school. And we can possibly make it to Target too.

Back home from fetching Caroline, I trudge upstairs to put a few stacks of folded laundry away, before keeping my promise to go outside and watch them play.

Caroline has bought an archaic, annoying Furby at a garage sale. I can't stand that toy. I put the noisy Furby into a dark basket of hand-me-downs that need to be sorted. "No like. Not fun," Furby intones. Too bad. I shut the closet door. Hard.

Scientists say that a four-year-old's voice is louder than those of 200 adults. Listening to Zoe's exuberant play, and Caroline's answering bossiness, I believe it. I feel the beginnings of a pounding headache.

I don't really feel like cooking. Again. I think I'll order in pizza. Everyone loves pizza. Especially me and Zoe. In fact, Americans eat more than one-hundred acres of it every day. I wonder what one-hundred acres translates to in pounds and inches. Never mind. I don't really want to know.

Sitting outside with the children, listening to the fading sounds of summer and the light-hearted giggles that always accompany bubbles and wading pools, I am very conscious that all this is fleeting. In another week, all the faded and cracking plastic wading pools, so bright and promising at the beginning of summer, will be abandoned on neighborhood curbs next to the bright green trash cans, bits of damp and dying grass clinging there, waiting to be hauled away and replaced by next year's batch.

The jingle of the ice cream truck trundles through our neighborhood, luring children outside. I see Vicki's door open and her two boys fly out in front of her. We wave. I again feel the odd, polite distance between us, but doing anything which requires depth just eludes me.

Caroline and Zoe look at me with interest, but not too much hope. What the heck? Indian summer won't last forever and in a few weeks, the ice cream truck will be a distant memory until spring. I scoot Eli's bouncy seat up next to the screen door, dash inside and rummage around in my change container, depositing wadded-up dollar bills and several shiny quarters in their outstretched hands. Seven hundred popsicles are made every minute at the Good Humor-Bryers plant in Sikeston, Missouri. That's a lot of popsicles.

It's almost 4:00 p.m. There's another loooong hour and a half before Max's day will end, and providing the bad guys have been cooperative, he will finally be home. These are the longest hours of the day for me. I may as well be a puppy, expecting someone home, tail wagging at the sight of someone new. For me, it's wagging my tail at the sight of a grown-up. Max can take over and then I need to run. I have to talk to Max. We need to talk. But I can't. How do I even begin to ask his version of Sergeant Rivers' and Thomas' reports?

At 5:00 p.m., I change my mind about ordering in pizza, collect the children and go into the kitchen to begin dinner. I'm actually going to cook something. No pancakes or scrambled eggs or canned soup or carryout pizza. I'm thinking shrimp sautéed in olive oil and a few crushed garden tomatoes, over wheat pasta. I'll make tea. A loaf of quick bread. Throw together a salad. I'll show Max I'm trying.

Why do they [whoever "they" are] call this happy hour? What is happy about it? This pre-dinner hour is more like mad hour. Everyone wants my attention. I feel shredded into pieces like a too fat bagel stuck in the toaster prongs, or poured out like a spilled pitcher of lemonade. The flies have sensed it and they've already landed.

Eli sits on a blanket near the kitchen table. Zoe has set up blocks at my feet by the stove. Caroline is vigorously smashing Play dough into my kitchen table, cutting it with my cookie cutters and offering me play bites of her creations every five minutes. Eli babbles, experimenting with the sounds he can make. Squeals tumble over coos, slide into showy octaves of all he is learning.

I juggle various pans, trying not to get the oil too hot, shape my dough into some semblance of a loaf, pour, measure and take stabs at having coherent thoughts.

Tonight. Max and I will talk tonight. I will try to be honest, but gloss over the worst of my thoughts, my one shared kiss. No point in hurting Max, right? I mean, anymore than he must be hurting in order to have threatened Thomas like that. Somehow I can smooth all this over. Salvage a marriage, try harder, be happier, still keep some part of myself. Can't I? *Can't I?*

Suddenly it's as if the children turn on me. "I want Daaaadddy!" Zoe wails and hiccups after banging her knee on the cabinet, then turning around and falling over her block tower. Bright wooden arches, half-spheres, columns and squares clack and scatter all over the floor.

I remember something my mother used to do when I was very small. "Bad cabinet!" I scold. "Bad, bad cabinet to hurt Mommy's girl!" I spank the edge of the cabinet and Zoe's tears halt.

Seeing that Zoe is getting all the attention, Caroline tires of her Play dough art. "Can you read me a story, Mommy? Huh? Can you?"

"Story! How 'bout *Red Fish, Blue Fish*? That's my favorite!" Zoe gets in her vote, jumping up and down and clapping her pudgy little hands.

Their noise startles Eli, who falls over and starts to cry. He scoots toward me in his silly, precious crawl.

The girls flank me with books, Caro lobbying for another chapter of *Junie B. Jones is Not a Crook*. "No! I asked for my fish book first." Zoe is adamant.

In a spurt of blatant immaturity, Caroline tries to grab it from Zoe and the fight is on. Now all of them are crying. In my imagination, I patiently turn down the dinner and go to the family room for a short round of Dr. Seuss and a few pages of Junie B.

In an alternate scenario, I strap Eli to me in a high-tech L.L. Bean back pack [which I don't even own] and assign the girls simple dinner tasks like putting the bread dough into whatever shape they want, or tearing apart lettuce for the salad.

In real life, I slide down the cabinets, sinking to the floor, Eli plunked in my lap, one girl on either side and we all cry together. Haven't I already done this? Cried in exactly this position earlier today? This is how Max finds us.

I can tell that he is assessing the situation just like he would if he were going to plan a SWAT operation. He immediately sees by looking at me that loud guffawing is not his best option.

"Um, sweetie," he is careful, pulling out his best negotiation skills. "It looks like you might be having a hard day. How 'bout dinner at *Pacino's*? My treat." He grins, looking devastatingly like the man with whom I fell in love.

He is once again my knight. Only his shining armor looks suspiciously like a holstered Glock.42. I refuse to think of my one guilty lunch meeting there with Thomas. Or the fact that once upon a recent time, that same Glock has been tossed on Thomas' desk. *Pacino's* is one of my favorite restaurants and I need to eat, keep up my strength for coming at least partially clean with my husband.

Still. "Oh, Max," I hedge, putting Eli down on the floor. "I already have dinner started, well, kind of, and the kids aren't ready," I gesture with my free arm and Max takes in Zoe's woefully mismatched short set. I'm simply too tired to argue with her about her clothing choices in this strong-willed do-everything-myself stage, and besides, don't all the books talk about how this will foster a healthy independence?

"Put what you've started in the fridge and use it a different night. Zoe looks marvelous!" His crooked grin is a statement all its own.

"And look at me, I'm just, I'm..." I trail off and Max silences my objections with a kiss. "I'll do you one better. Let me call Vick or your mom and see if one of them can watch the kids and I'll take my best girl out."

Alone time with Max. At a big person restaurant. I should be jumping at the chance, given how desperately we need to talk, but suddenly I feel nearly too shy to be with Max in such a place without the buffer of the children.

Mustering my best acting skills, I flash a brilliant smile. "That's so sweet, really. But they're missing you too and well, maybe this would be a better night to do the family thing. The girls like the kids' menu there. We'll talk later, Max. I know we need to. We really need to." I lower my head. What if Max knows that I know about the Sergeant's call to me? That I know what he's said to Thomas. What if that stops me? Worse, what if it doesn't?

Max seems so pleased by my uncharacteristic reasonableness and willingness to go out that he doesn't try and persuade me further. Typical Max. He doesn't tip his hand. He will say nothing to me until he is ready. As for Thomas? Max will have been ruthless, silent and thorough. I feel guilty anyway.

"Alrighty, then, Deena Bean, a family night it is."

"Yay! Yay! We're going out!" Caroline and Zoe are thrilled. Eli grins and blows spit bubbles.

Deena Renee, I hear my mother's voice, *A lady always, always puts her man first. You'll want a strong relationship when you have children.*

A quick giggle escapes my tightened lips as I imagine telling my mother to stuff it. As if.

Max takes this sound for delight and he hoists Zoe on his shoulders and takes Caroline by the hand. They go out to the van in a cloud of giggles, marching to the beat of their own happy parade.

I look at Eli, who has pulled himself up on my jeans and is wobbling, clutching the material in his chubby fists. Sweeping him into his car seat, I plant a raspberry on his deliciously sweet little tummy. He looks at me wide-eyed with that quizzical expression. "Come on, my little man, you need to make sure Mommy's a fun mommy tonight!" I am rewarded with a primarily toothless grin, his bottom two teeth resting like pearls in a pink velvet box.

Ignoring the guilt I feel at allowing Zoe out in public in such an outfit, I relax on the drive and begin to anticipate dinner where someone else will clean up after us and sweep the endless crumbs into a different dust pan.

Max and I are polite. I pull out my best questioning techniques, getting Max to share all about his day. Trying my best to listen. Before we know it, we are pulling into the parking lot.

Pacino's is packed. We wait for twenty minutes, not a terrible wait, but always a challenge with three small children who think dining out entails golden arches or cows that implore you to "eat mor chikin."

Our name is finally called and we gather up our little family and troop past diners dressed with far more panache than we can pull off. A tug at my sleeve causes me to turn around and swallow my dismay as I see Mother and Daddy seated in a booth, salads and garlic bread with olive oil dipping trays at the ready.

"Deena! Max! And my beautiful grandbabies!" Mother is effusive and Dad has already begun to pull out the extra three chairs at their oval table.

"Ma'am?" Dad flags down their waitress. "Could you please get us one extra chair and a high chair? That way you can just give their table to someone else."

Max and I look at each other and realize there is no gracious way out. We busy ourselves setting Zoe in a booster seat on top of her chair, unwrapping plastic packages of Crayons for coloring their kids' menus and buckling Eli into his highchair with an assortment of Cheerios and Gerber apple puff snacks on the tray.

Caroline is bending her grandpa's ear with tales of school and Max is trying to teach Zoe the Tic Tac Toe game on her paper menu.

"Deena, honey," my mother's usually bright voice is subdued, "are you alright?"

I sigh heavily. She means well; I don't even sense any criticism. "Thanks, Mother, for noticing. I'm just – I'm just having a bit of a rough time right now." I square my shoulders and take in a deep breath. "But it will all be fine. Life is just overwhelming sometimes."

As though she senses that I need some reserve or I will shatter, Mother uncharacteristically pats my arm, offers me some of that wonderful bread and engages Max in a story about work. Daddy and I talk a bit about the University and the rest of dinner passes in a blessedly uneventful blur. Could this be evidence that the Lord did indeed hear my three-word prayer?

Home again, home again, jiggety jig. I sit in the dim lamplight of the family room, rocking Eli and nursing him before bed. His little fist grasps my sweater and we cozy up together, basking in our own mutual admiration society.

My bare toes, the pink polish chipping off of my left big toe, push the braided rug in front of the rocking chair, absently polishing the floor. Eli makes the cutest nursing sounds and his eyes flutter open and shut.

Max is upstairs putting the girls to bed and I hear the muffled sounds of thumps, giggles, and occasional running. Max is a good daddy; he makes everything an adventure for the girls. Eli is too small to know anything other than that life is something very different when daddy comes home.

With a small contented sigh, Eli breaks the seal, his little mouth milky and contented. He nestles into my breasts, scooting his body as close as he can get to me. I wrap his favorite blankie securely around him, patting his Pampered buns, smiling at that one-of-a-kind sound and marveling at the fact this is how all my children have gone to sleep. If someone tried patting my backside while I was trying to sleep, it would be the most irritating thing in the world.

Reluctantly, I carry him upstairs to put him down for the night. Sometimes I feel like I could hold him forever. Even this little bit of letting go smacks of poignant loss. I lay him in his crib, lingering a moment, listening for his peculiar night sounds as he settles in. Butternut Squash winds himself around my legs, purring softly, padding to the end of Eli's crib and curling up in a tight ball on the rug. I bend down to pat him and head downstairs.

Max isn't far behind me. We settle in to our usual places, me in the oversized rocking chair, Max in his leather recliner. It's not like we've decided *not* to talk, but nobody's talking. I'm fairly certain this is not what you'd call a comfortable silence.

I'm pretending to read the style forecast in *Vogue* magazine, one of my Target purchases, which although small, mystifies even me. I'm not good at this unless I'm doing the sulking.

"Any good cases, lately?" And why does that sound like a really bad pick up line, since I'm already married to the guy?

"They're all good when I'm getting to figure them out." Max is trying to be jaunty but it comes across flat and distracted. He doesn't look up from his leadership book.

"Any of them you'd like to run by me?" He did this all the time when we were first married. He once proved that a death everyone else was certain had been homicide, was actually a suicide. When he put all the pictures [shielding me from the gory ones by covering them with index cards] into an album with commentary by each piece of evidence, outlining his case to present to the Sergeant, he asked for my input on questions. I remember being so thrilled that he trusted me with that.

"Nah. I got it for now." He goes back to reading and I lazily flip through a few more pages of *Vogue*. Where are the things that mommies can wear? Or people with real lives, for that matter.

I spot Max looking out the front picture window. He's checking something out but he's trying not to make a big deal out of it. After a few minutes, he leisurely gets up, stretches his back and walks the long way to the breakfast bar to pour himself more coffee. Thank goodness he switches to decaf at night.

I hear him in the short front hallway and then he appears in the family room again. This time he just stands right in front of the window waiting. Waiting for what?

"Max? What is it? Is something wrong?"

He waves me off. "Nope. Just wondering about this car. It's been driving by our house very slowly a couple of times and I've never seen it in the neighborhood before."

"'Curiouser and curiouser,' said Alice,'" I quote. "What's it look like?"

"Fairly fancy. A newer model Mercedes or something. Looks green or gray. I'm trying to check the license plate, but it looks like the bulb's burnt out."

"Kind of high end for someone who'd be mad at you," I joke. "Max, I need to ask you — well, to tell you that — Sergeant Rivers called me today." I am stumped for a way to continue.

"He did?"

"Yes, about Thomas and you and how valuable you are and … Max, we need to talk, I know we do. I'm just not, not…" Tears threaten again.

"C'mere," Max softens. "We will talk, Deena. I'm here. I will always be here."

I walk toward him and we stand together in an awkward Junior High dance position. We just don't know what to do with each other. I know something has to change; it *is* changing. I just hope it won't be like Humpty Dumpty and all of the king's horses and men can't put us together again. I don't know what to do. I only know I don't want us to be that broken.

Max's shirt soaks up my tears. And when he lifts my chin to tenderly kiss me, he starts to speak and then doesn't. When he turns to go upstairs, I go into the kitchen and scribble another list by the light of tiny yellow gingham lamp.

<u>Grocery List</u>
Hershey's syrup
Junior Mints
Diet Coke
Milk
Deodorant for Max
Mascara – try kind in ad?
Lunch boxes
Colored pencils
Pink Pearl Eraser
Wooden ruler
School scissors
Elmer's Glue
Loose Leaf Paper
Lunch drinks
Oreos
Baby Carrots
Yogurt
Colored Markers
2 pocket folders
1 inch binder
Kleenex
*finishing getting things on Zoe's pre-school supply list

Chapter 13

September. Included in its meanings are post-Labor Day back to school sales and lists of supply sheets. Freshly sharpened pencils, ruled paper and a box of pristine Crayons, lined up like elongated jewels in a box. This is the New Year for teachers, children and mothers everywhere. It breaks my heart that Caroline won't need a rest mat this year. How could my firstborn possibly be a first grader?

I am seated between Vicki and Super PTA MOM who but for the fact it's illegal, would sneak into grocery stores at night with a box knife and remove all the General Mills Box Tops for Education just so her kid's classroom could win the pizza party. Vicki and I roll our eyes together. Just another form of exercise between friends.

Whatever has been preoccupying Vicki seems to have abated and in my bizarre situation given Sergeant Rivers' phone call and my unsatisfactory questioning of Thomas, we have been dwelling too often in the Land of Distant Politeness, only occasionally talking on each other's porches, taking cautious brief outings with the kids. I take the eye rolling as a sign of amelioration on the whole situation.

When the meeting is over, Vick and I are reluctant to head back to bedlam just yet. "Starbucks," she shouts. "Last one there is a rotten egg!"

"You're on!" I race to my minivan and she slides smoothly behind the wheel of her trendy chocolate colored Ford Explorer with caramelly leather seats. I laugh every time I see her license plate: VENTI. She's serious about her coffee.

We wait in line for our venti vanilla mocha and pumpkin spice latte, and nearly the minute we sit down, Vick has morphed into Serious Concerned Friend. "Deen, I know I botched it, when I tried to talk to you earlier, and I've apologized. And you know I love you, but I think you need to tell Max about your attraction to Thomas. Red flags aren't just flying, girl, they're smacking you in the face! If you're right and there's nothing going on, then you need to tell him before it goes too far."

"Truth hurts, Vick. There's no point in worrying Max. And it's not going anywhere. It's not like I'm going to sleep with the guy! Besides, I've missed you. Let's not go there."

Vicki's eyes widen in surprise. "I wasn't accusing. Deena, you are my dearest friend and I couldn't bear it if you were, well, if I truly thought something was wrong and I didn't tell you. You need to be honest with yourself. And with Max."

Tears sting my eyes and pool over. "I am doing something about it. Lots of stuff has been happening that you don't know anything about because you've been too busy doing, well, whatever it is you're doing and I'm not ready to--" I push back my chair and snatch up my purse and stalk out the door. I've never done that. Not in our five-year friendship.

In the minivan, I slam the car into reverse and practically squeal out of the parking lot. The radio chirps out an advertisement listing the side-effects of a particular brand of sleeping pill. They actually mention drowsiness. Is this not the point? Seriously.

Glancing in my rearview mirror, I see the blue and red flash of a light bar and yes, it's for me. Could this night get any worse?

I pull over on the shoulder and fish my driver's license and insurance card from my wallet. My window is down and waiting when the officer arrives. I don't recognize him, but I know there have been a bunch of new hires. Before he says anything to me, I hand the cards through.

"Ma'am," he glances at me but the interior of the minivan is dark with only an odd green sheen from the dash lights. He looks down at my license and peers in again. "Oh. You're Max's wife. Recognize the name. You were speeding, you know. I'll let you go this time. Slow down and be safe." He hands my things back to me and walks back to his car, on the radio within seconds.

I punch the radio button off and adjust my interior lights, fuming and stewing all the way home. What a night. I refuse to consider Vicki's face with its hurt.

Back at home, Max looks up quizzically from the couch. All's quiet on the Western front. And thank God.

"Late meeting, baby?"

"Vicki and I went to Starbucks afterward." I take a measured breath.

"No problem, but I was worried. You should have called." I see the echo of suspicion from previous, less innocent times I've been late.

"Max. Just because I know someone will tell on me, I got pulled over. That takes even more time. Some new guy. He recognized the name and didn't write me a ticket. And I don't need a lecture from my best friend *and* my husband." I ignore the irony there; at one time I would have considered Max to be both. "I'm just going to go upstairs and take a bath."

"You and Vicki fought?" Max is so stunned by this news, he doesn't even inquire about the near ticket. "Wow. Anything you want to talk about?" Max's tender concern irritates me. I feel like Caroline, caught reading her beginner books under the covers with her flashlight after bedtime. I am even more irritated with myself. What happened to my resolve to get closer to Max? To come clean? It's a half step forward and three steps back.

I question his motives, though I shouldn't. I know Max and our needed conversation is still present in the room, expanding to fill up all the rooms of our life, an awkward box that no one knows what do with, and therefore, no one has yet opened it or moved out of the way. Max is simmering, which means Max's mind has never shut off. That's how he works.

"No. I don't want to talk about it." I'm curt and I can tell I've hurt him. And he doesn't know the half of it. "No. Thank you." I turn to go up the stairs.

"Well, then, if you're going to be mad anyway, you might want to call your folks. Your mom called here and wanted to talk to you." Oh joy.

Ten minutes later, I hurl myself into the bathtub, a major pout coming on. Major. In the steam, tears leak from my eyes and before I know it, I am sobbing. I have to leave the water running to drown out my noise.

My mother is going to Paris. They're going to go next month. Everyone goes to Paris in the spring time; they're going to do a fall tour. Of course she's taking my father with her, but still. That was a trip she knows I have long dreamed of. She prattled on and on about the tours they'll take through French wine country and the Louvre and going up in the Eiffel Tower and "oh the rich history behind the Arc de Triomphe and the view we're going to have of the Seine."

I am in full-out pity party mode. Never mind the fact that we don't get along. You can discard all of that when you're feeling hurt. She could have taken me. Waited. Something. I ignore more reasonable voices reminding me that this isn't the time. Baby Eli. No one to watch the children. I need to go with Max. Someday when we're using walkers and canes, perhaps.

It seems that everyone's life is more together, more interesting, less complicated and better than mine. Even as I know that cannot possibly be true, the thought takes over my mind and spreads like the jam melting from a knife dipped deeply into the jar and then left on the stove top when the oven underneath is baking something at 400 degrees.

I want someone who will just let me vent. Vicki. But I can't. I can't. I've blown it. Or someone who will just hold me. I know Max would do exactly that. He would be appropriately sympathetic and he gets the odd dynamics between my mother and me. But like an overtired toddler who doesn't like any of the choices offered him, I stubbornly want Thomas. Thomas who might not be at all what he seemed.

In real life, I would never dump all of that history and ugliness on Thomas [but I would on Max – and what kind of person does this make me?]. That wouldn't present the picture I want him to have of me. Funny. Feminine. Put together. Organized. And yes, desirable. Despite everything, I am clinging to something that has made me feel important. Wanted.

I have seen myself cry and it's not pretty. I'm one of those red-eyed, red-nosed, hair disaster criers, whose snot leaks through multiple Kleenex and whose nose honks when blown.

Max knocks gently [warily?] on the bathroom door. "Deen? I brought you some hot tea." I don't answer. "Aannd, a box of Junior Mints."

Now you're talking. I find myself responding with a small flicker of gratefulness. For Max. For the steady person he is. "Is there a bowl of vanilla ice cream to go under them?" A smile breaks through the stuffed up sound of my voice.

"Possibly." There's an answering smile in Max's voice. I don't deserve him. I absolutely do not.

I get out, towel off and slather myself with lavender-vanilla lotion and put on my soft pink robe. I open the door and for just an instant, think about taking the tray from his hands and disappearing back inside. Mother's ingrained training, even about manners to my husband, kicks in. *Deena Marie Brantwell you get out there and be gracious!* Ugh.

"Want to talk about it?"

"Oh, Maaax." It slides out Laura Petrie style like in the old episodes of the *Dick Van Dyke* show that I watched with Mother and Daddy growing up. "Mother and Daddy are going to Paris, and I spent the morning running errands, trying out different signatures on those little machines you slide your debit cards through. I thought I might be able to generate some excitement."

Max's mouth falls open. "Didn't work?" I can tell his curiosity is genuine and he's evaluating whether or not I've lost my mind and what this has to do with Paris.

"Actually, it did. They accept every single one. I signed as Doris Day and Jennifer Aniston and every possible forgery of my own name. I'm desperate Max. This is my life."

"I see," says Max. Clearly though, he does not.

"My parents are going to *Paris,* Max, Paris! City of lights. Romance. Adventure! I live in the land of Pampers boxes and naked Barbies. My idea of a thrill is scoring double coupons on Pampers and trying to see whether or not a clerk can catch me pretending to be someone else!" Max pours a small handful of Junior Mints into my gesturing palm and I take a sip of tea.

Max wants to laugh, I'm sure of it. But instead, for the millionth time, he extends grace. He holds me and I let him. Moments pass and he leads me to the bed, but not for the reason I think.

"Get some sleep, little Deena Bean." He tucks me in. "I'm going to go downstairs and do some paperwork for a while. We'll go somewhere…someday."

Still snuffling, I roll over on my side. "Night, Max," my voice is nasal and stopped up with a glut of tears and inexplicable misery. It's inadequate. It's all I can choke out.

******

I need to see Thomas. I need to see for myself what I thought I heard on the phone. There are still two days before our next meeting and like an addict who knows very well what she's doing is stupid, I make a plan anyway. I loathe myself for it, but can't seem to stop. I load Zoe and Eli in the minivan as soon as Max leaves to take Caroline to school, and drive out to campus. I tell them we're just going to walk around the lake and feed the ducks.

I know better. Thomas might be there again, walking and planning his lectures. We might accidentally-on-purpose run into him. And since Caroline's eagle eyes and tell-all mouth are safely at school, Zoe might be quiet about it this time.

"Hold my hand tight," I remind Zoe, trying to contain her energy and wheel Eli's stroller with the other hand. I've been working with her on holding my hand whenever we cross the street; she's far too independent.

"I have to do it by the lake too, Mommy?" I nod. "That's so I don't get hit by a duck, right?" In moments like this, I don't feel the pressing need to meet Thomas. My life feels sweet.

One leisurely lap around the lake, I promise myself. Just one. I will go home if I don't get to see him. I try to look around unobtrusively, nodding to the few students and other walkers, taking in a world that is gearing up for fall. The sun is curiously faded in color, covered by a haze of clouds, looking very much like a worn-down sucker, laid down on a napkin of sky.

The ducks look silver, gliding around in placid calmness, occasionally diving under the water for a treat. A college couple sit on one wrought iron bench, heads bent together over a text book, stealing glances at each other.

From a distance, I see a man exit a deep green car, lifting his hand in farewell as it drives slowly away. My heart quickens. Thomas. I barely glimpse the profile of a gorgeous redhead with creamy porcelain skin. Who is she? I've never seen him in that car before. Thomas' car is a grey BMW. Who *is* she? And who am I to act like a jealous girlfriend?

His hand lowers and he walks quickly toward the lake. In about forty yards, he will be to us. I stop the stroller and pretend to busy myself with something in its underneath basket. Eli reaches down and grabs my hair.

"Ow!" I raise my head, banging it on the rear stroller support bar. I straighten the rest of the way, frowning and gently remove three strands of hair from Eli's fist. "Son, that hurt Mommy."

The sternness of my voice causes Eli's little lower lip to tremble. I can tell he's going to cry. "Great, Mommy," Zoe scolds. "Now you hafta make Eli cry."

"Zoe Irene. That's enough. I didn't mean to make Eli..." my voice trails off and I can see that a well-polished pair of men's cordovan loafers have stopped just to our left. Thomas.

He looks down on us with a bemused smile. "Well, fancy meeting you here. It's the happy family, I see." The veneer of his charm has chipped through. "I'm assuming that you've come here to apologize to me privately on Max's behalf before our joint committee meeting this week."

I bark a laugh. Ducks quack in the background. Zoe has wondered off a bit, digging in the dirt with a stick, right next to a lovely carved bench. "Apol — you think I need to apologize for *Max*?" This is rich.

"Deena, I have mistaken your interest and your willingness to meet with me as something for which you are clearly unprepared. I don't want any trouble. I will see you at the next meeting." He inclines his head as a member of royalty dismissing someone from a lesser court.

He turns to walk away and I reclaim Zoe's hand and wheel the stroller in a U-turn. I am not going to go back toward that, that imposter of a man. How dare he? How dare he act as though I am the immature one? He is pusillanimous, one of my all-time favorite words on the incoming freshman vocabulary knowledge pre-test. Yes, the illustrious Dr. Hunt is just a well-dressed coward.

I start to giggle. At least I know what direction I *don't* want to go. In that delightful way that children have, Eli and Zoe giggle along with me in celebration of their mother's happiness, her own rare giggles, and this gloriously autumn day. I throw back my head and full out laugh.

I will go home and clean furiously until time to get Caroline. I will talk to Max. I will do whatever it takes. I whisper the first fragile breath of a prayer to a God I haven't approached for far too long.

******

It is seven o'clock. No Max. No phone call. The children and I have finished playtime, the pasta dish I started the other day, and they've had their baths as well. When the phone rings, I jump.

"Deena," Max's voice is weary. "I haven't had a chance to call earlier, lots of things going on here with these burglaries. I've been interviewing and well, you know how it goes. I'm sorry honey. I'm not sure when I'll get home."

I feel bereft. This is not how it's supposed to go. Max is supposed to be home and we've talked and we're well on our way to being us again.

"Oh, Max. I --," my voice catches. There is a dictionary's worth of words unsaid between us. A sonnet that needs to be composed. But this isn't the time. "I miss you. Come home. Be safe."

"Always." There is a wealth of words in that single one.

Zoe and Caroline have come to stand right next to me, their hands on my knees, peering up at my face. "Mommy? Is daddy okay?"

"Yes, girls, daddy's fine. He's just working on a case about some bad guys."

"I don't like bad guys," Zoe declares.

"But then, why are you crying?" Caroline wants to know. "You don't always cry when daddy is with the bad guys."

I can't help it. I laugh and cry. "I just miss daddy."

"We miss him too." They settle on my lap and I scoot them off. "Go bring me a Dr. Seuss and a Junie B and we'll read some of both, okay?"

"Yay! Yay! Mine first!"

"No, mine!"

And they're off. I scoot Eli closer to me on his blanket, spread with blocks and toys, reveling in his sweet scent and gleeful expressions as he bangs two plastic cars together. He is all boy.

Stories read, I tuck the girls in, nurse Eli and lay him gently in his crib. The length of him astounds me, compared to the tiny bundle with drawn up frog legs that we brought home just yesterday. His room exudes coziness with its chair rail border of Beatrix Potter bunnies and carrots, the softest knitted throws, little lamps, oversized rocker and baby blue toy box. Before I know it, we'll have to exchange bunnies for Thomas the Tank engine or Bob the Builder or some other big boy-themed room. I turn on the soft nursery light and pull his door halfway shut.

I sit up in bed, leafing through *Good Housekeeping*, straining to hear Max's side of the garage doors open, for a key in the lock, for something that lets me know he is home. I am listening so attentively that I must have fallen asleep and not even known it.

Looking at the clock, I see that it is nearly five o'clock in the morning. Groggily, I push my hair out of my eyes and stumble downstairs to see if somehow I've missed Max.

As soon as I reach the bottom stair, I know he is home. His dark dress socks are balled up in the corner by the basket of perky yellow mums. His gun and badge are lying at his place at the kitchen table and as I round the corner, I can see his feet at the edge of the couch. Max is sleeping on his side, brow still furrowed in concentration, his short hair reaching in every direction, a Chia pet gone mad. I cover him with another throw and just as I bend in to kiss him, I hear Eli's waking up snuffles from the monitor. Max needs his sleep.

******

I can't get back to sleep. I've fed, changed and rocked baby Eli back to sleep. He's snug in his crib and morning is fast approaching. Glancing out his window, I see the morning star, looking fuzzy edged, a star that hasn't quite woken up.

A half-moon sails along in the sky. A half-moon like I have half a life. Or is that a double life? No, not a double life anymore. I just need to find my way back to Max. Back into his heart. I am so confused.

Isn't this when girls talk to their mothers? As if. Even if my mother left me a letter with her dying instructions, it would consist of a proper To Do List:

- Don't forget to put starch in Max's collars.
- Take your father to Golden Corral every Wednesday evening before church.
- Get your thank you notes out on time.
- Never, never put tomatoes in the refrigerator.
- Stand up straight.
- Get your beauty sleep.
- I'll miss you.

She'd put that, wouldn't she, that she'd miss me?

Back in our room, I slide my notebook onto the bed, write a little, and jot a quick post.

September 30, 2010
Blog Spot Post by Pajama Mama

I have a confession to make, fellow moms. This morning while changing the sheets on my bed, I discovered and promptly threw away a ¼ inch pink Barbie shoe and matching miniature sun visor. Bad mother.

If you want to respond to today's post, please tell me about the most amusing things you've thrown away. I *really* need to be entertained today. You? Sigh.

Back to life. Good luck with yours,

Pajama Mama

P.S. By the way, what's the best piece of advice you've ever gotten from your mother? It seems I'm really in need of that too.

Comments:

Throw away? I'm a certified hoarder.
~Dust Diva

Why throw it away when you can have a garage sale?
~First Time Mommy

Shudder. eBay.
~Lexus Mommy

That's just a glorified on-line garage sale.
~Dust Diva

Advice. Hmm. Always wear clean underwear.
~Chocolate Guru

Send your thank you notes out right away.
~Formerly Hot

Gravel. Lots of it. Oh, and an empty lipstick tube full of dead flies.
Don't ask.
~Dust Diva

BTW, that was throw away, not advice.
~Dust Diva

LOL. I can only imagine.
~Pajama Mama

Logging off the computer, I try to close my eyes. It wouldn't hurt me to try and sleep for the next hour before the alarm starts clanging. I lie on my left side for about ten minutes. Restless, I huff aloud and roll to the other side. My mind will not shut down.

Throwing back the covers, I trudge to the shower. If I'm going to be awake, I might as well be up.

Within fifteen minutes, I've showered, lotioned, applied tinted moisturizer, mascara and a sheer berry lip gloss. Pulling on my favorite blue jeans and a pink oxford, I head downstairs. I'll try to make breakfast for Max.

As I add water to the pancake mix and slice bananas, a sleepy Max shuffles into the kitchen, plunking down on the breakfast bar stool in front of me. I offer a smile and pour him a cup of coffee. He lifts it in salute to my can of Diet Coke.

Scooting the mug to my side of the bar, Max gets off the stool and comes to wrap his arms around me. Eyeing the big bag of mix, he gulps a bit of coffee, blows, making a face at the temperature and grins at me. "Gourmet this morning!"

I shove my elbow into his ribs and playfully swat him away. The coffee mug thumps on the counter and Max grabs me with both arms. It's impossible to break his hold on me and I know it. "Bring your best, Deena Bean. Come on!"

This is us. This is what I want. But this will continue to be Act III, scene IV, unless we get to talk. I lean back and look up at him. Soon. Timing is everything, right? "Let go, Max, I'll burn these! What time did you get home?"

"Late or early. Depends on how you look at it. Ended up doing a stake-out in a neighborhood we thought would get hit next with those burglaries. Long story. I'll fill you in when I can."

"It's been awhile since you've done one of those."

"Been awhile since I've done lots of things." Max grabs a pancake straight from the griddle, slathers it with peanut butter, slaps some banana slices in the middle and folds it up taco style. His fingers toss it back and forth until it finally cools enough for him to wolf it down. "Thanks, hon. Gotta get back for a briefing." He kisses my cheek, waggles his eyebrows and dashes upstairs, whistling tunelessly.

"Nice having breakfast with you!" I call up after him. I hear him laugh just before our door closes.

Zoe and Caroline come down on their own, lured by the smell of pancakes and the pre-cooked sausage slices I have heating in a pan. "How're my favorite girls?" I squeeze them, kiss the tops of their heads, pull out their chairs, pour them tiny glasses of juice and add a gummy bear children's vitamin to each plate. Popping in a Go Fish CD, we jam to the rollicking tunes of "Snazzy."

"Can we take that in the car to listen on my way to school?" Caroline asks.

"You bet, Caro."

"Only I wanna get to the Superman song," Zoe requests.

I am prepared for an argument, but am pleasantly surprised when Caroline says simply, "That's a good one."

"I think Eli likes it too," I offer.

The girls giggle. Max brings down a freshly diapered, but still pajama-clad Eli and they giggle all over again. Max shrugs and blows us all kisses. "Got to run!" He jams his Glock and badge on his belt and hustles out the door. I put Eli in his high chair and scoot him closer to the window so he can watch the birds in the feeder. He loves that.

"Da!" Eli shouts and points. "Da!"

"Mama, son!"

Eli looks at me and looks out the window at the bird feeder. "Bir!" He would love to be able to say bird.

I can't help but laugh even though it seems Eli will never say 'Mama.' "That's right, Son, bird." He looks extraordinarily pleased with himself, bopping in his high chair to the beat of the song.

The music and laughter breeds a good mood which bolsters us all, spilling over into the morning like a fountain suddenly too full from a drenching rain. I hum while I load the dishwasher. Zoe and Caroline brush their teeth and hand me their hair bows without being asked. Eli kicks in his high chair, alternately pointing at the birds and trying to scoop up the Cheerios scattered across his tray with his tiny thumb and forefinger. That is a comedy show like none other.

I look around at my grandmother's blue willow ware platter on its stand and the homey kitchen with its blue and white with cheery red splashes seems especially dear to me today. Hauling Eli out of his chair, I kiss him loudly under the little rolls of fat on his neck and he chortles.

"Time to chauffeur your big sisters to school, little man." He rewards me with his now five-toothed grin and presses his forehead to mine, his own little gesture of supreme affection. I squeeze him, apparently a bit too tightly, for he arches his back and grunts. "Sorry. Love you too much." I kiss him again.

"Girls!" I call up the stairs. "Let's hop in the car! I think we can make it on time today."

"Yay! Yay! We're on time." Zoe and Caroline clamber down the stairs and I even remember to snag the Go Fish CD so we can continue our jam fest enroute to The Flannel Goose and Roosevelt Elementary.

We sing exuberantly and off key. "Is it a bird? Uh huh. Is it a plane? Uh huh. What could it be? It's me—ee!"

We drop off Caroline, who for a change has not only eaten breakfast at home, but has also brushed her teeth and her hair in the same morning. Yay us!

Vicki is still in her car after dropping off Canaan when we get ready to leave the pre-school. My heart tenders. I can see her on her cell phone, scribbling down something on a piece of paper with her free hand. When she clicks her phone off, I adjust Eli on my hip, walk over to her window, and taking a deep breath, I tap on it.

She glances up, her wide brown eyes and perfectly smooth cap of blond hair swinging around in surprise. I am prepared for censure in her expression, but there is none. "Deenie!" She rolls down her window and her smile is wide as she reaches for Eli.

I go ahead and boost him through the window and let them have their snuggle fest. Vicki adores Eli and the feeling is mutual.

After a few moments, she motions for me to scoot back and she opens her door to hand me Eli. I thrust out one hip and place him on it. "I've missed you," I say. Tears brim in my eyes. "I know that's stupid. We live across the street, but I – I haven't been a good friend lately. I haven't really shared my heart with you, and I certainly haven't listened to yours. I'm sorry." I swipe the back of my hand across my nose. "I'm a mess."

There are answering tears mirrored in her eyes. "Tell me something I *don't* know," she volleys in typical Vicki fashion. "Hey, wanna meet at Target and go shopping together?"

I laugh. "I was just headed there."

"Okay. I have to run by the bank real quick and do a few things afterward before pick-up or else we could just ride together. Ummm....let's say fifteen minutes by the entrance doors."

"Can't wait."

I have a few things I need to grab in town, but we'll head to Target first. By the time I wrangle Eli from his car seat and settle him into a cart, it should just about even out.

Pulling into the parking lot a few minutes later, I see Vicki's chocolate Explorer at the stop sign with her blinker on and an aisle over is Kay Tupper's ivory Jeep. Oh boy. I don't want to run into her, not when Vicki and I are mending our friendship over shopping and snacks.

I wave at Vicki and she pulls into a spot next to me and offers to carry Eli in the store. Cleaning off the orange plastic cart handle with the provided antiseptic wipes, she snaps Eli into the seat and laughs as he promptly sinks his little teeth into the hard plastic.

"Grosses me out every time," I say.

"This is your first boy," she responds. "Just wait – he'll do grosser stuff than that!"

Vicki pushes the cart into the snack bar/Starbucks area attached to Target's entrance and orders a vanilla latte for me and a pumpkin spice one for herself. I dig through my purse for my wallet, but she waves me off.

"My treat. This seems like something to celebrate."

A tender glance passes between us and I am reminded of the words of the song by Watermark about someone who has been on her knees in prayer for a friend – *More Than You'll Ever Know.* "You have spoken the truth over my life," is a phrase in that song that I love. This is what Vicki has done for me and I didn't respond well. But I'm getting over myself.

She reluctantly surrenders the cart with Eli in it to me and grabs a different one for herself. "Might as well stock up on some of the basics while I'm here. Their ad flyers had good deals on toilet paper, paper towels and tooth paste."

"That stuff is a thrill a minute. Right up there with bra shopping. Ugh. Why do the basics have to be so, well, so basic?"

We begin with a quick jog through the dollar section and Vicki tosses a few cute Halloween decorations in her cart.

"I know, I know, Miss Thang! You're always ultra-prepared. I wish I was that way." I shake my head at my organized, always thinking ahead friend.

"Yes I am. And, in your dreams, Deena Bean. Your talents must lie in another direction."

"Very funny."

We wheel companionably through children's clothes and I toss in a few cute plaid shirts for Eli.

Vicki sighs heavily. "I love looking at baby things."

"I know you do, Vick." I wish there was something I could say to make it better. She can get pregnant just fine; she just has a hard time keeping them to term.

She squares her shoulders resolutely, and off we go to meander around what's new for fall in the women's clothing section. I look at some sweaters and Vicki picks up some richly patterned scarves. If anyone could pull those off, it'd be her.

"Want to tell me?" she asks.

And I do. Right in the middle of Target. We huddle around a clearance rack at the edge of the store and I tell her about Sergeant Rivers' phone call, and mine to Thomas. About my conflicted feelings, not in the sense of wanting to give up on Max or my family, but my reluctance to give up a part of my life that seemed exciting. A place, a person that made me feel wanted.

Vicki squeezes my shoulders in complete understanding. She reaches in her purse and hands us both a Kleenex. Naturally they are printed with miniscule fall leaves and pumpkins. Only Vicki. We wipe our eyes and blow our noses. I'm so glad the store isn't crowded on a weekday morning before 9:00 a.m.

"Wanted, maybe," Vicki says, "but not cherished, Deen. He is nothing next to Max. Nothing. Max is over the moon about you. You are one blessed lady."

"I know I am, Vick. I think I just might need some help through this. Some reminding of what can happen when you are so completely stupid."

"You got it. You need anyone to tell you you're being stupid, well call me up – I'm your woman!"

"Gee thanks, Vick."

"Anytime, Deen, anytime."

We turn the corner and give the men's clothing and then the shoes a cursory glance. I hold up a pair of adorable argyle boots, but fashionable Vicki sticks out her tongue. "Unless you're Queen Elizabeth, getting ready to muck out the stables or take your Corgis for a walk on the manor grounds you can't wear those."

"Fine."

Next up are books and magazines. I could linger there forever. Not so much Vicki, who tends to favor parenting magazines and a light read by Debbie Macomber.

I on the other hand want to look at gothic romances, classic literature and peruse all of the up and coming authors in every genre possible. Maybe one day, mine will perch on a Target shelf. I can see it now, right under the cardboard banner reading, Book Club Picks.

One aisle over from where Vicki and I have parked our carts, I am nearly positive that I spot perky Kay. My body freezes. I am so not in the mood to be perked at. But I can't help myself. I am curious, because Kay is in the aisle that displays nothing but Harlequins! Who would've thought?

Vicki sneaks up by me and whispers with shades of melodrama. "Deena – do you have our suspect in sight?"

Little does she know, I actually *am* spying on someone. I hold a finger to my lips. Vicki's expression is priceless. I motion her to peek her head around the corner. Kay is so deeply engrossed in flipping through the book in her hand that she doesn't notice us. We back up toward the section of first readers and American Girl books and tiptoe off.

"What on earth?" Vicki asks when we are safely away.

"Beats me. I would have figured Kay went for deep books with tangled literary themes or the kind of thing that's featured as an Oprah Book Club pick."

"Well, we all need an escape, and they're not bad. I'm just surprised that's all."

I snort. "Perhaps," I place my hand over my heart playing up drama to the hilt, "perhaps she simply cannot bear Richard's overtime hours and the lonely life in her ivory tower, um, Jeep any longer and these help her to escape. Along with her manicures and visits to the chiropractor, of course."

Vicki rolls her eyes. "You are incorrigible. Here she comes!" We back into the Barbie aisle, slinking as though we've done something wrong.

"Vick – let's follow her!"

"Yeah, that's a great idea because we're oh so subtle with two bright orange carts and Eli." She snorts but then shrugs. "I'm game."

And for some crazy reason, we act as though we are eleven all over again and the last vestiges of tension that were wedged in our friendship like pieces of corn caught between your teeth, break free.

Grinning, we skulk behind Kay who is suddenly on a mission. She stops and gets a bag full of Almond Joy candy bars and a value pack of some sort of gum. The Harlequin is still in her hand and she drops that in her cart too.

Kay pushes her cart with extreme purposeful strides and lands a spot at the express checkout lane. We wait a few seconds until she seems busy, hiding behind some mops and cleaning displays next to the opposite end's checkout counters. Vicki snags the value package of paper towels from the end cap display, tosses our empty latte cups into a trash can and we get in the lane as far away from Kay as we can.

We quickly pay for our purchases and leave the carts, carrying Eli and two bags apiece. Blinking in the bright sunlight, we look for Kay.

A remote's unlock tone beeps from that row and sends us her direction. We watch as she climbs up, boosting herself on the Jeep's running board, impeccably dressed as always in a khaki walking shorts suit, cream flats and huge gold jewelry.

Vicki and I saunter over that way, intending to get a few cars away and see what she's doing. We edge closer to the Jeep and dawdle behind an extremely dirty four door car of indiscriminate color and dubious ability to run.

Kay sits in her car, book in hand, jaw moving furiously, not starting the car, not doing anything significant that we can see. Vicki and I look at each other perplexed. "What could she be doing?"

"I have no idea. Wait a few more minutes."

It's the pungent odor of stale sweat and cigarette odor that first alerts us that we are no longer alone. "Pardon me, girls. Mind telling me what you're doin' hidin' behind my car?" A filthy man with a cigarette dangling from his lips scowls at us. "Do I need to call the cops?"

I can't help it. I look at Vicki and we burst out laughing. "No, Sir. We're sorry. Just looking for our car," Vicki says. Forced to walk on, we end up on the passenger side of Kay's Jeep. She still does not see us.

She is sitting in her seat, candy bar wrappers littered around her, reading the Harlequin and, judging from the mascara ringing her eyes, crying. Crying! Perky, perfectly put together Kay Tupper is *crying*.

I feel bad now that we are scrutinizing her while she's in the assumed privacy of her car. But something niggles at me. It doesn't seem like she's actually reading the book; she hasn't turned a page since we've been standing there.

"Vick." I hiss. "Do we knock on her window or just leave her be?"

"I don't know. If she sees us leaving, it'll seem like we're snubbing her. Then again, this looks like a private moment."

"Yeah, either snubbing her or *stalking* her. I say we just say hi."

Kay makes the decision for us, looking up with red, swollen eyes. For a moment it seems like she is looking right through us. Then, as though her arm weighs a thousand pounds and it would take extreme effort for her to lift it and roll down her window, she slowly pushes the button and the glass glides smoothly down.

I am aware of so many things. The pieces of gum flattened all around us on the asphalt, some flattened blobs of gray, others pink. A stray wrapper. A sticky puddle of soda, spilled in front of her door. I feel sorry for Kay. Something must be really wrong for her to allow herself to be seen like this.

"Hello, Vicki. Deena." Her sigh is full of pain. "Could you guys, um, can you come in here with me for a minute?"

Vicki recovers first. "Sure."

Kay leans across the seat and opens the door and Vicki clambers up. I hand her Eli and climb in the back with our shopping bags. No one says anything and then Kay turns in her seat so she can kind of see both of us.

"Read this," she says, thrusting her leopard-covered cell phone at Vicki.

Vicki looks slightly alarmed. "Oh, Kay. That's your phone and I don't think--"

"Please. Read it. I can't stand to look at it again."

Vicki obligingly flips open the phone and goes to texts. Her eyes scan and widen with concern. "Oh, Kay, that's a really sweet message only, only…" Her voice trails off.

"Go ahead and say it – it's not meant for me." Kay's voice is sharp. "I might be 'Babe,' but I've never been there. How, how could he have had a wonderful time?" She buries her head in her hands.

"Can you guys fill me in?" My question is as clueless as I am. Vicki just hands me the phone. I read it and realize Kay's predicament with clarity.

It's so cliché as to be insulting. Another woman. A phony business trip. The necessary late hours. The sweetness of a text that is not meant for your spouse. The one with whom you share children, courtship memories and yes, well, shower mold.

No one deserves this. Not even perky Kay. And no, not my Max. Vicki passes Eli to me, but mid-pass, Kay reaches out. "Would you mind, Deena? If he'll come to me, it would really help me to hold someone. I've, I've barely slept all night."

"Oh, sure! He'll go to anyone," I say cheerfully, not meaning it the way it came out, which I realize the instant Vicki glares at me.

"Sorry." I mouth. But Vicki just rolls her eyes and Kay is too distraught to care. Eli promptly busies himself by grabbing her chunky gold necklace and stuffing it in his mouth.

"I wondered," Vicki clears her throat. "I don't want this to sound flippant, Kay, or like it's an empty thing, but I wondered if we might pray for you."

"Please, oh please do." Kay buries her face in Eli's shoulder and doesn't even flinch when he grabs a fistful of her hair. I reach over the armrest and untangle it gently.

Vicki and I each lay our hands on Kay's arms, and man! When the book of James says the prayer of a righteous man is powerful and effective, I am sure the writer is thinking of Vicki. Her eyes meet Kay's after the amen. "Kay. We will keep right on praying for you."

She includes me in this, naturally, but I feel so unworthy. I may not have met Thomas at a seedy motel at a business meeting, but I have engaged in flirting by text and coffee shop. I have allowed stolen kisses; not just allowed them but relished them for a season of brief insanity. It will be awhile before I feel as though I can be worthy of making such a promise to pray.

We walk in a very subdued, non-Nancy Drew mode back to our cars. Vicki hugs me and kisses Eli's cheek. "I know what you're thinking, Deen. And you're wrong. You've already been forgiven by me and by God. Now you just have to go after Max." I grip her hands and squeeze so tightly I can't believe she doesn't yelp. We don't need any other words.

I buckle Eli in and arrange my Target sacks on the floorboard. Shoot. Now I'm going to be late to pick up Zoe.

I am driving without my mind on the road in front of me. Suddenly, I see the flash of brake lights and in an instant, I have rear-ended the car in front of me. Naturally, it is a hearse from Berry's Funeral Home. In my uptight state of mind, a name that has always struck me as slightly off, now bites at my funny bone with hysteria. I'm trying to dial Max on my cell, but I am laughing and crying and trying to talk all at once.

Mr. Berry, the oldest of the three bachelor Berry brothers, gets out of the car. I roll down my window just as he curves his knuckles to rap on it. "Oh, Mr. Berry! I am soooo sorry. Are you hurt?"

"Not in body, young lady, not in body. But I am much wounded in my dignity. Driving a funeral car around is serious business. Serious business." He shakes his head in dark accompaniment, a punctuation to his words.

"Were you, um, were you transporting a body? I mean anybody? A *person*?" I try and correct every stupid statement I am making.

Lights appear in my rearview mirror as my cell phone simultaneously jangles with Max's ring tone. "Are you okay?"

"I am, Max. I just, um, I kind of ran into the back of Mr. Berry's hearse, but Eli and I are fine and there's a patrolman here that just pulled up."

"Deenie, do you need me? Because if you do, I am there in a heartbeat. If you are seriously okay…" I hear Max's portable squawking in the background and a flurry of desk noises. "Deen? Who is it that's there at the scene?"

I meet the badge that is now at eye-level. "Stockham," I tell Max.

"Let me talk to him." I hand Officer Stockham the phone. And listen in to his side of the conversation as best I can. Stockham nods. "Yes, Sir. Yes. Umm hmm. No, doesn't appear to be. No problem." He hands the phone back through the window to me.

"Mr. Berry. Mrs. Wilson. There don't appear to be any injuries to either vehicle or to any of you. Mr. Berry do you want to sign a complaint against Mrs. Wilson?" Officer Stockham is being diplomatic and very courteous.

"No young man, I don't believe I do. I wish you'd tell her to pay better attention when she drives though."

"Done. Mrs. Wilson?" Stockham peers at me sternly, rips off a white sheet of paper from his ticket book. "This warning ought to do it. Pay attention to the road for everybody's sake."

I know he doesn't mean anything by it, but the every*body* thing cracks me up and it's all I can do not to snort out loud. As it is, my breath sputters and chokes as I try not to let all the stress that's in me bubble out as inappropriate laughter. I glance down at the paper on which he has written: *Mrs. Wilson. Stop running into hearses or no body is safe!* My exhale releases as a full-fledged snort and Mr. Berry walks away shaking his head mumbling about the younger generation. So there you have it. I am still the younger generation, even at my ripe old age.

I'm miraculously only twelve minutes late picking Zoe up from pre-school and since I naturally forgot all about the grocery section in Target in order to play Nancy Drew with Vicki and spy on Kay Tupper, we now have to make a quick run into the grocery to pick up some eggs. Omelets for lunch. Maybe for dinner too. Quick. Easy. Cheap. Not pizza. I check the expiration date, open a carton and notice there's a little quality stamp on the top of each egg. I find myself laughing and then crying hysterically, trying to imagine how many I would break. I shouldn't be allowed near eggs. I've been on the verge of breaking other things, infinitely more fragile, more precious.

At home, Zoe decides she doesn't want omelets. "What then?" I ask shortly, my patience running as thin as the rug in the family room. "Peanut butter and jelly? Ham and cheese? What? Because those are your only options."

Sensing my frustration with perfect Zoe-ness, she tiptoes to reach my cheek. "Mommy, if I kiss you, *then* could I have more options?"

I can't help it. I laugh.

******

The bank of sulky clouds perches atop the autumn trees like an inky, petulant teenager. Goth clouds. Go figure.

It is Sunday morning. My best worst day of the week. I love the singing, seeing the people I love. But every morning is crazy. Up to shower, make time to nurse Eli. Pick out something that fits, or rather that I still think I look good in...But today I find myself avoiding it. Trying to make excuses not to go. Nothing wrong with Eli. Only had to get up twice during the night. The girls both look healthy and raring to go, fighting over the last of the Fruit Loops. Sigh.

Pulling into the parking lot, I laugh at the pithy saying for this week on the wayside pulpit: "Life stinks. We have a pew for you."

We've made it there on time. After greeting the spinster Rossman twins, squeezing Mr. Mac and getting my weekly allotment of Bazooka, we settle in our regular pew to listen to one of Pastor Sherman's lively deliveries. I hand Eli to Vicki and she nuzzles him, promising to take him to the nursery if he acts up.

Today's text is from II Samuel, chapter 11, about King David. And Bathsheba. Naturally. But, Pastor Sherman adds a slightly new spin, talking about modern temptations with their roots in age old desires.

"Make no mistake about it – when King David saw Bathsheba drawing her bath, he was thinking 'Man! What a view from *this* rooftop!'" He pauses with his excellent sense of timing, and the congregation laughs even while some squirm in their pews.

"Shoot," Vicki whispers to me. "I have to use the bathroom." She hands Eli to me and Zeke gives her a quizzical look.

Max nudges me and smiles. Usually we whisper about the sermon and give each other loaded glances when a topic hits home. Not today. I watch Kay's husband come in late and sit next to her. Richard whispers something and she acts as though she can't even see him.

All of us Bible study girls are supposed to meet next week at the hospital the Tuesday of Tandy's surgery. It will be interesting to get Kay's update then. For now, I pretend not to feel Max's nudge and shift Eli up over my other shoulder. Max drapes his arm around me and nuzzles Eli's sweet cheek with his hand.

"Doubtless, some of you out there are quite taken with the views from your personal rooftops. Let's be honest here. I won't kid you, sin can be *fun*. But it is *never*, never as fun as God's best for you.

The Apostle Paul acknowledges that temptation has been around since the Garden. It just doesn't have to give birth to full-blown sin. 'There has no temptation taken you but such as is common to man. For God is faithful and will not allow you to be tempted beyond what you are able to bear, but will with the temptation also provide a way of escape that you may be able to stand up under it.' I Corinthians 10:13. I'm quoting that from the King James Version this morning for special emphasis. That and the fact that I'm old enough that's how all my church camp memory work was done." He smiles as the congregation laughs along with him.

We want to think of ourselves as mistake makers, not as sinners. But we reap what we sow-- 'For the wages of sin is death...' You can count on it. Even a loving, forgiving God allows consequences. That's why God took David and Bathsheba's son. Ah, but God is gracious. You'll remember that Solomon, also their son, is the one to build God's temple. And it is through their very line that God would send His own son into the world to save us from our sins.

That's our message this morning. It's one of redemption."

Suddenly I can't wait to get out of church. Tears sting my eyes and I turn to the side the minute the closing hymn is over and the closing prayer said.

I busy myself arranging Eli, buckling him into the carrier, adjusting the diaper bag straps. Fussing over everything and nothing. Trying to make everything just so. Vicki slides back into the pew and glances at me quizzically. I know she is dying to ask if Max and I are okay. If I have confessed to him.

I shake my head at Vicki, even as I feel Max's hand on my back. He leans into my ear and whispers, "I love you, Deenie. You know that."

I'm unreasonably annoyed and even more annoyed that such a sweet statement makes me annoyed, that I can't even look at Max. My heart shreds anew. "Max." I am still fragile. Such irony, when Max is the one who deserves to be fragile. But then fragile and Max hardly camp in the same tent. He senses my quiet desperation.

He knows how I hate to fall apart in public and instantly changes the subject. "Where to for lunch? Did you plan something at home or would you like me to take my son and my best girls out?"

Max's phone vibrates. He opens it and frowns, reading a text. "Deena, I'm so sorry, but I'll have to take a rain check on lunch." He is rueful.

"How will you get home?"

"Sergeant Rivers is on the parking lot. He'll bring me home."

"Sergeant Rivers? What on earth is he doing working on a Sunday?" Even though I have not spoken to Thomas on a personal basis in several weeks and barely saw him at our last group meeting, the mention of Sergeant Rivers' name evokes our phone conversation and causes my heart to pound. Surely if there was something new on that front, I'd have heard about it.

"Another one of those first-degree burglaries, Deen. This one broke in thinking the folks were probably at church, but they were home. He hit the woman in the head; we might be looking at a homicide instead. Gotta go in." Max distractedly kisses the tip of my nose. "Tell the girls I love them too."

I watch Max's purposeful and yes, sexy, stride out of the foyer. Might as well go to the grocery store, put everyone down for a nap and hide from the world.

<u>Grocery List</u>
Frozen chicken strips
Catsup
Flour
Diet Coke
Toilet paper
Junior Mints
Vanilla ice cream
Cinnamon
Pepper
Garlic salt

And the fact that's it's time yet again for a trip to the store reminds me that the average kid asks fifteen times, "Can we buy this?" during a single shopping trip. Mine are far above average.

October 2, 2010
Blog Spot Post by Pajama Mama

How do you get your life back, fellow sleep, busy moms? What defines your worth? Are you putting your marriage first, or your kids first? I need your help, so write in from cyberspace and save me.

Back to my pondering life; good luck with yours!

Pajama Mama

Comments:

I wanna do "marriage first," but frankly, my kids are wearing me out.
~Formerly hot.

I feel that.
~Chocolate Diva

Pick your marriage. You'll have regrets when the kids are grown, if you don't.
~Mother

Chapter 14

The morning of Tandy's surgery is incongruently beautiful. I pull into the hospital parking lot and nibble at the rest of my Chick-fil-A breakfast biscuit with a large Diet Coke, of course. The food sits in my stomach like a smooth, cold golf ball; I am worried about Tandy. I take in the view from my mini-van windows, stalling as long as possible.

Jewel-toned leaves on overgrown limbs rub against the patient room windows as though trying to impress a record of their existence onto the pane. There's not a cloud in the sky and the sun bends low as though spying on me before continuing its climb into the heavens.

At 7:42 a.m. I reluctantly get out. We've all agreed to meet at 7:45. This is officially the last possible minute. Once inside, there are five of us from church, standing awkwardly around the edges of Tandy's room, trying not to step on any tubes, IV poles or bright red cords.

Vicki and I didn't drive together, because she had some kind of lab appointment earlier. We're standing together now though, visiting quietly. Tandy is just too sleepy for conversation. Kay, I note, is *not* here. The nurse comes in and frowns at our group.

"You need to go on out of here, they'll be ready to take her into surgery any minute." As though her words summoned the orderlies, two middle-aged men show up, tease Tandy about the stylishness of her surgery cap and collapse the railings to wheel the bed down the hall.

Her parents, John and Ann Miller, are in town to help watch her kids. Tandy's husband, Macon, is out of the country. The army has promised to fly him home as soon as possible, but the strategic mission he's on is top secret. Meanwhile, she's facing this without him.

John and Ann have come here this morning to kiss her before surgery, but she tells them she'd much rather they go back to her home with Matthew and Kelly than stay here with her. "You know how it is, Mom," Tandy says, her voice groggy with the relaxant they've given her. "I'll do much better knowing they're safe with you." Her mother hugs her with such tenderness, I look away, envious.

We stop at the end of the hallway, just before the entrance to the surgery waiting area. Her parents walk over to us and smile conspiratorially. "Since the kids were sleeping, the neighbor lady is with them right now. I'm going to let Ann sneak back over here later to be here when Tandy wakes up." John puts his arm around her shoulders and pats her in a completely male gesture of comfort. She briefly leans her head on his shoulder, then reaches up and pats his hand in return.

"Thank you," Ann says to all of us, "thank you more than you know for coming, for being here with my little girl..." She holds up a Kleenex, decorated with the signature pink ribbon of breast cancer awareness, to her brimming eyes. How Vicki managed to get a package of cute, appropriate Kleenex to Tandy's mother is just another of her wonders.

Miss Opal, elegance and class personified in her navy slacks with dainty chain belt and turquoise and navy striped sweater set, embraces Ann without a trace of awkwardness.

"Don't you worry about anything, Mrs. Miller. We'll stay here praying, and no matter what Tandy told you, she'll be thrilled to see you when she's in recovery. A girl needs her mother when she's hurting."

When they leave, the rest of us all sit in the uncomfortably brown pleather seats, linked together in u-shaped rows with metal arms. We've brought books, magazines and snacks. Miss Opal is the only one who has brought her Bible with her today. None of us really expect to study.

"Now then," Miss Opal begins. "We just need to pray and wait on the Lord to work!" Her voice is confident and you can tell just by hearing her that she expects it. "The Old Testament suggests to us that we can just lay out our requests before the Lord each morning and 'wait in expectation!' Isn't that grand? That's just what we'll do."

Her gentle glance takes in all of us in our not-so-glorious morning attire: sweats, haphazard pony tails, precious little make-up, old blue jeans and bulky cardigans in hopes of knocking off the ever-present chill that seems to come standard with hospital waiting rooms. "I don't see Kay, girls. A few weeks ago, she planned to be here. Does anyone know how she is?"

Vicki and I glance at each other. The news we've discovered isn't ours to share; besides, we don't have an update.

"We'll just add her to our list then." Miss Opal reaches out her hands in gracious invitation and we all join them together.

"Great Physician and Healer, Maker of the heavens and the earth, today we entrust to You not just our eternal futures, but the life of precious Tandy. Surely, You know best and we trust You, but You have told us to ask, so Father, we beseech You to spare the life of this precious mother. Comfort her parents and her little ones. Bring Macon home to her safely and soon. We can't wait to see how You will answer our requests. We are eager in our anticipation of Your glory. Amen."

Reagan Anne McCabe and Betty Mitchell, with her ever present bag of knitting projects, go down to the cafeteria for some coffee. I'm glad that Reagan seems so comfortable with Betty. In her late fifties, Betty seems serene and firmly settled in her walk with God. She's taken Reagan under her wing, helping her with the kids on occasion and keeping her spirits up.

Miss Opal's head is still bowed and Vicki's cell phone vibrates. She grimaces at me and steps into the hallway to take the call. I pull my little notebook computer out of my bag and power it up.

October 19, 2010
Blog Spot Post by Pajama Mama

I'm not in my pajamas this morning, girls. I'm in a hospital waiting room while a friend from my Bible Study group has a double mastectomy. I have no idea what to say and it's gotten me to thinking about what I would do if it were me.

I'm terribly afraid someone might only be able to say, "She was really good about picking up the dry cleaning." I'd rather be remembered for something a tad more significant.

On a lighter note, what kind of people design these hospital gowns anyway? If they can't go for modesty, could they at least work with us on some sort of pizzazz?

On with my worried, waiting life, good luck with yours!
Pajama Mama

Comments:

Worrying with you.
~Dust Diva

I'll pray too.
~First Time Mommy

Thanks, girls.
~Pajama Mama

I give Facebook a cursory look, jot a quick e-mail to Max's folks (yes, they will be coming to our house for Thanksgiving) and fire off another one to Sonya Weatherby with two more possible suggestions for the next committee meeting. She hasn't asked why I've been directing most of my e-mails to her and I haven't volunteered. When I log off, Miss Opal's kind eyes are fastened on me. She pats the seat next to hers. "Well, Deena, it appears that the good Lord has seen fit to give us some time together."

I drop the computer into my bag and plop down by her.

Though kind, those same eyes penetrate mine and I feel like they see straight through to my dirty heart. "How goes life for you these days?" she asks.

"Um, good I guess. Max is busy working on a bunch of first degree burglaries, so he's not home as much as we'd like. Zoe loves pre-school and Caroline loves first grade. Eli is with my mother this morning and he'll be a year old in December."

"Goodness, are they all so grown already?" Miss Opal smiles reflectively. "I'm glad to know about all those things, Deena, but I asked about *you*."

"I don't do much worth telling about these days, Miss Opal. Just home, laundry, block towers, Barbie fashion shows, story time and lots of cleaning up the remains of Eli's Zwieback teething biscuits."

"Those are very worthy things, Deena, *very* worthy." She waits on me. I squirm in my seat. "But how are you in here?" She taps her heart. "In your heart? In your very soul?"

From the corner of my eye, I see Vicki step back into the waiting room. She sees what's happening and even though I beseech her with my eyes, she begins to back out. "Do it!" she mouths. Great.

To my great astonishment, I do tell her. I don't withhold anything. I cry some and try to explain. Somehow, she pieces together my disjointed narrative and nods. She closes her eyes and for a moment I think I have shocked her, that she is shutting out the mess I've very nearly made of my life. "Miss Opal? I'm sorry, I shouldn't have…oh goodness, I'm so embarrassed, I…"

She holds up one hand. "You don't need to be sorry to *me*, Deena. You've already done your sorry saying to the Lord apparently, and you still need to square everything with Max, but not with me, Deena. Mercy! Do you think it's so terribly shocking that you would be tempted to sin? That you would feel unappreciated and forget to seek your worth from the One Who loves you more than life? Perhaps you felt you were exempt?" Miss Opal chuckles.

"That's an age-old story, precious one," she continues. "No one is righteous, not even one, the Bible tells us. Certainly, I am not."

"Miss Opal, I just can't see you doing anything wrong." I tuck my legs under me and turn to face her better.

She doesn't answer, but reaches into her purse for an old beaded pouch, made of blue silk. She unzips it and pulls out an obviously foreign coin and a wrapper from a piece of Bazooka bubble gum. She unfolds it, smoothing it gently against the fabric of her slacks.

"In 1953, just as the Korean *conflict*, the police action, as they liked to call it, looked like it was coming to an end, I did something awful. Maggie Sloan, Sadie Holloway and I were the best of friends in those days. One of the hometown boys was sweet on Maggie, but I was determined to have him for myself. He had been corresponding with her for the year that he'd been gone, and he mailed her a note, proposing marriage, with a ring, a coin, and a piece of his favorite gum. But as it happened, she was in the hospital for appendicitis and I picked up her mail that day."

I sat on the edge of my seat, spellbound as Miss Opal drew in a deep breath and continued. "I could tell by feeling the envelope what was inside, so I, I opened it. Wickedly, selfishly, I put that piece of gum in my mouth, took a walk out to Cole's Creek, threw the ring in it and never did give her that letter. Her beau was heartbroken and Maggie, thinking that he had lost interest in her while he was overseas, began seeing Elmer Chitwood. I went to the diner one night, after he'd returned home, waiting until Henry got off of work so I could tell him what I'd done. You see, I figured that since Maggie already had someone new, I could convince him that we were meant to be." Her eyes closed again.

"What happened?!" I couldn't help myself, interrupting and begging to know what happened next as though I just wanted someone to read the next chapter of a very interesting novel.

"Oh, he told me in no uncertain terms what he thought of what I'd done. I don't think he ever told Maggie, because he loved her too much and didn't want her to be unhappy and Maggie never treated me any differently. I was a fool to think telling Henry would make a difference after what I'd done. Later he married my friend Sadie and I – well, I never married.

"I keep this," she folded the Bazooka wrapper and placed it with the Korean coin back into the little beaded pouch. "I keep it to remind me that acting without God's blessing never works out."

I think about the Bazooka wrapper and suddenly it clicks. I press my hand to my mouth. "Goodness! You're talking about Margaret Chitwood and Mr. Mac's Sadie! Wait – you were in love with Mr. *Mac*?!"

She inclines her head. "I don't know that I ever stopped loving him, Deena. I just learned to love God more. I will be praying for you to do the same; for you to allow Him to capture your heart so completely there is no room for unfaithfulness of any sort. You let Him show you how to make it right with Max and you need to officially – *officially* – tell Dr. Hunt you are through. With him *and* with the committee." Miss Opal's eyes shine with compassion.

Reagan Anne and Betty come back up with Styrofoam cups of coffee just as Vicki steps back in. A surgeon enters a few seconds later. His eyes crinkle and he approaches our group. "I understand that you are here as family today for Tandy."

"Just a minute, doctor!" Ann Miller hustles into the room slapping on a name tag sticker that identifies her as Tandy's mother. "I've been watching my grandchildren for her and I want to hear everything."

"We believe that we've gotten every trace of cancer. Between the earlier radiation and this surgery..." He spreads out his hands and shrugs. "However, in about six weeks, we're going to do a few sessions of chemo just to make certain. She's in recovery now and she'll be happy to see her mother. She's going to be quite sore. I'll come by to check on her in the morning." He inclines his head and exits the waiting room.

Our little group hugs each other tightly, thrilled at the news. We agree to go home and allow Tandy this time with her mother in peace; we'll bring meals to her when she goes home, and for several weeks after. When I look around for Miss Opal, she has already gone.

******

The Tuesday after Tandy Walker's surgery, our Bible study group is relatively somber compared to our usual boisterous mood. Most of us take one of Reagan's pumpkin cream-cheese muffins and some of Miss Opal's amazing Chex mix. She uses real butter and some secret spice that she refuses to tell us about. Someone has arranged a garland of fall leaves in the center of a creamy tablecloth and set the coffee pot on a tray. Still no Diet Coke available, of course; it's a coffee-centered world.

There's some desultory conversation about the church's annual Harvest Party and the non-scary, Halloween alternative costumes. Christopher and Canaan are going as Superman and Thomas the Tank Engine, respectively. Vicki has crafted an adorable train caboose out of a copier paper box and blue Tempera paint.

Caroline and Zoe will be Dorothy and the scarecrow from The Wizard of Oz. Vicki rustles a sack under the table and shows me the darling little hat with doggie ears she picked up on the way here for Eli. "Just put a little black eye-liner on his nose and put him in little black sweats and he can be Toto!"

I grin. "Well, since Max is most definitely *not* the Cowardly Lion, I guess he can be Tin Man and what does that make me? The Wicked Witch of the West?"

"I plead the fifth." Vicki elbows me as Miss Opal begins soliciting prayer requests and passes around a sign-up sheet for meals for Macon and Tandy that will cover the next six weeks. The doctors have decided to postpone her three chemo treatments until the week after Christmas. These next few weeks will allow her to recover.

Vicki raises her hand. "I have an unspoken request. I'm just not ready to share, but I would really appreciate your prayers."

My eyebrows hit my roofline. "Tell you later," she whispers with a mysterious smile.

"It can't be anything bad or you wouldn't be smiling, but..."

Vicki puts a finger to her lips and turns around, pointing her nose in the air and directs all of her attention to Miss Opal.

"The kids and I are still hopeful, prayerful, but we are doing alright. Really, we are." Reagan shares. "Best of all, I have an interview tomorrow at Bountiful, that new bakery opening up on Main Street. The hours would be great and I think I'd really enjoy it."

"I think we all agree you should get the job, Reagan Anne," Miss Opal smiles. "Betty? Are you still watching her little ones?"

"I am and I'm loving it! With my grandchildren overseas and my sweetheart helping out in heaven, well, this is just what I needed." Betty smiles and pats Reagan's hand.

At the end of prayer time, Kay Tupper staggers in and collapses into a chair at the far end of the table. She has been seriously de-perked. In fact, I'd go for wilted. Additionally, she is tardy and unkempt. I can't help wondering how things are going between her and Richard. I feel sorry for her.

Miss Opal favors Kay with one of her glances that feels like a blessing. Her hands smooth the pages of her worn old study Bible as she clears her throat and begins today's lesson. "Girls, today we're going to talk about wilderness living."

The Bible study girls look around with a bit of confusion. There's not a 4-H or FFA girl among us. Perhaps Miss Opal is going to suggest a camping trip instead of the usual women's retreat?

"For us, this will not likely be a physical wilderness. Rather it will be the challenge of wilderness waiting, of wilderness wanting. You are waiting to be rescued. You are waiting for deliverance – from your circumstances, from your loneliness, from your desire for something. Moses waited in the wilderness. Joseph waited. In a literal pit of despair. Then he languished as a falsely accused man in a prison.

Daniel waited one night that must have seemed an eternity, in a den of hungry lions. Jonah waited three days and nights in the smelly belly of whale. Jesus Himself waited thirty years to begin what was surely the most important ministry ever and spent forty days and nights in a literal wilderness. Then He waited cruel hours on a cross, knowing that His Father could *not* rescue Him if He was to fulfill the plan for our redemption. He lay three days in the tomb, waiting for God's divine plan to culminate in a glorious resurrection." She pauses and assigns us to look up portions of these familiar stories.

"Precious girls, you are not alone in this experience. No matter how long or short your wilderness trek, it seems the longest and the loneliest to you when you are in the midst of it."

Regina Baker, a beautiful, African American, single woman and realtor who has recently joined our church, murmurs a hearty, "Umm, hmm, you got that right!"

Betty Mitchell's knitting needles click together as though they are echoing a heartfelt amen.

Tandy Walker's chair looks emptier than a chair should be able to look. But Vicki and I have both been over to deliver meals. She is in great spirits and yesterday, Macon arrived home. I think that has done her more good than all the treatments in the world will do.

Reagan McCabe pauses at the snack table, rearranging the muffins and scooping up a bit more Chex mix.

Kay isn't meeting anyone's eyes.

Vicki's head is bowed next to mine.

"Hear this, and *know* it, girls: help is on the way. Divine help. Cling to this no matter what comes your way."

My eyes are fastened on Miss Opal's. How does she always know exactly what it is that we need to hear? Never mind, I can see from her countenance that she asks God and just waits on Him to tell her. I want to live like that.

As most of the group files from the room, Kay looks up. "Miss Opal, Vicki, Deena – would you please stay just for a minute?"

Miss Opal goes to the door and shuts it, sensing Kay's need for privacy.

Kay dumps a brown handled sack full of Harlequin-type paperback novels out on the table. There must be thirty or so of the small romance novels, each with idyllic scenes of a man and a woman lip-locked in a romantic setting, on a picture-perfect country picnic or in front of a fireplace with children and a dog. Surely this is not a donation to the church library.

"Kay," Miss Opal ventures. "I'm guessing this has something to do with what you wanted to talk to us about."

"Yes," Kay sniffs miserably. "I'm repenting. I, I'm pretty sure these books have ruined my marriage. I think they made Richard run to another woman!"

"What?" Vicki is astounded. "Kay, I don't care what you've been reading, that doesn't make sense. Richard chose to be unfaithful."

"Hear her out," Miss Opal hushes the outburst.

"I know, Vicki, but what I mean is that this is *all* I read. When the children are napping, when they're at school. I've been so lonely at home and I get so caught up in my stories that I neglect Richard. I'd rather read one of these than talk to him. I've resented him working so much even though it means I have anything and everything I could want. I've compared him to the heroes in my books, even though I haven't exactly acted like a heroine." Kay sobs again.

"Kay. When we're lonely, we have all wanted a storybook hero. We've imagined that the worlds on paper or in our imaginations couldn't hold a candle to the vibrancy of real life." Miss Opal's assessment is right on target.

"I'm not sure you need to repent of reading," Miss Opal continues, "but perhaps you should limit how much and broaden the focus. Maybe you could read some Christian fiction and some books on marriage or on subjects that interest you as well. And of course, you can never substitute a storybook romance for the tender work required of the real relationships of this life."

Vicki hands Kay a package of Kleenex, this one is pale yellow with tiny lady bugs all over the tissues. I can only marvel. Vicki shrugs.

"Thank you, Miss Opal. Please pray for me and Richard. And Deena, I owe you an apology too," Kay says.

"*What?*" I squeak. "What on earth for?"

"Because I have been so envious of you. Your perfect marriage to Max. Your balance between calm and fun. Your friendship with Vicki. Your consulting work at the University. You seem so content! You have it all."

"Oh, Kay. No." I am humbled and well aware that appearances are not what they seem. "I have my own messes, and believe me when I say that Max and I are far from perfect. In fact, I think I've envied you. You're always so put together right down to your nails and your purses."

Kay stands awkwardly shredding her Kleenex and I step forward and hug her. Every trace of resentment and mockery slides away like after-dinner scraps down the garbage disposal.

Kay wants us to help her pack up her books and throw them in the blue dumpster on the back parking lot. We do and wave as she drives away, each of us praying with all our hearts that Richard will listen to hers

******

"Whew! We made it home just in time." Max is helping Caro and Zo unload their oversized pumpkins from the back of the minivan. They are chattering excitedly and asking when we can begin the carving.

The sky is being whipped as though it exists in an oversized blender. The leaves run from the wind in a violent game of chase. Max is determined to make up to us all of the hours he's been spending on those first degree burglaries.

It's amazing how life gets away from you like a runaway horse and just keeps on running, not even slowing down for conversations you really need to have, for marriage makeovers that are really essential, for repairing that which is precious.

Max is no wimp, but because he's Max, he plots his battles and moves with slow precision. He's all about strategy. And right now, he's all about those burglaries. Ten of them in the last two months, each one escalating in the risks they take, the things they steal, and the violence they're willing to perpetrate. Where is there room in all of that for an unhappy wife?

We're doing better, and yet... A few fat drops of rain smack my face and land with heavy plops on the concrete. I tug my raincoat around me and hustle around the van to get Eli out.

"Hang on a sec, Babe and I'll get him for you as soon as I get the pumpkins and my punkins," Max draws out the word and tickles the girls for maximum effect, "in the house. Then I can pull the van the rest of the way in the garage."

I scuttle on into the breezeway; hang my coat on one of the collection of old door knobs screwed to the mudroom wall for just that purpose. I walk on into the kitchen where Zoe and Caroline have already beaten me inside and are running around in excited circles.

"Mommy! Hey Mommy! Can we carve our pumpkins tonight?"

"I wanna be a carver! Could I get Daddy some newspaperses?"

The dough for baked cinnamon spice donuts is rising on the counter. I quickly wash my hands, cut them into the proper shapes and slide them into the oven, heating apple cider on the stove. The scent is intoxicating, embodying everything fall.

It's nearly impossible not to get caught up in their contagious enthusiasm. "Sure. Zoe girl, run get daddy a big stack of papers from the recycle box okay?"

"Caroline, why don't you help Mommy by climbing on the stool and getting everybody a mug down for cider, okay? There's my big helper." Caro makes a pass by my knees to give them a quick squeeze.

"I love the punkin patch, don't you? I love, love, love the way that daddy lets us pick out the biggest ones in the whole entire patch!"

"I love pumpkins!" Max pats me on the bottom with Eli draped over one arm, swiping a bit of leftover dough from the yellow striped bowl. "And I love your donuts too, Deena Bean." He waggles his eyebrows at me, incorrigible as always, hinting of desire.

Zoe comes in with her little arms full of crushed papers. "I couldn't see you daddy!" And then she giggles. "Daddy 'panked Mommy's bottom! Daddy 'panked Mommy's bottom." Caroline joins in the little sing song.

The timer dings for the first batch of donuts. I wrap a hot pad around the pan and pull fragrant donuts from the oven. I dip the strainer into the powdered sugar and dust them all. Max kisses my nose, sweet from the sugar, he says. I lean into his kiss. Savoring the sweetness of him; filled with bittersweet emotion.

I am tired of Neverland. I need to grow up and start living life as it is, rather than life as I wish it were. Miss Opal's words of caution and admonition rise to the surface, like apples in a tin bucket of water, bobbing and then being submerged. I think of Kay and remember that I cannot take Max and his stable faithfulness for granted; after all, look at me.

We sit around the white pedestal table, Eli in his high chair with bits of torn donut on his tray. After several rounds of cider and donuts, I put a sweater on Eli and we traipse out to the stone floor of the covered breezeway to carve the pumpkins.

"Who goes first?" Max raises his eyebrows in question.

"Zo can go first, 'cause I'm in school now, so I'm more used to waiting. We wait lots in school, Daddy. We wait at the drinkin' fountain and at the swings and we specially wait to go play in the gym room while Mrs. Rooney yells at us!"

"And I go to school now too," Zoe says importantly. "But I'll go first if Caroline wants me to."

Max winks at me over her head and Zoe tries with all her might to push the pumpkin across the uneven stones. She gives up and rolls it and we all laugh.

As always, we say the pumpkin prayer as Max carves. He cuts off the top of the pumpkin. "Lord, open my mind to your ways. Fill me up with You."

The girls push up their little sleeves and dig in, filling a pail with clumps of orangey pulp. "Take out all my fussies and frownies and make me a joyful child for You."

Zoe chooses triangle eyes. Max marks them with a carpentry pencil and begins to cut. "God, open my eyes to appreciate the beautiful world You've made."

During the cutting of the round nose, Max prays, "Lord, may my life be a fragrant offering to You."

Caroline sits back on her heels. "Daddy? What's fragrant mean?"

"Well, Caro," Max answers. "It means to smell good, like your mother." Max growls, crawling over her on his knees to tease me, pretending to sniff my neck like a wild animal. He gives me The Look and I am astounded again at his desire for me and his obvious love for me. Why have I been so inconsistent? So ungrateful?

As Max carves on a jagged mouth with spotty teeth, I say, "Lord, may my mouth speak Your truth and be filled with Your praises." I don't quite meet Max's eyes, but I can feel his quizzical look.

We repeat all the steps with Caroline's pumpkin and snap the appropriate pictures, including one of a now sleeping Eli with a white Baby Boo pumpkin resting on his miniature blue jeans.

I hunt the wax holder out of the junk drawer, add a pinch to the metal bottoms of the votive candles and help the girls situate them inside the pumpkins.

As Max lights them we all say it together: "God, make our lives shining lights that reflect You to a dark world."

I make a quick detour to lay Eli on a blanket on the floor next to the couch. Max and I each grab a pumpkin and the girls accompany us to the front porch so that our orange beacons can shine from the steps for a bit.

****

The next day, I am neither happy nor unhappy, going through the motions of breakfast and dinner with Max. I'm keeping up the traditions of summer's end and fall's apple pies and fragrant cheesy loaves of my homemade braided bread, lunch box notes for Caroline and the annual family outing to the pumpkin patch.

I went along on the expected hay ride, took the usual photos of the kids, and posed near the hay bales with Max as I have every autumn since our marriage. But underneath it all is a layer of impatience and I suddenly wonder what Thomas would think of all this. Does he have traditions? I want to know what they are and I wonder if I will ever shake these feelings entirely. How can I still be semi-entranced by this person that I don't truly know? Haven't I personally witnessed him being a jerk? And to me, no less.

Long after the children are in bed, and Max has cleaned up pulpy, pumpkin stained newspapers, I make my way upstairs. Max is still awake, waiting for me. His hands on me are warm, urgent. "Sweet Deena," he breathes against my mouth. "I know, I know that things are hard for you just now. I'm trying to understand. I'm planning some things...I just, well, I have to get this stuff at work wrapped up and I'm going to focus on you. *Only* you. Hang in there with me, okay?"

I study the depth of emotion in his eyes. How can I not trust this man? Love him? *Lord*, I pray, *give me the courage and strength to be honest with Max. To beg his forgiveness. Fill me with love for him. Give us a second chance.* I answer Max's request to hang in there with a kiss. His eyes go completely dark with want and we fall together in the timeless dance of love. He goes to sleep with his arms wrapped tightly around me. For once, his phone does not ring and I sleep too.

A sharp shard of light invades our room, slicing through the bands of wooden blinds. I am awake, fully awake way before Max needs to be up. The beam of moonlight falls on my shelf of Disney princess figurines. The romance. The ball gowns. The happily ever afters.

Max and I were destined for a happily ever after. I was certain of it. Maybe it's just that my view of what that looks like is wrong. I lie there for half an hour, crawl out from under Max's arm and head for the shower. Max stays asleep as I dress, wake the children and get them ready for the day.

He's already on the phone when he makes an appearance in the kitchen, kissing me with apology, hugging the girls and patting Eli in his high chair. "Da. Da." Eli bangs his little plastic bowl.

I wave at Max and bend down to Eli, capturing his little hands. "Say Mama, little boy. Come on!"

The girls look at me with interest, but Eli only blows a raspberry and shouts "Da Da!"

After school, I take a quick walk with the children and admire all of the papers in Caroline's take-home folder. Then I fix a quick snack and settle them in the kitchen so I can try and get something done. I sit in my office daydreaming instead.

"Mommy?" Caroline's voice pulls me back to now. "I only have ten pretzel sticks and I said I wanted twenty."

"Break them in half and then you'll have twenty." I smile as I resurrect this old trick from when Caroline and Zoe were two and wanted two of everything – one for each hand. Snap. One vanilla wafer, one graham cracker, one frosted animal cracker becomes two.

I'm a "Mike" from *One Fish, Two Fish*. I do all the hard work when going uphill. Thanks Dr. Seuss for this unforgettable picture of myself. Too bad snapping yourself in two doesn't work for mommies. I get up to answer the call for milk in sippee cups.

I sit back down and check my e-mail and laugh at Vicki's Facebook post this morning, describing her little ones' bout with an early flu bug.

Roses are red,
Violets are blue.
I have gum on my shoe
And the house smells like puke!

P.S. Yes, we have the flu; I'll stay away just in case.

Yep. Vicki is a poet in the making. And I'll need to check on her and the boys later.

I'm trying to write. Once again, random distracted by thoughts of Thomas invade my mind. What is it about him? I think it's just the mystery. I miss the process of discovery. I know everything about Max, I think. Thomas likes Mr. Goodbars. I remember the week that I bought him a bag of them at the grocery store and put them on his desk. He made such a fuss over my thoughtfulness, thanking me.

And then I think of all the lives – Miss Opal's, Maggie's, Mr. Mac's, Sadie's – who were forever altered by just one selfish choice.

Notification of a new e-mail appears in the corner of my laptop. I don't recognize the name, but it doesn't look like spam. When I click on it, there is only one sentence and an attachment:

"Don't get used to this."

When I open the attachment, I gasp. It is a picture, taken on the outskirts of the campus buildings, taken on the winding trail where I spent so much time with Dr. Hunt. The picture is of us, in profile, and we are kissing.

Heat flushes my face and guilt swamps me anew. When Max gets home I need to tell Vicki. No. I need to tell Max. I need…I don't know what I need.

It is eight o'clock and Max is home, but he might as well not be. Max is plastered to his recliner. I try futilely to engage him in conversation. I launch into a shallow, witty and selected recap of my day, asking him dozens of questions about his day. I am on a fishing expedition for news until I can decide how to handle this. He doesn't mention being copied in the e-mail I received.

Preoccupied doesn't come close to what Max must be. His lap is full of reports and he is either texting or talking non-stop on his Blackberry. It must be confirmation that now is not the time to tell Max about my having kissed another man. Anyway, I am obviously sadly mistaken in my childish belief that if my monologue goes on long enough, it might become dialogue. I've just succeeded in telling myself all about my day.

"Did you know that seven million cell phones are accidently dropped into toilets every year?" It's the last thing I mutter before I trudge up the stairs, my nose buried in a pile of clean folded towels.

"Did you say something, Deenie?" Max voices drifts up faintly after me.

My insomnia clings to me like a pernicious, itchy rash. I am out of sorts and out of focus. No matter how tired I am, I cannot seem to settle down long enough to go deeply asleep. Every time I close my eyes, I see that picture. It evokes a sick thrill of remembrance and a feeling of utter dread. Who else has seen that picture? What do I tell Max? Would he even believe me anyway?

I scoot out of bed, grab my bag with the computer and scuttle into the depths of my walk-in closet. Eerily bright blue light assures me that Windows is powering up. I connect quickly to the Internet.

October 29, 2010
Blog Spot Post by Pajama Mama

Night Thoughts 101: Maybe some of us could go in together and hire David Letterman to come play "Will It Float?" to entertain our toddlers and preschoolers. Anyone?

Too sleepy for depth life; good luck with yours,
Pajama Mama

Who am I kidding? I can't even be real in cyberspace. Quickly, I compose a second post.

October 29, 2010
Blog Spot Post by Pajama Mama

Serious Insomniac Night Thoughts: What is the stupidest thing that you've ever done? Does it ever keep you awake at night?

Wide awake now,
Pajama Mama

P.S. So far so good; my friend's cancer surgery seems to have gotten all of it.

Comments:

That's great news!
~First Time Mommy

Oh, yeah…stupid things. Stuck my spoon in the wrong bowl (At a restaurant. With my in-laws!) and accidentally fed my baby a bite of salsa instead of her sweet potatoes. What a face! I felt terrible.
~First Time Mommy

That's funny.
~Dirt Diva

Fell in love with the wrong man.
~Formerly Hot

Oh, goodness! My story's not even in the same league. I'm sorry.
~First Time Mommy

Don't be. Yours is the better story.
~Formerly Hot

It is four thirty in the morning as I write. The on-line version of *The Southern Hills Sentinel* pops up. The lead story is about the escalating first degree burglaries that are plaguing our little college town. Scanning the facts, I read that the woman whom Max feared might become a fatality is in stable condition. That the police are getting closer.

There's a quote in the article from Max: "While we don't want the public to panic or be overly fearful, we would ask for vigilance in calling the police department to report any suspicious people or vehicles in your neighborhoods." I smile a little bit knowing he will hate it.

The writer also lists the elements of burglary in the first degree and notes that in Missouri, it is a class B felony.

- "A person commits the crime of burglary in the first degree if he knowingly enters unlawfully or knowingly remains unlawfully in a building or inhabitable structure for the purpose of committing a crime…and he or another participant in the crime:
- Is armed with explosives or a deadly weapon or;
- Causes or threatens immediate physical injury to any person who is not a participant in the crime; or
- There is present in the structure another person who is not a participant in the crime."

An eye-witness description of one of the suspects being a white male, approximately 5'9", 180 pounds with a brown goatee remains unconfirmed.

The article mentions a few more scanty details and includes a side bar with a map of the locations of all ten burglaries. I wonder why the paper doesn't have more to offer and then I remember that Max has told me the media gets only the first page of the police report. Everything else is unavailable as long as an investigation is ongoing.

No wonder Max has been so preoccupied. Closing out the newspaper site, I log in to my yahoo account, pull *the* e-mail back up and open the attachment. I look at it again and zoom in. Something isn't right.

I call Vicki's cell phone, then hang up and call again in our secret emergency signal. Then I hurry to the picture window and kneel on the window seat cushions to wait. When I see her porch light come on and she appears on her steps, wrapping her robe tightly around her, I slip out the front door and meet her on our porch.

We sit down on the swing and I hand her the computer with the picture pulled up and a tiny flashlight. "This had better be good, Deena," she hisses.

"It's not *good* at all," I hiss back, "but it's for sure worthy of having you drag your carcass over here in the middle of the night."

She smooths the grainy printout of the picture on her lap and points the flashlight down at the image. Then she zooms in on the screen. "Hmm...Dr. Hunt, I see, but this, this is not you."

"What are you talking about? Of course it's me! Who else would it be?"

Her eyebrows raise in a sardonic salute to my stupidity. "Naturally," Vicki drawls, "Dr. Faithful himself couldn't possibly have kissed anyone else."

The neighbor's dog, Camelot, wanders into our yard, and lifts his leg, watering my hydrangeas. Vicki laughs at me. "You ought to let Camelot urinate on that picture. You need a dog!"

"It's too early for laughing, and furthermore, no way! You know my philosophy on dogs. We don't have one because I don't need something else living with me that doesn't listen. Camelot is a case in point; what's he doing wandering around loose at this hour?"

"Well, Wilson, *you're* out wandering around loose at this hour."

Vicki and I snort together and I am glad again to have such a friend. "Talk to Max, Deena. Do it soon." She hugs me tightly and I watch her walk back across the street.

The porch light blinks out. I bend down to adjust a pot of mums on the porch, turn and smack right into Max's hard, muscle-y, bare chest.

"Max!" I yelp, more than startled. "What are you doing out here?"

"I came to check on you. Are you writing? I heard the door open and clearly it's not a night for sleeping."

"Guess not. Let's go have some Junior Mints for an early breakfast," I offer.

Max makes a face. "Omelets."

Who am I to argue with one of Max's fabulous ham and pear omelets with blue cheese melted on top? I sit on the breakfast bar stool to watch, to figure out a way to tell Max I have kissed another man, and write out yet another list.

<u>Grocery List</u>
Sweet Potatoes
Yukon Gold Potatoes
*Have Max pick up the free turkey that city buys for all their employees
Canned Pumpkin
Sweet cream butter
Whipping cream
Vidalia Onions
Marshmallows
Pampers

Chapter 15

A spooked turkey can run twenty miles an hour. I'm not sure why I know this, or who even thought to clock the turkeys and determined they were spooked. I *do* know that since 1947, the National Turkey Federation and the Poultry and Egg National Board have given a Thanksgiving turkey to our President in a special White House ceremony. Most presidents have eaten their turkeys, but in 1963, President John F. Kennedy reportedly said, "Let's just keep him!"

In 1989, President George H.W. Bush officially pardoned the turkey for the first time; since then, subsequent presidents have followed suit. Caroline, Zoe, Eli and I have already watched the president pardon this year's turkey and Caroline thought it a riot.

She still wanted a turkey on our table though, and I assured her there would be. Why is it again that I volunteered to have Thanksgiving dinner at our house this year? Sigh. With both sets of parents. Triple sigh. Oh, yes, because Max is on call and it will be easier that way. Easier for whom? I haven't yet figured that one out.

I review our menu before writing it with window markers on a beautifully lacey-edged porcelain plate. *There you go, Mother. That's my own brand of elegance.*

Roasted Turkey
Whipped Garlic Mashed Potatoes
Sweet Potatoes with Mandarin Oranges, Marshmallows & Brown Sugar
Field Greens Salad with Brown Bread Croutons & Shredded Parmesan
Scalloped Corn Casserole
Green Beans with Bacon & Almonds
Cloverleaf Rolls
Pumpkin Pie w/ Whipped Cream
Chocolate Pecan Pie

Iced Tea
Coffee

My mouth waters in anticipation of a feast. This is the time of year that wreaks absolute havoc on my waistline. Ah, well, now there's a postable blog subject to which every woman in the world can relate.

Blog spot Post by Pajama Mama
November 11, 2010

Well, fellow moms, from raiding my girls' Halloween candy stash through Thanksgiving feasts, Christmas parties, New Year's buffets and Super Bowl snacks, I can feel my waistline expanding as I type. Come to think of it, I'm pretty sure my backside will follow suit, spreading like warm cookie dough.

So, I pose to you this imminently debatable question: Is it really yo-yo dieting if I plan to do it consistently for the rest of my life?
Share with me a favorite holiday recipe and then your best exercise tip. Moms with diet schizophrenia unite!
Here's to a laughing off the calories life!

Back to mine, have fun with yours,

Pajama Mama

Comments:
Is there a "Laugh Your Way Slim" class instead of Zumba?
~Formerly Hot

Nope. Cowgirl up.
~Lexus Mommy

I have eaten all, ALL, of my kids' Baby Ruths. There were a lot.
~Dust Diva

Chocolate pumpkin cheesecake. Ok, the whole thing.
~Chocolate Guru

You crack me up!
~Dust Diva

November has seen more middle of the night call outs for Max for two more burglaries. They seem more vicious, more random and they're taking more things than ever. They're getting careless, is what Max says. That's when they make mistakes and that's when they'll be caught.

The whole department is holding its collective breath, being as proactive as they can with their leads, and hoping for a break soon. The edginess is nearly palpable, as fear creeps into homes during the dark velvet hours of night. Things always seem worse, scarier in the dark.

The day before Thanksgiving, Max stays home. I call it doing penance in advance; he's the detective on call for Thanksgiving Day. We slept in and feasted on Max's wonderful omelets. I contributed brown sugar bacon and fresh pineapple drizzled with honey and vanilla yogurt.

It's kind of fun having him here, hanging out with us after all the extra hours he's been putting in lately. Stupid burglaries. Surely, they'll take a break for Thanksgiving. The girls don't have school and he's entertained them all day. They've jumped in piles of leaves, cooked gourmet grilled cheese sandwiches for our dinner and made turkeys out of construction paper, tracing their little hands, and under Max's dubious supervision, using copious amounts of glue.

Zoe and Caroline run around shrieking for no apparent reason, stopping for frequent hugs. They have been missing their daddy. Max seems content just to hang out, watching me prepare the side dishes since he's already lugged the big turkey out of the freezer to thaw.

I am mixing up stuffing while Eli naps. I have donned a pink and white gingham apron, full of eyelet trim and retro flair. It's something I rarely use, but then again, I'm not usually cooking like this. Max sits across from me on one of the rattan woven bar stools, leering playfully at me.

"Looking sexy, Deena. I'll have to do something about that when the kids are in bed. Maybe wear *just* the apron."

"Who's wearing the apron, me or you?" I stick my tongue out at him. "Max, look at them." I point to Caroline and Zoe who are running circles around the kitchen and waving their turkeys at me, pretending to gobble. "As if that's going to happen anytime soon. Besides, I've got so much last-minute cooking to do, you'll probably be fast asleep."

"I am a patient man, Deenie. Very patient." He raises his eyebrows suggestively and I can't help but laugh.

"Keep them out of here, Max or I won't be able to finish your favorite chocolate pecan pie."

Max filches a pecan out of the small mixing bowl on the counter closest to him. "I'm not giving up." To the girls, he bellows, "Here comes the turkey tickler!" They shriek wildly, anticipating a rousing game of chase with their daddy.

The baby monitor on the table shows a few lights and I fear Eli is going to wake up early from his late afternoon nap, but after a few half-hearted snuffles, sleepy silence pervades. Whew.

The doorbell chimes at the same moment my cell phone, charging on the counter, pings with its distinctive text message alert. "I'll get the door, Babe," Max promises. I can see him walking in front of the staircase, one girl attached to each crooked arm. Max loves his girls.

Wiping my hands on the dishtowel, I look at the text. *Deena. Sorry. I want to talk to you. Personal issues. Shouldn't have treated you like that. Name the time. T.H.*

Right now? Seriously? No way. I am not going to answer and I'm going to tell Max about this and about the kiss. Tonight. I absolutely have to. I shut the flip phone and place it back on the counter.

"Deena Bean! Vick's here. She wants to talk to you for a second," Max calls to me. Eli cries full out at all the commotion and noise. "I'll get my boy." Max starts up the stairs, the girls close on his heels.

"Vick! Come all the way in, silly. It's pretty chilly out there."

Vicki wipes her feet on the pumpkin patterned hooked rug and after I hug her, follows me into the family room where she perches on the edge of the denim slip-covered club chair.

"Sit down," I urge. It's as though she's too antsy for normal sitting.

"Can't." She looks as though she's bursting, but there's absolutely no rushing Vicki, so I just wait.

"Deena," Vicki's voice emerges raspy, full of emotion. "Remember when I told you I would tell you something, but I wasn't ready yet?"

I nod my encouragement. "Yeah."

"Well, the morning of Tandy's surgery, I had to be at the hospital's out-patient lab at seven."

I frown. She hadn't said anything about why she'd made an appointment until now, and in the flurry of Tandy's surgery, I had forgotten to ask. If something is wrong with my dearest friend. "What's wrong?" I steel myself, willing myself to be the most supportive friend ever. I'll cook for her every night. Drive the boys to school. Shave my head during her treatments if it comes to that.

"Nothing that won't be fine in about," she releases her breath as if she'd been holding it just to push it out into the world's largest helium balloon. "In about, oh, seven and a half more months." She reaches into the pocket of her classic lavender cardigan and produces a tell-tale stick with two pink lines etched clearly in the little window. Now she giggles. "I couldn't help it, I had to just show it to you!"

My eyes widen and I leap up from the couch to hug her again, squealing. "But Vick – how did—I thought you couldn't--"

"It happened the usual way," she smirks and then sobers. "The reason I went to the lab is that we've been trying this experimental drug that helps keep the baby and it tests the optimum levels of something or other and they told me it looked good and ooooooh!" She clasps her hands together and then touches her stomach in wonder. "My official due date is July 8th. They've told me this will have to be the last baby after the trauma of last time, but Deenie...I never thought there would be another baby after Canaan."

"Oh, Vick. I am thrilled for you, I truly am." My eyes fill, mirroring hers. I am so thankful there isn't anything wrong with her. "I hope you have a little girl."

Her face goes all dreamy. "That'd be sweet, but oh, Deena, I'll just take any baby at all."

"I know you will, precious friend." I hug her tightly.

"Well, I'd better scoot, my in-laws just got in and who knows what's happening in my kitchen. When is all your company coming by the way?"

I roll my eyes. "Mother and Daddy will get here early so she'll have time to boss me before the meal and show me all of their Paris trip pictures, I'm sure, and Max is going to pick up Dora and Daniel from the municipal airport at six."

"The Double D's!" Vicki laughs, using my pet name for my in-laws. Dora is a bit on the plump side and I'm pretty certain that is in fact her bra size. "Hang in there, Deenie." She steps out on the porch.

"You too. Take care of your little bean and tell Zeke congratulations, and the boys Happy Thanksgiving!"

"Happy Thanksgiving!" She waves, her cheery voice echoes through the screen and I watch her fairly float across the street.

"What did Vicki want?" Max appears with Eli, happily kicking in his tiny jeans and the forest green sweater that Grandma Dora knitted for him.

"Hey there, little man." Eli reaches for me and we snuggle before he wants down. He scoots and crawls toward the rug where Caroline and Zoe have just sat down with their baby dolls. "She's expecting, Max! Her doctor found some new medicine that is supposed to help reduce the imbalance they suspect caused her miscarriages. She's thrilled. Due in July."

"That's great news! How about you? You ready for another one?" He flicks his index finger at my apron and grins.

"Max! Not funny at all. And no, at least not for several years."

"Fine by me, as long as we can still engage in the activity." He mimics a smoldering bedroom look from an old black and white film. "I've been working too hard, Deena."

"I know, Max, I know." The moment is jarred by Eli's loud squealing and the girls' vigorous protests. Eli has one baby doll by the hair and another one's foot in his mouth. Caroline has launched into a lecture about taking care of toys, which Eli obviously ignores. Zoe is grunting, trying to wrest hers away from him and Eli is surprisingly strong, squealing and growling, fighting for one of his big sister's toys.

Max sighs and kisses my cheek. "Later." He walks into the family room with his purposeful sexy stride. Bending down to Eli, he unfastens little hands from the doll's hair and removes the foot from his mouth. Eli stiffens in anger. "No, son," Max's voice is deep and patient. "Let your sisters play. And we'll get your trucks."

"Tuck!" Eli shouts, easily distracted.

I turn to finish up in the kitchen, already planning sandwiches for supper and the best way to talk to Max.

Twilight falls and together Max and I bathe the girls, read them stories and sit all together on the couch watching our annual tradition: *A Charlie Brown Thanksgiving*. It's been a satisfyingly family day. After we tuck them in, I come back downstairs, a homey fire crackling while I rock Eli. I prolong the moments for as long as possible; when I lay Eli down, there will be no more excuses.

Upstairs, I kiss Eli's cheek before tucking him in with his lovey, listening a moment more as he grunts and wiggles himself into just the right position in his sleep. I check on the girls, watching them in their innocent sleep, Caroline's hands curled above her head, mouth barely open, a sweet rose; Zoe sprawled out, a limb in every possible corner. Listening to their deep, even breathing, my heart overflows.

I linger a bit in the master bedroom. I've brushed my teeth. Reapplied a bit of the pink gloss that Max favors because it's not too goopy. I don't change my clothes. What does one wear to tell your husband that you've been unfaithful? Sweeping my hair back from my face, I lean close into the mirror that hangs over my dresser, inspecting myself. There are little lines that weren't there this time last year. I look at my eyes. They are tired, but I see hope reflected there. Breathing deeply, I also breathe out a prayer for my talk with Max to go as it needs to.

Downstairs, Max has turned off all of the lights except the lantern lamp nearest to the couch. The fire snaps and hisses; its brightness reflects in the picture window, bathing the window seat in jumpy light. Vicki's porch light winks at me and the moon scuttles behind the blanket of November clouds. The vanilla pillar candle is lit, illuminating the wreath of miniature rosehips and grapevine which circles the wooden holder, and casting shadow puppets on the creamy walls.

Max turns his slow, full smile on me, lighting up when he sees me. The familiar curl of desire in my belly is dulled by the ache of what I must share. "There's my best girl," he says, patting the couch cushion beside him.

I hesitate in the doorway, looking around the cozy room and Butternut Squash resting curled up on his soft cushion by the fireplace. Smart cat. The grandfather clock that belonged to Max's great grandmother, given to us by Dora and Daniel on our wedding day, chimes nine o'clock.

The air smells of vanilla and the faint scents of all the cooking I've done today. I wipe my sweaty palms on the front of my blue jeans. This familiar scene is dear to me, but after tonight, it won't seem the same, perhaps for a long while. This is my doing. I have tainted it with my stupid chasing after some ridiculous sense of importance; a fleeting pseudo-flirtation that was anything but harmless.

"Alone at last," Max sighs, clasping his hands behind his head, utterly relaxed. "Deena? Come here."

I sit down, formally and upright, knowing I don't communicate the depth of what I'm feeling nor am I behaving like the object of his desire. Max puts an arm around me, running his fingers through my hair, massaging my neck, urging me to relax into his embrace.

Puzzled, he turns to face me and gently moves my shoulders until I have no choice but to look at him. "Deena?" he whispers, a question from his heart rather than his lips. He leans toward me, his hands reach for me and his eyes close. I know he means to kiss me.

"Max." I still his hands at my waist. "Max, no. Wait. Look at me. I need to tell you something."

In the space of a breath, such a fragile thing, I sense Max's demeanor immediately shift into work mode. He is on guard, wary, alert. He waits for me, yes, to confess. I could almost feel sorry for one of his suspects. Except I'm the suspect, and Max only suspects how far this has gone.

"Max, oh Max. I know that you've wondered about the texting, that you cared for me, for us, enough to confront Dr. Hunt, uh, Thomas," my breath comes shallow. I am desperate for this to be done. "That means a lot to me; maybe more than you'll ever know. But Max, I cannot stand another minute without telling you, without being totally honest."

I cannot help myself. I start to cry. "Max, I, we –we kissed. I mean Thomas kissed me." I shake my head. "No, that's not entirely truthful. I let him kiss me. I kissed him back. It was just once, Max. But there's an e-mail, someone has a picture of--"

Max's face might as well be a statue, molded of concrete and rebar. He stands up from the couch abruptly. He walks to the picture window and looks out. I hurry over to him and grasp his arms. They are inflexible steel; he flinches at my touch. That more than anything, shreds my heart. "Max, please..."

He turns to me, looks at me, slowly shaking his head. "I cannot believe it, Deena. Another man kissed you, *kissed* you!" His voice is terrible. Loud. He scrubs his hands over his mouth as though erasing any memory of our own kisses, turning away. When he turns to face me again, he is cold, silent.

"Max, please, please let's talk." I am sobbing so hard, my breath hiccups and my whole body shakes with chills. "Max! Say something!" I touch his arm again and he jerks away from me.

"Don't touch me right now. And I don't have anything to say." For the first time in our marriage, Max leaves in anger. He walks to the entryway; I trail behind him, begging pitifully. Ignoring me, he grabs his car keys and within seconds I hear him squeal out of the driveway.

Sinking down onto the cold stones of the breezeway, I sob. *Max, Max, please come home. I love you. Please forgive me.* Too late, I realize those are the words I did not get a chance to say.

I don't know long I sat there, sobbing, listening to the pieces of my world breaking apart. When I stand my legs are stiff and my face feels so dry it might crack. I haunt the downstairs, listlessly moving things around, moving from room to room. Max's gun and badge are on top of the refrigerator. That he didn't take them with him tells me more than anything how hurt and upset he is.

I look at the pewter framed pictures of life with Max. A silly one of Max giving me a piggyback ride, impulsive romance in our college days. The one Max snapped of me, young and hopeful on the porch of our honeymoon log cabin in the Ozark Mountains. Max and I grinning down at a bundled Caroline, as he wheels me out of the hospital. Christmases. Anniversaries. Life captured in unforgettable moments.

I drag myself up the stairs, peek in on each of the children and then stand under the hot spray of the shower, trying to wash away the ugliness, straining to hear any sound of Max's return. I cry myself into a fitful sleep of sorts, waking every few minutes.

Around 2:00 a.m., I hear something I can't place. It sounds so odd, that I push myself up on one elbow, holding myself completely still, my heart beginning to pound, holding my breath so I can really listen. A low dragging sound. Maybe it's just my fight with Max combined with my overactive imagination, especially after reading the story about the burglaries the other night.

Carefully, I swing my legs over the side of the bed, reaching for my cell phone on the nightstand. This noise cannot be Max. I hear it again. Dragging and a muffled pop. I never would have heard it all the way up here if I hadn't already been awake.

My heart hammers. I frantically dial Max's cell number, sliding to the floor. *Answer. Answer.* At the sound of his voice, my breath rushes out. "Max, oh Max! I heard a noise, no—I *keep* hearing it and I think someone is breaking in!"

"Deena. I'm headed home anyway. I'm just a few blocks away."

"Max, Max, hurry! I'm so scared."

"Listen to me. Call 9-1-1 on the other phone. Go get the kids and get in our closet. Do *not* leave our room unless you hear my voice."

I dial 9-1-1, tell the dispatcher something, and hang up, forgetting her request to stay on the line. For an instant, my legs refuse to obey. I snatch my robe from the foot of the bed, get up and start to head for the girls' room first, but then I hear breaking glass. My mouth fills with a dryness so bereft of moisture it feels as though someone has stuffed it full of cotton balls.

Glass tinkles sharply from what must be the door in the stone breezeway. I'm not sure what I'm doing, but I yank the ties on my robe and start down the stairs, thinking I can't let someone come upstairs, completely disobeying Max.

There are footsteps moving and then I hear tires screech, running and Max's voice. "I'm a police officer! Freeze! Freeze!"

Loud scuffling and cursing draws me like the heroine in any thriller to the one place she shouldn't go. He does not have his gun. Oh, dear God, Max has rushed in without his gun! Max is exchanging punches with someone whose shape I cannot make out. I stand there, rooted to the spot. I hear sirens and my knees sag with relief. Back up for Max. Armed back up.

I want to go check on the children, but I can't tear my eyes from Max. I move backward around the corner toward the stairs when someone runs full-force into me, knocking me into the edge of the wall. *Two of them?* This registers at the same time I scream. "Maaaax!"

Front my place on the floor, I see Max look over his shoulder. I can feel his split-second debate. He can finish this fight or he can check on my screams. *Why didn't I listen to him?* In that moment of hesitation, the bad guy scrambles up and runs.

Max crosses the floor in a few quick strides. I hang on to him like I'm drowning. He holds me for a second. "I'm glad you're okay. Go check on the kids." This is my fault. All of it. Max would have gotten at least one of them if it hadn't been for me.

In another second, our house is swarming with cops and Max goes with them to do their thing, looking at footprints, giving descriptions, wishing he could join the guys outside in the chase.

******

Thanksgiving morning, I set the table with my mother's ivory damask table cloth and carefully arrange each place setting of my Old Country Roses china; my mother's choice at the wedding registry, not mine. The girls' turkey hand place cards are a quirky addition, each guest's name Crayoned in sloping block print. I smile at all of the lines on Zoe's capital 'E.'

The turkey has been in the oven since I tiptoed down at nine o'clock this morning to put it in. Max is still asleep, or giving a good imitation of sleep, on the couch. Our house had been an official crime scene all through the night. I am hoping to talk to him before the children awake; we *have* to come to some sort of understanding before we have a house full of company.

Aesthetic preparations all done, cranberry salad chilling in the refrigerator, I look in on Max again. He has not moved for the last hour. I dash upstairs to get ready. Grey slacks, a pink fitted tunic with black trim sewn on the cascade of ruffles down its front. Black ballerina flats complete my look. It's one of Max's favorites.

I splash my face with cleanser and water, then hold my can of Diet Coke against my face, trying to reduce the puffy carousel of luggage under both eyes. Vitamin C cream, foundation, blush, grey eyeliner, pink lip gloss, a sweep of silvery eye shadow and mascara. That will have to do. The day is slightly overcast, so maybe if I light enough candles, no one will notice I've been awake more than half the night crying.

The girls, Eli and I spend the rest of the morning upstairs in their rooms, creeping around the house as quietly as we can, letting Max sleep as long as possible.

When I finally take a break and walk into our bedroom with clean laundry to put away, Max is there, towel in hand. "Max," I try a tentative smile. I am *so* glad to see him. "Do you know anything from last night?" I want to know about the burglars and about us.

"Just wait, Deena." He holds up a hand. "I can't get into this right now. I'm showering and going to get my folks. If you need help around the house, I'll help you. But we just need to get through the day."

"And then, Max?" I choke out.

His eyes close. "I don't know, Deena."

Oh, Lord God. Hold me up. I don't think I *can* do this day.

Precisely at five o'clock, the doorbell rings. I've already let my folks know that dinner will be a bit later after all the excitement at our house, although I was sketchy on the details. Caroline and Zoe make a beeline, jumping up and down. I busy myself in the kitchen and Max lets my parents in. I hear the low buzz of conversation punctuated by Caroline and Zoe's gleeful exclamations.

Taking a deep breath, I wipe my hands on my apron that only yesterday was a source of Max's flirtatious attention. Walking to the entryway, I see my mother, glowing and sparkling, dressed in brown slacks, heels and a mustard-colored sweater topped with a border of autumn leaves. She has a little bag for the children. The girls are already dipping in. There is a package of Thanksgiving-themed Shrinky Dinks, those plastic shapes you color and then shrink when baked. I haven't seen those since childhood. These have little holes through the tops so they can be tied with ribbon and used as ornaments.

"Mother," I lean forward, anticipating a kiss on my cheek, but she hugs me instead. "Where on earth did you find Shrinky Dinks?"

"Cracker Barrel, my dear. They have everything."

"How's my girl?" Daddy hugs me tightly. "And you know you're getting old when you've actually seen everything Cracker Barrel has on their walls in *use!*"

Everyone chuckles politely. Mother and Daddy can tell something is awkward, but they don't know what it is. Max sets Eli on the floor. Eli promptly uses the edges of mother's brown slacks to pull up, banging his free fist on her legs to get up.

"I'll gladly hold you there, Eli," Mother scoops him up. "And I brought something for you too." She nuzzles him and produces a colorful plastic teething toy, shaped like a turkey. I have to hand it to her; she knows how to find anything for any holiday.

"Why don't you go on into the family room? I've already started a fire and I hate to leave, but I've got to go pick up my parents at the airport." Although it's only a ten-minute drive, Max clearly wants to get out of the house.

"How are Daniel and Dora, anyway?" Daddy asks.

"You can ride along with me, if you want to," Max offers.

"I think I will." Daddy is always up for anything. But first, he leans in and hugs me. "I'm sorry you were so scared last night." I squeeze him tightly before he lets go.

"Deena, do you need anything while we're out?" Max offers perfunctorily.

"I think we have everything, but thank you." I am subdued, not quite looking at him so I won't cry.

"We'll be back in about a half hour or so, then." Max does not kiss me good-bye.

"Deena!" Mother calls from the family room. "Come join us."

I poke my head around the corner. "That's okay, Mother. I know the kids are loving spending time with you and I've got a few things to check on in the kitchen."

Caroline and Zoe have already ripped open the package and are sitting on cushions at the trunk which passes as our coffee table, coloring turkeys, pumpkins, pilgrims, Indians and cornucopias. Eli is on her lap and mother looks like she's having a ball.

As I'm taking the taper candles out of the freezer, a trick mother taught me to help keep them from dripping, she walks in, carrying Eli. "The table looks lovely, Deena, and everything smells simply delicious."

"I'm using your candle trick," I offer, surprised that she has not once bossed me or said anything critical. I place the tall burnt orange tapers in the ivory holders, arranging a pumpkin here, a gourd there, in the center of the table cloth.

"I saw that. It's good to know you don't ignore everything I've taught you."

"Mother, I don't ignore everything and why did you have to say that? I really don't want to argue with anyone else today."

Mother's antennae are on high alert, evidence by the high arc of her immaculately groomed brows.

I sigh and turn back to the stove, stirring the sweet potatoes, which are just about to boil over.

Mother walks around the stove to where she can see me. Eli grunts and kicks to be put down. Mother bends and gently lets him loose. She reaches over and smooths the hair back from my eyes, which takes me completely off guard. "Deena, sweetheart, what's wrong? Obviously, the break-in, but it seems more than that. A girl can talk to her mother, you know."

Well, some girls and some mothers, but not us and definitely not about this. "I'm fine, Mother. Thanks for your concern. It's just been busy preparing all of this and--" I wave my hand in the air vaguely. "After all that happened last night, I'm tired."

"Very well, if you don't want to talk, I certainly won't force you to." Her heels click on the laminate back to the hushed carpet of the entryway and on into the family room.

I sit on a breakfast bar stool, watching the potatoes, staring at the duct-taped refrigerator door handle, watching the clock, trying to concentrate on what time I should put in the rest of the side dishes in the oven in order for us to eat on time.

I leaf through a few pages of *Country Living*, suitably chastised by the picture-perfect tables, meals and decorations. I think about posting on my blog before our meal, but just can't muster anything intelligent to say. The break-in at our house is definitely off-limits.

Zoe rushes in with her sheet of Shrinky Dinks, showing me her creations with pride. "Those are fine, Zoe girl, just fine! We can bake them after Mommy finishes dinner."

Her little hands rest on my knees and she looks at me. "Mommy, your eyes look all funny. Didn't they get enough sleep?"

I laugh. "Probably not, sweetie. Mommy had lots of cooking to do." She seems satisfied with that answer.

"Okay, then, I'm gonna go back and color with Nana!"

The oven timer goes off. I slice the sweet potatoes and cover them with marshmallows, brown sugar, butter and mandarin oranges, already hearing my arteries slam shut. I am draining the mashed potatoes when I hear the flurry of foot stomping and luggage dropping in the stone entryway. Dora and Daniel have arrived. Which means Daddy and Max are home.

Dora bustles into the kitchen and hugs me with gusto, stepping back and appraising me with her overwhelming warmth. "Deena! You just get prettier every time we see you! Daniel, come here, doesn't she get prettier."

"She does," my father-in-law Daniel is comically quiet next to Dora's chatter as he steps over and hugs me.

"Dora, Daniel. I'm so glad you got here safely! My mother is in the family room, if you'd like to sit a while. Dinner's not too far away."

"Mercy!" Dora says. "We have been sitting on that plane from Des Moines to Southern Hills. I'll just run in and squeeze those grandbabies and then I'll stay in here and help you. I thought that little plane would buck us out what with all that wind."

"Just enjoy the kids, Dora. Seriously, I don't need any help."

"Don't have to tell me twice! Hope you don't mind, Deena, I brought the children a little something." She grabs Daniel's arm and off they go. What is it with grandparents and presents?

Obviously, Max has not told them about last night's burglary attempt in our home.

Max stays behind in the kitchen. I can feel him looking at me and I feel seared through with guilt, like a steak getting its final marks on a summer barbeque grill. Here we are, like two enemy adolescents, stranded at the Junior High dance, isolated from the merry making group in the next room.

The sounds of laughter, Eli's strident grunts, Zoe's little girl explanations and Caroline's delighted squeals, thrilled to be in at least the partial center of so much attention, provide us with a modicum of cover.

"Max, we can't go on like this. We have to do something. It's Thanksgiving and I--"

"You should have thought about that before you decided to make out with another man." Max cuts me off, letting his anger show.

"That is *not* fair, Max!" The tears threaten again. "If you stayed in here just to torment me, I, I feel awful, you have no idea. I wanted to talk to you, but you haven't exactly been around." Anger of my own slithers out of nowhere.

"Stop it." His voice is deadly quiet. "Just stop it. You don't get to be angry. You don't get to be…" He throws up his hands in defeat as his dad comes around the corner.

"Kids," Daniel's voice is friendly, concerned. "Everything all right in here?"

"Fine, Dad." Max's voice is weary. "Deena, is it about time to change Eli and get the girls washed up?"

No, I want to say, it is *not* time. It will never be time as long as I have to spend an entire holiday dinner with both our parents and our children watching us sit in our usual places, acting as though everything is normal when it is not and I am not sure when it will be.

Instead, I untie my apron, use one of the strings to blot my eyes and say brightly, "That would be great! Daniel, would you mind changing Eli?"

"I'll get Dora to do it." Daniel wrinkles his nose at the thought of a diaper change and leaves, as though aware this is no typical married couple spat.

As the grandfather clock chimes out seven o'clock, we are gathering around my table, flickering with candlelight, festive with turkeys and elegant with the arrangement of fall mums and greenery and the classic charm of china.

The grandmothers are seated together, Eli's highchair between them, Zoe and Caroline on either side. Butternut Squash curls himself under the high chair, a spot that is still warm from the where the newly-departed sun shone through the window. Daddy and Daniel look a bit bereft. Max and I seat ourselves at our usual spots.

For a moment, the awkwardness is suspended until Daddy says, "Max, if you don't mind, I'd like to say grace for us today." Daddy clears his throat and from force of habit, my hands extend to Max on my left at the head of the table, and Daddy on my right.

"Most holy God, we are thankful, *I* am thankful to be here today, gathered in my grown daughter's home with my precious, healthy grandchildren, my son-in-law and his parents as well. We are indeed blessed to live here in a land of plenty. We are thankful for the wonders in the world, not the least of which are Your grace, Your mercies that are new every morning. Thank you for the privilege of being able to give thanks in this land of the free. Amen."

Well, I'll be. I have never heard my daddy pray quite like that before. He gives my hand an extra squeeze and then he winks at my mother. Winks at her! Mother is *not* the sort of woman one winks at.

After grace, Max gets up to carry the heavy turkey over on my grandmother's beautiful blue willow ware platter. I'm so glad she gave that to me. Max sets it on the table with the rest of the food to the accompaniment of oohs and aahs. I start passing the side dishes while Max carves.

"Mommy," Caroline prompts, "aren't you gonna have everybody say their thankful stuff?"

"Sure thing, sweetie. You start."

"I am thankful for all my grandmas and grandpas here and for the presents." Caroline twists her wrist back and forth to show off the sparkly beaded bracelet from Grandma Dora.

"I have one too, see?" Zoe boasts.

"Zoe Irene," her sister scolds. "You are *still* an interrupter. It's not your turn and I wasn't done with my thankful stuff."

"Girls," Max remonstrates, gesturing with the carving fork, "I am most thankful when my girls are not fighting." The grandparents chuckle.

"Anywaaaaay," Caroline continues, "I am thankful for lots of food and marshmallows and for Eli and Zoe, mostly, and for Mommy and Daddy."

"All good things, Caroline," Grandma Dora praises.

"My turn, right, Daddy?" Zoe, of course.

"Your turn." Max concentrates on carving and begins to lay slices of moist, fragrant turkey on everyone's plates.

"I am thankful for Miss Carrie and my pre-school and for Mommy's pretty bare table with little rugs on it before she put Thanksgiving stuff on it."

"Placemats," I clarify for the confused grandparents.

Dora and Daniel are thankful for their health and their friends and for their safe travel here to be with us.

My father reminds us that he's already listed everything in his prayer.

"I am thankful for second chances," my mother says simply. What on earth?

"My family," I say through a throat so constricted by tears that I'm surprised my words do not squeak. I hop up and busy myself with tearing up little pieces of turkey to put on Eli's highchair tray, even though I know he is flanked by two grandparents who would be thrilled to do it.

"Max?" his mother prompts.

"I am thankful for promises kept," he says pointedly, though nobody but me realizes it. Max's voice sounds exactly like that of a novice reader. Careful diction with no enthusiasm at all.

And with Max, who is normally a fabulous conversationalist, mad at the world, (well, ok, just with me) the table talk stalls for a moment.

"How was Paris?" I ask, knowing that mother has saved her pictures until she could properly put them in an album, and naturally would want to bring them today. This, I figure will be great table talk and I won't have to do a thing.

To my great surprise, Mother and Daddy exchange the look of lovers, and she giggles, deferring to him.

"We, well, actually your mother and I don't have any pictures, but do we have quite the tales. On our last evening in Paris, we made reservations to dine at the top of the Eiffel Tower. Your mother insisted that we take pictures from the observation deck. As we stood there admiring the view, another tourist jostled us – it was quite crowded—and the camera flew over the side."

I gasp. "Daddy, Mother, you have to be kidding me!"

Dora groans, "Oh, Stephanie, Samuel – that is just awful!"

"Well it should have been," my mother says, "but for some reason I just got so tickled! There went my beautiful new digital camera, sailing off the tower. A member of the staff saw it happen, took a picture of us at our table and printed it out on the gift shop computer. I bought a beautiful frame for it after dessert, and the rest of the night, Samuel and I just spent walking along the Seine, sitting on benches, sipping coffees and having a sweet at one of the sidewalk patisseries, until it closed. It was the most romantic, healing thing ever."

"That it was." My father smiles at her. "Stephanie looked beautiful."

My mother blushes. Blushes! I am trying to picture my mother and daddy holding hands, walking around Paris in the moonlight. And *healing*? What an odd word to use about the vacation of a lifetime.

"What's new with you and Daniel and Iowa?" mother asks.

"Well, nothing *that* exciting," Dora laughs.

The conversation drifts and wafts, settling into hollows, climbing on the peaks of the children's laughter and inconsequential but sweet retellings of their little lives. Only Max and I seem like outside observers of our own family meal. Every now and then, I glance surreptitiously at Max, but he always seems to be studying his plate with frightening intensity. I can tell there won't be any more headway between us until his parents are in bed tonight.

As I am getting up to clear plates and get out the dessert dishes for the pumpkin and chocolate pecan pies, I hear Max's cell phone vibrate insistently. That won't be good.

"Oh, Max," Dora complains. "Don't pick up that silly thing. It's Thanksgiving!"

"I'm on call," Max reminds her, already getting up with his phone. I don't say anything about it. We've had more celebrations interrupted by the police department…the only time they couldn't reach Max was on our honeymoon. I don't dare complain today.

I turn from the sink, watching Max carefully. I see him scowl and spring into action. "That was an automatic text from dispatch for burglary detectives on call. We've got one right now; I have to go."

Max crosses to the counter and turns up his portable radio to better hear what's going on. He grabs his keys, snatches his gun and badge from the top of the refrigerator and jams them onto his belt. I am just a foot away from him at the counter, pie server in hand.

I wait the space of two heartbeats. Surely, after everything that has happened – after the danger of last night-- he won't leave to go on a call without kissing me. "I'm sorry, Deena." He looks at me for just a second and snags his portable. The back of his hand brushes mine; I can't even be sure it was on purpose.

The portable shrieks. "All units dispatched to burglary in progress, reporting party states shots fired. I repeat, shots fired." And Max runs. In a matter of seconds, I hear the tires of his on-call unmarked police car squealing out of the driveway.

My hand goes to my heart. Be still. Max is now going to a shots fired call and we have not even kissed good-bye. "I love you, be safe," I whisper.

In my mind, I hear Max's ready response. "Always." Resolutely, I turn back to the counter, ready to serve pie. Oh, Max, you didn't get any of your favorite chocolate pecan pie.

"Okay, then, who wants pumpkin and who wants chocolate pecan?" I call out brightly.

My mother appears beside me, taking orders for which kind (Daddy and Daniel want a piece of both; Dora says she shouldn't, but well, Thanksgiving only comes once a year) and carrying the plates to the table.

When I am seated, Dora asks, "Deena, aren't you having any dessert?" I shake my head. She eats the bite that is on her fork and closes her eyes in bliss.

"Mommy? Daddy didn't kiss us bye-bye." Zoe grouses, a bit confused.

"I know sweetie. Daddy had to be in a really big hurry to catch a *really* bad bad guy!"

Caroline sighs. "I don't think you should ever be in too big of a hurry for good-bye kisses."

Tears sting my eyes for the millionth time; my daughter has been unwittingly poignant.

"What was that," Daniel waves his fork for emphasis, "What was that auto text Max was talking about, Deena?"

"Oh, that's a relatively new thing, part of their CAD system. An automatic text lets all the officers on call get the information at the same time the call comes in from dispatch. That way they don't have to wait for dispatch to get a hold of them; it really steps up the response time. It could be for homicides, drug busts, or in Max's case right now, something about these burglaries that have been happening here."

"Max was telling us about that on the phone last week. I can't believe they've gotten so bold as to operate in broad daylight," Dora says.

"Actually, we think it was that same pair that broke in our house last night." I give a shaky laugh.

"What?" Dora is aghast, placing her hand over her ample bosom, near her heart.

"What happened, Deena?" Daniel is all concern.

"I don't want to talk about it just now with--" I gesture toward the children, noting Caroline's ears ready to take in every word.

"That's frightening, Deena, and despicable." Dora again, but she nods in understanding. I know she'll get the details from Max or Mother later.

"That is the truth. What is the world coming to these days?" Daddy and Daniel commiserate about the state of moral decline. I push my chair back and begin to clear dessert dishes.

"Look at that," my mother whispers and points. Eli's little head is on his high chair tray. He's fallen asleep amid the crumbs of dried out turkey, carrot pieces and bits of roll.

"Here you go," Dora brings Mother a damp cloth, and wiping him off, mother graciously hands Eli to her.

"Go ahead and put him down, if you'd like," Mother offers.

"I'd like nothing better!"

Mother volunteers for dish duty. Daddy and Daniel retire to the family room to stretch out in front of the fireplace and football. The girls skip along happily. I recall reading that since 1920, the NFL has made a tradition of football games being played on Thanksgiving Day. I wonder if *their* wives are any happier about that than police wives are about their husbands being on call.

Mother is loading the dishwasher and I am brushing crumbs off the table before taking the cloth outside to shake it clean and launder it when the phone rings.

"Shoot. Mother, could you please get that before it wakes Eli? That boy can sleep through a house demolition before he could sleep through a phone call."

She smiles at me. "You were the same way." She quickly dries her hands and answers. "Hello, Wilson residence. Certainly."

She holds the phone out to me, her other hand covering the receiver. "It's for you. He said it's important."

Brushing my hands holding all the crumbs I've cleaned up back onto the tablecloth, I take the phone from her. "Hello?"

"Deena?"

"Yes."

"This is Sergeant Rivers." As soon as hear his voice, I can tell something is wrong; my knees are water. Next to having a police car pull up in my driveway, a phone call like this is what I have dreaded the most.

"I am calling from the hospital. Max--"

I slide down the wall; all I hear is an incessant buzzing in my ears. Max must have been shot. Mother takes the phone from me and for once, I am thankful for her take-charge manner.

"Yes," she says. "A hit and run?" She is puzzled, then, "I understand. We'll get her right there."

"Deena, honey, I need you to pull yourself together." Mother wipes my face and is more tender than I've ever known her to be.

"Was Max shot?"

"No. It was apparently a hit and run; they'll have more details for us when we get there. Max is stable, but apparently has some serious injuries, possibly internal bleeding."

As though the phone call were a magnet drawing them, daddy, Daniel and Dora have come into the kitchen. An organizational pow wow begins; I am thankful for the presence of these people in my life who can step in when I am literally falling apart. Mother quickly dials a number from my list beside the phone. I hear her greeting Vicki.

Caroline and Zoe, are apparently asleep on the couch, victims of sugar crash and the tryptophan effect of too much turkey. "I will take the children across the street to Vicki's house," Mother decides. "They don't need to be at the hospital, and as soon as we know what's going on, one of us can come back and rescue the Hamptons."

"Thank you, Stephanie. We would like to be at the hospital with our son." Daniel's voice is husky and he squeezes Dora's shoulder.

"Samuel, would you please drive Deena to the hospital? She's in no condition to be driving." Mother's bossiness, back to life. "Vicki says she'll be praying," she adds for my benefit.

"What about Dora and Daniel?" I manage.

"They can help me settle the children and we'll be just moments behind you."

"Sounds like a good plan," Dora says, though I know she must be anxious as well.

"Deena, if I could use the keys to your van--" Daniel. He squeezes my shoulders.

"Of course."

I get my purse and kiss Caroline and Zoe, praying for the performance of a lifetime. "Girls," I whisper, gently shaking them awake, "Daddy got hurt at work and Grandpa Wilson is going to drive me to the hospital. You're going to get to play with Christopher and Canaan," I work on my enthusiasm, "because hospitals are, they're--" I start to choke up and Daddy rescues me.

"Boring! Little girls wouldn't have any fun there. In fact, I'm going to try and get back to you as soon as I can." He hugs them both and hands them over to Mother.

"Girls, come upstairs with Grandma Dora and me. We'll get a few playthings together and you can show me what all needs to go into Eli's diaper bag."

They are still sleepy and so do not protest too much, but at last Caroline pins me with one of her looks. "Mommy, Daddy will be okay won't he? Because we didn't get to tell him good-bye and I love you, be safe."

I wish I had the answer for that.

Daddy drives me to the hospital and I think that no vehicle has ever driven so slowly. He has the car radio turned onto the local Christian station and the words to a Rich Mullins song drift across the airwaves. *"We are not as strong as we think we are."* And I sob. No, I am not strong. Deena Brantwell Wilson. I am Deenie. I am a little girl. A child of God who has so desperately lost her way that I almost don't recognize myself anymore.

I start praying, bargaining with God as the car chews up the ribbon of road. *Father. I've been so wrong. If you just won't let me lose Max, I'll….I'll….*

Snow flurries scud across the pavement as though they *want* to put on the brakes, but can't. It seems a sorry visual picture of my life. I've been trying to stop myself from idiocy but have been blown along by an unseen force. My wants. My emptiness. My pity party to whom all my unmet needs have been invited as guests. Party's over.

If I were writing today, I'd post only this:

Blog Spot Post by Pajama Mama
November 25, 2010

Oh, Cyber Girlfriends…life is uncertain. It's impossible to write when you're sobbing.

I hope I have a life when this is over.
Pajama Mama

And my cyber-friends would respond. I know they would.

Comments:

I don't know what's going on, Pajama Mama, but hope everything will be much better than you expect.
~First Time Mommy

Ditto.
~Lexus Mommy

That goes for all of us.
~Dust Diva

Me too.
~Chocolate Guru

Absolutely.
~Formerly Hot

I see Max briefly, on a stretcher, through the glass emergency room doors, as they were rushing him to more tests. He looks like the inner workings of old-fashioned electrical board, tubes and wires running everywhere. I long to touch him, but I am shepherded to the family emergency waiting area.

In the waiting room my eyes roam over everything restlessly. I glance at the paper, folded back to the obituaries. Senseless losses reduced to a few words. My mind already starts composing. Stop it. Stop it. Max will not have one of those things. Not yet. I won't let him. I have too many things to be sorry for. To tell him. To change.

Surgeons are consulting on Max's condition. They need to check for internal bleeding. They tell us all that might be wrong in indeterminate medical terms. Then Sergeant Rivers comes to fill us in.

"Apparently Max arrived on the scene right as one of the suspects was fleeing the house. The owner had interrupted the burglary, and fired a shot. The suspect returned fire twice and ran. Max's car rounded the corner just as the driver of the getaway car gunned it. Max got t-boned at the intersection. He managed to give a description of sorts before losing consciousness. We've just received news that the driver has been apprehended, but they are still looking for a second man who jumped out of the car and ran. They're running the tags to check on the registration and they hope to ask Max some more questions as soon as it's allowed."

"Did *you* see him, Sergeant Rivers? Do you think he will be--?" I am desperate for reassurance.

"Deena, I think Max is in good hands. I'll leave speculation like that up to the doctors and we'll make sure the bad guys get put away."

I thank Sergeant Rivers and he pats me awkwardly on the shoulder, promising to keep us posted.

Restlessly I pace the path worn in the once-ornate rose patterned carpet. From the clock to the vending machine to the couch. Back again. I feed the machine a steady diet of quarters, provided to me by Daddy who has patted my hand helplessly, but steadily each time I light on the couch for a few minutes.

I have bought baked Cheetos, only to break them all into nervous pieces. I've consumed a gallon of Diet Coke, built little piles with my Junior Mints, and nibbled around the edges of several packages of Nutty Bars. I stare up at the clock and down at my watch willing them to tell me something. It's ten o'clock. 10:22. 10:38. 10:47.

With sudden clarity, I see my stubbornness and my idiotic choices as if on the big screen. It wasn't Thomas I wanted at all. It never was. Rather, it's Max that I've been missing. Yes, we've lived together, but I was missing mystery. I was almost duped into trading it for the temporary giddy thrill of want. I hadn't counted on the tossing and churning, the sea change that staying at home has been.

I've made my self-worth hinge on completely wrong things. Yes, I've continued to be in church and at Bible study, but without my heart in it. And when God is left out of any equation, the result is one messed-up product. I will do anything for another chance with Max. I want to beg him to forgive me.

I love you Max. I love you to the max. I do.

Max's parents have arrived, hugged me and sat silently on a green vinyl couch at one end of the waiting room. My mother glides in right behind them, regal in her pair of deep daffodil colored pumps that seem almost incongruous with the season. The shimmery bronze yarn outlining the autumn leaves on her sweater glows under the fluorescent lights. As always, she is the bastion of Emily Post correctness in manner and dress. Of all things, she leans down and kisses Daddy's head, bending to whisper something to him. It seems Paris has worked a magic spell. Daddy goes over to join the Double Ds on the ugly green couch.

Mother takes her place next to me. "Try not to slouch Deena, dear. It helps to act strong at a time like this." Her voice is low, trying not to make public our conversation in a waiting room that alternately fills and empties like the sea at high tide.

Childish though it is, I shrug away from her. "I don't think my having good posture is going to help, Mother."

"Deena. Honey. Max is going to pull through this, and you will be stronger than ever. I understand more than you think I do."

"Really, Mother? What is it you think you understand? How could you possibly?"

"This is how I know. You might have been too young to remember…" She trails off, looking for a moment as if she were watching a painful movie in her mind.

I can't *imagine* what she's going to tell me.

"Your father and I – when you started school, I fell apart."

Mother fell apart? I press my mouth together. I guess my expression said it all because she straightens her shoulders.

"Anyway, you had been my world and I didn't quite know what to do with myself. I threw myself into activities and I felt neglected as your father threw himself into his work. And I, that is to say, that I didn't always make the best decisions. I have been observing you and Max and well, you know, in a town this size, one hears rumors. It caused me to remember how it felt to be so lonely and feeling isolated at home and I…" Her fingers twist her rings around and around.

"Mother, did you *cheat* on daddy?" I question incredulously.

"Deena." This, sharply. Her expression silences me. "It wasn't entirely what you're thinking, but it was certainly not right. Not appropriate. Your father and I did go to counseling. It helped some. And it made me, *makes* me, want more for you. Sometimes, we need to let go, just like with my camera, sailing over the balcony. Otherwise we are too busy documenting our lives, trying to make it so picture-page perfect, that we forget to live them. To savor them. I didn't want to be in that season of my life, Deena. I have so many regrets. I don't know that we got entirely past my 'indiscretion' as your father referred to my, my infatuation."

"Mother? Who did you...?" But I realize it doesn't matter. What I don't understand is why she became so standoffish, why the elementary school years that I remember were all so formal, so odd. That's when I became a daddy's girl.

"You are wondering," mother continues, as though I have spoken out loud, "why it seemed that I withheld myself from you. Why my mothering was so distant. Stoic."

"Well, yes."

"Oh, Deena." She presses her finger tips to her eyes. "It was so very wrong of me. I thought perhaps if I didn't care quite so much, or at least appear to care so much, about anyone, I wouldn't get into trouble. I would make everything so perfect and work on improving myself so much that I wouldn't be tempted by anyone else, and I couldn't be hurt by your busyness and growing up or by your father's long hours. I just shut down on the relationship level and put everything into appearances. I didn't want to *be* hurt or hurt anyone else ever again. When Caroline was born, and then of course Zoe, and Eli – why, I felt as if I had been given a second chance!

"But it was not until this trip, Deena that your father and I sorted out some of our issues. His withholding of genuine forgiveness; my tendency to try and make everything too perfect. I am fifty-eight years old and I am just now figuring that out. It's exhausting to want to be anyone other than who you are, Deena. To envy things that no one can truly know the truth about. I need your forgiveness too." She is silent, waiting for me.

In a flash of a memory, I see a little girl sitting on a hard, black lacquer bench trying to color, her feet not able to touch the floor, shiny shoes swinging back and forth. It was a counselor's office. Mother and Daddy were inside and I was outside waiting. I feel what it is to wait. I am waiting again now. Waiting for a chance.

Why would I withhold from my mother what I want so desperately from Max? I put my arms around her. "Yes, mother," I whisper, "I do forgive you."

"Thank you," her whisper is a lovely, fragile thing, and I feel the wetness of her tears on my shoulder.

I think of the beautifully engraved plaque in Vicki's entryway: *The shortest distance between a problem and a solution is the distance between your knees and the floor.* And in the dirty, chaotic waiting room, I hit them.

Last summer, I finally got around to reading Mitch Albom's book, *For One More Day.* In the introduction, he writes of wanting to return to a day; to repeat or change something about it. If you've ever done that, then you "know you can go your whole life collecting days, and none will outweigh the one you wish you had back."

I know exactly which one I want back. I begin my litany of promises to God all over again. How I will apologize again to Max. How I will be a good mother, a more grateful person, a more involved person, in my church, in my house, with my children. But most of all, with my husband. I want to feel his arms around me. I want to beg him for forgiveness. I want a second chance.

Oh, God, how I have wasted my days.

Dr. Thornton comes into the waiting room. All of us stand. He shakes Daddy's hand and Daniel's and smiles kindly at me. "Mrs. Wilson. We've been able to determine that the internal bleeding we feared is not present. Max did need a few stitches in his head, and we've had to immobilize his left leg for a bit, to give it a chance to heal, but other than a mild concussion and a bruised rib or two, he's a mighty lucky fellow. He'll get a nice stay in the hospital with us for another day, and then we'll send him home with you."

"Not lucky. Blessed." Daniel asserts. The doctor nods in acquiescence.

"When can we see him?" This, more than anything is my heart's cry, now that I know Max will be okay.

"They just took him up to the fourth floor. You can go ahead, but only two at a time please. He's exhausted and likely still very groggy from all the pain meds."

"Deena, you go ahead and go on in. Then Daniel and I will go." Dora hugs me.

"I'll just wait for you, and take you on home, Deena Bean. We can see Max tomorrow. Give him our love." This from daddy. Mother has already left to get the children and put them in their own beds.

"Dora, let's just stay here with Max tonight, let Deena go home and get some rest. She can come back in the morning." Daniel.

I want to protest, but I know I won't be able to talk to Max tonight. I push the elevator buttons, surprised and grateful to be on there alone. I watch the lights change under each number as I go from the first to fourth floor. Will he be awake? Will he realize I am there? Will he forgive me?

Walking down the hallway, I glance at the ugly green room signs. They're the same ugly green as the waiting room couch, with tan numbers and little white dots with the numbers in Braille. When I reach it, the private room is dark except for the sliver of light balancing underneath the bathroom door.

A Southern Hills officer is standing across the hall at the nurse's station. When he sees me, he comes over. Officer Judson, the tag reads. Lovely. I recognize him as a newer guy who once stopped me for speeding. "Mrs. Wilson. Looks like those burglaries might be connected to a drug operation. One of us will be staying at the hospital until we can talk to Max, possibly in the morning." He must have seen my look of dismay. "I'll wait here. Give you some privacy."

Max's bed is at the far side of the room; the bed on the opposite of the filmy curtain is empty. A large window faces the south parking lot. The moon looks like a shiny ice cube, dropped and melting in the puddle of the dark sky.

Tiptoeing, I stand at the edge of his bed, drinking Max in with my eyes. There is a neat gauze bandage above his right eye, close to the hairline. In better times, I would have teased him about his rakish appearance. His leg is propped on pillows, immobilized from his knee on down. A walking cast, they called it. The tubes and wires have all been removed now, except the IV, taped to his wrist.

Silently, I move to his side, ready to smooth my hand across his forehead, longing to kiss his cheek. The IV pole is closer to the top of the bed, a series of blinking lights glide across a control panel. He is bare-chested, gauze wrapped tightly around his ribs as well. He seems to be sleeping, but I so need to touch Max. As I bend over, a strong hand snakes out of the covers and grabs my hand, encircling my wrist so tightly that I cannot move it.

I gasp, inhaling sharply and let out a startled shriek. Within seconds, Officer Judson and a night nurse are in the room.

"It's okay; it's my wife." They back out of the room. Max's tone cannot be mistaken for anything other than an order.

Even in pain, Max's wits are about him, his reflexes are razor sharp. When he speaks to me, I notice again the raspy quality of his voice, left over irritation caused by the tube that had been down his throat.

"Deena. I'm sorry I hurt your wrist. I didn't know it was you until my eyes adjusted."

"Who did you think it was?" I am shaken and weariness washes over me.

"You never know." Max sighs heavily. "I could tell someone was there and my instincts just kicked in. Let's start over."

"Hello, Max," I oblige. "I am so glad, so very glad that you're, that you're…" I sob all over again, picturing the phone call, being so afraid that I would lose Max without ever having the chance to tell him again that I am sorry. That I love him.

"Come here." He turns on the tiny light built in to the side of his bed so that I can see him wince when he tries to scoot over. I can't imagine how much his ribs must hurt.

Gingerly, I sit down on the bed. Now that he is awake, I am afraid to touch him, to press a kiss to his cheek. I feel as though I have lost that privilege.

"I know you need to get home. Not much good for talking now." His voice is growing slurry with exhaustion.

I nod miserably, tears dripping from the end of my nose. "Max, I just want to tell you again how sorry, sorry, sorry I am. That I love you. Please, Max, please forgive me."

His eyelids flutter, fighting against sleep. "I do…" Love you, I finish the sentence for him. That's what I think he might have said. "Tomorrow."

Pressing my lips to the top of his head, I turn and run from the room, not even stopping to say anything to Officer Judson or to Dora and Daniel. In the lobby, Daddy is waiting. He has the car already pulled up to the doors. We do not speak a word the whole ride home. That alone is a comfort.

It is a fitful night and when I wake up the sun is overly bright. The smell of coffee and bacon floats up the stairs. A quick glance at our iconic clock radio tells me it's 9:00 a.m. When I listen outside the children's rooms, I can see that all of them must be taken care of by a variety of grandparents, so I risk a quick shower, dressing in dark jeans, boots and a pink sweater with little ties at the waist. Max has always liked it on me. He says the tassels on the ends of the ties are entertaining. I fix my make-up, both eager and dreading going back to the hospital.

Mother is at the stove, putting the last of the bacon on a paper-towel lined plate. "Good morning, Deena. I hope you rested well. There's some fresh-squeezed juice at your place. Daddy has already been to pick up Dora and Daniel from the hospital and looked in on Max for a bit this morning."

"How's Max? Where are they now?" I yawn, grabbing a piece of bacon and gulping my juice while standing up. This earns a small frown from mother, but she bites her tongue.

"You'll want to see Max for yourself." She smiles. "Your father went out to get a newspaper. Caroline and Zoe are with him. Daniel and Dora are asleep in the girls' room. I guess the extra hospital bed and the recliner weren't all that comfy."

"They're on the little twin canopy beds?" I moan. "I meant to air up the extra Queen-size mattress and completely forgot about it."

"Don't worry, honey, I don't think they care right now."

"Where's Eli?"

"You'll have to see that." She motions toward the family room.

I tiptoe in there and Eli has fallen asleep on the floor, Zwieback toast in one hand, using Butternut Squash as a pillow. Squash's tail swishes across the rug in dreamy contentment, not bothered at all.

"Doesn't that beat all?" Mother has followed me. She grins and shakes her head. "That was so cute, I just covered him up and let him stay."

I gape at her.

"Deena Marie Brantwell Wilson! I am learning."

"Whoa." I grin back at her. "Doesn't *that* beat all?"

"Don't be cheeky!" She waves the bacon tongs, still in her hand, at me. "I'm still your mother."

I lean down to kiss my boy. I really, really want to see the girls, but I can't wait another minute to go to Max. Popping a stick of gum (from Mother's purse) in my mouth, I hug her and grab my car keys. "Thanks, Mother."

By the time I am parked, there are metal pin balls chasing each other through the corridors of my stomach. My boots thunk on the hard tile of the lobby and the elevator seems to crawl. There are voices in Max's room and when I get to the doorway, all I see are uniforms. Male laughter rings out and Max groans. "Cut it out, guys. Laughing feels terrible right now."

"Suck it up, Wilson."

"Hey, those stitches will make you look like a real cop!" That has to be Stockham. I recognize his voice from the day I ran into Mr. Berry and his hearse.

"We'll let you know more as we find out. Rest up." Sergeant Rivers.

When they turn to leave and see me, they all mutter subdued good mornings. I imagine Max telling them everything and I cringe. Sergeant Rivers stops while Stockham and another patrolman file past. "Max will have a lot to report, Deena. He looks a lot better this morning." He raises his hand in mock salute. "Back to the station. Take care."

For a moment, I hesitate, unsure of what to do. Finally, I come the rest of the way into the room. The harshness of daylight reveals that Max has indeed been fortunate. There is dark bruising edging from beneath the bandages around his rib cage and a shadowy bruise outlines his temple and the area just below his stitches.

I am just about to speak when I hear a noise in the hall. I look over my shoulder. A figure wearing a familiar black wool overcoat stands awkwardly in the corner of the door frame. Before I can process, Max is shoving himself up on one elbow.

"Too bad for you, I survived; now get out."

Thomas? "Max?" My voice is an inquiry directed at one or both of them.

Thomas clears his throat. "I've already been to the station this morning. I have no idea why they think it was *my* car."

"Your tags. Next time you won't be leaving," Max barks.

"Wait a minute! They let me go. I wanted to explain, to say that--" Thomas is flustered and as inarticulate as I've ever heard him.

Sergeant Rivers enters the room again. "I was just going to place Dr. Hunt here under arrest. But new information just came in. The green Mercedes, license plate 562 TOG, does check to one Thomas Hunt, but somebody didn't bother to read one line down on the registration. It's also registered to Caryn Hunt. Imagine that." The Sergeant fixes his steely gaze on Thomas.

Thomas turns crimson. "Deena, I can explain."

Sergeant Rivers snorts.

"I thought your wife was *dead*! What about the baby?" I turn a disbelieving, furious gaze on Thomas. I cannot believe this. What a sad, twisted story to invent. "I don't think there's an explanation possible for that." I'd feel even more stupid if that were possible.

Thomas turns around abruptly and leaves. Run, cowardly liar, run.

"Apparently that's a little story he likes to tell when he's decided to make a new conquest," Sergeant Rivers explains. "As far as we have been able to determine, there was no such accident involving his wife. Mrs. Hunt mainly lives back in Ohio, but she's getting a bit tired of the long distance 'romance'," Rivers snorts again. "She decided to do some detective work of her own."

Sergeant Rivers hands Max a report of some sort.

Max scans it. "Tinker's Car Repair. Hmm…employs Jeremy Burk and Chip Cassado. Jeremy's the one that fit my description; I identified him this morning. But Thomas Hunt's car and the driver we arrested last night…sorry, Sarge. Not making the connection."

"Drugs'll do that to you, Wilson." I will never get used to cop humor. Sergeant Rivers continues. "Caryn Hunt, Thomas' wife, brought her car there for repairs. She called *us* to make a report because they were taking so long and wouldn't give her a straight answer as to why. Mentioned that her husband was a professor out at the University and she's in town for a long visit.

"Turns out Burk and Cassado used this car for the last two burglaries and damaged the bumper. They hadn't had time to repair that. When she asked us to look into it, someone finally put it together this morning."

"So Chip Cassado was our other guy?"

"Looks like. He matched the description of another eye witness. Looks like preliminary reports on that footprint matched the one at your house too. A team's getting ready to serve a search warrant. Those two will have to find someone else to carry on their burglary stunts; turns out they've been pawning all this stuff to help support the new drug operation over by the ridge area, the one the task force has been just about to bust."

"And Tinker?

"He's clean. He's just ticked that he had to gainfully *un*employ two mechanics. And Wilson, if it hadn't for you getting out of the car when they shot at you, managing to get a shot off and giving us that description despite your injuries…well," Sergeant Rivers clears his throat gruffly, "good job."

Good job? Someone shot at Max?

"*Max*? Someone *shot* at you?"

"Only a bad guy who didn't much feel like going back to prison. I just nicked him in the calf."

"Just enough to slow him down during the manhunt. Hard to climb a tree with your leg messed up." Sergeant Rivers guffaws.

I'm still absorbing this, my thoughts zigzagging like a pinball on the loose. I remember the tall redheaded woman who dropped Thomas off near the lake one day. Max might have been killed! The night that Max thought he saw a vehicle with that description at our house. I shudder. Gracious! They could have been casing our house long before that night.

"What about the other matter?" Max queries.

Sergeant Rivers looks around, clearly uncomfortable.

"Deena, could you give us a minute?" Max isn't really asking. It worries me that he wants some information without me.

I turn around and step back out in the hall. Kay Tupper and Tandy Walker, of all the unlikely pairs, are standing at the nurse's station, asking about Max's room. "It's right here," I offer.

They turn around, Kay holding a bouquet of candy bars. Max will love it. "Hi! We won't stay. Just wanted to make sure Max is okay. It was on the news last night."

I step over to hug Kay and then carefully hug Tandy. "How are you?"

She smiles her sweet smile. "I'm wonderful, Deenie, truly. Just a bit tired still."

"I bet. You and Max both."

Sergeant Rivers leaves the room for a second time. Curiosity will likely kill both the cat and me if I don't ever get the chance to talk to Max without this parade.

"Go ahead," I gesture toward the room. "Pop in and say hello."

Kay and Tandy walk in and set the candy down on the table that slides under Max's hospital bed. "We're leaving. This is all we wanted. Seriously." Again, Kay does all the talking.

"I've been praying for you, Max." Tandy says shyly.

I wave to them, thanking them again. My turn at last. Suddenly I feel awkward and shy.

"Deena, I remember you being here last night, but I was kind of out of it."

I cross closer to the bed. "Yes, you were," I laugh softly, "but not out of it enough not to grab my hand when you thought I might be a bad guy." My tears start up again, thinking about all that might have happened.

"Sorry about that."

"No, Max, I'm the one who's sorry." My tears flow in streams. "All I could think about after Sergeant Rivers called was what I would do without you. What I would do if I never got the chance to tell you again that I love you, that I'm sorry. Oh, Max! I need you to tell me that you forgive me!"

It seems like hours before Max speaks. "I'm not going to lie to you, Deena. That's not something I ever expected to happen to us. It will take me awhile to trust you again, to recover. But, I do forgive you. I *choose* to. Yesterday taught me life's too short not to try."

He opens his arms, holding one hand out to keep me from crushing his ribs. I fall into them, as carefully as I can, marveling at the treasure of grace.

******

Max's first Sunday out of the hospital is a postcard autumn day. Though the chill of winter is just days away, the warm blanket of sun cozies up the world. Caroline, Zoe and Eli all seem to understand what a gift this is, going as a family for the first time in a long time where our bodies, hearts and spirits are all in accord. The first hymn has begun as we make our slow way into our usual pew. Naturally, Max refuses to stay home. Mr. Tough Guy and all that. "When all around my soul gives way, He then is all my hope and stay." The music swells.

Mr. Mac slides out from the end of our pew, gesturing for us to claim that spot. He kisses my cheek and hands me a Ziploc baggie chock full of Bazooka. His warm smile blesses my heart. He slips into the row in front of us, right next to Miss Opal.

Vicki gives me a glowing smile of welcome, Zeke at her side. She has been a gem, watching the children, bringing us brownies and her wonderful homemade macaroni and cheese. I look around at my church family. The music buoys my spirit, picking me up and bearing me away to a place that is ever trustworthy. Ah yes, "On Christ the solid rock, I stand..." After all the sand of this year, today is solid.

<u>Grocery List</u>
Bandages
Paperback by Louis L'Amour for Max's stocking
Jelly Beans
Wrapping paper
Milk
Junior Mints
Cucumbers
Salad greens
Pistachios
Potatoes
Cream
Pampers

Chapter 16

On the first Wednesday of December, I rise early and dress carefully, choosing a beautifully tailored grey pantsuit that finally fits me again. A red camisole, a nod to the season, peeks out from the lapels. I pull gray pearls that swing on little silver hoops through my ears. They are my mother's gift to me from Paris. I will need a little bit of Paris this morning.

It has been eleven days since Max's accident; nine wonderful days since we've brought him home. Max's parents went home that same day, promising to return at Christmas. We'll save Eli's big 1st birthday celebration until then.

Eschewing breakfast, I brush my teeth, splash water on my face to rinse the dot of creamy cleanser. I apply make-up sparingly. Rosy tinted moisturizer and shimmery blush. A cherry red lip gloss. A hint of fawn-colored shadow with the barest coat of mascara. I look at the pink tube. Maybelline's Great Lash mascara is a classic. They started marketing it in 1971 and it still sells at a rate of one tube every 1.9 seconds. That's more staying power than lots of things I could name.

I step back and then lean into the mirror, checking my face for signs of lines. For signs of weakness. I bow my head in a silent prayer and plead for resolve. I don't want Thomas, but I no longer fool myself into thinking I can camp near the enemy's fire without being burned. God has been teaching me that. I'd like classy resolve while I'm at it. Ending my prayer on a sigh, I slip my feet into classic grey pumps.

When I walk into the bedroom, Max is propped up on his side watching me. His stitches have been removed and the bruises are fading. But he still has two weeks at home before returning to light duty. "Want me to come with you?"

"No, thanks." I sit on the edge of our bed. "I've got it. Really. It's just something I need to do by myself."
"Max?" I continue. "Could I ask you something?"
"Sure."

"That day in the hospital, what was Sergeant Rivers telling you?"

"I asked him to find out about the picture on your e-mail. The one of you kissing Thomas." He says this without flinching.

"What about it?" I stare at the floor.

"Deena, look at me." I raise my head and he continues. "I know you kissed Thomas, but that wasn't you."

"What?" Didn't I have this conversation with Vicki?

"It was a picture of Thomas and his wife, Caryn. It was taken on campus during this most recent visit. They traced the computer that sent it to Sonya Weatherby."

"I knew she didn't like me, but, I don't get it. Why would she do that? Send me that picture?"

"She didn't do it. Caryn Hunt asked her take it and then used Sonya's computer at the University to send it to you, but with a different e-mail address. She and Sonya had been talking, and Sonya shared some gossip about you and Thomas. Caryn got your e-mail from Thomas' committee list, used Sonya's computer and was hoping to rattle you a bit. In fact, it was her that drove by our house that night in the green Mercedes. That is one messed up couple."

"Oh, Max. I don't know that I can talk; look what I did. Why did you even ask about that?"

"You didn't need evidence out there to trip you up or hang over you and I wanted to know. We all mess up, Deena Bean. It's going to take some work, but I'm in. I'm always here for my best girl, whenever."

"I know, Max. I really do." I rise, stretch and bend back over the bed to cup my hand around his cheek. I haven't yet initiated any real kiss. It would feel awkward.

The beautiful drive to Southern Hills University has never seemed longer. Or shorter. I feel perspiration gather under my arms and I quickly flip on the Christian radio station. Pastor Sherman's voice is on, a pre-recorded sermon clip, advertising our new service times. "Do you know what the hardest temptation is that you face? It's the one you don't give into." The DJ plays a beautiful chorus next and I love a line in it. "You are more than the sum of your past mistakes." Yes! How thankful I am.

Driving past *The Rooster*, where Thomas and I sat putting away morning pastries and Boss coffee, I test myself to see whether or not there's a twinge of nostalgia or a prickle of regret. Nope. Their sunshine logo with its rising rays and perky slogan, "See the morning!" just makes me smile at the clever phrasing.

I *am* seeing the morning. Truly seeing it for the first time in a long, long time. Mornings don't represent chances at the University, or stolen moments with fraudulent happiness; they are God's representation of second chances. His mercies are new every morning and they will get me through this one as well.

I pull into a parking space and pull my parking tag from the rearview mirror. I won't be a committee member anymore; I'll just be a visitor on campus like anybody else.

I walk up the beautiful old staircase and into the conference room off the main library, filled with determination. Thomas looks up from the massive oak table, catches my eye and immediately excuses himself.

"Give me a moment," I tell him. Facing the committee, I thank them for the opportunity I have had to work with them on the literature pairings. "I will always love literature, and who knows, I might come back to teach someday, but for now, I love my family more, and they require more of me during this season of my life. I am resigning. I wanted, I needed to tell you in person."

I look around at all of them. Jeremy Templeton, busily eating today's offering of brownies, leads a light smattering of applause for me. Clare Samuels says, "You will never be sorry."

Even, it seems, Sonya Weatherby gives a slight nod of approval. "Thank you for your work, Deena. Your insight was always superb," John Claxton offers. I will miss this mixture of tweed, stuffiness, book dust, lemon pine wax and academia. But that's all.

"It was my pleasure." I mean that only in the purest most literary sense of the word. Examining my heart, I know that it is true. Thomas doesn't factor into anything more than a harrowing lesson learned.

In the hallway, I face Thomas. "I resigned from the committee, Thomas."

"I gathered as much, Deena. I, I am sorry about Max."

"Thank you. He is doing quite well. I am sorry as well, Thomas. Sorry that you feel the need for someone other than your wife; sorry that I was such a poor example. But I do need to tell you that what you did, what you are doing is unacceptable. Get some help. We all need it sometimes."

He brushes past me to go back into the conference room, muttering something that I don't even want to hear.

Shaking my head, I walk down the beautiful, wide old steps to the bottom floor of the library and the exit onto the commons. Looking around, I contemplate all the stories that have been told, written and lived out in places just like this all over the world.

I am uncertain about what the future holds, but at least now I know what I *want* it to be. I lean for a moment against the 800s label of the majestic shelves' Dewey decimal system. That is my favorite section to visit. It is as familiar to me as the back of my hands. Literature. Austen. Bronte. Steinbeck. Harper Lee. Dickens. I can feel someone's presence behind me just for the space of a heartbeat before warm, firm hands cover my eyes.

"Guess who." My heart stops for a breath. I turn and my eyes widen. "Care to go get a Diet Coke with me, Beautiful?"

I snort. "Beautiful, Max? I don't feel very beautiful." I take in his cropped hair without the slightest hint of grey. Those laughing eyes with sexy crinkles around their edges. The healing stitches. His broad shoulders. "Age looks good on you. On me old just looks…well, old."

"You look great to me."

I snort again. "Yeah, well I quit having a waistline the same year I quit listening to Bruce Springsteen."

Max laughs his sexy booming laugh and the librarian at the circulation desk glares at us. "That's your problem. You should never quit listening to Springsteen."

He guides me through the center courtyard maze just outside the library and down a shortcut path to the minivan. For a moment, I wondered who he's talked into bringing him here and who is watching the children. Max reads my thoughts. "Vicki has the kids and Mr. Chitwood dropped me off."

Max opens the door for me and gets around amazingly well to his side. I can't remember the last time he's held open a door for me. We've been too busy juggling babies and diaper bags and car seats and parallel lives.

He leans over to punch the CD button and a familiar song fills the air. It is our song, the one that played the first night he ever kissed me.

"You remembered," I exhale the words so they hang on air like the puck in the air hockey tables of the student lounge. "I love you to the max," I whisper for the first time in a long time, but still not loud enough for him to hear me.

"No, Deenie. I just never forgot." He kisses the tip of my nose. "I want to kiss more than that, but my ribs won't let me in this car. Let's hurry home." Max puts the car in reverse, and as we head home, he holds my hand tightly between us all the way home. The music of our song sweeps through the car and my heart, purging it of the heaviness.

Our song ends and Max reaches over to turn it down. At a stop light he turns to me.

"Catch me up on your life."

"I lost the Christmas auction on eBay."

"Who won?"

"Somebody whose on-line name is 'Lexus Mommy.' I think she's the same one who leaves comments on my blog sometimes." I huff. "Naturally Minivan Mommy loses to Lexus Mommy."

"What were we bidding on again?"

"That ancient Fisher Price popcorn popper that Zoe really wanted. The one Miss Zieman at the pre-school wouldn't part with."

"Hmm."

"I know. I offered her fifty bucks for it too!" I'm indignant.

"Come here."

I scoot toward Max. "I love you to the max." My words are only a breath. His hand twirls my pony tail. He tilts my face up again.

"I love you to the max," I whisper again, this time loud enough for him to hear.

When the car pulls into the driveway, he gets out of it as quickly as he possibly can, given his injuries. He opens my car door and without saying a word, leads me through the garage, through the stone breezeway, up the stairs and into our room.

Pulling the ribbon from my ponytail, Max gathers me to him and seals his mouth to mine, claiming me. Red hot sparks are nearly visible. "Always be mine," he whispers against my mouth, laying me back on the bed. "Promise me."

"I will never be anyone else's." His hands reach for the buttons on my suit, his mouth urgently on mine again. Max is reclaiming me, really, as his. And that is all I want to be.

******

Tuesday, December 14th is our last Bible Study meeting until after the New Year. Prayer time is more like prayer and praise time than it's ever been. There's a thrill of newness in the atmosphere. It springs from this time of year and it seems to have soaked into the fibers of the carpet and the oil paintings of Bible scenes on the walls.

We gather around a festive snack table complete with a bowl of holiday spice punch and an ice ring of holly floating inside. Someone has lit candles.

We have given Miss Opal a card signed by all of us along with a gift certificate to Delia's Downtown Diner that she is always reminiscing about. Miss Opal has a small gift for all of us as well. They are all tiny boxes, wrapped in red foil paper that glimmers under the fluorescent lights and are topped with miniature gold bows. We are like little children and cannot wait to open them, fidgeting and whispering about what might be inside.

Pretending that she doesn't notice, Miss Opal smoothes her hand across the pages of her Bible, a gesture which has come to endear her to us all. God's Word is her treasure. "I'm going to open with a quote today from Hannah Whitall Smith. 'The greatest burden we have to carry in life is self; the most difficult thing we have to manage is self.'

"In different ways, I believe we have all found this to be true this year. I would like us to finish out with a reminder that because of the Gift born to us this season, we are equipped with everything we need to be overcomers of our selves. To release that burden to the One who is able to carry us. To deliver us. To help us finish strong.

"Let's turn in our Bibles to Hebrews, chapter 11, that great Hall of Faith. It contains so many story clips of the ordinary men and women whose lives turned out to be heroic because of their faith. Listen: 'By faith, Abel…by faith Enoch…by faith Noah…by faith Abraham…by faith Isaac…' Twenty-six times that all important word is mentioned in this chapter. That would almost lead me to believe that's important, girls!"

We all giggle. Miss Opal's gaze becomes tender. "You may open your boxes."

The table tears into them, gasps and oohs and aahs echo in the room as we reach in and take out the tiniest, perfect charms, replicas of candles, with the faintest sheen of red where the flame is represented.

"I pray you will wear these on a charm bracelet or a necklace so that you will have a reminder to always carry the flame, never let it die out. Finish this race by faith. May you carry Christmas in your hearts and the Light of the World ever before you."

When Miss Opal finishes, there is not a dry eye in the room. She asks us to share what is on our hearts before we go.

Kay Tupper reports that she and Richard are seeing a counselor. Things are far from perfect, but they do have hope. She has put herself on a book diet, a thing that makes us all laugh.

Tandy Walker has just finished her treatments, insisting on finishing them earlier than her doctor suggested; she just wanted them over. Macon hopes to return at Christmas and will not re-enlist.

Reagan Anne McCabe got the job as assistant baker at Bountiful. We all cheer. She has learned to have an "odd kind of peace" about single parenting and says she would welcome suggestions for some meaningful Christmas traditions that will help her and the girls focus on Jesus' birth. I smile at Vicki, because I know Kay will be all over that.

Regina Baker is dating someone she met while showing a house. "That man is fine! He loves the Lord and I'm just trustin' in those possibilities. Um hmmm. He's fine." Her beautiful caramel skin glows as though she's attempting to hug a special secret to herself but it spills out.

Vicki shares the joyful news of her pregnancy and passes around a grainy black and white ultrasound picture. Her glow surpasses that of any candle.

I tell them that I have resigned from my committee work and that I am finding a surprising peace about staying at home. I also share with them something I have not told anyone besides Vicki. I have been diligently working on my manuscript and hope to have a novel out to several editors and agents by the end of the year.

"I can't wait to read it!" Kay enthuses. "I will be book skinny by then!" She's referring to her reading diet, of course. We all laugh again.

Vicki is going to take over Bible study in the spring for Miss Opal. And, Miss Opal, well, she and Mr. Mac are going to spend some time together, free of all of their usual duties to see whether or not anything might develop between them.

Imagine that, after all these years! I guess that just proves that we are never too old for second chances. I will be rooting for them all the way.

Vicki and I stop by for Starbucks on the way home. I left Eli with mother this morning, knowing this would be the last study before the long holiday break. "Vicki," I lean across the table and squeeze her hands. "I am so, so happy for you."

She cannot quit smiling. "I know it and I thank you, but I am just as happy for you. You and Max. Max being safe. And I better get a copy of that book you're writing before Kay does!"

"We'll see," I tease.

We finish our lattes and I tell Vicki I'm going to get Eli without even looking at anything to buy while I'm this near to Target. She laughs. "I'm not getting in my car until I see you leave!"

I pick up Eli from my mother's and try to make an excuse for leaving quickly without telling her about my writing. It seems too precious a thing to share yet, though our relationship is getting better.

At home, I feed Eli and then set him on the floor on a blanket, his blocks and trucks all around. He is obviously not in the mood to take his nap. As I am typing on my fledgling manuscript, Eli peeks around the corner of my desk, pulling himself up on the wall. I swivel in my chair and grin at him. He answers me with a huge answering smile. Nearly six teeth!

After a moment, he lets go of the wall and stands on his own. I hold my breath. His arms flail and then balance at his sides like a miniature tightrope walker. He steps toward me. One. Two. Three steps before he wobbles and plops down on his little Pampered behind, delighted with himself. I applaud, sweeping him into my lap.

In a few moments, I will pick up my precious girls from school and a few hours after that, my husband will come home, not on call, and will spend the entire gloriously ordinary evening with us. I can't wait to tell him about Eli's first steps.

We think we're trying to write our life stories in full, rich chapters at a time, but really, we can only write a sentence at a time. My cup overflows.

Grocery List
Candy Canes
Christmas lights
Hot Chocolate packets
Chocolate Syrup
Candy Sprinkles
Wrapping paper
Baby wipes
Baby bath
Baby lotion
Milk
Cheerios
Chicken Nuggets
Yeast
Flour
Sugar
Brown Sugar
Peppermint flavoring
Pecans

Chapter 17

I curl up on the window seat to read the devotional that Mr. Mac and Miss Opal have given me together as a Christmas present. Though they've never done such a thing before, their thoughtfulness touched me as much as the pieces of Bazooka taped all over the wrapping paper tickled me.

Stark, bare branches shiver in the wind, rattling like bones. The few stubborn leaves still clinging to the trees are wrinkled like forgotten wads of brown paper that missed the trashcan. The sky is pewter grey. Apparently, the sun has ducked out to attend a party on the other side of the world.

My devotions are healing this morning. Wrapped in my grey sweats and fuzzy pink cardigan, I feel small and newborn. Fragile, but with growing strength. I have the chance for a different beginning with Max. New and fresh like the dusting of snow covering our lawn and frosting the roofs outside the window.

"All of us have become like one who is unclean, and all our righteous acts are like filthy rags…like the wind our sins sweep us away." It's from Isaiah 64:6. I am so grateful not to have been swept away, but to have been gently blown back home by the breath of the One who guides the very winds.

I am savoring the peace of the morning after the tumult of the past months. Max took Caroline and Zoe to school; they were ecstatic to be dropped off in a police car. Eli is down for his early nap and I am left to my own devices, contemplative and content.

The window seat showcases the windows that have framed so many of my heart pictures: the children playing in the snow, jumping in the leaves, running through a summer sprinkler. Max, wiping the sweat from his forehead as he mows, bursting into a grin when he sees me coming out with a glass of sweet tea and a handful of his pistachios. My best friend driving up to her house and looking over to wave before going inside.

Heart pictures of me holding up each of our children, crooking a finger, pointing, "Look — Daddy's home!" It was always said with such joy and anticipation. Max might not have come home. I could have disappeared with the slow sucking squelch of the machines at the hospital during Max's stay, or with my own determination to run from what I thought was the loss of myself. I will not think of these "what ifs."

Curling my legs beneath me, I sip cocoa from the huge candy cane stamped mug that Max bought for me last Christmas. Butternut Squash curls up at my feet. The fragrant Douglas fir is bedecked with plaid bows, plenty of tinsel and a treasure trove of memories disguised as ornaments. Packages flank the nativity set with the crèche holding baby Jesus in the very center of it all. The tree lights wink at me and peace floods my heart.

Staring out at the snow, I immediately think of David's words of repentance and his plea to the Lord after being confronted about his sin with Bathsheba: *"Wash me and I shall be whiter than snow."* Snow can cover a lot of ugliness. Trash. Discarded, forgotten things. Dirt. The deepest snow in the Midwest was eighty-eight inches in Minnesota in 1969.

I sigh with newfound contentment. It's amazing how much things can change in almost a year. In the center of the long narrow trunk which serves as our coffee table is an early Christmas present from Vicki: a replica of a centerpiece I have always admired at her house.

A tiny lighted glass church is on a bed of fake snow with miniature evergreen trees and two snowbirds around it. This peaceful scene sits on a pewter stand covered by an etched glass cloche. Last winter I might have looked at hers and felt trapped like those covered birds.

Eleven months later I don't see myself as trapped, but rather protected. Held at this place in my life by the Lord's big, ever present, ever capable right hand. He covers me and shields me from anything I might think could be a safer place than here.

As our Bible study leader, Miss Opal reminds us, life is grand. Every precious, crazy, loud, sticky, wild and wonderful day of it. God is so good.

In counseling last week, Pastor Sherman quoted something I'm just now beginning to get. "Life is lived forwards, but understood backwards." Max and I have been meeting with him a few times a week, with mother and Vicki taking turns watching the children. Pastor Sherman is helping us understand how we could have gotten to the point where I could have justified cheating in our marriage.

I lean against the chilly window pane and remember our most recent session. Pastor Sherman leaned back in his heavy oak chair with the leather stuffing on headrest and seat. His hands were steepled behind his head and he closed his eyes just for a moment. For some reason, I felt newly nervous.

"Let's pray together first." We all bowed our heads; three together in strong agreement.

"God of second chances, we praise and bless you for intervening mightily in the lives of this precious couple, Max and Deena. Thank you for giving them a tenacious faithfulness, stopping them at the brink of a much worse disaster. Make our work here as productive as though we could see You in this room, and bind these two together for as long as you give them breath."

"Amen." Max echoes, and squeezes my hand lightly. I press myself tightly into his side as though shrinking myself into him will make everything go away.

"Deena," Pastor Sherman begins, "we've already addressed some of the tougher issues: what factors led to this emotional affair; what you felt you were lacking from Max; what Max needs from you; what you need to do to repair this as a couple — what boundaries need to be in place.

Though the work on any marriage is ongoing, particularly when a breach of trust is involved, I think with just one more specific piece of this puzzle, you'll be ready to work this thing out and I fully expect to be present for the celebration of fifty years of wedded bliss!"

His confidence and enthusiasm infuse me with warmth and zest for this new beginning. I sit on the edge of my chair, my fingers winding in and out of Max's big strong ones. Max places his free hand over mine to stop my fidgeting.

"Deena, what I want you to tell Max is what you most need from him now."

I am so close to Max I can hear his almost indiscernible intake of breath. It's the lone expression of Max's nervousness, a misfit companion to mine.

My chin drops. I look at Pastor Sherman and then into my chest I murmur. "I want Max to fall in love with me again." My throat catches with sobs that are all clogged in my throat, desperate for their chance to come out, like the traffic trying to turn left on Main Street at rush hour in the places where there is no stop light. My eyes cannot meet Max's deep ones.

Pastor Sherman leans into his desk. "Deena, I don't want you to tell *me*; I want you to look at Max and tell *him*."

Tiny rivers of water are gathered in my lower lids and I feel my chin quiver. My voice hitches and I softly breathe, "I need you to fall in love with me again." My eyes can barely meet Max's gaze. He so didn't deserve what I've done to him. To us, really.

As close as my next heartbeat comes the solidness of Max's reassurance: "Deena," his voice is a well of tenderness. "Deena, look at me." He gently takes my face in both of his huge hands. "Deena, I can't do that."

My stomach does a jackknife and I straighten up. Pastor Sherman's confusion is palpable. We wait for some explanation from Max.

"I can't because I already *am* in love with you. I've never stopped falling."

Pastor Sherman clears his throat. "Max, there's no escaping what we've worked on. *Show* each other love. Don't just tell."

But launching myself sideways, I throw my arms around Max's neck and his kisses rain all over my cheeks, absorbing, tasting my tears. Such a gift considering I have surely been the cause of many of his. Grace. This is my grace.

Pastor Sherman clears his throat, rises from his desk and places one hand on each of our shoulders. "Well, that's definitely showing. I think we're done here." Shaking his head and grinning, he exits.

Max tugs me up from one of the tan club chairs and hauls me against the strong length of him. I am nearly on my toes to meet his lips. His mouth moves on mine with vehement passion. I am dimly aware of the u-shaped floor to ceiling bookcases filled with commentaries and austere looking biblical research texts. It smells a bit dank and musty, a combination of a basement after rain and the archival stacks in a big city library.

Milky white light from the muted night mode bulbs in the office complex hallway mingle with splashes of red from the exit signs to form patterns on the floor. It seems surreal. Not the setting I would have chosen after such a revelation.

But that kiss. Oh, that kiss. In it was the very breath of new beginnings. Of promises past. Promises kept. Promises broken. And the promise of forever.

Blog Spot Post by Pajama Mama
December 17, 2010

Well, cyber girlfriends and fellow sleepy moms, this wraps up the journey through my first year as the stay-at-home mommy of three.

I was so wrong about so many things, chiefly about my identity lying in what anyone thought of me: my colleagues, my parents, my readers, even my husband.

I am only anything by God's grace. He has placed me here for just a few short trips around the sun. I'm not going to live for anything but Him [not even shopping trips to Target]. I've been working on surrender in the spiritual realm and standing up for the real me in this one. So far, so good.

It's a sweet life; may God pour His sweetness on yours.

Pajama Mama

Comments:
I'll miss this. It's been a great year.
~First Time Mommy

All the best chocolate in your life.
~Chocolate Guru

May your dust bunnies be few! Seriously, thanks for being real.
~Dust Diva

We'll be on-line anytime you need us to give you a laugh. Thanks for all the ones you've given us.
~Formerly Hot

Thanks, girls. Keep your eye out for my book. I hope it'll be in stores one day.
~Pajama Mama

How will we know it's yours?
~Dust Diva

Trust me, you'll know.
~Pajama Mama

****

My mother went with me to Bible study the week before last, and we've been having lunch on Friday for the last two weeks at the Target snack bar, no less! Our tenuous mother-daughter bonding is every bit as much a second chance as mine with Max. I can't believe I have never known the things I am discovering about my mother until now.

Christmas, they say, is the busiest time of year for plastic surgery. Mother has agreed to hold off on having any "work" done. In fact, Daddy told her she didn't need to change a thing. She's been growing, as have I. We've been talking a lot more lately, and even though I'm far from enjoying her company, I think we're discovering some common ground. We actually have fun sometimes!

And I really can't believe that I came so close to deceiving myself about the truth of my marriage. I am astounded that I was kept from even greater sin. That Max would know all this and take me back. That we are going to go on a real date – a weekend away, actually-- for the first time in nearly a year.

Thanks to Max's parents' early gift of Christmas cash and the promise of babysitting from my parents, Max is planning something magical. Max is back at work, his leg growing stronger every day, his bruising nearly gone. He is, however, more than ready to be back on regular duty.

I have always loved this time of year, but this year I love it even more. Eli will be old enough to tear into boxes and paper, loving those things more than the presents. What a contrast to last year when he was still sleeping twenty-two hours a day.

Caroline and Zoe, like most children their age, make celebrating a joy. Absolutely everything delights them: secrets, shopping, visiting Santa, making lists, making cookies, making me crazy.

UPS will deliver about 22 million packages on December 19, its busiest day. I think of the gifts in them, the thrill that always accompanies the delivery of a package to a porch, and smile.

If my life were a novel, Max would be whisking me away to Paris for Christmas and we'd renew our love in the City of Lights at the same time the world celebrates the Light of the World. Since it is real life, after all, we're not going to Paris.

We are, however, going to stay at Big Cedar Lodge. As Max says, "Who cares about the expense, I'm going away with my best girl!" And do I feel guilty about my children even for two days during the most wonderful time of the year?

You betcha. But I'm going to do it.

It's about time for me to finish packing, but after devotions, I got side-tracked and went in to type some more quick paragraphs in my novel. Before I know it, several hours have passed. I will have to hustle to pick up the girls; it's an early out day.

Eli and I scurry into The Flannel Goose, fleeing from the chilly air. Zoe meets us with a happy squeal. "It's almost Christmastime, Mommy! And Miss Carrie says it's supposed to snow some more." Her arms wrap around my knees for a spontaneous hug of joy.

Everywhere, there are parents and preschoolers calling out, "Merry Christmas! Merry Christmas!"

"That will be so much fun!" I take Zoe's hand in one of mine and little Eli's mittened one in the other; he wants to practice walking whenever he can.

"Can we have some hot chocolate? And a candy cane? And a fire?"

"Slow down there, Zoe girl! I'm sure you can."

Pulling into Roosevelt Elementary, the air is electric with giddy children, about to be let out for the long Christmas holidays. They wave homemade ornaments, glittery snowmen, empty lunch boxes and colorful scarves. I spot Caroline who is fairly dancing.

"Mommy! Is this the night that Nana and Papa Brantwell are coming to spend the night? Can you tell them we can have some popcorn?"

"That could be arranged."

"Yay! Yay!" Caroline and Zoe chime in together and Eli hunkers his little bottom to the floor bouncing up again like his favorite Jack-in-the-Box. "Yay!" he parrots.

"Mommy, do you even think you could share some of your Junior Mints to go with our popcorn?"

I look at Caroline's expectant upturned face. "I'm sure of it."

"Oh, thank you, Mommy! We're going to have a grandparents' sleepover!"

We walk our way to the minivan, a merry clump, all excited for different reasons, but which are very much bundled together as the best parts of this season of joy.

At home, they eat pretzels and drink hot chocolate, talking about all the treats they will get to have with my parents here and in charge. The doorbell rings and I have to laugh at my parents, here an hour early to begin watching the children.

"Sorry," my mother smiles, "we were getting excited."

"Nana!" Caroline and Zoe scamper to the door and Eli protests loudly from his left behind spot in the high chair.

"Do you want me to get a fire started, Deenie?" Daddy asks. "It's getting mighty cold out there."

"That would be great, Daddy." I kiss his cheek.

"We wanna go watch Mommy get all dressed up, okay Nana?" Caroline asks.

"But don't get your feelers all hurt, Nana, 'cause we'll get to spend lots of time with you after." Zoe is ever concerned about others.

"You go right ahead. Eli and I will supervise Papa while he builds the fire."

"I heard that." Daddy pretends to grouse. "I don't need any supervision."

I hold out my hands to my girls and they walk up the stairs with me, admiring the greenery, the red bows, the twinkling lights and the festive touches everywhere. It's true, I realize — the season never grows old.

In the master bedroom, I brush my teeth, carefully apply my make-up and go to my closet to take out a beautiful new dress. Slipping it over my head, I feel exactly like a princess. The fitted bodice is threaded with tiny pink and silver beads. Silver and pink panels fall from the waist to the middle of my calves.

I put the silver Paris hoops holding grey pearls in my ears, tuck a beautiful nightgown, underwear, toiletries, jeans and sweaters into my overnight bag. I let Caroline and Zoe put in my make-up bag and curling iron and zip it up.

"Ooh, Mommy, you look so pretty!" Caroline gushes.

"Why are you gonna date Daddy again?" Zoe wants to know.

I smile. "Because I love him. And even mommies and daddies need to go on dates."

Zoe frowns. "But you don't have any shoes on!"

For a moment, I hesitate. I hadn't thought of shoes. I've just been thinking of our seven o'clock dinner reservation at the Candlestick Inn, perched high on the bluffs overlooking Lake Taneycomo and the glittering lights of Branson Landing. What a perfect evening; what a romantic start to our Christmas getaway.

"That's a good point, Zoe. Girls, let me think." And then I remember. In a shoebox are a delicate pair of silvery, strappy sandals that I wore with a dress on our honeymoon. Max loved that dress and those sandals. For some reason, I just haven't worn them again. They will go perfectly with this dress.

"Close your eyes, girls. No peeking." I hear them giggle as I pull the box down from the top recesses of my closet and slip them on, adjusting the shimmery elastic on the back of the straps.

"Okay, you can look!"

The looks of delight on their faces form a heart picture I will never forget. "Daddy is gonna be so glad he gets to take you on a date." Zoe approves.

From the noise downstairs, I can hear that Max is home. I hear his voice, greeting my parents and Eli. His bag is already packed and downstairs; he will want to leave right on time. My heart pounds with excitement, and I wipe damp palms on the sides of my dress.

"I'll carry your bag for you, Mommy," Caroline decides.

"That's sweet of you, Caro."

"Then I wanna put her perfume on for her." Zoe picks up the pink bottle from the dresser. I obligingly hold out my wrists and tilt my head back as she sprays my neck and wrists.

"Thank you, Zoe girl."

"You are very welcome," she tilts her nose up imperiously and my two girls escort me to the stairs.

"Wait here!" Caroline commands.

Zoe thunders down the stairs right behind her. "Daddy, close your eyes. No peeking."

They nod at me and I descend. Halfway down, they instruct Max. "Okay, now you can look!"

Max's gaze devours me with appreciation. He whistles at me and takes my hand to turn me around. "I can't wait," he whispers, for my ears alone. He kisses Eli in my mother's arms, hugs the girls and says aloud, "I'll back the car out." Taking our bags, he goes to retrieve the Wilson family chariot.

"What do you think?" I ask of Daddy, Mother and Eli.

Eli lunges for me. "Ma ma!" His little hand pats my shoulder.

My eyes fill with tears. "Little man! You finally said it! You said Mama! Good boy." I kiss him, tightly rocking him back and forth.

"Here you are, Deena Bean." Daddy wraps my cream-colored coat around my shoulders. "You look beautiful."

"Thank you, Daddy." I hand Eli to him. "Be good son, I'll miss you." I bend down to my sweet girls, kissing their noses. "Thank you for your help, girls." Their faces are beaming. My heart camera is taking pictures like crazy.

Mother looks at me with approval. "It's lovely, Deena."

Butternut Squash pads in from the family room and meows his own compliment. I bend to scratch behind his ears and he purrs. Taking a deep breath, I pick up my evening bag from the bench. "Time to go!"

I open the door and step out onto the porch, trailed by all of them. The timer clicks the lights on, and the garlands, roofline and miniature potted Christmas trees flood the porch with magical light. Fat, lazy snowflakes have begun their dainty descent from the heavens.

"Yay, yay! It's snowing again!" Caroline and Zoe are ecstatic.

The headlights of the car spotlight the falling snow. Max honks the car and gets out to meet me at the edge of the sidewalk. "We're going to be late, beautiful princess!" He calls.

"I'm coming!" I wave and blow kisses, going down the porch steps.

"Deena, wait!" Mother steps out a bit farther, squinting as though to see better. "I didn't realize it was snowing. You can't wear sandals in the *snow*!"

She means well.

"Princess Deena, your chariot awaits." Max is growing understandably impatient.

And so, I raise my eyes to the heavens, to my Audience of One who washes us white as this snow, catching flakes on my lashes and tongue.

Giggling, I bend down to remove my sandals and hook them over my fingers, walking barefoot in the December snow down the sidewalk, toward the car where my Beloved is waiting.

Grocery List
Travel size vanilla candles
CD of love songs
Sexy new bra & panty set
Manuscript boxes
Ink cartridge
Pampers – Walkers!

Epilogue

At three in the morning on July 5, Vicki gives birth to an eight pound, twelve-ounce baby girl. Deborah Faith Hampton. At the hospital, a few hours later, I linger a bit longer after the rest of the Bible Study girls have gone home.

I want to hold baby Faith all to myself. "She's Deborah, after the prophetess and leader of Israel, and Faith, like Miss Opal reminded us to have in order to finish strong. I never want to forget that," Vicki told all of us. It suits her. I look at her perfect peachy baby face, upturned nose, and thick cinnamon colored hair.

Vicki is propped up among a mound of pillows, wearing an adorable blue checked pajama set, having flat out told the nurses that she will not wear one of those hideous gowns. Zeke is out getting her something to eat from *Pacino's*.

She looks at me fondly. "I'm so glad you're here, Deena Bean."

"Where else would I be? Besides, I have something for you."

"What could you possibly have? You've already brought Faith the tiniest, most adorable swimsuit ever, and you've brought me enough of your secret stash of Nutty Bars to last until school starts!"

"Well, you won't need any more now that you have your very own little Debbie," I quip.

"Very funny."

"Well, I wanted you to be the first to see it, besides Max."

I walk over to the table by the door and produce a square package of plain brown paper. I've tied it with twine for effect.

She opens it carefully, turns it over and squeals. "Deena! It's here! You did it." She pats the space next to her on the hospital bed. I carefully sit down with baby Faith.

Together, we look at the beautiful glossy cover featuring the glow of Christmas tree lights through a window, a sidewalk of shimmery snow, and the silhouette of a bare-footed woman with pink polished toes, holding a pair of silver sandals.

"I love the cover, Deena."

We admire the title font in bold curling letters:

Barefoot in December

A Novel

By: Deena Brantwell Wilson

"This is your advance copy, Vick. It's going to be in stores next month and there'll be a special CBA release that will coincide with Christmas. I'm so excited! But, read inside the cover."

She opens it and reads the dedication aloud.

*This book is dedicated to all of my Tuesday Morning Bible Study
girls who, in their own ways, drew me ever closer to the Father,
whose love will not let me go~*

*Miss Opal, Tandy Walker, Reagan Anne McCabe, Regina Baker,
Betty Mitchell, & Kay Tupper, but especially, my dearest friend,
Vicki Hampton, who is faithful with her wounds for my own good,
and who always believed I would do this.*

*And to my husband Max, with whom I fall daily more in love;
Our three Blessings – Caroline Elaine; Zoe Irene & Eli Jackson*

*And most importantly to the God of Second Chances,
Author of all our stories, including the best one, not yet released,
When we will never have to read the words:*

THE END

Book Club Questions for *Barefoot in December*

Prepared by Sharris Hayes, Reading Specialist teacher in Southwest Missouri

Character Questions

1. Deena- Do you think Deena is a typical new-to-staying-at-home-mom? Can you relate with her thoughts, circumstances and possibly, even her betrayal?

2. Max- Max is a loyal man, who obviously loves Deena very much. Do you think his reaction to Deena's affair was realistic? Do you have a husband/boyfriend like Max?

3. Vicki- Can you empathize with Vicki's desire to have another baby? Do you have a friend like Vicki or know someone like her? Do you think she should have kept Deena more "accountable"?

4. Thomas- Thomas was a sweet talker, who had his own best interests in mind. What was going on in Thomas' life that made him stray from his marriage? Give your opinions of Thomas.

5. Pastor Sherman and Miss Opal have significant influence on Deena's life. Which of their sermons, counseling quotes or Bible study lessons most affected you?

6. Which of the Bible study gals was your favorite? To which could you most relate? [Kay Tupper; Tandy Walker; Reagan Anne McCabe; Miss Opal; Betty Miller; Regina Baker; Deena Wilson; Vicki Hampton] Why?

Discussion Questions

1. Early in the story, Deena muses, "It seems odd to me that so much of mothering, which after all, is born of romance, or at least passion, strips one of the same." Do you agree with this statement? To which incident of stay-at-home mothering could you most relate? Talk about some ways that you have kept your romance alive after children.

2. Only one of Deena's three children are in school; the other two are at home, one in diapers. Could you relate with this scenario? Have you ever felt like you were at your breaking point? What did you do or are you doing to keep yourself sane? Have you experienced the tug between work and home?

3. Vicki confronts Deena about her "meeting" with Thomas, at Pacino's, with eye-witness evidence. Even so, Deena brushes it off as an innocent work meeting. Deena even says to herself, "Crow with a side of evidence is a hard meal to eat and I'm not feeling terribly hungry yet." Have you ever been at this place of denial, whether it be an affair, spending too much money, gossiping, or flirting? Would the affair with Thomas have happened if she had been more accountable to someone?

4. Deena's blog seems to be an outlet for her as she is home with the children. Do you have an outlet like this that is just "yours" to work on in order to gain perspective?

5. Deena has a secret Target card. Do you think that keeping secrets from your spouse is ok, once in a while? Do you think this secretive behavior may have led her to rationalize the affair?

6. Thomas and Deena's relationship escalated quickly into something inappropriate. What are some things she could have done to prevent this? What were the warning signs?

7. What do you think the consequences would have been if Deena and Thomas had become physically intimate? What would the consequences have been if they walked away from their marriages?

8. What was the motivation behind Thomas' desire to be with Deena? What was Deena's motivation behind wanting to be with Thomas?

9. Deena's relationship with her mother is strained, to say the least. In the end, she finds out that her mother isn't as perfect as she thought. Are there people in your life with whom you have a strained relationship that you might see differently now? They may have baggage that you do not know about. Do you have personal experience with such a person and yet see them differently now that you know their story?

10. Everyone has a story. There may be especially much to be learned from older couples. "Modern temptation is rooted in ancient desires." Did it surprise you that Miss Opal manipulated Mr. Mac and Maggie's correspondence? Have you ever been manipulative in order to gain something you desperately wanted?

11. Deena kept putting off talking to Max about the affair until it was almost too late. Is there anything in your life, in your relationships, that needs to be talked about or something that needs to be said before it's too late?

12. Were you surprised that Thomas showed up at the hospital? Was the connection between Thomas' car and his wife a surprise?

Devotion Questions

1. In the Easter Sunday sermon, Pastor Sherman points out that "because we have a Savior who has conquered death, our ultimate enemy, we can rest assured of victory over any other problem we will ever face." Deena thinks to herself, "There in that sanctuary, surrounded by other believers, it is easy to believe that I too am a conqueror." Do you sometimes find strength only in those around you or in yourself instead of relying fully on God? Do you truly believe that we have that same power that raised Jesus from the dead within us? Would we live more boldly if we did?

2. During Tuesday morning Bible study, Miss Opal refers the girls to Hebrews 12:11. "No discipline seems pleasant at the time, but painful. Later on, however, it produces a harvest of righteousness and peace for those who have been trained by it." Kay pipes up with something about getting on the treadmill, but Miss Opal redirects to their spiritual lives. What are some things that can derail us in our lives and cause us to doubt, especially when God's discipline is in a painful area of our lives? Can we be so brave as to give it ALL to God, even those parts of our lives that we don't want to hand over….just yet?

3. Pastor Sherman's sermon refers to David and Bathsheba in II Samuel Chapter 11, and the Apostle Paul's words about temptation being around since the Garden. "Modern temptations have their roots in age old desires." He also mentions that this temptation doesn't have to give way to sin and that God always provides a way of escape (I Cor. 10:13). However, we try to rationalize our sins and pretend that this all doesn't apply to us. None of us are immune to temptation. How do we sometimes rationalize sin in our own lives? Do you look at yourself as a mistake-maker instead of a sinner?

What are you willing to look at and work on in your own life that you need to turn over to Him?

4. "We think we're trying to write our life stories in full, rich chapters at a time, but really, we can only write a sentence at a time. Sometimes just single words really. Sometimes it's just a groan, something we can't utter, but the Holy Spirit takes over for us and tattles about it to a merciful God; thankfully, He is a superb translator." This quote is referring to Romans 8:26 that says, "In the same way, the Spirit helps us in our weakness. We do not know what we ought to pray for, but the Spirit himself intercedes for us through wordless groans." What have you tried to write in advance of God's pace? Take some time to meditate and focus on Him each day. If you have a difficult time knowing what to pray for, the Holy Spirit will intercede on your behalf. What a wonderful promise!

~~~~~~

Reading *Barefoot in December* is like having a long-overdue heart-to-heart with an old friend. Grab a Diet Coke and learn with Deena how to cope with the discontent that threatens the happiness of so many women today. Dagnan's acute insight and vivid language create a treasure of a novel.

-Stephanie Reagor
Writer and Stay at Home Mom

About This Book

She stayed at my book table, at the end of a line of twenty or so women, wanting to talk, to share their journeys as wives and mothers. Mascara tracked down her cheeks like the inky footprints of a mischievous raccoon. A handful of Kleenex was balled up in her hand. Other mothers shared similar stories: funny anecdotes about their children, their former or current careers, loneliness, laughter, occasional drifting from their Beloveds; I could tell hers would be different.

Indeed, this young woman broke my heart and planted the seed for this novel. She was a wife and mother like the rest of the conference attendees, but she was poised to wreck everything and she didn't want to. Her husband travelled. She felt alone and lonely much of the time. She had begun talking to someone who was single and gave her the attention she craved. "I just don't know who I am anymore, "she sobbed into my shoulder. "I can't see him anymore, can I?"

"No, sweet girl. You can't." "But," her eyes raised to mine, pleading. "Shouldn't I at least call him and tell him why?" I shook my head and saw that she knew the answer to that. She was at a crossroads. I prayed for her and watched her walk away.

And the character of Deena Brantwell Wilson was born. I wanted her to be real. To struggle. To love her children and her husband and be conflicted about the source of her worth.

At the end of it all, I wanted her to choose right. To dig deep. To hang on to her commitment. To fall in love with the God of Second Chances and repair her relationship with her Beloved. And she does.

Deena reflects the choices, the craziness of life, and the realness which besets all of us in certain seasons of our lives. Above all, I long for us to remember that our worth, our beauty, our identities lie with the One Who loves us best and Most. Always. Oh, how He loves us.

****

I am extra thankful for my own tribe of book club/accountability girls whose friendship speaks truth into my own life. Look for the "insiders" sprinkled throughout this book. Thanks for forcing me to finish it by choosing it as one of our selections!

To the Bible Study girls at the high school where I teach, for faithfully praying.

To the Playground Therapy girls from Harry S Truman Elementary, where we hung out when our Blessings were younger and smaller, and I guess we were too.

To Sarah Joy Oaklief for her brilliant suggestion to add a readership and their own unique voices to follow Deena's **Pajama Mama** Blog.

For my baby sister, Angie, and one of her dear friends (and mine), Special Stephie, for being my first readers.

To my family – for my tender past, my crazy-wonderful present, and a future that God holds. Remember **Revelation 21:4** – let's meet in the back right- hand corner of Heaven.

About the Author

Cindy Sigler Dagnan has been married to her Beloved for 23 years. They are the parents of 4 Blessings, a son-in-law and are Nana & Bup to 3 little grandsons. An author, speaker and high school teacher, she has been a guest on **Focus on the Family** & **Phil Waldrop** radio programs and has spoken or sung in 30 states, Taiwan & Austria. Speaking engagements have included the North American Christian Convention, Missouri Christian Convention, Hearts at Home Conference, various women's retreats and marriage seminars with her Beloved. She is passionate about Jesus, family & chocolate. Book her for speaking with the Robinson Agency. The author of 6 previous non-fiction books, including *Hot Chocolate for Couples*, this is her first novel. Cindy loves to hear from her readers and hope this book blesses your life!

Connect with her @

Cindy Sigler Dagnan Author
@DagnanCindy
CindySiglerDagnan

Made in the USA
Middletown, DE
01 July 2022

68038669R00199